The BONES
of GRACE

Tahmima Anam's debut novel, *A Golden Age,* was shortlisted for the Guardian First Book Award and was winner of the Commonwealth Writers' Prize for Best First Book. Her follow up, *The Good Muslim*, was shortlisted for the 2013 DSC Prize for South Asian Literature. She has been published in the *Guardian*, the *Financial Times*, and is a Contributing Opinion Writer for *The New York Times*. In 2013, she was named one of *Granta*'s Best of Young British Novelists. Born in Dhaka, Bangladesh, she now lives in London.

Also by Tahmima Anam

The Good Muslim

A Golden Age

The BONES of GRACE

TAHMIMA ANAM

CANONGATE

This paperback edition published in 2017 by Canongate Books

First published in Great Britain in 2016 by
Canongate Books Ltd, 14 High Street, Edinburgh EH1 1TE

www.canongate.co.uk

1

'All of Me' Words and music by Gerald Marks and Seymour Simons © 1931,
Reproduced by permission of Bourne Co/EMI Music Publishing Ltd,
London W1F 9LD

Tomas Tranströmer, 'The Blue House', from *New Collected Poems*
(Bloodaxe Books, 2011). Reproduced with permission of Bloodaxe Books
on behalf of the author.

British Library Cataloguing-in-Publication Data
A catalogue record for this book is available on
request from the British Library

ISBN 978 1 84767 978 9

Typeset in Bembo by Palimpsest Book Production Ltd, Falkirk, Stirlingshire

Printed and bound in Great Britain by Clays Ltd, St Ives plc.

For Roland Lamb, again (and always)

And for my sister Shaveena, who, though she arrived late, saved me from the loneliness of one

Without really knowing, we divine; our life has a sister ship, following quite another route. While the sun blazes behind the islands.

'The Blue House', Thomas Tranströmer

Contents

I saw you today, Elijah. You were crossing the road. There is a building on the corner of Mass Ave and Harvard Street that looks like a miniature version of the Flatiron Building in New York. You had your back to the building, and when the little white man began to blink, you stepped off the sidewalk and onto the street – that's when I saw you. You made a little gesture with your hand that made me think you had seen me too, that you were waving, but it was a small motion of your wrist that meant nothing – you were just bruising the cold November air, and before you caught my eye, I bolted.

I knew it would only be a matter of time before we ran into each other. Cambridge is a small town and the orbits are modest. I've been back three months, and every day I've swept the corners of my vision, hoping and not hoping, as the warm days turned to ice, that it might be you in that charcoal coat, your legs in that pair of loose-fitting trousers. Your voice ordering the coffee before mine.

Diana has brought me back. She is here – or, at least, a very small part of her is here – in my hand. Her ankle bone is paler and lighter than I had imagined – time has robbed it of its weight – but her presence is nothing short of a miracle, here in this lab, in this town where my dreaming of her and my dreaming of you began. When we left her behind in Dera Bugti, I never thought I would see her again. I thought the mystery of the walking whale would remain in the ground forever, one of the secrets we were never meant to unearth. But earlier this year I received a message, written in Urdu and translated, reluctantly, by my mother:

Dear Miss Zubaida Haque,

Here is a gift from our departed friend. I do not understand why a man would give his life for such a thing, but perhaps you will. He got a letter out, asking me to recover his treasure and send it to you.

I have no choice but to dispatch my duty to a brother and comrade. We scoured the desert for your Diana, and now I am sending her to you, piece by piece. I do not know what these bones mean, but if you are reading this, you will know that our friend had a parting wish, and that I have endeavoured to fulfil it.

I didn't want to believe the message was real – after years of silence, could it be that Zamzam was helping to finish what we had started? But there was no other explanation, no other possible reason for this stranger's message, and he had used her name, Diana. I replied, listing the department's details, offering assistance to cover the transportation costs, the formalities that would have to be completed in order for ancient fossils to cross borders. Then I boarded a plane, I came here, and I waited.

When the box arrived, it was wrapped in several layers of duct tape, and inside, within folds of newspaper, encased in a layer of red matrix, was Diana's double-hinged ankle.

I closed my fingers around the padding and felt the sting of tears in my eyes. I knew immediately that this wasn't just the fulfilment of a dream I have so long desired yet had taught myself to renounce; it was also a way for me to make a final plea for you. Diana is the reason I left this town, and Diana is why I have returned. I think of her as a spirit of comings and goings, a beacon that leads me across continents and through time. I live in hope that she will lead me back to you.

I suppose I must have been composing this story in my head for some time, but as I held Diana's bone in my hand that day, a flood of words came to my mind, and I rushed home and wrote them down. I have been living in a state of waiting, Elijah, for this moment, this opportunity for reckoning, and Zamzam, from beyond his grave, has granted me my wish. Diana is here, and I have seen you, and now I can take account of the whole thing – not just of you, the great love of my life, and not just of *Ambulocetus*, but also of Anwar, the man who led me to my mother, and of *Grace*, the ship that was ground to dust before our eyes. There is a whale, a woman who gave up her child, a piano, and a man who searched so long and hard for his beloved that he found me. But you have interrupted me too soon. I am not finished yet, and until I do there will be no way for us to wend our way back together.

You were ahead of yourself, Elijah, standing in that intersection before you were meant to.

The Preludes

The first words I ever said to you were: 'When I was nine years old, I found out I was adopted.' And you replied: 'Aristotle was an orphan.' And I said: 'So was the Prophet Muhammad.' That evening, the music and the heat of late summer had made me recall the day my parents had finally confessed the thing that I had, even as a small child, always suspected. I remembered that after my ninth birthday party, when the guests had gone home and what remained was the smell of fried chicken and torn corners of wrapping paper and the scatter of fallen potato chips, my parents told me that they had adopted me two years after they had married and fifteen years after the war. I hardly ever thought about that day, but, on the evening we met, I recalled it clearly: my father had built a piñata that had emptied its candy onto the lawn, and a boy from my school had taken the piñata stick and chased the other boys into a shady corner of the garden where the cobwebs were as thick as books. I remembered being sandwiched between my parents as they narrated the story, remembered each holding one of my hands and telling me about wanting so much for a baby and the miracle of finding me, remembered that I developed the sudden urge to vomit, that my vomit was candy-orange, and remembered especially the colour, because in those days there was no flush in the evening and I'd had to pour six mugfuls of water from the bucket into the commode to make it go away. It came back to me in a flood on that hot night in Cambridge that sat heavy on all of our shoulders, late summer and the semester about to begin, the campus sparse. I was preoccupied with the final preparations for my trip to find a complete skeleton of the ancient whale *Ambulocetus natans*, and my memories mingled with thoughts of packing away my apartment and the journey I was about to embark on, imagining the dig, the moment of discovery, the possible unveiling of a fossil that had already changed the way we looked at the relationship between the land and the sea, and in this interlude, between the memory and the anticipation, a crack appeared, a pause in which everything slowed down, an in-between moment that was neither here nor there – and into that crack fell you: a man with piano hands and the smell of cold weather on his collar.

I had gone, as you of course know, to a concert at Sanders Theatre. I sometimes spent evenings in that wood-panelled auditorium, and on that night, on the eve of my departure, I allowed myself this indulgence as a coda to my seven years in America, immersing myself, as I was often wont to do, in sounds that would always resonate, despite, or perhaps because of, their unfamiliarity. I usually forgot the music, except once, when Yo-Yo Ma played the Bach Cello Suites. The event was more of an interview than a concert so he only played for a few minutes at the end, but it was brief and magical, and the only time I had wished to share the experience with someone else.

So it was my last night, and my last concert. I found, when I arrived, that it would be the Shostakovich Preludes.

I had heard of Shostakovich, but other than the name I didn't know anything about the music. I saw a grand piano on stage, then the lights went down and I was surprised when a slight woman emerged from behind the curtain. She was older, possibly in her sixties, and she wore a long skirt and had her hair tied into a grey knot that hung low on her neck. She began to play short pieces of perhaps five minutes each. I found the music pleasant but unexciting. It would begin on a romantic note, but somewhere in the middle it would become distant, almost intellectual. I couldn't connect. At one point I became aware of a man to my left: of you, Elijah, of the way you tapped your hand against your knee, the frayed material of your jeans where your fingers rested, your sandalled feet and the canvas bag that sat under your chair.

Though I turned to look at you a few times, you didn't glance back. Aside from your hand, the rest of you was very still. I wondered at your stillness. I followed your eyes that were fixed on the tight pool of light around the instrument, on the float and hammer of the woman's fingers, and as you gazed so seriously, you compelled me to do the same, to really listen to the music. At the end of No. 4, I felt the fraction of an earthquake open in my chest, and after No. 5, which was tender, then triumphant, the tremor rose, so that when the music stopped, I felt it making its way up towards my neck. And that is when the memory returned to me: the birthday party, the confession, sleeping between my parents that night, their anxious breaths mingling over my face. Before I knew it, my cheeks were wet with tears, and it was all I could do to stop myself from sobbing out loud as the next piece began. I held my arms tight around myself, attempting to contain whatever it was that was erupting, and finally you turned around and saw that I was crying, and, though it was dark, I could see from the outline of your face that you were perfectly solemn and had registered no alarm. You put your palm against the sleeve of my shirt, the warmth of your touch radiating from my arm all the way across my shoulders. At your touch, I felt calmed at first, and then, when the music ended and you lifted your hand away, I experienced a piercing loneliness, the loneliness of being the sole inhabitant of my body.

We had our first exchange, which, looking back, is an odd thing for two people to say to one another as introduction, but which at the time felt perfectly natural. Your voice was deep and mellow in the quiet. You took my hand, and the blood rushed to that hand, leaping beneath my skin as if to leap out and mingle with yours, and this is how we sat for the rest of the first half, my heart hammering in my chest as the hour came to its end and the lights went on in the auditorium.

In the sudden brightness I noticed you were very pale, with blue eyes and a beard that was neither messy nor particularly trimmed. I rubbed my face, willing the evidence of my tears to disappear. I pulled my hand away, seeing the people file out for intermission and wondering if anyone had recognised me. You asked me if I would like a glass of water, and I would have said yes, but I worried you would disappear and I would never see you again. Finally, the lights went down and the second half began. This time the audience seemed restive, people shifting on the shallow wooden benches that angled around the stage. I thought again about the matter of origins. Not so much about where I was from, but of the fact that, in my twenty-five years, I had lingered so little on the matter. How few questions I had asked – none, really, possibly because of the fierce love of my parents, which I had reciprocated without question until that very moment. While all of this was cycling through my mind, the concert came to an end with an energetic blur of the pianist's fingers and a triumphant hand-stretching series of chords. The crowd rose to its feet, a meadow of standing figures, and the applause went on for a long time, but there was no encore, so the lights came on eventually and the concert ended. As the auditorium emptied again we both rose, and you stepped towards me and leaned in, letting other people pass on their way to the exit. I inhaled your scent: wood shavings and trees that survived snow. A cold-weather smell on this, the hottest and closest of evenings.

We considered one another. You fixed your eyes on me as if we were the last two people left in the world. I had never seen a gaze like that, so direct, so unambivalent. Most people like to be in at least two places at once, but you – you were standing there as if roots had grown around your feet. I could hardly bear it, so I said, 'All right, then. Goodbye.' You laughed at this, and, relieved, I laughed with you. We made our way to the exit, and I thought for a moment about inviting you to stay the night with me, but instead I suggested we go to the Korean café for a cup of tea. I hadn't eaten dinner but I wasn't hungry, and you didn't mention food either. We walked up Mass Ave and ordered iced tea, and I asked for tapioca pearls in mine and you looked at me with a question in your eyes, and I explained that I had been introduced to bubble tea in Bangkok, which was a short distance from Dhaka, Bangladesh, where I was from. 'A snack at the bottom of your drink,' I said. 'Try it.'

You told me things about you, things that seemed irrelevant at the time, but that I recalled later in order to make better sense of our meeting. You said you had once built a fountain out of used water bottles and that, a few years ago, you had participated in a staged reading of *Ulysses* that had lasted one hundred and seventy-six hours. I found myself attempting to match the eccentricities of your stories and only coming up a little short, beginning with the story of my parents' confession, and how afterwards they never mentioned it again, and that I had never asked, because, in the way of children, I knew the subject had simultaneously been opened and closed.

You had recently dropped out of a doctoral programme in Philosophy. Why, I asked, and you told me, as if you were realising something only at that very moment, that it was no longer important to you. What would you do? You weren't sure. You might travel, see something of the world. Or you might practise the piano for a few years. You seemed very sure of yourself, in the way you held yourself and carefully paused before you spoke, and yet the things you told me betrayed a man with little ambition or certainty, a man with nothing to push against and hence adrift in a sea of infinite choices.

When I looked around, I saw that we were the only two people left. I was about to suggest we go somewhere else and decided instead that we should wait until the café closed and we were forced to leave. Your gaze was still fixed on me and I shifted in my seat. You seemed comfortable with pauses in the conversation but I needed to fill the silence, so I told you about the dig. 'I'm going to Pakistan next week,' I said. 'I'm going to dig out a whale fossil.' I told you that I was joining an expedition to find the bones of *Ambulocetus natans*, the walking whale. 'We're hoping to bring an entire skeleton back. The pelvis will tell us a lot.' I matched my pace to yours. Every word came out slow and deliberate. The word 'pelvis' sent a charge through me.

I asked about your family, and you told me the kind of story I had never heard before, that is, the story of perfect American people. Parents both professors at Harvard, now divorced but still great friends, three brothers and a younger sister, a house in Porter Square, a grand piano in the living room, lemonade in the refrigerator, a kitchen that smelled of wood and chamomile (the last details made up, but close to reality, as I would soon discover). No wonder you were lost. With nothing to resist, you floated like a fallen leaf. Then you said, 'My grandmother died last month. Every night I go to Sanders and I listen to the music. When there isn't anything at Sanders, I go to the Boston Philharmonic, and, sometimes, to the movies or to Shakespeare in the Park or to the Hatch Shell.' I reached out to touch your knuckle with my tea-cold hand. You seemed pleased by my touch, yet you didn't return the gesture. I told you that I had never been close to anyone who had died. Then I said: 'I know this will sound strange. But when I remembered my parents telling me I was adopted, it felt like a death. Like there's a person I've been my whole life and she's a fake, a ghost.'

'It must be hard, not knowing.'

'I'm afraid of what it means. And I feel alone in the world.'

'Loneliness is just part of being a person. We long for togetherness, for connection, and yet we're trapped in our own bodies. We want know the other fully, but we can't, we can only stretch out our hands and reach.'

It was so close to what I had felt an hour or two ago, when you had touched me and then untouched me, that I said, 'I think that's the best thing anyone has ever said to me,' and you smiled, your lips disappearing into your beard.

You said were pleased to have been given the opportunity to say the right thing. Then you asked me to tell you more about Dhaka. 'I don't know anyone from Bangladesh. In fact, I can't say I know any whale-hunting Shostakovich fans from any country.' I was charmed by this description of myself. I said you should come and see the place for yourself. You said you would like that. I told you how my parents had met during the Bangladesh War, that it had been the event that had framed their lives, and mine. We talked about that for a bit, and I gave you the potted history of my country I had narrated many times in the last seven years.

The café closed and we stepped out into the night, which was bright with heat and cones of streetlight. We drifted slowly towards my apartment. There seemed an infinite number of things left to say. We hesitated at the top of my street, reluctant to part, and, if I had paused to think for a moment, I may have had a premonition of what was to come: breaking your heart, finding my mother, *Grace*, the end and the beginning, the pulling crew, the discovery of love and its abandonment, and my telling you this story of our love, and of Anwar, and my mother. But I didn't pause, and the clairvoyant moment passed me by, and so we said an ordinary goodbye, promising to meet in the morning. When we parted, I felt my mind freeing itself of the story of my birth and turning to more graspable things, the dig I was about to go on, the fossil that was waiting in the earth, the lip balm and magazines I needed to buy before I departed.

You will wonder, as I often have, about the precise moment we fell in love. Was it on *Grace*, after you played the piano, or was it before that, the moment I saw you through the print-smudged glass at Chittagong Airport, or in your parents' living room, or as we parted that first evening, Shostakovich soaring in my music-mind, turning around as you walked away so that I could see you retreat with slow steps in your sandalled feet and hippy trousers?

But I should tell you now that it was not that night, because that night, I did not believe in love. I knew, of course, that it existed. I knew that it was the central principle around which most people built their lives, and I wasn't foolish enough to assume that it was something I could avoid entirely. But I did not believe that I lived in an age when a great love was possible. Everything about my life was too easy. I could love whomever I wanted, and marry or not marry them, or change my religion, or get divorced multiple times and have children with three different fathers if I wanted. I came from what you might call a traditional society, but I was not in thrall to that society. What I was in thrall to was the past. This had to do with my parents and the war they had been in, and, as a model for love, for what was possible between two people, they had set an example that fixed in my mind the notion that the epic thing, the one that went down in legend and song and was anointed with passion that lasted beyond beauty and youth, was something that only happened to other people, people that came before me or were born into magical, troubled times. I didn't believe that I was immune – of course I would love, and be loved – but I had proposed to myself a life that respected its historical moment and demanded something less, something tamer than those deeper furrows and interruptions of the heart.

As for you, if you had asked me, I wouldn't have been able to give you a single reason for your interest in me. I told myself this: (a) I would make an amusing anecdote for you later. Hey, you would tell yourself, I met this Bangladeshi palaeontologist and we listened to Shostakovich and then

Nina Simone and she loves *Anna Karenina*. What're the odds? Or, (b) you felt sorry for me. Or, (c) you were actually a social outcast, totally unlikable and in desperate need of company, and I just couldn't see it. There was, of course, another option, which was that your interest in me was genuine – but I couldn't really fathom that, because I would have had to change my own understanding of myself and admit that I was what you were looking for, and that would have been beyond my imagination.

Now that my estimation of myself has taken a significant battering, I can say this: you did love me. You loved me from the very start. It could have been because you found me beautiful, or interesting, but more than that, it was because, although you bore none of the outward signs of being anything like me, we were, in fact, very similar. In me you saw embodied all the things you had felt about yourself: that you had been born into the wrong family, that there were things within you that had yet to be voiced and you might, if you were lucky, find yourself uttering them in my presence. In other words: we were nothing, yet everything alike. And you had the wisdom to see that from the start, even if I didn't.

As I approached the apartment, I could hear music spilling out onto the street, and then I remembered my goodbye party. I called Bettina, the anthropologist I had lived with since my first year, and my closest friend in Cambridge. 'Sorry.'

'You're late,' she said.

'I met someone.'

'An Amphibian?' 'Amphibian' was our code word for people like us. Bettina was Argentinian, born in Queens, had grown up in Buenos Aires when her parents had decided to un-immigrate themselves, gone to college in Paris, taken several years off and backpacked through China, where she had been bitten by monkeys, and landed up here, in Cambridge, by which time her parents had returned to their place in Astoria, chastened by the more exciting side of the planet. 'Amphibian' signalled people in between, people who lived with some part of themselves in perpetual elsewhere. 'No,' I said. 'Waspish, by all accounts.'

'Honey, if you're going to cheat, at least put some colour in it.'

I tried to conjure Rashid's face in my mind, stoking my memories for a feeling of tenderness, arousal, something – but nothing came, so I said, 'It's not like Rashid and I are married.'

'Where are you? I can hear music.'

'I'm on the porch.'

'We can unpack this later. Hang up and come inside.'

Bettina had installed an air conditioner in the living room the summer before, and, though the apartment was crowded, it was cooler than the street. I scanned the room and saw my lab partner, Kyung-Ju, and a few other graduate students from my department, but it was mostly anthropologists, the coolest and most depressed social scientists, huddled together in small clusters. I caught fragments of their conversation, complaints about the new department chair, a journal article one of them had failed to get published, a new class on semiotics, the fraud that was Slavoj Žižek. I had gotten to know them well; they spent a lot of time at our apartment, drinking tea and watching television ironically. My own friends from the Department of Organismic and Evolutionary Biology, on the other hand, preferred to get drunk on weekends, letting themselves into the prep lab or falling asleep between the shelves of the Invertebrate collection.

Bettina often joked that I was in the wrong department, but there was something pleasantly straightforward about scientists, and I found I could live among them without giving much away, and, in those days, hiding in plain sight was what I did best.

I caused a stir as I moved through the crowd. A cheer went up from somewhere in the kitchen. Bettina, larger than me in every way, bones and height and volume, enveloped me in a smothering hug and passed me a plastic cup of sangria. 'So what happened?' she asked, pulling her thick hair into a ponytail.

I plucked an orange segment out of my cup. 'It was so strange. I was listening to the music, and there was this guy there, and then I started to cry.'

'It was bound to happen,' Bettina said, fanning her face. She liked to act as if nothing could surprise her when it came to men. I took a large gulp of sangria and followed her into the living room. Bettina and I had met a few weeks into my first fall at Harvard, when I had decided to take a shortcut through Tozzer Library on my way to the Museum of Comparative Zoology. I entered the building, expecting an ordinary arrangement of books, but instead came upon a very dark room, and, when I dove further in, the lights suddenly came on and illuminated a totem rising two, three storeys into the gallery. I was terrified and let out a small yelp, which Bettina, a few feet behind me, witnessed and found hilarious.

We started talking and she mentioned she was looking for a roommate. At the time I was living in a tiny room in one of the dorms off Kirkland Street, and the walls were so thin I could hear my neighbour, a doctoral student in Political Philosophy, clicking her retainer into her mouth at night. It turned out Bettina's first choice, a law student whose boyfriend lived in New York, so she would only have been there a few days every week – absence being the holy grail of roommate desirability – had backed out at the last minute.

Our first weeks together were awkward, because Bettina seemed to inhale all the oxygen in the apartment, but it didn't take long for little tendernesses to grow between us. One day I offered to make dinner, and Bettina fell in love with the one dish I could cook competently, which was dal with spicy omelette. And then, in the first cold snap of the year, I caught the flu, and Bettina made ginger tea and introduced me to TV I'd never seen before, like *Buffy the Vampire Slayer* and *Gilmore Girls*. After that, we shopped at Trader Joe's on the weekend, went to the occasional movie together, and even sat in on each other's classes. (I accompanied her to Homi Bhabha's seminar on melancholia, and she came to my Analytical Palaeontology course. She claimed I got the better deal, and I had to agree.)

Bettina's parents had helped her buy the apartment, a two-bedroom flat on Trowbridge, when she had started graduate school. I brought back a few things from Dhaka after the first winter holiday, a clock made out of recycled paper, a length of cloth studded with small round mirrors creating a partition between the living room and the kitchen. We found a battered sofa on the street and dragged it inside with the help of Bettina's boyfriend, a master's student at the Ed School, who was dispatched a few weeks later when she grew bored of him. We named the sofa Edvar, after him, and the armchair, donated by an aunt of Bettina, Maude. The apartment was warm and more like home than I had ever imagined I could be in America, and, looking around, I realised it would be a long time before I had a place of my own again.

'The palaeontologists are hanging out by themselves, as usual,' Bettina complained, collapsing on Maude.

'The anthropologists are doing their best to look intimidating.'

'And failing.'

I took another sip from the plastic cup and felt the warmth of wine and sugar spreading through my body. I wanted an excuse to talk about you. 'So this guy, I haven't seen him around campus before. Turns out he's a Philosophy grad.'

'What's his name?' Bettina asked.

'Elijah Strong.'

Bettina rolled her eyes. 'Seriously?'

'Seriously.' A thought suddenly occurred to me. 'Unless he gave me a fake name. Do you think he gave me a fake name?'

'Definitely. In the meantime, there's pie.'

I replayed our conversation in my mind and decided no, you hadn't lied, Elijah Strong really was your name. Later that night, I would look you up and find a photograph taken before you'd grown your beard and made you look very young, and for a moment I thought it wasn't you, but of course it was. 'Pie?'

'As American as. I turned the oven on in this crazy heat to lure you back to our shores.'

We had been debating for months about whether I should return to Cambridge after my fieldwork. In the end, I had decided I wouldn't. I could just as easily write my thesis in Dhaka, where I could be closer to the dig and closer to Rashid. I had decided this despite knowing the world was full of doctoral students who never finished their degrees. My ambivalence was compounded by my lack of determination to stay in your country – I'd never dreamed, like others I knew from back home, of living in America. When I was a teenager, I had once visited New York with my parents. My father had a cousin on Long Island, and we stayed in the guest-room of a two-storey house off the highway. I recalled an impressively fluffy wall-to-wall carpet and large rooms that smelled of onions. I had wondered why all the women covered their heads and why there were framed Arabic inscriptions on the wall above every doorway. When an alarm clock belted out a canned Azaan, I had not been able to stop myself from laughing. My mother had scolded me, but I knew she was secretly judging too, that in her mind an immigrant was someone who had abandoned their country.

That was all I had known of America before landing in the small college town I had chosen for my undergraduate degree – it was before my parents' fortunes changed, and it was the only place that had offered me a scholarship. Those four years were spent in misery, frigid winters and lonely weekends, marooned among other international students with no car. It wasn't until I discovered palaeontology, and the whale, that it began to crystallise in my mind, the prospect of making a life for myself, here where people cared about the bones of animals that had lived far before memory or human ambition. Still, I couldn't shake the image of that house on Long Island, the way all the people from home clung to each other. To my parents and to Rashid, I said nothing about the allure of living here; to my friends, like Bettina, I explained that there was no way I would settle anywhere but Dhaka. My parents were there, I was an only child, and they had lived through a war. To construct my loyalties in any other way would constitute a betrayal, and I was, above all things, aware of my commitments.

I spotted Kyung-Ju and Brian, a boy from my cohort, and pushed through the crowd to them. My lab partner was drunk, her thin, bluish-black hair sticking to her forehead. 'Hello,' she said. 'Ready for your big dig?'

'You had enough to drink?'

Kyung-Ju clawed the air. 'I'm the Asian tiger. I'm the Asian tiger.' The slight animosity that had rippled through the lab when I had been chosen over the others to work on the dig in Pakistan had turned brittle over the course of the spring. Underneath it all was the implication that I had been chosen because I had a Muslim name and spoke a few words of Urdu. No one had been allowed near Dera Bugti since the start of the war in Afghanistan in 2001, but somehow the leader of the expedition, Professor Bartholomew Jones, had been granted permission to dig around the Western Suleiman. If we were successful, we had a chance to make a significant discovery in the field.

All the graduate students in my department had applied for the place. I had waited until the last day to submit my application, uploading the essay with minutes to spare. And, instead of describing all the technical skills I would bring to the team, I painted a picture of the world as it might have appeared to *Ambulocetus*: the landscape of the Early Eocene Era after the extinction of dinosaurs, home to the whale who both walked and swam, an amphibian that was also a tetrapod, a creature embracing its duality, its attraction to both the lure of the seas and the comforts of land. I had sent off the essay and decided to think very little of it, telling myself I would have to do my thesis research in a library while secretly believing they would choose me, not because of my name, but because there was poetry in *Ambulocetus*, and she demanded someone who would understand that. Kyung-Ju had congratulated me after the announcement, but I knew it was particularly difficult for her. She worked harder than me, had an encyclopaedic knowledge of the Eocene, and answered to parents who, unlike mine, took a daily interest in her progress.

I tried to grab the cup from Kyung-Ju's hand. I knew she had a crush on Brian and I didn't want her to embarrass herself.

'My mom was so mad,' Kyung-Ju said, dodging me. 'It was bad enough I wanted to study palaeontology, but I couldn't even be the best at it.'

'I just got lucky.'

'Don't sweat it, Kyung-Ju,' Brian said, 'you get to stay here with the rest of us, while Miss Glamourpants gets her hands dirty.'

Brian threw his arm casually around me, his unshaved chin bristling against my cheek. I smelled whisky. His beard reminded me of the concert, your fingers entwined in mine. I let a small sound escape my lips. Brian lingered, leaning towards me, and I thought about kissing him, because I wanted so much to kiss you. Brian had asked me out during our department orientation, and I had laughed it off, saying we had only just arrived, there would be plenty of time for romance. He hadn't repeated the offer, and soon everyone knew about Rashid. I pushed him away gently now and wrestled Kyung-Ju's paper cup from her hand. 'That's enough,' I said. 'Here, eat some cashews.' I steered her towards the sofa, supporting her head as she leaned against the armrest.

'I wanted it more than you,' Kyung-Ju said, her voice cracking.

'I'll whisper your name into the dust,' I said.

I wandered onto the porch, wishing you'd given me your

phone number. I would call and tell you about the party, the people spilling onto the tiny patch of grass in front of the house, Kyung-Ju's head rolling forward onto her arms, the smell of cigarettes and baked fruit. I pulled my phone out of my pocket and started sending Rashid a text. It was a few lines long before I gave up, unable to capture the thread of feeling that had begun to unspool inside me: a sadness at having to leave this place, which I had always treated as temporary, and a parallel restlessness, an eagerness to go because the conversations were folding back onto themselves, and I was thinking about the woman who gave birth to me, tucked away in some part of my country, and that, out of loyalty to my parents, I would probably never know, because the word biological was terrifying to them, and had never been uttered.

Bettina came through the door with two of her fellow anthropologists, Suzu, who wore her blonde hair in a pile of dreadlocks, and Chandana, an Indian woman I had never particularly liked. I wondered who had invited her. 'Hey girl,' Bettina said, 'we've been looking for you.'

'I was dealing with Kyung-Ju. She's drunk.'

'I know. She threw up in the kitchen.' Bettina leaned against the railing, while Suzu pulled a red packet out of a small purse she wore around her neck. Chandana joined me on the porch step, sitting a little closer than I wanted her to.

'Brian's taking her home now.'

'I don't think she's used to drinking,' Suzu said. 'What did you put in that sangria?'

'Nothing,' Bettina said.

'She's rebelling,' Suzu said. 'Do they drink where you come from, Zubaida?'

'Yes and no,' I said, recalling the parties I had gone to

in high school, where the booze was in plain sight. 'Officially, no. But everyone drinks.'

'Everyone? Surely not everyone. Not the farmer, or the rag-trade worker,' Suzu said, lighting a cigarette.

I rolled my eyes. 'When I said everyone, I meant everyone I know.'

'Zubaida doesn't like us to have stereotypes about Bangladesh,' Bettina said.

'Like what?'

'Like that it's full of fatwas and poor people,' Bettina said, looking to me for approval.

I was feeling contrary, so I said, 'Except that it is.'

'Oh, fuck that. You spend three years lecturing me and now you've what, changed your mind?' The scent of Suzu's clove cigarette enveloped us in a spicy, acrid fog.

'Suzu,' I said, 'it's like 1993 in your mouth.'

'So you're saying your country is portrayed accurately in the Western media,' Bettina persisted.

'It's exactly like that. Political in-fighting, radicals on the loose, child marriage, and climate disaster around the corner. No one should want to go anywhere near it.'

Suzu turned her thumb ring around and around. 'I have no idea what you guys are talking about,' she said.

'That's because you're smoking that shit,' Bettina said, waving her hands in front of her face. 'Zubaida met someone.'

Suzu dropped her cigarette and pressed it into the grass. 'I thought you had a boyfriend.'

'I did. I do.' I wanted to change the subject, so I turned to Chandana. 'What about you?' I asked. 'Dating anyone?' She was one of those Indian women who adorned herself with enough silver jewellery to set off a metal detector. Her ears were pierced in multiple locations, her nose had a ring with a chain that connected to her earring, and her bangles chimed every time she raised her arms. Bettina hadn't given herself permission to make fun of her until I started calling her 'full bridal', because, as far as I knew, only a fully decked out Indian bride would wear a nose-ring like that. I assumed Chandana had many sexual conquests, that she would marry an ethnomusicologist or a sculptor, but she said, 'Oh, my parents will only approve if I marry a Tam-Bram.'

I knew what she meant, but Suzu and Bettina did not. 'A Brahmin boy from my home state, Tamil Nadu,' she explained.

'That doesn't make any sense,' I said.

'Doesn't it?'

'So how does it work?' Bettina asked.

'Every few weeks I get a phone call, and it's some banker or doctor on the other end, and he's the nicest guy in the world, and so boring he could put a rabid dog into a coma. And then we go out on a date to an expensive restaurant, and then I go home and tell my parents he's not the one.'

'Do they mind?' Suzu asked.

'What restaurant?' I asked.

'Oh, I've been to them all. Craigie on Main, Aujourd'hui. They like their French food, even if they're vegetarian and can only order the cheese soufflé. Once a guy even flew me to Miami. And my parents like to see me trying.'

'How do you get anything done?'

'It's very time-consuming. I almost failed my comps.'

'What happens if you fall in love with someone?' Bettina said.

Chandana and I rolled our eyes at each other. 'I was dating this white guy last year, and my parents found out and they totally freaked. I mean, my mother had to double up on her blood pressure medication. It wasn't worth it.'

'That's terrible,' Suzu said.

'Oh, it can't be that bad,' I said. 'Craigie on Main is a really good restaurant. Rashid took me last year.'

'So you're going to marry this guy or what?' Chandana asked.

'Yes,' I said. That moment of clairvoyance was finally catching up with me. 'I've known him my whole life, my parents adore him. And he's sexy as hell, everyone's always telling me how lucky I am.'

'You should've broken up with him years ago,' Bettina said.

'It just gets harder when your parents are attached,' Chandana said.

I put my head on Bettina's lap and thought for a moment about what it would've been like if I had ended it with Rashid. We had been together since high school. When he'd gone to college in London the year before I left for America, I had told myself I would give it six months, but I found Dhaka dull without him, and when I left for college myself, I found his telephone calls, made precisely on time every morning before I went to class, comforting through that first, long New England winter. In March, which your people call spring, but when the ground is still as hard and white as a funeral, he had come to visit, renting a car and driving up from Boston, bringing a suitcase full of things he had smuggled through customs and cooking khichuri and potato bhorta in the tiny kitchen in the basement of my dorm. That was when I think I decided – watching his fingers casually wrapped around the top of the steering wheel as he drove me through snow-banked roads. After he finished university, he moved home to join his father's business. He was always there when I went back for the holidays, taking my parents out for their birthdays and anniversaries, filling something of the emptiness I had left behind. There were sometimes men I liked, men I flirted with, but no one I could ever imagine bringing home, because home is where I knew I must eventually end up, no matter how long or sweet the wandering.

And that, Elijah, is the story of our first meeting. I have had much time to dwell on it. I been able to recount every beat of our encounter, to revel in that moment of possibility. Perhaps the memory is as clear to you as it is to me; perhaps you recall that I had a bruise below my knee that you commented on at the café, and I explained that I had never learned to ride a bike and my roommate was trying to teach me before I left. Perhaps you recall our mutual love for Nina Simone and telling me that your parents had once taken you to a concert when you were six, that you regretted deeply when you were older that you had slept through the whole thing. Perhaps you will remember every detail, as I do, though the alternative is more likely – that you have erased the entire episode from your mind, because you never think of me, and even when you do – even if you remember picking up a ten-dollar bill from the sidewalk, a note that fell out when I took my keys out of my pocket – it won't be with tenderness, but with regret. Either way: here, three years later, is the story of our meeting, and falling in love, and breaking up, and all the messiness in between. Here is every detail recorded in my mind and amplified by remorse. It is an ethnographic field study and an apology for the way I behaved, and a chance for me to give you a comprehensive account of exactly what happened – because, though we were together for so much of that time and I felt like I was telling you everything, I realise now that there was much you didn't know, that even when you are closer to someone than you have ever been or thought you could be, there will always be silences and ellipses and things you should have said but were too afraid to admit. And somewhere along the way – I have not yet decided where – I will also tell you about Anwar, because his story is as important as ours, the three of us woven together in ways we could never have dreamt.

I had arranged to meet you in front of the Science Centre, but when I got there, ten minutes late, you hadn't arrived. The heat had already sliced through the day; the fountains were on, and a few people were milling around the curved stone bench. There was a woman pushing a child in a stroller and a man in a black suit with a newspaper spread out between his hands, and the clown who usually hung around the entrance to the subway. I wasn't sure what to do, so I circled back through the Yard, walking slowly, so that I could be sure you would have arrived by the time I returned. Then I thought, what if you didn't show up, what if you walked away and I never saw you again? I rushed. When I crossed the gate out of the Yard, the man in the black suit looked up from his newspaper and I realised that you were him, and you saw me and you waved. My heart was beating so fast I thought I might crack a rib. I waved back.

'Well hello there,' you said, in a tone so warm and friendly it could have been the greeting of an old friend. You wore a formal white shirt and a striped tie. The comb-tracks were visible in your damp hair. I wanted to jump for joy but instead I stood restless in front of you. 'What were you just doing?' I asked.

'Nothing,' you said. 'Just sitting. In fact, I was thinking about you.'

'I was thinking about you too,' I said.

You broke into a smile. I decided not to ask why you had dressed up. You said you knew the best breakfast place in Cambridge, and I said I'd had a bowl of cereal but I could always eat again. I liked the fact that people in your country took their breakfast seriously. Back home I could get ice cream at midnight, and there were fruit stalls on Mirpur Road that sold mangoes until dawn, but there was never anywhere to go in the morning. No omelettes or hash browns or complicated types of toast. I followed you out of the quad, up Quincy and down Mass Ave, past the Korean café and the wine store that I had always been too intimidated to enter. You took off your jacket and folded it neatly over your arm. We ducked into a small, unlabelled restaurant with a blue awning that I must have passed a hundred times but never noticed. The air conditioner was on full blast. You found us a table at the back and sat down, careful to restrain your tie as you pulled your chair forward.

'Mass Ave Diner,' you said proudly, sitting with your face towards the sun. Against the backdrop of the undertaker's suit, the blond tangle of your hair was electric. Eyes little moons of blue light. I forced myself not to stare at you, taking in the plastic tablecloths and the large, egg-shaped man behind a flat grill in the open kitchen. Rashid would have never brought me somewhere like this; he would have taken me to an upscale brunch place on the other side of the river after reading reviews on his phone. Now you were talking to the waitress, your tone intimate, meeting her smile. The waitress left with a wink and a sneaker-clad pirouette.

We talked. You started with the story of the time your parents had taken an extended sabbatical and moved your entire family to Vermont. You remembered breaking the ice by throwing rocks into the well, keeping bees and pigs and growing your own vegetables. Your parents tried to start a small business – Strong's Sweet Nectars – selling honey and maple syrup, thinking that they might leave it all behind and stay out there for ever if things worked out. But the experiment failed: the bees swarmed and disappeared one day, and the syrup crystallised, and your mother grew tired of washing diapers by hand, and they packed everyone up and drove you all back to Cambridge, and central heating, and running water, and eventual divorce. You were nine. The place was still there. You returned occasionally and retreated from the world, not speaking or meeting another person for days, sometimes weeks, on end.

'I could never be quiet for such a long time,' I told you. 'Doesn't it make you crazy?'

You said something about how the world became very loud when one stopped talking. Then you told me about the trees in Vermont, how they gave up their sap, and the wild turkeys that roamed the valleys, and the ice-cold lakes into which you and your brothers and your sister liked to plunge. It was all very exotic to me, because I had never been camping with my parents or jumped into anything deeper than a swimming pool. Going on the dig was the most adventurous thing I had ever contemplated doing. Thinking about it now conjured an image of another person that lived inside me, someone to whom the word 'intrepid' would be frequently attached.

The waitress came back. We had forgotten to order. I think I may have reached for the menu, but you looked at me and said, 'I'm going to order for you because there's this sandwich and I know you'll like it. Best sandwich in the world.'

'A sandwich for breakfast?'

'Not a sandwich for breakfast. A breakfast-sandwich.'

You turned to the waitress and ordered. 'Just egg and cheese for me, Betty. Coffee? Orange juice? You drink coffee, right?'

I shook my head. 'Sorry. I hate the stuff. Do they have tea?' You asked Betty for tea. 'With milk and sugar,' I said. Behind the open kitchen, the egg-shaped man poured a large spoonful of batter onto the grill.

You said, 'Tell me about the whale dinosaurs.'

'Well, the thing about whales is that they went the opposite way to everyone else, evolutionarily speaking.'

'What do you mean, like they walked first and then swam?'

'Yes. The whale's earliest ancestor, *Pakicetus*, was almost entirely a land mammal. Sort of like a coyote. Ten million years later, you have *Basilosaurus*, who had nothing but a trace of the amphibian left in him. The intermediate species are what interest me.'

'The intermediate species. I like that. So which ones are in between?'

'There are a few, but the one I'm looking for is called *Ambulocetus*. It was discovered about twenty years ago, but no one has been able to bring back a complete skeleton. That's why I'm going to Pakistan.' We talked awhile about *Ambulocetus*. Even though I had explained this story many times, to many people, I felt as if I was revealing a secret about myself. This was a feeling that would return to me many times in your presence, of giving away more than I intended to. It was neither unpleasant nor comfortable.

The food arrived. The sandwiches looked small and pale sitting alone on their heavy porcelain plates. The tea was in a giant mug, the orange juice in corrugated-plastic cups.

I picked up the sandwich, which was almost as high as it was wide, and took a bite. The egg came loose between the layers and spilled onto my chin, the plate. I was embarrassed, and tried to keep my lips closed, alarmed by the intensity of flavour and volume in my mouth.

At this point, I believe you may have thought you'd committed a faux pas. You said, 'There's sausage in that sandwich – you don't eat pork?'

I allowed myself to hesitate a little before laughing. 'It's all right,' I said, 'just don't tell my parents.'

You pulled the plate from me. 'I'm so sorry.'

'I'm joking. Really, I am. My parents don't care, they're not religious. Give me my sandwich.' I pulled the plate back. You asked if I was Muslim, and I said yes, I was, but that I came from a family of sceptics. Nationalism was the religion in our household. 'They're communists. Sort of. The Bangladesh war changed them.'

I think I may have mentioned at that moment, by way of explanation, that my mother drove an ambulance during the war. I wanted to bring up the subject of my adoption again. To repeat that my parents were not my only parents, that I had other parents, parents I had hardly thought about until last night. The image of your home – the cabin, the maple trees – was deepening in my mind. I could smell pine and hear the clamour of your family. Your story made my story into a sad one, and I began to regard you with some envy. Also, I could not understand why you were suddenly in limbo, after having had what appeared to be such a privileged life. You mentioned again that you'd been to India, that you might like to go again.

'I had a friend from there, I went to visit her family. And then we travelled together to Nepal, and Bhutan.'

I sprang back into the moment. I wanted to ask you the name of this girl. I crossed and uncrossed my arms, trying to find the most casual, relaxed pose I could to express how much this story was not bothering me. I told myself that people fell in love with you all the time. You were cartoonishly handsome. Even your forehead was sexy, big and flat and serious. I tilted my orange juice till there was nothing left at the bottom of the cup, and then, not being able to resist, I said, 'Was she your girlfriend?'

'She was, for a long time. But it was over by the time I went to India.'

'Did you break her heart?' The longing to be that girl, drawing you towards me from across the continents, was so strong I felt a surge of blood to my legs.

'No.' I would learn, over time, that you were the master of the meaning-burdened one-word answer.

I looked into the pools of your eyes, the light ring of your eyelashes, allowing you to see inside me. 'Last night, you looked so beautiful when you cried. I've never seen anyone cry like that,' you said.

'Can I ask you now why you are dressed so formally?'

'Today is my grandmother's funeral.'

You told me you had sauntered into an internet café in Pondicherry, ready to write a long email to your family about that town, the fort and the little shacks on the edge of the beach where you had admired the sunset, each evening a different shade of pink, and you were thinking how different the sun was there, bigger yet somehow further away than in Vermont, where it stood alone without the frame of clouds. And then you discovered your father had been trying to reach you for days, calling all your friends and asking if they knew where you were. But you had travelled to Pondicherry alone – Reeva, the girl, had left you in Mysore and gone back to Delhi. As you told me this story, that lost expression came over you again, the one I had seen last night as the lights came on in the auditorium, and now I wanted to tell you I was looking for something too, something that couldn't be found in the ankle bones of a whale. You pulled your chair forward and pressed your chest against the rim of the table.

'How terrible for you,' I said. 'I'm so sorry.' And we stayed that way for a long time. And then I told you. I hadn't meant to, not right then, but it just came out. 'There's something I should have said yesterday. About me.'

'What's that?' I had slipped off my sandals and I was sitting cross-legged on the chair, but now I straightened up and planted my feet back on the ground.

'I have a person – a boyfriend – back home.'

'Really?'

'His name is Rashid.'

'Rashid,' you repeated.

'We've known each other our whole lives. We'll probably get married or something,' I said, letting it all come out in a rush. 'Of course, not that you care, or anything, I just – I just thought, since we just met—'

'I wish I'd met you before.'

'I didn't want to give you the wrong impression.'

Our sandwiches had been devoured, the mugs emptied. The waitress returned, tore a page from her pad, and left it on the table. I couldn't tell if you were disappointed. Were you? Or perhaps, with the death of your grandmother, you were unable to register much of anything at that moment, your every feeling crowded by some other feeling. Even now, when I think back, I wonder if our story would have ended differently if I had told you at some other moment, or in some other way.

'So,' you said, inhaling deeply, 'what were you planning to do your last few days in Cambridge?'

'Nothing much. Finish at the lab, return some library books.'

The meal was over. I put my palms on the table. 'Thank you for breakfast.'

'I wish it was two weeks ago,' you said again. 'Or last year.'

'Me too,' I replied, believing I meant it more.

We looked at each other, wondering what to do next. Finally you said, 'Would you like to come to my grandmother's funeral?'

I tried to imagine what would happen if my grandmother died and I brought you to her funeral. 'No, I don't think so.'

'How about later? We're having lunch at my mother's.'

I didn't want to meet your entire family, not like this, but I wanted an excuse to see you again. I said, 'I thought about last night, and it all made sense to me. It's because I'm going, and I'm not sure when I'll be back – something like that.'

'You're an intermediate species, like *Ambulocetus*.'

'Exactly.'

'Maybe if we'd met under different circumstances, we might have decided to see what it was like. To be together. But if that's not on the cards, that's okay. I still want to spend time with you. Is that all right?'

'Of course,' I said. 'I do too.' I was unsure if I had gotten what I wanted. Without being coy or hesitant, you spoke about our being together, and accepted with equanimity that we would not be. I should have been relieved – an awkwardness averted – but instead I felt disappointed, as if the conversation had hurried past me and I had failed to hail it down.

You asked if I had ever heard the Goldberg Variations. I hadn't. 'You remind me of number thirteen,' you said. 'Shostakovich is okay, but Bach is the source.'

I had to go to the MCZ and pack up my lab.

You checked your watch. 'Call me when you're done,' you said. I wished you good luck for your grandmother's funeral. I wanted so much for you to hold my hand, to put your arms around me like you had last night, but the moment, if it had ever existed, had passed, and so I settled for walking back down Mass Ave with you, the sidewalk warm beneath our shoes, everything brilliantly cloudless above.

I shared a large, brightly lit room on the ground floor of the Museum of Comparative Zoology with six other graduate students and a visiting professor. A bank of windows faced out towards Kirkland Avenue. Everything smelled of old wood. When I arrived to pack up my desk, Kyung-Ju was photographing the ankle bones of the *Pakicetus* we had borrowed from the University of Michigan, and I could hear some of the others in the back room with the scanner. The lab had been my home for the last three years, and after breakfast with you I found myself indulging in a moment of nostalgia, because I knew now that whatever happened on the dig, I would return to Dhaka, and that meant the end of late nights in here, over-sugaring my tea and arguing about when the Tethys had finally dried up. The department was moving anyway, to a brand-new facility on the other side of the quad.

I had first discovered the whale while leafing through an article in *National Geographic*, which my parents, like so many of their generation, dutifully collected. Photographs of *Ambulocetus*, with her hind legs and long, slender mouth, fascinated my younger self. I was naturally curious about origins and unusual digressions in history, such as a whale who walked and also swam, while all the other animals were pulling themselves out of the sea and making their homes on land. My mother had not been pleased. 'Fish?' she kept saying, when I told her I was doing a PhD in Evolutionary Biology. My mother had been an ambulance driver and a revolutionary and the kind of woman who stood in front of picket lines. She had been in a war. And I was hiding behind very large sea creatures. But what was my alternative? Medicine, like her? I was good at science, but I did not like bodies, at least, not the ones that hovered between life and death, the scale tipped by my hand – too much responsibility, that – or English?, my love of novels started young, deepened by the lack of company, and although my parents' shelves were on the dry, political side, I read Ibsen and *The Last of the Mohicans* and *Bleak House*, and, too early, *Jane Eyre*, and there were totems in those books: with every age I recognised the clues that would lead me, Gretel-like, through life, but who wants to know and be known like that? Not me. Jane was poor, obscure, plain, and little, I did not want to know her, or the her that lurked within me. Hiding in plain sight, that was my habit, or maybe I should have been some kind of humanitarian, but the reasons against that should be obvious by now, because I would have been looking around the corner for myself, the subject and object at the same time. Bettina would have said it was possible to auto-anthropologise, but that sounded too much like 'apologise'; I would have spent the whole time feeling sorry for all the people I would never become, trapped in guilt like my mother, and again we return to her, because she made everything possible and impossible.

So, you see, there was nothing for me but those skulls and bones and taxonomy and strata, Hutton's earth, with 'no vestige of a beginning, no prospect of an end', that was what I chose: the earth with its hot centre, and its rocks that threw up history, and bones, enduring bones, skipping back to a time when I couldn't be found.

'Ready for departure?' Ju said, holding the camera at arm's length and clicking. She smelled strongly of soap. Neither of us mentioned the night before.

'Not nearly,' I said. 'Though I finished packing the apartment late last night when I couldn't sleep.'

I had brought a small carry-on suitcase with me the week before, when I'd begun putting away my papers. Now I started with the filing cabinet next to my desk. There were old articles I had photocopied; course syllabi; teaching materials for Archaeology 101, which I had worked on as a tutor for three semesters, winning rave reviews from my students; essays; transcripts; the whole catalogue of my three years as a graduate student. I threw most of it away, keeping only a thin file of papers that related to the dig. Around midday, I sped up, clogging the blue recycling bin and bequeathing my model of the 50 million-year-old *Rodhocetus balochistanensis* skull to Ju. We hugged goodbye, Ju holding on for an extra few seconds by way of apology, and I promised to keep in touch. I took out my phone and dialled your number, but there was no reply. I thought I'd sit under one of the big oak trees in the Quad for a few moments before trying you again, but when I went through the double doors, dragging the suitcase behind me, there you were on the steps. You had removed your jacket and rolled up the sleeves of your shirt, and for a brief moment I imagined you making love to your Indian girlfriend and how your forearms would have straddled her body and how she must so desperately miss those forearms, in fact, was probably thinking about them at this moment, that she and I must be having the same dream, and how much she would hate me for being closer to your forearms than she, thousands of miles away in Delhi. Poor girl. Poor Delhi.

'Are you all right?' I asked. You passed me a pamphlet, printed on craggy recycled paper. *Clementine Alexandra Rowena Morris. Cartographer, Adventurer, Poet, Activist, Mother, Dancer, Artist.*

The day had cracked open, the sidewalks shimmering in the heat. We walked in silence, struggling with the upward slope of Mass Ave as it neared the wider streets of Somerville. You stopped to look in the window of an origami shop and we discussed paper, and folding, and cranes, then we turned into a side street, and you led me to a pale yellow house with rocking chairs on the porch and wilting daffodils in the front yard. The sort of house I had walked by many times, Obama posters in the window, the smell of laundry and Thanksgiving, modest, Protestant, indifferently grand.

The door was open. A few people stood on the porch, and, as we approached, one of them waved and called out your name. I saw a tall man with wide shoulders and a square, friendly face who shook my hand and introduced himself as your uncle, and as we passed through the front door and more guests said hello and patted you on the back, you took my hand and guided me through. People's shoes were noisy on the wooden floorboards and their voices rose up to the high, white ceiling. The house was bright and frayed and bigger than it had seemed from the outside. We entered a room at the back with tall windows and double doors that opened onto the garden beyond.

Immediately you pointed out a woman who you said was your mother. She was slim under long, loose layers of black and dark grey, with tousled hair and a pair of eyes that matched yours in warmth and colour. You told her my name and she smiled distractedly and asked me to make myself at home. I gripped your arm, and we turned towards an older woman with a narrow face. She held out a thin hand, the bones close to the surface, and you told me she was your great-aunt.

'Hello,' she said. 'I'm Autumn, Clementine's sister.' Her voice was reedy and English.

'Zubaida Bashir. It's lovely to meet you.'

'I met Zubaida last night, at the Shostakovich,' you said.

Autumn asked me if I was a musician. Although they must be around the same age, she could not have been less like my grandmother. Nanu had fewer lines around her eyes, but in her manner she was much older, her ironed saris, the pearl necklace she always wore around her neck, and Autumn, though her face was craggy and she had a slight tremor in her hands, appeared as though she took long walks in the snow. I told her I was no musician, but a palaeontologist.

'Fossils! You know, Elijah's great-great-great-grandfather was the original Indiana Jones.'

Of course he was. I looked around me now, at all the people in black dresses and suits. On a sofa that faced the garden, three men who looked almost identical to each other and to you were crowded together, playing Scrabble. They must be your brothers. I realised I didn't even know which one you were in order of age, but, even as I asked myself the question, I knew you must be the youngest. Ezekiel, Erasmus, and Eric. Hello. Hello. Even sitting, they were almost as tall as me. Their teeth gleamed in their faces.

No one had asked me if I wanted anything to eat, so when you let go of my hand and moved towards the piano, I made my way to the table and found mismatched casserole dishes, pie plates, and baking trays holding lasagna, cold salads, cheeses, and sticks of vegetables. There was an open bottle of wine on the sideboard and a woman pouring herself a glass asked me if I wanted any.

A loud, rhythmic tune exploded from the piano. 'Thelonious Monk,' you called out above the crowd, 'Grandma's favourite.'

'Oh, stop that now. Play something with a tune,' someone said, but the crashing jazz continued. The woman who had offered me a glass of wine now asked, 'Where are you from?' She had a milky, freckled face and a beautiful mouth, her long hair pulled into a French braid.

'Bangladesh,' I said, then realised she was asking how I came to be there. 'I'm a friend of Elijah.'

'You know, my grandma once made us watch a documentary about Bangladesh. And we spent the next few weeks chanting "Joy Bangla".'

'That's something of a national slogan.'

'Grandma was an old leftie.'

'You must be Elijah's sister.'

'That's right. Ada.'

When she leaned down and hugged me, I wanted to cry.

'I recommend the tuna casserole. My mother is a terrible cook.'

In the meantime, you had started to sing. 'Imagination is funny/ It makes a cloudy day sunny.'

Ada joined in, with a strong, practised voice. 'Makes a bee think of honey.' She led us to the piano and then you were sitting side by side on the stool. Others circled you, and the chorus of voices was sweet and loud.

I stepped back, holding the plate of tuna casserole, watching your back sway to the music, and then I drifted away, down a corridor and past a pair of swinging doors into the kitchen. I found the countertops worn and scrubbed, the whole place smelling of old trees. I leaned against the wood-burning stove for a moment, enjoying its warmth even on this very hot day, before examining the photographs on the fridge. A collage of willowy, beautiful people smiled indirectly at the camera, holding dogs and babies against backdrops of mountains and dark lakes. I opened the fridge and found an open tin of cat food and a jug of lemonade crowded with spears of fresh mint.

The song had finished. I liked how no one noticed as I came and went. When I went back inside, a wave of warm air swirled through the room, the smell of lavender drifting in from outside and settling on the furniture. I saw, then, that there was a large portrait of your grandmother displayed on a side table. Someone had pencilled her features, a strong jaw and wide-apart eyes and a pair of dark-rimmed glasses. She wore a small smile, as if she had just seen someone she knew and was about to wave hello. Beside the drawing there was a notebook on which people were writing messages. I looked closer. *May you be as treasured above as you were among us.* And: *Tell God it's getting hot down here!* And: *Grandma, as you left the planet, you sent me a gift. Thank you.*

A few people carried plates into the kitchen and I heard the sound of water running. I found your mother reclining on the sofa. The sun zigzagged against her face. Your brothers were outside, huddled together beside an old swing set. In a gazebo at the back, I spotted Autumn sitting on her own, and I wondered if I should go and talk to her. A man was narrating a story about how Clementine had crashed his parents' wedding dressed as a camel. I watched you as you listened to the story – you had obviously heard it before – and I wondered what it was like to be so sure of your provenance, to talk about ancestors whose lives were documented, birth certificates and university degrees and marriages officially registered. To be told a straight story that you knew was true. Me, I couldn't look at another living person and see something of myself, the angle of eyes, a gait, a particular texture of hair, or identify the things I hated about myself, the smallness of my breasts, the weakness of my ankles. The kink in my hair had no echo. In a culture where people commented freely on everyone's looks, people rarely said anything about mine, because a simple phrase, 'how beautiful you are', couldn't be followed by, 'just like your mother'. Just like who? To whom did these long bones belong, the tone of my skin? Not to the ancestors collaged onto my history.

I laughed with everyone else as the man described the look of shock on his parents' faces, the judge at the registrar's office standing up and ordering them to leave.

'We should go,' you said, appearing behind me. You had changed into shorts and a red T-shirt with Chinese lettering on the front. 'Zubaida has things to do.'

'I didn't get to say a proper hello,' your mother said, pulling her glasses from on top of her head.

'I'm leaving in a few days,' I said.

'Well, that's a shame.' Your mother put her hands on my shoulders and regarded me, and I wanted to ask her if I could stay, to walk up the stairs and fold myself into the blankets on her bed. 'Here,' she said, as if reading my mind, 'take this.' And she pulled a necklace over her head and then over mine. It was made of old buttons, each one a slightly different shade of blue. I kissed her on the cheek and said goodbye. Outside, a pair of brown cats had draped themselves on the porch. The air was packed tight in the heat, everything quiet and solemn.

Meeting your family changed something between us. I saw the way you wrestled with your brothers, punching them on the arm by way of hello, and how everything was so perfectly dishevelled in your house. And I could imagine almost every day of your childhood, because it would have been documented in films or on television – in that way, you had probably lived a deeply unremarkable life, had experiences without specificity, and that had bothered you, the way my own past grated at me. All the things that irritated you were things that I had longed for, and all the things you longed for were things I took for granted. I fingered the necklace your mother had given me. It was so light around my neck I could hardly feel it, and I sought that, that lightness and impermeability, things passed from person to person with little significance.

'I was Clem's favourite,' you said, in answer to my question. 'I'm going to miss her.'

'Was your father there?'

'I didn't want to overwhelm you.'

I was suddenly hungry. You suggested we return to Harvard Square and have lunch. We debated the merits of Felipe's and Chipotle's, both of which I had frequented over the years and would miss, and at that point I remembered I had left my suitcase at your house and I stopped in a rectangle of shade, asking if we could go back.

You told me to wait there, and jogged backwards. A few minutes later you were wheeling the suitcase down the street. When you stopped I closed my eyes and I thought you might kiss me lightly and tenderly on the forehead, as if you had been kissing me for years, as if we had lived together in a house and raised children and frowned over the sagging roof and made French toast on Sundays.

'So tell me again,' you said, putting your hands into your pockets and leaning back on your heels. 'About your boyfriend.'

'There's nothing to say, really,' I said, taking the suitcase from you and starting to walk again. 'He's lovely.'

'How does he feel about new friends?'

I imagined how I would describe our meeting to Rashid without making it sound as if I had done something wrong, which I hadn't. Not yet. I thought about the ease with which I had just entered your home. I had, since arriving in this country, assumed an air of being able to float seamlessly from place to place: a grateful guest at Thanksgiving dinner, a girl from far away who understood everyone's jokes because her English was so good. It was better to render my difference invisible, brush over the small discomforts I occasionally felt, always too cold in the spring when everyone wore T-shirts, occasionally emphasising a syllable (I once mispronounced 'intestine', making it sound like 'Lichtenstein' to a table full of laughing Americans). You held me in a very tight gaze now, in a way I don't believe I had ever been looked at, and I found myself struggling to speak, and still I believed there was nothing for me to regret or be ashamed of, because, though the feeling had the intensity of being sexual, it was something altogether different – not a churning but a quieting, as if I were being put back together, piece by piece. I felt the sidewalk burning beneath the soles of my feet, and the sun high and bright above, and, thus framed by a day that seemed to stretch over my whole life, I declared to myself that you were the best friend I'd ever had.

'What should we do next?' you said.

'We should go and look at the Glass Flowers.' I'd had the idea in the kitchen at your mother's, and I was hoping it would be a new discovery for you, even though your tenure in this town had been far longer than mine.

You paused for a moment, then exclaimed: 'Oh, the Glass Flowers! My grandmother used to take me. Did I tell you that? How did you know?'

I was thrilled. 'I took a chance.'

We went back down Mass Ave, stopping for a pizza at Hi-Rise Bakery. All my clothes were sticking to my skin. I complained and you bought me an ice lolly from a convenience store. When we reached Kirkland I relaxed – this was where I was most comfortable, among the red-brick buildings, the courtyards and the small, triangular gardens.

The receptionist at the Museum of Natural History gave us two small metal pins to attach to our lapels. I led the way up the stairs to the top floor. 'I want to show you something,' I said 'before we see the glass flowers.' We went through the displays, past the ancient Rhino and the *Glyptodont*. We paused in front of the domed shell of *Stupendemys geographicus*, the giant tortoise, and I told you the story of how it had been transported in pieces. In the *Vertebrate* room I led you to the giant glass cabinet that held *Kronosaurus*. I'd seen it many times before, and I knew its murky history – that what we were looking at was probably an incorrect reconstruction, but it always took my breath away – something about the whole swimming reptile, all the way from its enormous maw to its pelvis to the articulated bones of its fins. I held out my hand with a flourish. You read the caption. 'So this is what you're up to,' you whispered. 'One-upping this guy.'

'Something like that.'

The glass flowers sprang up from inside the display cabinets as if they had just been cut out of a field. Tiny filaments of wire held the petals and stems together. Without context, they sat like silent pearls in the felted hush of the museum.

'I haven't been since I was a kid,' you said. You read the plaque, illuminated by a small lamp attached to the wall. 'Leopold and Rudolf Blaschka.'

'Father and son. It took them almost fifty years.' I had forgotten how much they were about sex. Stamens and ovaries and modes of reproduction. And they were bigger than I remembered.

I considered telling you that you were taking something away from me right now, standing there with your fingers wrapped around the handle of my suitcase, staring at the glass cactus as though the pink flower blossoming from its side were some sort of miracle. I considered telling you my parents liked to tell stories that would make them feel better about the adoption, for example, that I resembled my maternal grandfather, whom I had never met, that I had his height and his small eyes, which made me look a little Mongolian, and his curly hair. There was an old joke in the family that my grandfather was descended from Genghis Khan. I had never heard anyone tell this joke apart from my parents, who forced a couple of laughs out whenever they said it, and then looked at each other and willed the whole thing to be true. Then I turned nine, and they confessed everything, and by then I was old enough to know we would never speak of it again. But I didn't say anything like that. Because, for the first time

I could remember, I didn't care where or who I came from. I didn't care if I was an amphibian or a member of an in-between species because I belonged here, in this moment, with these fragments of moulded glass, and little else mattered.

On the way down, you stopped on the second floor and leaned against the banister.

'So now you've seen the Glass Flowers,' I said. 'Again.'

'I don't want to say goodbye.'

I thought about the night I had lost my virginity, Rashid sneaking into my bedroom while my parents were at work, the ceiling fan muffling our sounds, the way my knees felt wobbly for days afterwards, the guilty, exhilarated glances we had given each other in school the next day.

'I would like to see you every day,' you said.

'I'm leaving on Friday.'

'That's ages away.' You were holding your hands wide apart to indicate the vast amount of time between now and then. I worried if I spent another minute there, on those steps, with you, I would be rooted for ever, that I might live and re-live this moment for the rest of my life. 'We've got tomorrow, and the day after,' you said. 'And on Friday I'll take you to the airport.'

In all my years in America, no one had ever taken me to the airport. Or picked me up. Bettina had offered, but I had always said no, not minding as I passed through the arrivals gate without scanning the crowd for a familiar face. I'd had a twenty-hour plane ride to morph into an anonymous student, landing at Logan Airport along with the Argentinians and the Koreans, getting our bags checked in case we'd attempted to smuggle in Mama's dulce de leche or kimchee. And when I departed, I took the T and then the Silverline. I banked on the fact that no one would miss me, that there were people on the other side to whom I mattered more. So when you offered to take me to the airport, because I had spent years in this country without allowing that sort of intimacy to blossom, and because I was leaving now, probably only to return once, I threw up my arms and said, 'okay,' for the first time in seven years not wishing I was somewhere else.

The next morning we met at the Science Center and walked again to the diner. We ate the same sandwiches. You confessed to an addiction to coffee, I an addiction to chips. By chips, I said, I mean French fries. The space yawned and narrowed between us like an accordion. We shared a love of Russian literature, and, recently, Shostakovich. I confessed I was a fan of *Buffy the Vampire Slayer*, and you replied that your childhood was bereft of television, sugar, and most forms of processed food. You said the house in Vermont had no running water or electricity. I told you my ancestors had worked very hard to get running water, thank you very much. I drew a parallel with the whale, saying, you white Americans, going backwards into the sea when everyone else is happy to be on dry land. Ah, but your fascination with the whale suggests you see the benefits of bucking history, you countered. I smiled at that. You said again that you would very much like to see where I had grown up. And I wondered what I would ever do with you if I did take you home. There was a reason I had chosen Rashid, and that reason sat inside me like a stone. I was thinking now that you would say something about your grandmother, but you didn't, and I had no idea if this was the way people displayed grief in your family, by making new friends and laughing and showing them sandwiches. Falling in love and calling it friendship.

In the evening we went to the apartment. Bettina was stirring something on the stove, and when we entered, she said hi, turned down the gas, and went into her room. Small signs of the party still remained – the faint whiff of whisky on the tabletops, the kitchen bin overflowing with blue-and-white plastic cups. I avoided looking at you or talking to you, finding myself wishing I hadn't stripped the bed that morning. It was only 8 p.m. and there was the whole evening to fill. Wordlessly now I pulled a few ice cubes out of the freezer and poured us each a glass of water. You were scanning my almost-empty bookshelf, your hands in your pockets. I passed you a glass and we drank water in silence, your eyes still trained on the few remaining books. There were three copies of *Anna Karenina* I was waiting till the last minute to pack away. I wondered if I should offer you something to drink other than water, a glass of wine or something. Then Bettina came out of her room and asked if we wanted some vegetarian chilli. 'Have we met before?' she asked you.

'I don't know,' you said.

'Do you run the ArtSpace?'

'Actually, yes.'

'What's the ArtSpace?'

'It's a Bacchanalian gathering of very talented people.' Bettina explained. 'Supposedly they are making art, but I've heard rumours.'

This conversation made me feel terrible. I opened the fridge and found the sangria. I pulled it out and drank it straight out of the jug, the lip of glass fat against my mouth. The two of you looked at me and I saw that you were the same, growing up with giant cartons of orange juice and Christmas carols in December. I told myself to calm down. Then I announced, while you and Bettina were discussing whether we should all walk over to Church Street for an ice-cream cone: 'I don't understand what's happening.'

'We're ganging up against you.'

'That's what I thought.'

Outside, the air was muggy and you began to hum the song you had sung at Clementine's funeral. At the Brattle there was a late showing of *The Big Sleep*, and you declared we must go. I tried to get Bettina to join us, but she said she had some reading to do and wanted to turn in early and headed home with a scoop of mint chocolate-chip. I don't understand mint chocolate-chip, I said. It tastes like cold toothpaste. You asked me if all the things I had wondered about these last seven years in America were just coming out now. No, I said. Mint chocolate-chip is the only remaining mystery. The theatre was only half-full, and we found seats towards the back. As soon as I hit the velvet cushion, I regretted myself. I could see what was coming as the lights dimmed, a flashback to the moment at Sanders when we held hands in the dark – was it only the day before yesterday? – and now, two hours in a cool theatre with Lauren Bacall, who, Bettina had just informed me, was the sexiest woman ever to grace the screen, and here she was, her voice pitch dark, a rasp against wood. I was finished. 'I need popcorn,' I said, jumping out of my seat and bending forward as I excused myself past the knees of the other people in our row. In the lobby of the theatre I bought a drink, and as I was paying I realised I was still holding my ice-cream cone, and that the ice cream had dripped onto my wrist. I threw away the cone and licked my wrist, recalling Bogart's long and narrow face, the hat pulled over his forehead. I re-entered the theatre, and when I sat down you didn't look at me or say anything. I concentrated on the film and understood very little. At some point you whispered to me, with a small laugh, 'You forgot the popcorn', but I didn't see the humour in it, I only wrapped my fingers around the armrest, as if to say, please don't hold my hand. And you didn't.

The Dig

I dare myself to wait for you at the intersection, but you are never there. The triangular building juts into the street and the sidewalk beneath it is empty of you. Sometimes I walk to Porter Square and on the way I look down the street in the direction of your mother's house. I think about ascending the four wooden steps and ringing her doorbell, but the distance between the thought and my finger on the buzzer is vast and unbreachable.

In the meantime, there is this. I spend my days deep in the belly of the new building, three storeys down where the corridors smell of nothing and the lights are brilliantly white. All the specimens have been transferred to vast metal drawers, and it is not unlike a hospital morgue. I've heard people complain, but I don't mind: I like the idea of Diana coming back to the world in this neutral, unghosted space.

The fragments arrive at irregular intervals. Suzanne Williams has completed the first specimen, and I'm looking at Diana's ankle – the double-pulley that connects her to our herbivore, land-dwelling mammals. It is perfectly intact. Suzanne is one of the best preparators in the country; for years I had only ever passed her in the hallways of the old building, a tiny woman with a grey ponytail and a fierce

53

silence around her. Now she sits hunched beside me in the prep lab, her fingers delicately separating bone from matrix, the tap-tap-tap of her tools like a metronome.

I scan the bone and send the images to Bart and Jiminez. Often I stop and consider what I've been given, that Diana in my hand is a miracle, a testament to everything we are as humans – the scientists who uncover the past, the artists who imagine it, frail, delicate beings who seek immortality even as we realise we are mere pinpoints in the long chapter of our own history. At night, I turn my thoughts to our story. Piece by piece, I put it together. All the other voices clamour to be heard – my mother, and Anwar, and Mo, and the other life I might have had if things had taken a different turn. You don't know Anwar, do you? Not yet. You are wondering who he is. I say his name but say nothing more. Perhaps I should tell you now (no, he is not my father). He is a man who revealed to me the entire history of my being, and, having done so, released me from all the things I believed I couldn't do, wasn't entitled to, because my past was a mystery. That is all I will say for now. Anwar will tell you the rest himself.

I went to Dera Bugti, even though until the last minute I was convinced something would happen to prevent the trip from materialising. Was I secretly hoping it would fall apart so I could stay in Cambridge with you and repeat our little rituals all summer long? Or was it, perhaps, a slight premonition that this was the start of a downward cascade, only a brief interlude on my way home, and home, too, was not going to be my ultimate destination, that other, final place more barren than anywhere I could have imagined?

I am rushing. Let us take it one miserable location at a

time. Here I am now, on the bus to Dera Bugti. The open window whips my hair into gravity-defying tangles I will later spend hours righting. Eventually I will give up, and in a few weeks I will let it all turn into a giant, dust-cemented knot. On the seat beside me is Jiminez, who collected me at the airport. Jimmy and Professor Bartholomew Smith, the leader of our expedition, arrived early to set up camp. Jimmy looks more like a heavyweight boxing champion than a palaeontologist. He tells me straight away that he's an ex-army man and that he's done three tours in Afghanistan, as if he's used to having to explain his shoulders, the pyramids of muscle climbing up his neck. The bus is only half-full and I am the only woman on board. I'm dressed in a long-sleeved tunic and a black veil that covers my head and most of my face. I also have to hold in my pee because there's nowhere to go, and I'm too embarrassed to tell Jimmy that's why I'm not drinking water. 'Take a sip or the desert'll suck you dry,' he says. His voice is kinder than his bulk would have you imagine.

It's a long ride. I sleep, wake, listen to the playlist you made for me before we parted, write little notes to you in my mind that I will never send. Like this: what if you came with me? I think of the grand piano in Sanders, brass feet blending into the gold tones of the savannah. The veil, so close to my mouth, amplifies my breathing. We pass fields of millet. It isn't all bare: spiky green bushes are dotted all over the rolling hills, with occasional bursts of colour, like the Translucent Honeysuckle, *Lonicera quinquelocularis*, which Jimmy points out when we change buses at Kashmore. I consider asking for the toilet, a dull pain spreading through my lower stomach, but I don't want to leave Jimmy's side. I realise, too late, that I'm not the adventurous type.

★

'How shall we keep in touch?' you asked at the airport, the smell of detergent and tired bodies our little anthem of departure.

'The world presents you with an infinite number of possibilities,' I said. 'Text, email, phone, Skype. And sub-possibilities. iMessage, WeChat, WhatsApp, Snapchat.'

'Your knowledge of the genre is impressive,' you said.

'I am never less than a thousand miles from someone I love.'

'Letters?'

'The post is abysmal. It'll be ten years and I will have missed something crucial. Imagine the regret.'

'Smoke signals?'

I had no reply to that.

'Something encrypted,' you explained.

'I'm afraid I won't get it. We have to make up the rules before we start.'

'Okay, how about lines from *Anna Karenina*?'

'Too depressing.'

'*Moby-Dick*?'

'I've never read *Moby-Dick*.'

'What kind of a cetophile are you? No books, then.'

'How about songs?'

We looked at each other. There was only one answer. 'Nina Simone,' we both said at the same time.

'I may stray a little,' you said. 'I can already think of a few standards she didn't cover.'

'You have something of an advantage.'

'True. But you'll catch up. Consider it an education.'

'In restraint, or music?' Because there would be so much more to say.

'Both.'

Before my plane took off I looked up a list of jazz

standards. 'Love Me or Leave Me'. 'Darn that Dream'. 'Jonah and the Whale'. 'Every Time We Say Goodbye'. 'I Wish I Could Know What It Means to be Free'.

Professor Smith was leaning on a bolster, talking to a man in a beard and cap. 'It's a damn shame about *Baluchitherium*,' the professor was saying. 'It could have changed everything.' Changed everything is the holy grail for people like us. We look for the bones that will rewrite everything we have known about our history. We look for the ear of *Pakicetus*, the ankle of *Ambulocetus*, the spine of *Rhodocetus*. I knew what he meant – *Baluchitherium* may have yielded such bones, but it was never fully examined.

Everyone in the small world of cetacean palaeontology knew that Professor Bartholomew Smith had spent his entire career in this part of the world. That he spoke the regional dialect and dressed in the manner of the local tribesmen, in long cotton tunics and embroidered vests. Now I was seeing this something of a legend man in the flesh and finding him weathered and small, his body as if recently unpacked from within a very small space. He had a betel habit that had turned his mouth a lurid colour of red.

He saluted me with a hearty 'As-salaam alaikum!' I was cheered by the warmth in his voice and I liked him immediately, his manner open and slightly clownish. He insisted I call him Bart and he poured me a cup of creamy tea, which I accepted (in case you're wondering, I pissed like the proverbial racehorse the moment I got to camp).

'This is Zamzam,' Bart said, introducing the other man. With narrow shoulders and a timid face, Zamzam appeared out of place, though he must have thought the same about me. I had removed my veil and the dust was making my eyes tear, and I had already developed something of a tic, rubbing the back of my neck to get rid of the grit that had started accumulating there. I sniffed, blew my nose into a crumpled tissue, and exchanged polite hellos with Zamzam. On the bare ground was a pot of curry and a platter of stone bread. I was offered a plate and helped myself. The bread lived up to its name and was very hard, but the curry was delicious, sweetened by dried prunes.

Bart went on about *Baluchitherium*. My eyes stopped streaming and I tried to remember everything I knew about it – I recalled it was discovered in Dera Bugti by an Englishman at the start of the twentieth century and was thought to be one of the largest mammals ever, a rhinoceros-like behemoth who roamed the earth 30 million years ago. Young, then, compared to *Ambulocetus*.

'A group of French archaeologists dug it out of the ground in '99, and it was decided the skeleton would be moved to Karachi for examination. In the meantime, they stored it in the home of the tribal chieftain of the time, you know, Akbar Bugti. When the army raided Bugti's home, they blew up his compound, killed him, and everyone thought they'd wiped *Baluchitherium* off the face of the earth,' Bart said.

I didn't know the end of the story. 'What happened?'

'Bugti had all the bones stored in metal containers, the bastard!' Bart slapped his hand against Zamzam's back. 'That's why we've got to get *Ambulocetus* out of the ground and put it somewhere safe.'

Ambulocetus tells about the moment, somewhere around 50 million years ago, when whales began to swim. The earliest ancestor of the modern whale, *Pakicetus*, was discovered several hundred miles north of here, in Punjab. *Pakicetus* drank fresh water, had a marine-mammal ear and swam in the shallows. The last time this area had been excavated, Gingerich had found *Artiocetus clavis* and *Rhodocetus balochistanensis*, the two specimens that had proven that whales evolved from Artiodactyla, split-hoofed, plant-eating mammals such as cows and hippos. And Thewissen had found many specimens of *Ambulocetus* in 1992, but no one had been able to bring a full skeleton back from the field.

'Gingerich was here in 2000, but they shut him down when the war in Afghanistan started,' Bart said, removing a folder from his backpack.

I had been meaning to ask Bart about this. For over a decade no one had been allowed anywhere near here. 'How did you get permission?'

He pulled out a sheet of paper from the folder and wielded it with a flourish. 'Aha, here it is.' He cleared his throat. 'Imagine, if you will, *Ambulocetus*, the sun on her back, the edge of the water lapping at her thick skin, the temptation to plunge within too great, the secrets of the ocean beckoning.' I cringed at hearing my words read back to me, checking to see if Jimmy and Zamzam were laughing or, worse, staring down at the fat coagulating on their plates, embarrassed for me. Bart went on, in the manner of a hazing ritual: 'Her secrets lie within her bones: her hips, her protected inner ear that allows her to hear underwater, the length of her femur. These are the clues that will tell us who she is, so long a mystery beyond the reach of science.'

My face burned. 'Seriously, though. I thought this area was strictly off limits.'

Bart flung my application back into the folder. Then he pulled a tin box out of his pocket and selected a heart-shaped sheet of betel. 'You know countries like this,' he said, folding the betel leaf into a triangular packet and popping it into his mouth. 'You gotta find ways to get around.'

'Bart's been working on it 24/7,' Jimmy said.

The professor pulled at his scalp. 'Got the greys to prove it.' He chewed in silence for a minute, then said, 'You have to keep everything in balance.'

I waited to see if he would explain. 'You describe *Ambulocetus* beautifully,' Zamzam said to me.

My eyes started tearing again and I rubbed them roughly, wishing I'd never taken liberties with the whale's story. 'My parents didn't want me to come,' I said, my voice unnecessarily loud. 'They said it was too dangerous.'

'Danger is relative,' Jimmy said.

'No one wants their kid to grow up and hunt fossils,' Bart said.

'Your parents have nothing to worry about,' Zamzam said. 'I can assure you.'

'Anyway,' Bart said, 'we have our secret weapon.' He fanned out his fingers behind his head and gave me a broad smile, displaying his betel-stained teeth. Then he closed his eyes and appeared to dismiss us. I didn't ask him again how he'd received all the right permits and approvals, how he'd gotten the blessing of the local tribesmen, and he wouldn't have told me anyway, that he had made a set of agreements that were held in place through a careful balance of bets and payments. He would have considered it an acceptable procedure; after all, according to him, in countries like these, some transfer of human life would be unsurprising, a kind of ransom to which we would all be subject, and lines had to be crossed to get at the treasure beneath our feet.

Jimmy showed me around the rest of camp. The tents were arranged in a semicircle around a central area that served as an open kitchen. Bart and I were each given our own tent, and Jimmy and Zamzam were sharing. There was a cook, a driver, a pair of guards, and a few local men who had been recruited to help us to break through the dense red shale. When our predecessors had mined this area, the bones they had found were encased in layers of red-bed sequence that were as hard as cement. If we wanted to get a complete specimen out of the ground, we would have to first quarry the area with our tools and then blast through the rock with explosives. Zamzam was in charge of the dynamite, which he kept buried in a tin trunk on the southern edge of the site.

Later, after I'd eaten another round of curry and stone bread, I ran into Zamzam outside the makeshift toilet. He was holding an empty can of water. The evening was cool and quiet. I had taken an antihistamine and I was feeling slightly better.

'Have you seen *Stupendemys geographicus*?' he asked.

I felt myself light up. 'Just a few days ago. You know it?'

'Only photographs. How fortunate you are to have seen it for yourself.'

He was right, I was lucky: I had walked the hallways of Wilson and Gould, seen *Kronosaurus* and *Stupendemys* and the Glass Flowers. Held hands with you. I wondered what had motivated him. 'What made you come?' I asked.

'My father thought it was a terrible idea.'

I smiled. 'Tell me about it.'

'Some other time, perhaps.'

He darted away and I looked back to see him walking at a fast pace towards his tent, the night sky above us lit up with a fraction of moon and a dense scatter of stars.

We started at dawn, driving west in a pair of jeeps with a tiny pink sun at our backs. I noticed our guard was wearing something of a uniform this morning, a half-sleeved shirt and a pair of light khaki trousers. The gun tucked into his belt was visible when he turned his back and adjusted his turban against the wind. The hills were jagged, softened occasionally by plumes of wild shrubs. Against the horizon we could see a thin scattering of acacia trees. The Suleiman range appeared to retreat into the distance, though we were actually approaching it – a trick of the savannah – and finally we stopped at a site about two hundred yards across, marked off by Jimmy and Bart as they had prepared the location.

Jimmy was a sedimentologist – he would examine the bed of the Tethys for the environmental context of *Ambulocetus* and try to re-create the landscape from which the shale had been formed. The hired men would use sledgehammers to bring down large chunks of red rock and then Zamzam, Bart, and I would sift through each one, examining the broken stone with bits of bone and teeth scattered within it like flecks of white confetti. From the first moment the physical exertion was soothing in its simplicity. We baked in the heat, fierce even at this early hour, and, though it seemed there was no movement in the air, soon our skins were dusted red with the powder of the dried sea. That first morning went by very quickly, and we returned to camp for a late lunch, remaining inside as the afternoon blazed, cleaning, sorting, and setting up a rudimentary system of cataloguing what we had found.

I lasted a week. On the second Monday, Bart found me leaning against a rock with my head between my knees and ordered me off site. I was dehydrated, and the sunburn behind my neck had blistered. One of the guards offered to drive me, and I sat next to him in the front as he raced the jeep back to camp, speaking to me only once, to ask if I needed a ride to the hospital in Multan. I said no and spent the afternoon on top of my sleeping bag, angry at myself for succumbing to the environment. I had a lot to prove – not just to the others, because I was the only woman there, but also to myself, to my sheltered childhood, to my parents and even to you, Elijah.

I had decided that my week with you was the start of a new me. I would use it to turn myself into the sort of person who knew exactly what to expect from the world. I would no longer be the pampered only child of two doting parents. When I died the invitation to my funeral would say 'Palaeontologist. Adventurer. Rock-Slayer. Amphibian. Ninja'. I would be difficult to surprise, intractable. Even funny. Yes: I would develop a sense of humour, a dry, intimidating one. I kept repeating the word 'Ninja' to myself, smiling until my lips cracked.

I turned on my phone and of course there was no signal. The battery was almost dead, but I scrolled through my song list and chose the Nina Simone version of 'Here Comes the Sun'. I felt a strong desire to hear your voice, to tell you about this place, the searing pain at the base of my neck where the desert had pierced my skin, the aniseed scent that followed Zamzam around everywhere as he chewed on stalks of wild fennel, and the packed crimson rock that held its secrets so close. You realise, don't you, Elijah, that this is the way you worked your way into my heart? Not just in those days together in Cambridge, but in the aftermath, when I couldn't stop talking to you, when every turn of my story included a footnote of conversation as I pictured how you might respond, the way the desert light would catch your hair, the effect of the parched, history-heavy air on your voice. What would you have made of all of this, the green flags of our tents on the lunar surface of this ancient place, our little argument with time? That is, I know now, how people fall in love – in the words they recite to each other, the images they weld out of their abbreviated encounters, narrating themselves into the sort of connection that they will later refer to as fated.

In the evening, Zamzam and Jimmy brought me dinner and some sachets of oral rehydration salts. Zamzam put a sachet on the ground next to my sleeping bag, and I thought I heard his footsteps retreating, but he was rummaging around in my backpack, looking for water. He tore the sachet open and poured the contents into my flask.

'Did you find anything?'

'Only the murmurings of ghosts,' Zamzam said.

I opened my eyes and noticed that his face was leavened by pale-green eyes. 'I'll be back on site tomorrow,' I said.

Jimmy said, 'When I was in Afghanistan, I passed out at least a dozen times. This kind of dry heat can kill you.'

Zamzam finished making up my saline water and dropped the flask beside my sleeping bag.

I was eager for them to go, but they seemed to want to stay until I'd finished eating. I took a bite of bread and felt it turning back into dough in my mouth. 'What was it like out there, in the war?' I asked.

'Paid off my loans,' Jimmy said.

'My dad was in the army once,' I offered.

'Was he a Mukti Bahini?' Zamzam asked.

I nodded, surprised he knew the Bengali word for 'freedom fighter'. 'Bangladesh used to be a part of Pakistan,' I explained to Jimmy. 'My father was in the war of independence.'

'Fighting for a cause.' Jimmy said. 'Wish I knew what that was like.'

I put the plate down and took a large gulp of saline, its sweet saltiness reminding me of the time I had contracted food poisoning from eating a stick of roadside sugar cane. 'Thank you,' I said. 'I feel better.'

Zamzam put his hand to his forehead in a gesture of farewell. I recognised something – a mournful yet euphoric expression I often caught on my parents' faces, the look of a person who believed they could remake the world. I sometimes thought, when I looked at Zamzam, that he was trying to tell me something. But I was tired and a little light-headed, and as soon as he left I closed my eyes and stopped thinking about him.

The next morning Bart announced we'd be spending the day at camp. No, it wasn't on account of my heatstroke – we were having a few guests for lunch. When I emerged from my tent, I saw a seating arrangement had been made around the middle of the campsite, with plastic sheets and tablecloths covering a shady patch near the cooking area. The bolsters had been brought out from Bart's tent, and there were even table settings, tin mugs and plates arranged in a semicircle. Bart rolled a cigarette, smoked it, wrapped a betel, chewed it, swallowed, and started all over again with the tobacco, all the while shouting orders to the workers to clear up the site and hurry up with the cooking. The smell of singed meat and baking bread spiralled around us.

Bart said it would be better if I wore the burkha and the face veil again, so I did, and then he said something to me about keeping a low profile, which I gathered meant that I should either stay in my tent or not talk to anyone. I was going to ask Jimmy who exactly we were expecting, but I hadn't seen him since breakfast.

A convoy of jeeps arrived just after noon. The men, about a dozen, greeted Bart warmly, embracing him, then holding their palms to their chests. Jimmy and Zamzam approached, and, as they made their introductions, Zamzam fell to the ground and touched a man's feet. The man put his hand on Zamzam's head, and when Zamzam stood up they hugged. Someone came around and served stone bread and roasted goat. From inside my veil, I observed how the men were expert at positioning themselves so they didn't have to remove the guns slung across their chests even as they ate: Bart spoke to them in Balochi. Occasionally, someone told a joke and everyone laughed. Zamzam didn't say a word; neither did Jimmy. Tea was passed around, then tobacco. The man who had touched Zamzam's head stood up first. His face, lined as if with a fountain pen, was beautiful in a ruined sort of way. He made a speech, and then, his shoes heavy on the plastic sheet, he paused and waited again for Zamzam to come over and touch his feet. Then he led the others into their trucks and they drove away, copper dust trailing behind them like breaths from a dragon.

'What did he say?' I asked Bart, and Bart said, 'You will look after my brother's son.'

It was finally explained to me that Zamzam was the son of one of the most influential tribal chiefs in the area, a man called Didag Baloch, who was said to be a possible successor to Bugti. The older man who had come was not Didag Baloch himself, but his brother, Abrar Baloch, Zamzam's uncle. I spent the rest of the afternoon in my tent again, but thought about Zamzam differently after that, deciding we had something in common, the sense that we had been cast far from our provenance. What did Zamzam's father make of him, an unferocious man more interested in bones than in the fate of his people? Did his father remind him that it was his duty to wrest his land from armies, governments, and copper prospectors, that this work was insignificant in comparison? I said none of this to Zamzam, but when we passed each other that evening, as roofs of light slanted over the savannah, I made sure to look him straight in the eyes as if to say, I know who you are, I know all about it, every last hammer of doubt.

And then we found Diana's tail. Or, rather, Zamzam did. A few weeks after the visit from his uncle, Zamzam came running to where Bart and I were chiselling. He'd found a fist-sized bone that looked promising. We abandoned what we were doing and started quarrying carefully, paring away the surrounding stone to a radius of about three feet. Another, slightly smaller bone was lodged a few inches away. We worked on, ignoring the afternoon sun as it roared above us, and, slowly, like fairytale crumbs, the outline of bones in ascending size began to emerge from the rock. We were on the fifth when the light faded and Bart called it a night. All day we had hardly spoken more than a few words to each other, but as soon as we set off back to camp we spoke at once. Had anyone noticed the notches on the third bone? And what was the size telling us, the distance between vertebrae? Once we reached the end of the spinal column, the pelvis wouldn't be far away. Please let it be intact. Let it be perfect.

Zamzam suggested we blast the area immediately but Bart said he wanted to take his time with the hand tools first. They went back and forth a few times, but Bart insisted, so we set ourselves upon the area, chiselling through the sequence from dawn till sunset every day. In the evenings we staked claims on a name. From the beginning I thought of her as female, and the others seemed to agree. It was Jimmy who suggested the name Diana, after the Roman goddess of the hunt. Crouching over her the next day, Zamzam whispered a prayer over the eight vertebrae of her exposed spinal column. 'What's he doing?' Jimmy asked.

'These are bones of grace,' Zamzam said, lifting his grass-coloured eyes to meet mine.

I woke the next morning to the sound of Bart's voice. 'I have to keep him here,' he was saying. And another voice – Jimmy's – saying, 'You have to tell him,' and Bart said he would, he just needed a few more days. 'Let's get to the pelvis,' he said. They seemed to go back and forth a few more times, their voices quieting as they reached an agreement. 'Fine,' Jimmy said finally, 'but it's on you, Professor.'

A journalist arrived with a cameraman, making us pose around Diana with our tools. Bart carefully brushed away a layer of dust and exposed Diana's pelvis. The journalist cheered, and, in the tent that night, Jimmy and I drank cheap whisky while Zamzam sipped on a Pepsi, and we talked about the journal article we would co-author. I couldn't sleep, dreaming of the weeks and months that would follow, chipping away the matrix, preparing the fossils, taking them back to Michigan and mounting them at the Museum. I couldn't wait to tell you. My labours would soon be on display, like the Glass Flowers, and people would come and wonder at them and make up stories about my mythical creature. I felt my fate being determined, here in this dry, inhospitable land whose very dust was created long before history. The next afternoon, one of the drivers brought us the newspaper from Quetta, and on the front page was a photograph of Bart, the light in his eyes making him almost beautiful.

We kept going. In my excitement I thought little about the conversation I'd overheard, and within a week or two it had faded from my mind. Things had a tinge of the hallucinogenic about them. Inch by inch, we pared away the rock that encased Diana. It was late October now, and the afternoons were cooler, so we worked through the day, stopping only when the light faded to grey. Our quarrying was almost finished, when, one evening, as Jimmy and I were cataloguing small bone fragments, Bart entered the tent, followed by a man in an army uniform.

'I want a detail of your activities,' the man said to Bart, looking around and drawing a circle with his finger that encompassed it all. He was wearing a cap and ironed trousers. Multicoloured lapels.

'I told you,' Bart said, 'we're just scientists. We look for fossils. We found one a few weeks ago.'

'It was not in your daily report. We had to read about it in the paper.'

Bart looked around him. 'This isn't the place to discuss it,' he said.

'We will decide what is the place.'

The man went to Bart's table and ran his hands through a pile of paperwork. A few sheets slid to the ground. I wondered if my story about *Ambulocetus* was among them.

'General Alam no longer trusts you to give him what you promised.'

'We are about to make history.'

'You are no longer free to make your history here.'

At that moment, Zamzam entered the tent. In his hand was a chisel. Bart looked at the officer, then at Jimmy and me, and then at Zamzam, who turned around and attempted to run. He made it two steps when the officer took hold of his arm and flung him to the ground as if he was no more than a small dog. Then he crouched down and held Zamzam by the throat. Zamzam gasped for breath, hacking unproductively at the officer's foot with his chisel.

It comforted me to recall the last woman I had met, an auntie who had sat beside me on the flight from Doha.

She had asked whether I was married, and I had felt compelled to tell her I was engaged to a very nice man from back home. I tried to bring it to mind now, her hairspray scent, the way she called me 'darling'.

'Do you know, Professor, the punishment for harbouring a terrorist?' he said, his knee on Zamzam's chest.

'Please call my father,' Zamzam whispered. The officer punched him, and Zamzam's face swivelled sharply. I found myself moving towards him, taking a piece of cloth from my jacket (used, yesterday, to dust our half-discovered treasure), attempting to staunch the blood flowing from his mouth.

The officer turned to me. 'Please remove yourself, madam.'

'He's only a curator,' I said.

The officer tilted his head. 'What else would he be?'

'Leave it,' Bart said, when Jimmy rose to his full height, dwarfing the rest of us. 'There's nothing we can do.'

'He hasn't done anything,' I repeated. I didn't know why I was talking.

Jimmy came towards us and I was afraid and hoping he would start a fight. He pulled me away as the second blow landed on Zamzam, aimed at the exact same place, a wound upon a wound, and that was when a drop of blood travelled onto my retreating hand. Jimmy carried me to my tent.

'Don't move,' he said, pulling down the zip.

I waited inside.

I heard Zamzam being dragged out, his soft struggling, boots against the sand, a car door slamming shut. Within seconds they were gone. Jimmy unzipped my tent and pulled me out. I must have been crying, but I don't remember exactly, just that everything became blurred. Bart was arguing with one of the soldiers, and the soldier was just standing there and staring down at him, and after a few minutes Bart followed him into a jeep, calling out to us to take care of Diana.

Jimmy and I debated what to do. We could try and get her out of the ground. Zamzam had showed us how he was going to wire the site, where exactly he was going to place the dynamite. But even if we were able to control the blast, what would happen after? We had no way of shifting the bones, no hope of getting across a border with them. We had no other option but to cover the fossil over as best we could. For months after, this decision would continue to haunt me.

Jimmy and I drank the last of the whisky and spent the afternoon hiding Diana. We filled in the quarried area with sand and packed everything down with shovels. We removed the cordon, the markers, the outlines we had drawn. Our movements were hurried and messy. Jimmy rolled a cigarette and we passed it back and forth. Finally, when it was too dark to see, we gave up and made our way back to camp. I tried to make a few phone calls on the satellite phone, but I couldn't get through to anyone. I even tried you, Elijah. I remember thinking you would have known what to say at this moment, that you wouldn't go on about what a bad idea it had been to come here in the first place. I had an awareness of being in danger, but mostly I thought about Zamzam. I wondered if he was dead, or if he was somewhere that made him want to be dead. And I feared for Diana, that she would, like *Baluchitherium*, remain entombed, never to be fully known.

Jimmy rifled through Bart's things and found another bottle of whisky. We kept drinking. I went over and over in my mind the look on Zamzam's face when that second punch landed, the fight fleeing so suddenly from his features. Of course the more I thought about it, I realised it wasn't

71

his arrest that was strange, it was our being there in the first place. Jimmy told me about the arrangement that Bart had made with the army. He had promised to keep an eye on Zamzam in exchange for permission to excavate, and he had promised Didag Baloch that he would try and find out General Alam's next move. He had played both sides, but he hadn't bargained on Zamzam's worth, that the army would have wanted more – they would have wanted Zamzam himself, because Zamzam would give them leverage, something to bargain with in their battle for the area. Jimmy was cursing himself, saying he had tried to warn Bart, but Bart had promised him he'd had it all under control.

All this time, Zamzam had been our secret weapon. Our little talisman against the dangers of the desert. Now that he'd been arrested, perhaps his father would come to us, search through our carefully documented collection of broken geology for a clue to the betrayal of his son. I was too full of regret to fear this, wishing I had paid more attention, had somehow got the measure of Zamzam, or Bart, before this very moment when it was all too late.

In the morning Bart returned in an army jeep. It was unclear whether he'd been arrested – he wasn't in handcuffs, but there was a man with him and whatever this man told him to do, he did. Below his forehead, his face had collapsed into troughs and craters, and he had stopped chewing betel so his mouth was pale and undefined. We were ordered to dismantle the camp. 'I'm sorry,' Bart murmured to me. 'I'll write to your adviser and explain.'

We packed our things into the jeep. The driver wore metal-rimmed sunglasses and blasted the air conditioning. He drove us down to Sui, where we boarded a tiny plane for Sukkur, where we changed to another flight bound for

Karachi. At the ticket counter in Karachi, we changed our reservations, paid the airport taxes, and made declarations on our customs forms. Chisel. Hammer. Liquid plastic. There were no samples, no fragments of Diana encased in rock; we had just left her there, unmarked and unprotected. Jimmy repeatedly asked Bart if there was anything more we could do for Zamzam, if there was someone he could call to pull strings and get information on where they were holding him. Bart, a dead look in his eye, didn't reply. He kept glancing at the man who had accompanied us from Dera Bugti. At one point, Jimmy declared he wouldn't get on the plane, that he would remain in Pakistan until Zamzam was released, and Bart hushed him, putting his hand on Jimmy's enormous forearm.

My phone had found a signal and I read: *Fly Me to the Moon*.

When the flight to Dhaka was announced, I said goodbye to Bart and Jimmy at the gate. It wasn't until I entered the bridge that I realised the dig was really over, that we would never get Diana out of the ground or discover her true age, that there was a man in a cell somewhere and that we were leaving him to his fate. And to you I replied: *Nobody Loves You When You're Down and Out*.

Zamzam's mother stood outside the Quetta Press Club for sixty-seven days after his arrest with a photograph safety-pinned to her dress. Then she went in front of the High Court. In Islamabad, she set up camp with other parents of the disappeared. Jimmy sent me links to the articles that had been written about her, mostly by local papers. They called her 'the Mother of the Missing'. Then, years later, after we had long given up on knowing what had happened to him, Zamzam was returned to his family, his face barely resembling the portrait she had carried around, his face barely resembling a face at all. But somehow, from wherever he had been, before he died, Zamzam had managed to get a message out. And someone had received this message and through the network of people who had known about the dig, they had arranged to commit this last act of rebellion, sending me Diana, bone by bone. I want to believe it was his father, a powerful man now with nothing left of his son but this last wish. I want to believe he was sorry for wanting a different sort of child, one who would take on the mantle of a fighter, and that it was he who had sent out the order to retrieve Diana from the ground, to pack her up and send her to me. I do not claim to be this man's only act of resistance, but perhaps his most idiosyncratic, the one that makes the least amount of sense but reminds his comrades that there are scientists as well as revolutionaries, and both of these are men of the soil.

Homecoming

Anwar told me that it wasn't until he almost died that he realised he needed to find the woman he had once loved. I've thought about that a lot in the last few years, that if Anwar hadn't worked on that building site, he might never have gone looking for Megna, and if he hadn't done that, I might still be in the dark about my past. I've only ever been a hair away from being utterly alone in the world, Elijah, and it was Anwar who shone a light where once there was only darkness.

I now have a confession to make (another one? But yes). This isn't the first time I have been back to the place we met. Not the first time I've stalked these streets, hoping to run into you. I was here last year for Bettina's graduation. Early summer and the streets pink with fallen apple blossoms. Everything looked the same. Bettina had accepted a job at Stanford, and I helped her pack our little apartment into a U-Haul she was going to drive all the way across the country herself. When I expressed some concern, she assured me she was equipped with addresses of a carefully curated series of men she could call on the way – an insurance broker in Hartford, an engineer in Las Vegas, a creative writing professor in Iowa City. I waved as she drove away, holding on to the first edition of *One Hundred Years of Solitude* she had given to me as a parting gift. That was last year. When I wrote to tell her I was coming back, she offered to let me rent the place. I pay her a fraction of the sum she could get elsewhere, but she insisted and I don't have the will to refuse. I bought a futon and taped a photograph of Nina Simone on the wall above my head, but otherwise it is completely empty.

You don't care about any of this. The present is full of mundanities. What happened next, Elijah? The dig ended and I had to go home. My parents came to collect me at the airport. I was quick to regress to childhood patterns and greeted them meanly, keeping most of the episode to myself, already smothered by their worry.

On the plane I had sat next to a man who repeatedly asked me if I was Japanese. I had closed my eyes and pretended to sleep and seen Zamzam's face and wondered whether his anger at his father had made some part of him long to be caught. Zamzam's father wasn't unlike my own father, who had joined a movement to break away from an old country. My father was called a freedom fighter because his side had won and now he had a passport and a parliament and a vote, none of which Zamzam would ever have. Zamzam would die in that prison, and the world would remain divided between people who had countries and people who did not.

'My baby's home,' my mother said.

'I don't want to talk,' I murmured, depressed at the sight of her.

My message to you was: *Baby It's Cold Outside*. And, a few minutes later, you replied: *You Go to My Head*.

I folded myself into the front seat and leaned my head against the window, immune to the sight of my city, the airport road flanked on either side by fields of paddy, electric wires dangling low across the highway, and the watery air making everything heavy and indolent. 'Rashid said to phone him when you land,' Ammoo said.

Rashid had already sent me several text messages. I begged him not to come. 'Not today,' I said. 'I'm tired and I look terrible. I'll see you tomorrow.' He appeared in the early evening. I had struggled to wash the sand out of my hair, so Bashonti, our cook, was putting olive oil on my scalp.

'I told you to wait,' I said.

'You're full of shit,' he replied.

Bashonti released my hair. 'Bhaiya, look at this mess.' She pointed to my face, the rings of sunburn around my eyes.

Rashid was wearing a waistcoat over his shirt that emphasised his slim frame and the bulk of his upper arms. He had cut his hair short and changed his aftershave, but the rest of him was the same, his square forehead, his deep-set eyes and slightly flared nostrils. Looking at him, I remembered he'd had a bar installed over his bedroom door, that he pulled himself up on it every morning before going downstairs to eat breakfast with his mother. I was comforted by the sight of him, and I thought about resting my head against his shoulder, forehead to clavicle, and how reassuring that would be, but I couldn't stop thinking about Zamzam, and Diana, and the end of my life as I'd known it.

'Tell me everything,' he said.

Outside, I heard the sound of a neighbour scolding someone, a child perhaps or a servant. The blood pumped against my scalp where Bashonti had been aggressive with the brush. I'll never be a palaeontologist, I wanted to say, but I knew he wouldn't be able to pretend convincingly that this mattered to him. 'One of the people on my dig got into trouble and they had to shut it down,' I said.

We ate dinner together, Rashid and my parents and my flattened hair, Bashonti piling rice onto his plate. Rashid spoke mostly to Ammoo, telling her about the new factory he and his father were opening out in Savar. After dinner my parents claimed they were craving ice cream and made a point of letting us know they would be gone for an hour.

When I was twelve we went to Thailand with Rashid's family. My father's business hadn't yet taken off, so we stayed at a modest hotel across the street from the beach, even though Rashid's parents could afford much better. Rashid spent the entire holiday watching a Test series between the West Indies and Australia while I lay in the hammock under a tree beside the kidney-shaped pool. One day, while I was staring up at the sky and thinking about Sylvia Plath's suicide, Rashid nudged me with his foot and said, 'Let's go swimming.' And, even though I had been waiting desperately for him to notice me, I knew there was nothing I could say that wouldn't embarrass me later, so I ignored him, picking at the jute fibres on my hammock. 'C'mon,' he said again, tapping the top of my head, 'it's so fucking hot.' It was thrilling to me that he would say the word 'fucking' out loud, and to me. 'I don't know how to swim,' I said, still not able to look at him. 'It's okay,' he said, 'you can just float.'

I lay flat on my back, and he put his warm palm on my spine and ran me around and around the pool. We did this for what felt like hours. Later that year, when my parents bought an apartment on the other side of town and I struggled to make friends at the new school, Rashid took me under his wing, not embarrassed to be seen with me in the morning before the bell rang, waving to me from where he stood in front of the wicket, handsome beyond belief in his cricket whites, and when he ran the ball up and down his leg and made pink streaks on his uniform, I thought I would suffocate under the weight of my crush, but I didn't, I just kept feeling his hand under me, his steady presence, teaching me to swim, to belong, to fit in. I don't tell you this story to hurt you, Elijah, but to explain that the idea of leaving Rashid was like the idea of leaving behind my childhood, and, because I was a person whose life began with her own life, and not, like you, with a family tree that stretched back generations, I clung to every piece of my past, unable to forget, or let go, of a single thing, and maybe if Zamzam hadn't been arrested and we had managed to get Diana out of the ground, I would have been able to move through this moment with greater confidence, the confidence to break old threads and strengthen new ones, but now, in the shadow of this spectacular failure, I became, again, an obedient orphan.

Rashid was all over me, kissing my face and my neck. 'I can't believe you're home,' he said. I leaned my head against him for a moment, but it was not as I had imagined.

I had, a few minutes earlier, received this from you: *Ne me quitte pas.*

'Oh, jaanu, don't be mad. I can't be happy to see you? What's the matter?'

'It's nothing.' I looked down at my hands. I didn't know how to put it, I didn't even know what I wanted, so I said, again, nothing, and then it was too late: Rashid was rolling down the sleeves of his shirt and buttoning the cuffs, as if he had at some point decided to punch me and then changed his mind. Then he said, 'Let's go to Sally and Nadeem's. You'll feel much better after a drink.'

Nadeem passed me a gin and tonic and said, 'What's new with you, sister?' and I replied, 'I'm all fucked up,' and Nadeem laughed, raking a skeletal hand through his hair. In high school he'd been Rashid's best friend, but Rashid had left for university in London while Nadeem had stayed behind to join his father's business. In the summer holidays we would come home to find him perpetually stoned, playing video games or chasing his Pointer around the back garden. There was a quick downward spiral, and a year spent in rehab, and then, much to everyone's surprise, Sally agreed to marry him, and they moved into a flat and became ordinary.

'You're a strange girl,' Nadeem said to me, tilting his whisky in my direction.

Sally passed around a plate of Bombay mix. 'So you back for good this time?' she asked.

Rashid cupped my knee. 'I'm not letting this girl out of my sight.'

'When's the wedding?'

I wanted to lunge at her for bringing it up. 'Everyone wants to know,' I said. I noticed a streak of pale hair across her forehead and changed the subject. 'Did you dye your hair?'

'My cook did it. She's a genius.'

The gin and tonic was making me woozy. I felt a surge of revulsion for Sally and realised I had spent my whole life with these people, and I thought again about Zamzam, and Diana, and you, Elijah. Were you thinking of me? What would you make of this apartment, the leather dining chairs, the white baby grand against the sliding doors, Gulshan Lake glittering in the background? My tongue was sweet and heavy in my mouth. I relaxed, allowing the memory of our days in Cambridge to float around in my mind. 'It's a bit radical,' I said, going back to Sally's hair.

'Well,' she announced, 'I'm fucking pregnant.'

'Shit!' Rashid said, slapping Nadeem's shoulder. 'Come here, man. Let me hug you.'

I tried to think of something nice to say. 'Congratulations,' I managed.

'You'll be next,' Nadeem said.

I would be next. I considered Dhaka, this neighbourhood with big houses behind high gates, this over-air-conditioned apartment, and I was overcome with affection. A part of me was still back on Trowbridge Street, or eating ice cream with the Atlantic summer at my back, talking about jazz and Shostakovich and breakfast sandwiches with you, or out in Dera Bugti with a chisel in my hand. But I was at ease for the first time in months, at ease standing on what I knew instead of the strata of meaning I was capable of imposing on every situation. With these people who had known me all my life and not at all, I didn't have to talk about Zamzam, or the expedition, what I was going to do with my life, who I was going to become or who I had been.

Sally said she wasn't going to give up drinking, though she sent Nadeem and Rashid to the balcony to smoke. 'I'm terrified,' she said to me when we were alone. 'My vagina's going to be the size of a drainpipe, and even my tits will go back to being tiny in the end. What's the point?'

Sally, whose nickname came from her last name, Salehuddin, had always had a habit of making things sound worse than they actually were; in reality she was an optimist, insisting to her parents that Nadeem would someday grow up and become a good husband. I had attended their wedding, Sally buried under a thick layer of foundation, her parents hovering behind the wedding dais with fixed smiles on their lips.

'It won't be so bad. I hear they can be pretty cute.'

'When they're not crying all night and vomiting in your face.'

'So why are you doing it?'

'Not everybody's like you.' I knew what Sally meant, but I let her finish. 'Perfect boy, everything you could possibly want. This baby means Nadeem stays out of trouble, at least for a few years.'

'Then what?'

'I'll pop out another one.'

'That's your grand plan?'

'I didn't go to Harvard. It's the best I could do.'

No one would let me forget I'd gone to Harvard.

Over whisky-laced coffees, we listened to Nadeem strum his guitar. 'You're different,' Sally murmured to me, her chin on my shoulder. Not as different as I could be, I thought. But I said: 'I'll be back to my old self in no time.'

I did not return to my old self. Every morning I woke up with a jolt and realised I was no longer in Dera Bugti. This reminded me of what it meant for me to be here, safe, in the arms of people who loved me, that the price for this safety was the life of another man. I was longing for more than the few cryptic messages we occasionally exchanged, but I was so diminished that I was convinced you would find me dull and unworthy of your notice, and anyway, I had still not found the words to describe what had happened, not even to you.

When I wasn't obsessively Googling 'whale prehistoric arrest Zamzam Baloch disappeared', I was lying about the apartment and not answering Rashid's phone calls. He sent me messages asking if he could come to the apartment, but I never replied and he stayed away, though I imagined him bumping into me when I took long, pathetic walks around Tank Park or pushed a shopping cart under the blue lights at Unimart. I was very hungry and frequently on the verge of tears. My father knocked on my door every morning and asked if I would have breakfast with him. I almost always said no.

My mother was distracted by a new job. I was thankful for this, because I knew that if she turned her attention to me I would be forced to put words to what was happening. In Bangla they refer to women like my mother as dhani morich, because the tiniest chillies are the hottest. My mother is tiny and terrifying. During the war, she drove her ambulance every day to Salt Lake, the refugee camp on the outskirts of Calcutta, where all the exiles were stacked into unused sewer pipes. She gave them vaccines and bandaged their wounds and held their hands as they lost their children to cholera. I believe her whole personality was built in that moment – only seventeen and having to look death straight in the eye – but she must have always been that way. My grandmother paints a picture of a girl who was more stubborn than a trapped fishbone, a girl who tried to cut down the guava tree in the backyard because it had given her a scratch the last time she had tried to climb it. But the war was fundamental, a kind of birth not just for the country but for all the too-young people who had willed the country into being.

My parents are now, forty years later, starting to come to terms with what that war has done to them. All the good things – their marriage, woven with the broken threads of what they lost; the sweetness of knowing their lives have meant something, for they are not, like so many, plagued by the pain of insignificance. And the bad – both their brothers lost, my father's on the battlefield, and my mother's, later, to religion; the fear that they may not, after all, have gotten it right, because every time the country falters, they take it personally, as if there was a tainted seed planted then that corrupted all that followed.

Recently they have been given a chance to take account in a trial for the men who aided and abetted the army. The word 'genocide' is in my home like the word 'highway', or 'acorn', may be in yours. My mother has given up her medical practice and she's helping to gather research for the prosecution, travelling across the country to interview survivors and witnesses. She exists in a shroud of other people's memories as she gently, patiently coaxes out their stories and writes them down. She is remote and sad and emerges rarely, as if from a deep sleep, and in these moments she is joyful, as if she is discovering, for the first time, that the war was won after all. And then, inevitably, she withdraws into those dark places. My parents whisper to each other at night, out of earshot. They follow the trial, every episode, every motion, every witness. Me, I don't want to know. I seek the connection, but resist when the opportunity is offered. My heart is a nomad, still, after so many years of being in this country, child to these parents.

Can you ever know, Elijah, the feeling of being from a place you wish you could hate but are forced to love? Can you know what it is like to be from a country that everyone else is trying to escape? It is like running into a burning building. If you ask me, I'll tell you all the things I love about it – the smell of paperbacks in the winter, the cold-but-warm gust of monsoon air, the burnished wood on the desk I had as a teenager, dark from the oil of my skin, lying under the ceiling fan on my grandmother's bed, the taste of egg and parathas in my mouth. The love exists, but its domain is small, located in the particular bodies of particular people. My parents fought a war for this country, that is how much in love with it they are. There is a memory at every turn, an affection for every change in season, roots in the ground so deep you would have to tear them apart to separate person from place, body from soil. But not me.

One day my mother returns from the courthouse and she puts her head in her hands and cries as if someone is beating her. I stand a little apart and watch her shoulders sagging. My father goes to her and puts his arms around her and they sit that way for a long time. They see me and we look at each other and I stand there and they don't ask me to enter or leave and I don't enter or leave. I have witnessed it before, this thing that passes between them like a current, the knowledge that needs no explanation, and I know that she is remembering something, or remembering it through the story of someone else, heavy with what she knows and what she has recently learned, because it is always worse than she remembers, and every memory takes something away from the rest of her life, because she came away unscathed, and the burden of being who she is – whole – weighs heavy on her. She is a person with guilt at the very core of her being, and she spends her days compensating others for the fortune that brought her a life, a marriage, me. She is a moral economy all to herself, painted in tiny strokes of the past.

Someone had been nearly acquitted that day. They hadn't been able to make the case against him and he had gotten off with a light sentence. With a change in government, even this small verdict might be overturned, and the man might walk free. On the streets, there were protests, and people painting their faces in green and red, and children with rope around their necks, holding up signs that read

HANG THE BASTARD. My parents are not the only ones who want a reckoning.

What would you do with this messy history, Elijah? Your chamomile-scented home, your overfed cat, lemonade in the refrigerator, and that family tree, so august, no mystery blood, no revolutions, Indiana Jones an anchor in your provenance.

That afternoon, your message had read: *Don't You Pay Them No Mind*.

'Your mother and I are worried,' my father said. Ammoo had left early for a field trip to Barisal, and we were on the balcony overlooking Gulshan Lake. I looked down and saw the green water, the rim of garbage that lapped the shore, the necklace of apartment buildings that sat at the edge of the water on the other side.

'I don't know what to do,' I said. 'I keep asking myself and I just can't tell.' I remembered seeing a drowned cow in the lake soon after we moved in, and I had returned again and again to the balcony, watching with disgusted fascination as its intestines burst out of its body and floated into the reeds.

'Why don't you come to the factory? They love it when you visit. In fact, you could come and work for me.'

'You would give me a job?'

'I could use that Harvard brain.'

'Ammoo would have a stroke.' I found myself laughing with him. After years working for the government, my father had decided to go into business, and it was Rashid's father, Bulbul, who had lent him the money to open a textile factory. Freedom Fabrics foundered for the first few years, the costs outweighing the little profit it earned, but it rose to success when Western clothing importers realised my father's factory was one of the few that paid a decent wage and didn't employ children. They put Fair Trade labels on his clothes and sold them at department stores and boutiques, the price tags printed on crumpled brown paper. By the time I'd finished college, our financial circumstances had changed dramatically, but Ammoo and Abboo remained conflicted about their increasing wealth, because it interfered with their idea of themselves, forged all those years ago during the war. They kept to their Spartan lifestyle, driving their old Toyota, holding on to the battered cane set they had been given as a wedding gift. Their one concession was the apartment in Gulshan, and they had only bought that on the urging of Rashid's parents, who had themselves made the move across town years ago.

'I'll think about it,' I promised, remembering the last time I had been to the factory, the rows of sewing machines, the smell of kerosene and cotton, women bent over their work, plastic barrettes in their hair. Abboo reached out and held my hand, and I glanced at the stub which was all that was left of the finger he had lost in the war. Then he was looking out at the water, shaking his wrist to loosen his watch. I felt like there had never been a moment such as this one, and I was about to ask him to tell me something about the adoption, something he hadn't yet told me, something that would break it open and make it all right to talk about. But he cleared his throat and a lone fish broke the surface of the lake and the moment passed without commotion.

Ammoo flew back in time for dinner, strangely elated. We avoided asking her about the trial or the witnesses she had gone to find. Anyway, she wanted to talk about yoghurt. 'The food in Barisal is incredible,' she said. 'I tasted a superlative sweet doi. And the fish was also excellent.' The fish reminded her of something. 'Where's Rashid?' she asked. It was Friday, and Rashid always came to our house for dinner on Fridays.

Bashonti had made egg curry. I put a piece of egg in my mouth and chewed slowly. 'I didn't really feel like seeing him tonight.'

'Why not? Dolly said we should start thinking about setting the date.'

'Oof Ammoo why?'

'Why not? Is something the matter?' Ammoo peered into my face. 'Something wrong between you?' She sometimes liked to act as if my engagement to Rashid was the only good thing in her life.

'I'm on the verge of a spectacular failure – can't you see that?'

Abboo reached over and put his hand on my shoulder. 'Okay, sweetheart, you take your time.'

Ammoo poured herself a glass of water. 'What do I tell Dolly?'

'All I ever wanted to do was find that stupid fossil,' I said.

She took a gulp of water and put her glass down loudly. 'It's fine,' she said; 'you people do whatever you like.'

Your latest message to me was: *Trouble in Mind*. In my head I still couldn't resist telling you about every small thing that happened, but I had replied simply: *Don't Let Me Be Misunderstood*. I played the music you gave me, listening for clues as to whether I would ever see you again, telling myself it shouldn't matter, but knowing that it did, more than I could admit, and I thought again and again about Zamzam, and all the choices people made about their loyalties, and I knew that, no matter what I did, there would always be that tug in another direction, a headwind that would cast a sweeping and overwhelming doubt.

My father's village was three hours out of Dhaka and at the last minute I had agreed to accompany him to the wedding of a distant relative. I had played kabaddi with the children, watched my cousins fish in the pond beside the family compound, and finally, with leftover biryani packed into the trunk of the car, we started for home. It was early evening, and we'd had good luck with the traffic, so we were maybe twenty minutes from Chowrasta, the main intersection leading into the city. The light was softening and fading, and beyond the narrow highway and the string of shops were neon fields of young rice. Suddenly the car lurched, then stalled. Our driver, Abul Hussain, switched off the engine, then restarted it. The car whinnied, then shuddered to a stop. Abul Hussain turned around and said, with a tremor in his voice, that we had run out of petrol. He had meant to fill the tank in the morning and forgotten. He eased the car to the side of the road and then bolted out, making for one of the roadside shops to get help.

'Stay in the car,' Abboo said, following him. I opened the doors and let the evening air drift in. After a few minutes they both returned. The petrol station was several miles away. Abul Hussain would start walking and hope to find a rickshaw on the way. I got out of the car and wandered over to a vegetable cart, admiring the neat pyramids of gourd, pumpkin, and eggplant. Ammoo would be happy if I brought home some vegetables – she would say, oh, the marrow is so much sweeter outside of Dhaka – so I tried to get the attention of the man selling them. I was about to pay when I heard someone calling my name, and because I was in the middle of nowhere and the sun was about to set, I spun around with an aggressive word on my lips and saw that it was, in fact, Rashid, smiling down at me, a halo of hair framing his face.

He hugged me, his shirt stretched across his shoulders. 'What are you doing here?' I asked, my mouth against his ear.

'Your father called me,' he said.

I smelled his skin beneath soap and aftershave. 'Thank you,' I mumbled. He continued to hold me, unlike him to care so little that people on the street had begun to stare.

That morning, Jimmy had sent me a link: BODY OF DISSIDENT FOUND OUTSIDE OF QUETTA read the headline. Though the man bore marks of torture, the authorities were refusing to tender any sort of explanation. Zamzam's mother, Jimmy wrote, was still striking outside the Quetta Press Club. Abboo was getting ready for the trip to the village, pulling on his sneakers and ordering Bashonti to pack a bag of oranges for the drive. I asked if I could come with him, and he was of course overjoyed, assuming it was a sign of my recovery from whatever strangeness had gripped me since my return from Pakistan, but the road out of Dhaka, the children swarming around my knees, tilapia in the pond, all these images were meant, if not to erase, then at least to soften the picture of Zamzam, face down in a ditch, as dead as *Ambulocetus*.

Rashid had sent his driver in search of Abul Hussain – they would soon return with the petrol. He suggested we wait together at a small restaurant down the road. 'Why did you call him?' I whispered to Abboo as we climbed into Rashid's jeep, but Abboo didn't reply.

We took our seats on a row of plastic chairs in the restaurant, which was nothing more than a long, narrow room jutting out of the highway.

I said I needed to wash my hands, and the waiter pointed to a hallway. The bathroom was disgusting. There was no lock so I leaned against the door and dialled your number. I had 300 taka of credit on my phone, so if you answered I would only be able to talk for a minute or two. After three rings, I hung up. I splashed water on my face. There was no paper. I rubbed an arm over my face and headed back to the others, trying to form the sentences I would have to say to explain it all to Rashid, to appear calm and in control, as if my ignoring him for the past few weeks was part of some premeditated plan.

'It doesn't matter,' he said. 'You don't have to take everything so personally. Let's just focus on the good news, which is that you're here sooner than we thought, and forget about everything else.'

Forget everything else. How sweet that would be, how wonderfully pleasant. 'I'm an idiot,' I said. I examined him closely, his mother-of-pearl cufflinks, the untroubled way he bore himself. At the table he passed around the small glasses of tea, and I heard Abboo sighing as leaned back against the chair and closed his eyes. At that moment my phone buzzed and I thought it might be you, so I pulled it out of my bag. It was Jimmy. *It isn't him*, the message said simply.

Rashid and I went out the following night, to a Chinese restaurant we had frequented in high school, and afterwards we went to Movenpick and shared an ice cream in a cup, and he thought to provide two spoons, and I wondered if I was sharing that ice cream with you, Elijah, if we would have shared a spoon with no concern for who was eating more of it, and this thought, for some reason, made me want to shout out to no one in particular that I was being presented with an impossible choice. Then it was Sally's birthday, and we all took a boat ride together on the Buriganga. On the third evening, Rashid brought up the subject of marriage, and when I asked why, he said, 'Because that's what we were always going to do.' To you I wrote: *I Think It's Going to Rain Today*. And you: *Cry Me a River*.

I deleted your playlist from my phone and humoured Rashid while he talked about moving into a flat. I began to suspect that was an imminent end to my problems, an end to living and reliving a scrap of a week, obsessing about Diana trapped in the ground, imagining the look on Zamzam's face as he was loaded into the back of that van. The lie upon which my whole life rested. All of it.

In the evenings Rashid and I sat on the balcony and swatted mosquitoes, sometimes sharing a cigarette, staring out at the lake and the scatter of buildings on the other side. Sally's pregnancy was starting to show, and the four of us went to parties where Rashid mixed cocktails and held me while we danced. I liked that he was a poor dancer and I could look into his eyes as he made jerky movements with his arms. He sneaked into my room a few times, leaving without a trace before morning, not even his scent lingering on the sheets.

Early one Friday morning, when the traffic was thin, we drove out of the city to Savar and stood under the sail-shaped war memorial. He had brought breakfast, a thermos of tea and a pair of stuffed parathas wrapped in foil. It was cold; we huddled together under our shawls. By this point I had stopped thinking about you entirely, or at least that's what I had told myself, trying to turn it into a happy, light memory, like a preamble to something, but not the substance of life itself. It had been a month since you had written: *Do I Move You?* And I had not replied.

Rashid and I walked past the memorial, to the rectangular pool at its base. The path was paved in small red bricks. Pink lotus flowers floated on the surface of the water, which was deep green and opaque.

'So, you going to marry me, or what?' We were at the far end of the pool now, and I looked over at the memorial, the white folds of concrete rising up to a triangular point, and I remembered once when my parents had driven us out here and I had soiled my pants, and Ammoo had made me stand up in the back seat all the way home. I didn't often worry that my parents would send me back to wherever I had come from, but that day, somewhere in my mind I feared they might, and I had gripped the seat in front of me in terror, wondering if the driver would be directed to drop me off on the side of the road and pull away because, although Abboo and Ammoo had promised to love and look after me as if I were their own child, I had crossed an imaginary line.

Rashid reached out from under his shawl and took something out of his pocket, and when I glanced down at his hands I saw that it was a small velvet box with an engagement ring inside.

The week before, I had written to Bart to ask if there was any news about Zamzam or the dig, but he hadn't replied, and now I felt the years fall away – the long episode in America, the evenings of music, the sweet cold of New England winters.

Rashid was directing me to sit at the edge of the pool. 'We don't have to live here, you know. We can live in London. And we'll travel anyway.'

The implication that I was not at home in my own country irritated me. 'What makes you think I don't want to live here?'

'You want to live here? Great. Makes my life easier.'

'You think I don't fit in?'

'It's fine, Zee, don't worry about it. I just meant, you know, it's nice to get out once in a while.'

'Because you're rich, so we can take holidays in Bangkok and Dubai?'

'What's wrong with Dubai?'

There were a million things wrong with Dubai, and I could start listing them, but if I did I knew we would have to break up, so instead I said, 'I want to live here.' The concrete was cold; I tightened the shawl around my shoulders. Rashid passed me the flask and I took a long sip of tea.

'Okay. That's settled, then. We live here. Together.'

I took another sip. 'Did you put whisky in the tea?' I reached out and held his hand under the shawl. 'I feel tipsy.'

'Let me take care of you, Zee.'

I looked up and saw that the sky was greying and thickening. It would rain on the way home, and we might get stuck in traffic. 'Let's do it as soon as possible. How about January?'

His arms shot up. 'Yes!'

So this is how it happened, Elijah. As Rashid and I made our way back to the car, what passed through me was relief, because now we could all stop pretending there had ever been any other future in my stars, and for the first time in a long time, all the ways in which I felt the absence of my mother, the mother that knew the seedling-me – the me that was here before I was here, a flutter in the guts, that voice of knowledge and doubt – was silent and obedient.

At my door, Rashid asked if he could spend the night. 'Your parents are asleep. And anyway, who's going to give them a grandson?' he winked. 'Gotta practise.'

'I'm tired,' I said, evading him. 'It's been a long day.'

'You're killing me!' he said, holding my gaze, holding my elbow in his palm, holding every year we had known each other in the outlines of his face. I imagined him turning on his heel and marching back to the stairwell, jiggling the car keys in his pocket, his irritation dissipating within moments of leaving me, so I relented, undressing in silence at the foot of the bed and letting him fall asleep with his back turned to me, and all the time I was thinking of you, and what it might be like to be with you in this bed, whether you would be as serene in sleep as the man beside me now.

The next day, I went to visit my grandmother. The traffic in Dhaka is unimaginably bad, and it took two, sometimes three hours in the car to get to her apartment in Dhanmondi, which left about one hour for playing rummy, gossiping, and eating the vast number of snacks Nanu could conjure up at a moment's notice. She was waiting for me in a starched blue sari, smelling comfortably of pressed roses and talcum powder. Pithas – sweet steamed rice cakes – were already waiting, covered with a piece of foil to keep them warm. A teapot and a pair of apples joined them on a tray.

'I told her to make them after you arrived, but she wouldn't listen,' she complained, referring to the cook she had recently hired. 'So stubborn. Let me look at you.' She examined my shalwar kameez, nodding in approval.

'So,' she said, shuffling the cards, 'you want to bet money, or just keep it friendly?'

'I'm getting married,' I said.

She flung the cards aside. 'Finally! Somebody brings me good news. Is it that boy?'

I bit into a pitha. 'Yes. Dolly auntie's son.'

'Good. Your mother will be so happy. She told me you came back and ignored him.'

'I did, and then I changed my mind.' It sounded strange when I put it this way, as if I was returning to a bowl of leftover soup. 'He's very sweet.'

'Your mother used to tell me she would never get married.'

'And what did you say?'

'I told her marriage is wonderful, and children are even better.' She pulled off her heavy glasses. Nanu had been a young bride, and then a young widow, and anytime she mentioned her husband, an expression of such grief and longing came over her that it was as if she had just lost him the other day. And yet, she could have made an excellent case for being a woman on her own. There was a lightness to her, humour and joy, that she hadn't passed down to my mother. She had a regular bridge date with her friends, and hosted a monthly kitty party, in which her cousins and neighbours pitched in their savings, so that one person could win the whole lot once a month, names pulled out of an old pillowcase and celebrated with sweets. And she spent as many hours reciting from her Qur'an as she did in front of the television, watching old Hindi films and singing along to the musical numbers.

'Is he nice to you?' she asked, wiping her eyes.

'Very nice.'

'That's the most important thing. And so handsome.'

'Extremely,' I said.

She asked me a few more questions about what kind of wedding I wanted. Winter or summer? Outside or inside? And what kind of a mother-in-law would Dolly auntie be? She advised me to push Rashid to move out of his parents' house. 'It's always better that way, you won't argue about the cooking.'

'I hate cooking anyway.'

'But you would still argue about it,' she laughed. Then she looked at the clock on the wall and said, 'Will you wait here? I'll come back in a few minutes.'

It was six. She was going to turn on the television for her favourite soap, an Indian series about a villainous mother-in-law and her twelve obedient sons.

'Go,' I said, 'I'll be fine.' I looked down at my phone and saw: *I Get Along Without You Very Well (Except Sometimes)*. I didn't know that one, so I looked it up and played it on my phone.

> I get along without you very well
> Of course I do
> Except when soft rains fall

I lay down on the sofa and gazed up at the ceiling. Nanu's chandelier swam above me. I could hear the crude violin chords of her soap opera.

> I've forgotten you just like I said I
>   would
> Of course I have
> Or maybe except when I hear your
>   name
> Someone's laugh that's just the same

I turned off my phone and stuffed a pitha into my mouth, washing it down with a swallow of cold tea. The cook came to take the tray away, but I waved her off. I bit into an apple. After what felt like a long time, Nanu returned.

'You won't believe,' she said. 'A car accident, and mother-in-law dead.'

'She'll come back.'

'No. The car was burnt, everything.'

'You'll see.'

'Why are you lying down?' She put her hand on my forehead. 'Are you feeling okay?'

'Don't worry.' I looked at my phone. 'I have to go.'

'Go, go. Or traffic will eat you.'

'I'll come next week.'

'Come just before prayers, the streets will be empty then.' She unlocked the door. 'Bye, Nanu-jaan.'

'Have you told your mother?'

'Not yet.'

'Tell her quickly. You know I can't keep a secret.'

Diana's femur is encased in a thick layer of matrix. Suzanne and I have been debating the best way to prepare it, and I have persuaded her to use an acid treatment. She makes a three per cent acetic acid dilution and we slowly lower the femur into it. Then we place it under the hood and wait for the acid to do its work. It has to be watched carefully; as soon as it dissolves the final layer of matrix, it has to be removed, and the acid washed numerous times. We want it to eat through the matrix but leave Diana in peace.

Suzanne continues to pare away at the ankle bone with a tiny chisel. It's slow work, but she doesn't seem to mind. She chips away, fragment by red fragment, until we see the white of bone. Then she uses a brush from a make-up bag she never lets me touch to clear the last layer of dust. Every few hours we step back and admire her, and the world that preserved her so perfectly, pristine bones and her exquisite red blush.

Bettina has invited me to spend Thanksgiving with her parents, so tomorrow I will take the bus down to New

York. I wanted to stay at the lab but I was afraid that, with Cambridge vacant, I would spend the entire weekend wandering the streets, calling out your name. It is too soon to let my desperation get the better of me. Until you hear the whole story, there's no point bumping into you on the street and cracking my chest open as you brush past me, or, worse, pretend not to know me at all. I haven't really even begun, and there is also Anwar, waiting in the wings, with his own story.

Let me tell you, instead, about one of my ancestors. My great-great-uncle Kashiful Muslehuddin Ali, whose nick-name was Khoka, had once loved a Jewish girl. All his life the family believed there was something not quite right about Khoka: he was overly sentimental, lamenting the number of indentured farmers that starved when the harvest was lean, that he fussed over the goats when they died of the cold, that he moaned over the waste of food whenever there was a banquet. His mother believed it was because he had spent too long in the birth canal, her most difficult labour, and when Khoka came out, he was blue in the face and didn't seem to have any life in him. In fact, the midwife had pronounced him dead, and his mother had curled herself onto the bed when she heard a small cry coming from the black-and-white-tiled floor where they had left him. When he came of age and refused to behave like a man, she blamed that blue tone for making her spoil him.

Years later, unmarried and without a vocation, having proven himself unable to handle either the family accounts or the management of the estate, Khoka took a flat in Calcutta, where he purchased a motorcar and frequented the theatre and Firpo's, a restaurant on Chowringhee Road. It was at Firpo's that he met Rachel Mosel, a Jewish-

American dancer who had come at the behest of the proprietor, Signor Firpo himself, to teach the young women of Calcutta how to dance. The specially sprung floor at Firpo's, which was much advertised in the newspapers of London, was shamed by the badly executed foxtrots of the women of Calcutta. Even the very modern ones, who came in dresses rather than saris, danced badly; so did some of the memsahibs who had been too long in India – their ankles were graceless, their arms flapped about without purpose. So Miss Mosel, who Signor Firpo had met in New York, was drafted in for this very special and delicate task, and, that is when Khoka met her, and for some reason no one in the family was able to fathom, she chose him from among all the young men who instantly fell in love with her.

When Khoka brought Rachel to the estate in Bardhawan – when it was still at its glorious peak, when the Grand Trunk Road was indeed very grand, and the Howrah–Delhi railroad track was still pristine, before my great-grandfather mortgaged the estate, then sold it, before the family's fortunes declined swiftly under the influence of gambling and speculation – his mother regarded Khoka and decided that perhaps there was something enchanting about the gentle slope of her son's forehead and his full-petalled mouth, and that Miss Mosel would have been charmed by the way he noticed every beautiful thing. But this new awareness did not make Khoka's mother agree to the match. She marshalled the family against him, cut off his allowance, sold his Daimler, and stood over his head while he wrote to Rachel to break off the engagement. *I regret to inform you, my dear Miss Mosel, that it will not, after all, be possible for me to marry you.* Twelve hours after the letter had been dispatched, Khoka walked to the railway station, removed his neckerchief and lay down on the tracks, letting the 6.05 Delhi train, which was then called 'the Spear of Kali', glide over his slight frame like a spoon through Signor Firpo's famous Scotch broth. And there ended the sad romance of Kashiful Muslehuddin Ali, the only man in the history of my family to have ever ventured beyond the boundaries of his home in search of love.

Although I had agreed to marry Rashid, we would not be officially engaged until we'd made a public announcement, and, before that could happen, we had to have a party. It was decided that we'd have it at Rashid's house, which was five minutes away on the other side of Gulshan Avenue.

When they first moved to this part of town over twenty years ago, Dolly and Bulbul had built a modest bungalow with a lawn at the front and back. As Bulbul's business expanded – into steel-making, glass-making, shipbuilding – so did the house. Dolly was constantly renovating, exchanging the shuttered windows for aluminium frames, putting marble floors in place of mosaic tiles. Soon other buildings sprouted up on either side of them, and their rooms were plunged in darkness, so instead of tearing the house down and starting all over again, they simply added to the original building, leaving the lower floors to the servants and poor relations from the village. Bulbul had political aspirations, dreamed of someday using the space to hold district meetings, and to this end, he'd had the floors replastered in red to evoke the wide, colonial-style buildings in which such meetings had been held for generations, peasants squatting on polished cement floors and pleading with the Big Man.

Dolly answered the door herself, wearing a spun-sugar concoction of a sari that seemed to make her seem perfectly round from almost every angle. She was beautiful in an exaggerated sort of way, with big, bulging eyes and a full mouth. Behind her, the hallway was lit by a giant chandelier. She stood back and looked me up and down. 'Oh, I'm so glad you wore the pink jamdani,' she said, 'it goes so well with the set.' Earlier that day, she had sent over a rectangular red box that contained a pair of bell-shaped gold earrings and a matching necklace, the arrival of which had prompted a trip to the beauty parlour. 'You can't see the earrings if you don't put up your hair,' Ammoo had said. Dolly led us up the stairs and to the roof terrace on the top floor, where her husband was sipping whisky with his feet submerged in the swimming pool they'd had installed earlier that year. The floodlights and the water enveloped us in a pulsating blue gauze.

Bulbul called out to Abboo. 'Come, Joy,' he said: 'nothing like soaking your feet in this muggy weather.' It wasn't muggy at all; in fact, it was almost December and even a little chilly, but Abboo obliged anyway, edging his way to the swimming pool and rolling up his trousers.

'Zubaida, dear, will you join us?'

'Thank you, uncle, but I should probably—'

'You ridiculous man,' Dolly said. 'She'll ruin her sari. Let's go inside.' She pointed to a glass-walled room next to the pool, decorated in orange and gold. We sat down on the sofa and I looked up at the ceiling. I had been here before, but the house was strange to me now, all buffed up and shining, flowers wrapped around the banisters and bowls of potpourri on every tabletop. My mood turned sour. Dolly had sprayed the room with a heavy dose of rosewater and it was reminding me of a funeral.

'I'm so glad we decided to keep it small,' Ammoo said. She liked to reinforce the fact that she was in the throes of a good decision.

'I did have a lot of trouble keeping out the crowd,' Dolly said, 'but you're right, I'm glad it's just us.' She screwed up her face, delighted, then immediately frowned. 'Only thing is, my other darlings are not here.' Rashid's younger brother Junaid was away at boarding school in Singapore, and his sister Ruby lived in New York.

'Where's Rashid?' I asked. He had sent me a text message an hour ago and signed it *Your future hubbs*, which had made me feel slightly sick.

'He's gone off to get something or other. What will you have? Spring rolls? Fried shrimp? Coke, 7 Up?'

'Anything's fine with me,' Ammoo said. 'Zee?'

I didn't reply. I kept my eyes on the ceiling. 'I'll have a Coke,' Ammoo said, her voice high and bright.

'Are you nervous, my dear?' Dolly asked me. 'How about a drink?' And she winked.

'White wine?' I suggested.

'Zubaida, really,' Ammoo said, because I had ignored her look. We both knew Dolly didn't mean it when she offered me alcohol, but I stood my ground, watching while Dolly walked over to a polished wooden cupboard and turned the lock on a small refrigerator, returning with two glasses and a sweaty bottle of Chardonnay. 'Now, first things first. Do you want Army Golf Club or the Radisson?'

They were going to host a joint wedding reception. I turned to my mother and said, 'You want me to get married at a golf club owned by the Bangladesh Army or at a five-star hotel?'

Ammoo got up, moved to the seat next to mine and squeezed my elbow. I turned my head away and found myself looking at a cabinet crammed with porcelain figurines. 'Radisson,' I said. 'The food's better.'

'Only thing is, they won't let you bring your own biryani,'

Dolly said, 'which is so annoying. Hotel biryani is never as good.'

Ammoo nodded vigorously. 'You're absolutely right. It's more expensive too.'

'Oh, don't worry about that.'

'What I mean is, it's more expensive but it's not as good. Of course, the Radisson ballroom is very nice.'

I snapped to attention. 'I hate biryani.'

'Rashid adores biryani,' Dolly said. 'But never mind, we can do it at the Radisson.'

'Oh, I guess I don't mind, then,' I said, pretending as if Rashid's love of biryani was news to me.

Dolly took a sip from her glass. 'We don't have to. We like to be a bit different.'

'How about an afternoon wedding?' I said. 'We can have lunch. Fish, even. That's different.'

'Oh I don't know, darling.'

'Zubaida,' Ammoo said.

'What?'

'What's gotten into you?'

'I don't want to change my name,' I said, choosing one of the many things that had been bothering me.

'But sweetheart, won't it be nice to have the same last name as all of us?' Dolly said.

I waited for Ammoo to come to my defence. 'I suppose it's my fault,' Ammoo said, 'since I kept mine.'

'Well who knows what my name really is anyway,' I said. All the sound went out of the room.

A man entered with a tray of fried things. I picked up a spring roll.

'Of course you don't have to change your name,' Dolly said.

I tore my eyes away from the cabinet and found Ammoo

struggling to retie the bun at the back of her neck, pulling out and reinserting a series of black pins.

'Okay,' Dolly said, smiling. 'Problem is this. Children should not be involved in the planning of weddings. Why don't you go and see what the fathers are doing, Zubaida? Babu will be here any minute.' Dolly liked to call Rashid 'Babu' and sometimes 'Baby Babu'.

Abboo and Bulbul were drying their feet by the pool. 'Is that wine in your hand?' Abboo asked.

'Transgression,' I said, raising my glass.

Rashid appeared, holding a small rectangular packet and looking pleased with himself. I was struck by his confidence, as if there was no chance of things not working out as they should. For the twentieth, hundredth time that day, I pushed aside the thought of your voice and what you would have said about this party, my pink sari and my lacquered hair. 'Where were you?' I asked him.

'Getting my secret weapon,' he said, leaning in and kissing me on the cheek. He smelled strongly of cigarettes.

'So, uncle,' he said, turning to my father, 'how's the garment business?'

'Good, good.'

'You know the other factories are always complaining that you pay your people so well you make the rest of us look bad.'

Rashid passed the packet to his father, who unwrapped it carefully. Abboo sat up on his pool chair. 'You know what a full wage costs? Only three crores more per year. Nothing. It's the least we can do for taking the sweat from their backs.'

'You're still a leftie,' Bulbul said, rolling a cigarette.

'Something like that.' Abboo turned to me. 'Now I'm mostly handling domestic crises.'

Rashid put on a Beatles compilation and the two older men wiggled their ankles. The cigarette went back and forth.

'They're smoking pot,' I said.

Abboo passed the packet to Rashid. 'Here,' he said, 'you have my blessing.'

Rashid pulled a few leaves apart and shredded them between his fingers.

'This isn't going to end well,' I announced.

'Don't worry, be happy,' Rashid said, turning towards me with a pipe and a lighter. He leaned in, cupping his hand over the pipe and lighting the small brown tangle.

I inhaled. 'I love you,' I whispered, thinking I might like to get my feet wet after all.

It was time for the ceremonial part of the evening to begin. Dolly called me back inside and summoned her maid, who appeared with a garland of lilies and roses. The garland glistened, heavy with petals and the water that had been sprinkled on to keep it fresh. 'Wear this,' Dolly said; 'it will make you look like a bride.' I was intimidated by the word 'bride', so I obeyed, dipping my head and allowing Ammoo to drape the garland around my neck. Then Dolly, working quickly, slipped a veil over my head, securing it with a hair pin. We made our way downstairs, the veil and the garland slowing me down, Dolly's hand grasping my elbow, the rosewater smell fading as we descended.

Downstairs, in the vast living room, I saw both my grandmothers: Nanu, dabbing her eyes with a handkerchief, and Dadu, my father's mother, sitting erect and formidable with a plate of pistachios on her lap. Sally stood up when she saw me, and I gave her a small wave. The other assembled guests were a blur of silk saris and dark jackets. Dolly led me to a sofa and told me to sit down. Rashid appeared beside me. He had changed into a blue kurta, a present from my parents. He kneeled in front of me and held out his hand. I was moved by the tremor in his fingers as he removed the ring box from his pocket. It was the same ring he'd brought to Savar, but I had to wait until the ceremony to start wearing it. Now he held the velvet box in his hand and said, 'Will you marry me?' and I nodded, and everyone clapped, and he slipped the ring on my finger, and Dolly handed me a glass of milk with crushed almonds. Then Bulbul led us in a short prayer, which ended with everyone passing their palms over their faces, and Rashid sitting beside me, nudging me with his elbow the way he used to when I was a kid and the thought of touching him made my stomach tighten.

Rashid and I sat in one place while people came up one by one and congratulated us. We ate fried bread and sour potato curry. Sally, who had pinned her sari under the swell of her pregnancy, came to tell me I looked beautiful but also like I had been given a cancer diagnosis. 'What's wrong, bitch?' she said. 'Supposed to be all happiness and sugar.'

After most of the guests left, dinner was served in the dining room. Dolly's sister Molly, her husband, their son Faisal and their daughter Eliza were there, as well as Bulbul's mother. Everyone hugged each other again and said congratulations. The long mahogany table had been laid out in red and gold. Bulbul took the head of the table and invited my father to sit at the other end. 'Oh no,' Abboo said, 'I couldn't,' so Rashid took his place instead, leaving me between Molly and her son, who had the habit of drumming on whatever surface he could find, in this case moving between his knee and the gold-trimmed plate that he found in front of him. Having accepted my father's invitation to get stoned, I was extremely hungry. It occurred to me that this may, in fact, be a regular habit for Abboo – how else did he manage to appear so relaxed under any and all circumstances? Yes, of course, he must be a habitual smoker – why hadn't I seen it before? Good for him, I said to myself, he deserves it, it's not as if he gambles or stays out late or is ever mean to anyone. I looked over at my father and gave him a meaningful wink, then tuned into the conversation. Bulbul was making a toast, welcoming us into the family, and then we all raised our water glasses.

'So,' Molly said, 'Rashid told me you study physics.' She had applied orange nail polish to every other nail, and French-manicured the ones in between.

'No, not really – I'm a marine palaeontologist.'

'It's all the same, no? Microscopes and all that.' She picked up her fork and dipped it into the salad that had just been served by a waiter in white gloves.

'Sure,' I agreed. I looked over at Ammoo, who was sitting next to Bulbul. She was flanked on her left by Rashid's uncle. After the salad we were served roast duck, followed by mini tarte Tatins, which were warm and delicious. I kept myself entertained by asking Molly about her beauty regime, which consisted of daily facials with various fresh fruits and vegetables, a weekly wash and blow-dry, and special treatments such as bleaching her face and neck when she had somewhere in particular she needed to be. 'I used to go to Dazzle,' she explained, 'but the girls were getting too smart. They know everyone by name. I said na, none of this friendliness. So now I go to Neelo's.'

I nodded. From across the table, Dolly called out to everyone, 'I'm getting another daughter!' She curled her hand around her mouth so her words would travel to the other side of the room.

'Poor Dolly, always wanted more girls. I tell her, boys are

better, no talk-back. My Eliza, she has such a mouth. But Alhamdulillah, she is a good girl.' Molly, like a lot of women of her stature, used religious words like punctuation. When someday Molly's children got older and started taking drugs, or if she ever had a health scare, or her husband started fooling around, she would start peppering more of her speech with God words, Alhamdulillah, Mashallah, Inshallah, etc.; then she would start praying conspicuously, tucking a mat under her arm whenever she went to a party, then maybe she would take a five-star holiday to Mecca, uploading photographs of herself smiling in a burkha, to which her friends would comment, 'Mash'Allah', using the apostrophe in the appropriate place to show that they too understood God's punctuation. My father, still an atheist, had explained this to Ammoo and me numerous times, and we had all giggled about it, sitting around the table on the balcony and wondering what people would say if they could hear us. I let out a small laugh now, but Molly didn't notice, she was telling me how well Eliza was doing in school, that all the teachers loved her and that she had even received a prize for attendance.

After the tarte Tatin, the waiter passed around small dishes of ice cream while taking everyone's order for coffee or tea. I looked around the room. Abboo was in conversation with Molly's husband, who owned three garment factories and always wore a Bluetooth earpiece. Ammoo was concentrating on her ice cream, and Rashid was showing Eliza something on his phone. After the waiter retreated, Rashid stood up and called everyone to attention. 'I have a gift for my future in-laws,' he began. From behind his chair, he produced a rectangular package wrapped in brown paper and passed it to my father. 'Be careful,' he said, 'it's fragile.'

We gathered around as Abboo tugged at the jute string

that held the wrapping together. He pulled the paper away. The framed photograph was an enlarged black-and-white, showing two young men with their arms around each other. They looked at the camera and smiled. They were dressed in matching drainpipe trousers and one of them wore a bandana around his forehead and held up two fingers in a peace sign. In the background, grainy and grey, was the ornate façade of Curzon Hall, the science faculty where they studied. When Abboo looked up, his eyes were filled with tears. 'Where did you get this?'

'I met an old freedom-fighter friend of yours, and he had this photograph in his collection.'

'Thank you,' he said. 'I never took many photographs with my brother. I will cherish this.'

A hush fell across the room as my parents embraced. 'Thank you,' I mouthed to Rashid. He winked at me and I felt a wave of affection for him. And then Bulbul led us in a round of applause, and the tea arrived, Molly's phone rang, and everyone leaned back in their chairs and allowed the evening to come to an end.

And that is how, dear Elijah, I was engaged to be married to someone other than you. I sent you a message without encryption that evening: *I am engaged*, it said, and, seconds later, you replied: *I Hold No Grudge*.

Dolly convinced my mother to take a few days off so we could do the wedding shopping in Calcutta. Ammoo had spent the weeks after the engagement party in Sirajganj, where she had met a group of Birangona women who had been kept in rape camps during the war. The women were in their sixties now, but they still lived together in a shelter that had been set up for them just after independence. She went at first for one night, and then decided to stay for a week because two of the women had recently died of ovarian cancer and she wanted to set up a screening clinic with the local health department. She called and said she might try and persuade the Health Minister to come down. Did you know (her sentences often started this way), the Pakistan Army used to shave their heads because they might use their hair to hang themselves. I did know this, she had told me many times.

In college, after taking a class on Feminism, Selfhood, and Subjectivity, I had read Andrea Dworkin and decided that I had been the product of rape. My father had raped my mother and my mother had given me up for adoption because the sight of my face made her want to be sick. I walked around with this heavy, sludgy feeling in my bones for a few weeks. I practised saying to myself in the mirror that I was the product of rape, wondering how I might introduce such a subject in conversation, deciding it would most definitely give me some cachet with certain types of people. Sometimes I felt like taking a little razor to my skin, maybe my arm or the inside of my leg. I tried it a few times, but I was disgusted by the sight of my own blood, and the relief was only temporary, and eventually I returned to the thought less and less, reminded only when my mother brought up the subject of rape, which she did more often than you would imagine a person does in the course of ordinary conversation.

In Calcutta, Dolly got us rooms with connecting doors at the Grand, and I could hear them talking and giggling while I watched reruns of *MasterChef Australia*. We sat on velvet stools at fancy boutiques and were shown one sari after another, while the word 'trousseau' was whispered among the salesmen. Later, over ice cream, they told me that at university they had one fancy sari between them, borrowing it from each other for special occasions. Of course, the sari was Dolly's — Ammoo couldn't afford such luxuries — but that isn't how they remembered it. I guess that is why, after so many years, they were still best friends. Ammoo had risen to the top of her profession — people addressed her as 'respected Apa' — and Dolly, in the meantime, had become a rich man's wife, nothing but the accomplishments of her children to brag about. Ammoo reminded Dolly of the women they had expected themselves to become, back when the war made their dreams expand out of their little lives, and Dolly was the loyal friend who had seen her through a revolution and its aftermath. I finally understood why they were inseparable, why they had been plotting for years to bring me and Rashid together, because together they formed a single set of hopes, and that is why I had to accept the plot so faithfully, why, in my mind, there seemed no alternative. It wasn't so much doing what was expected of me, like Chandana's Tam-Bram marriage. For this was no arbitrary match, it was the culmination of decades of dreaming, an erasure of history as much as a mark of victory, and in its shadow, I was insignificant.

When Rashid and I were in high school his older sister Ruby sometimes helped me sneak into their house, leaving the downstairs door open and ushering me through the unlit corridors to his bedroom. By the time we got engaged, she had changed her mind. I suppose she had calculated the precise number of handsome, rich, decent bachelors in Dhaka and decided her brother, who had never crashed his daddy's car or spent a fortune on drugs or gambling, was too good for an old love.

Ruby had a tattoo of a camel on her left breast and

dressed like she owned the whole world. She once wore pink cowboy boots under her sari. It was Eid and she propped her feet on the coffee table at her house and showed them off, knee-high, heavily embroidered, and with pointy toes that looked like they could commit murder. After college she had married a weak-chinned American and settled down in New York City, coming home on two-week holidays to distribute lavish presents to the entire family. As soon as the wedding date was set, she booked her flight and started emailing me photographs of the sequined saris and lehngas she wanted to order from a Pakistani designer who lived in her co-op. I was never going to wear a lehnga, and this sparked a polite, cool correspondence between us, with Rashid acting as mediator. He always took my side, at least in private, and found a way to get me what I wanted without letting Ruby know she was being turned down. He was expert at this sort of diplomacy, and when I expressed annoyance at his unwillingness to get into a fight with his sister, he would say, 'Isn't it better this way? You got your sari, didn't you?'

Ruby arrived the week before the wedding and we decided to surprise her at the airport. When she came through the gates the first thing she said was, 'There isn't going to be enough room for my luggage.' She smiled and shrugged at the same time, tilting her head to the side, and Rashid put his arms around her and lifted her off the ground. Her hair appeared to be recently blow-dried, and I was reminded of the time she told me she never washed her hair in winter except at the salon. Rashid had had the driver bring a second car, so there was, in fact, enough space for Ruby's luggage, which followed her out of the airport in three carts. 'I had to get all the things for your trousseau,' she said, shrug-smiling, 'you lucky thing.'

Ruby sat in the front with Rashid. 'How's Matt?' I asked, leaning into the air conditioning from the back.

'Oh, he's fine. He's bringing the kids in a few weeks. I can't stand being on a plane with them.' She turned around and winked at me. Then she put her hand on Rashid's knee and said, 'Little brother! Never thought you'd actually do it. How are the parents? Is Mummy having a fit?'

'She's driving everyone crazy.'

'Bet she forgot to make my favourites for lunch.' She twisted around again. 'See? You're already ruining my life.'

I was hoping Rashid would offer to drop me off at home, but he drove straight to his house and I stood by awkwardly while Dolly and Bulbul and Rashid and Ruby and Junaid, who was home from boarding school, all hugged and said how good everyone looked, despite the tension of the upcoming wedding. They ordered tea in the garden. 'Now I can relax,' Dolly announced, leaning back on a rattan chair. 'Your father is completely useless and the servants are outdoing themselves with stupidity.' They exchanged complaints about the staff while Bulbul nodded off, dropping his newspaper onto the grass. Junaid's phone beeped and he stood up to answer it, nodding briefly at me and loping off.

I was wondering if anyone would notice if I slipped away when Ruby rolled out one of her suitcases. 'Don't look!' she barked. 'I'm just going to give you a preview. Just one.' She handed me a shoebox. I peeled off the lid and separated the tissue. 'Don't you just love them?' Ruby said.

Dolly picked up the lid. 'Ferragamo? Sweetie, you shouldn't have.'

The stilettos were gold and bronze, with a thin strap across the toes and another around the ankle. 'Thank you,' I said, pulling one out. 'They're beautiful.'

'You hate them,' Ruby said.

'Oh, no, not at all, they look – very weddingy.'

'That's exactly what I was thinking, it's so hard to find designer shoes that work for our clothes. Ammoo and I are always complaining when we shop in New York.'

'Very right,' Dolly said.

'But if you don't like them, you should just say. We're sisters now, after all.'

'Oh, no, they're great. I just – you know I'm not used to wearing high heels, so I might have a little trouble walking.'

Ruby nodded enthusiastically. 'I knew you would say that.'

'You're so simple,' Dolly said.

'But anyway at the wedding you won't be running around, you'll just be sitting there, so it won't matter.'

'That's true,' I said.

Ruby used both hands to place the shoe in its box. I stood up. 'I should let you rest, Ruby,' I said.

'Oh, I don't have time to rest,' Ruby said. 'We're going to talk to the biryani guy today, aren't we, Mummy?'

Dolly rubbed her eyes. Rashid was looking down at his phone and frowning. 'Daddy, did you hear about the strike?' Bulbul shook himself awake and they leaned over the phone together.

I took my leave, kissing everyone on the cheek. 'We have to go to the parlour,' Ruby said to me, 'those eyebrows need gardening.'

On my wedding day, I thought of Rokeya Sakhawat Hossain, who had written a novel, *Sultana's Dream*, about a world in which men and women changed places. It was 1905, and Rokeya was waiting for her husband to return from a business trip, and to impress him with her command of English (which he had taught her), she wrote a short novel. Because in Rokeya's real world, women wore veils and lived sequestered lives, in her imaginary world, it was the men who were trapped, the men who were locked away. The women, led by a benevolent Queen, ruled using science, technology and the wisdom that comes from having something that is hard won.

Rokeya's story made me think this: how many novels were written to impress a beloved? And: how did she, trapped in her zenana, push her eye to that better place and see all that would someday come to be, and imagine the things we would never have? Rokeya was my mother's hero. She dropped her name like other people invoked Jesus or Allah. If Rokeya could do it, she said, so could we. Begum Rokeya had done so much with so little. She championed the education of women, started a school, went from village to village to recruit students, gave speeches in parliament, fought her dead husband's family over her inheritance, and cracked jokes at dinner parties. And she was a widow, having lost that husband early in life. Perhaps Rokeya reminded my mother of her own mother, also a widow, also from that generation when things like going to school weren't taken for granted. Now, on the wedding dais, I thought of Rokeya, of my mother, and her mother, and all the women who had done what their mothers had told them to do, and those who had flipped the world around, making prisons into meadows.

After the reception we drove to Rashid's house, which was draped with strands of light that stretched out onto the sidewalk beyond the gate. Inside, Ruby was taking over the whole room, happy because she'd convinced me to wear a gold chain across my forehead and fasten it to my hair with a safety pin, annoyed because I'd refused to wear three necklaces staggered on top of one another so that the ornaments would have started at my navel and ended high on my neck, triumphant because now that I was part of the family she could boss me around and tell me what to wear. In the midst of all this happy/unhappy, Rashid picked me up and stepped over the threshold with the embroidered nagra shoes he wore to match his wedding sherwani, lowering me down so that I could dip my feet into a wide bowl of milk. Then rice was thrown over our heads, prayers whispered and blown over us, already the post-mortem of the reception in full swing – was the biryani a little oily do you think, yes, Reeta S had decorated the hall beautifully, excellent choice of orchids and white roses, doesn't our Rashid look like a prince – and my parents were nowhere to be seen, because I was theirs now, Rashid and Dolly and Bulbul and Ruby's, wearing, as tradition dictated, not a stitch of my old clothes, dressed head to toe in things Rashid's family had given me, right down to the gold thong Ruby had chosen from a New York lingerie boutique, the most uncomfortable, scratchy thing to have ever touched me.

A big show was made of ushering us into the bedroom. I was buried under so much make-up, my sari pinned together with so many safety pins, that it took a full hour for me to undress. I looked at myself in the mirror in my blouse and petticoat, dark streaks across my eyelids where the liner had been difficult to remove. I stepped into the shower to wash out the hairspray, struggling to untangle the complicated bun at the back of my head. When I came out of the bathroom in my old sweatpants and T-shirt instead of the silk negligée I'd been given, Rashid was on the armchair with an opened bottle of champagne. He had removed his shoes and socks, and the top button of his sherwani was undone.

'What, no sexy nightie?'

'Sorry. I'm tired.' I had decided to say it now, because if I waited any longer it would seem as though I was hiding from him, and for all the years that stretched ahead, I wanted it known, as a matter of record, that I had been honest from the very first day. I looked into his face, as familiar to me as my own reflection, his curved nose and flared nostrils, dark, heavy eyebrows, the impressive eddy of ink-black hair. 'Listen, there's something I have to tell you.'

He reached under my T-shirt and pulled me towards him. 'Later,' he said, his mouth arching towards mine.

I brushed his lips lightly. 'No, really. It will just take a minute.'

He sighed, folded his hands on his lap. 'Okay, Mrs Khondkar, I'm all ears.'

'Don't call me that.'

'I'm just saying it out of love.'

'I'm sorry. Look, we have to talk about this, because we're married now, and someday there might be children, and these things need to be out in the open.'

'So serious.'

'I'm not Ammoo and Abboo's biological child.' I took the champagne glass from his hand and drained it. Immediately it made me light-headed. 'I'm adopted. My parents never told anyone. They only told me once, when I was nine – it was my birthday – and we never talked about it again.'

He reached down to the floor and picked up the bottle. When he turned to me again he was smiling. 'Sweetheart, I know.'

'What?'

'I've always known, Zee. My parents told me years ago.' Rashid was still chuckling as he refilled the glass.

I took another sip and let the words sink in for a minute. 'All this time?' I gestured with my hand and a dribble of champagne spilled onto my lap.

'Listen,' he said, taking the glass from my hand, 'it's nothing. My parents know, and nobody minds. I love you. Everyone loves you.' He kissed me on the forehead. 'Now I want my wedding-night fuck.'

Nobody minds. There was generosity there, and something else – forgiveness, maybe. I didn't know what I had to be sorry for, but I was sorry, and he was telling me it was all right. I tried to imagine the conversation he would have had with his parents – when? – about how to handle the story if it were to get out, if other relatives got involved and questioned the wisdom of forming an alliance with a girl of uncertain provenance. Maybe they had even discussed it with Ammoo and Abboo. What had my parents said? Were they grateful because the Khondkars were willing to stand behind them, to legitimise their daughter by sanctioning the marriage?

Elijah, I thought back at that moment to what you said to me about the longing of the soul. The loneliness of being only in one body, when the spirit wanted nothing but communion. You didn't try to make me feel better, you made my fears seem unremarkable, just another small instance of the universal need for kinship. But Rashid was trying too, in his own way, pressing his lips against my neck, grazing my breast with the back of his hand. I allowed myself to enjoy his caresses, his hand firm against my back. We kissed. I tasted champagne and the familiar tang of his breath. He passed me the champagne again and I took another swig from the glass, the fizz going all the way to the back of my throat. Our bed was decorated with roses, and garlands were suspended from the ceiling and taped to the wall. Everything smelled pungent and slightly rotting. Rashid peeled back the bedcover and lay me gently on the bed. We made love quietly, both tired from the day, and, although we had done it before in this room, the smell of the flowers and the fresh paint and the lingering heaviness on my face and the thought that everyone else in the house knew what we were about to do weighted and dulled the ordinary gestures of sex, and afterwards Rashid got up to fold his clothes and brush his teeth, and by the time he came back to bed I was almost asleep, so that I was only vaguely aware of his hand on my hip, his breath behind my ear.

In the morning my parents arrived as guests in my new home. The cook piled chicken korma onto my plate, and Dolly gave me the key to the drawer in my closet, telling me to lock my things away in it whenever I left the upper floor of the house, in fact to lock the bedroom door itself because you never did know with the servants. It suddenly occurred to me that though Rashid and I had grown up within a few minutes of each other, so that moving into his house should have felt like little more than moving from one end of my parents' apartment to the other, it was another world, here in the three-storey building with the swimming pool on the roof, locking doors behind me, korma for breakfast, a fleet of cars in the basement, a suspicion of servants, because you never did know, except that I did know, and what I knew made me bitterly sad, the conversation from the night before grating on me as I remembered the pity and absolution in his voice. It was only the first day and already I felt the depths of the mistake, touching me like the ink from a stray pen in my pocket.

Every night there was an invitation to a relative's house for dinner, and, the following Friday, a visit to a factory that Bulbul owned. Occasionally there was the thrill of closing the door behind us and sneaking in a quick kiss, and once or twice Rashid played some of our favourite songs on the music system he had set up around our bed, and we held each other under the canopy of drying flowers, and in those moments there was the feeling of being out of context, away from the brocade saris and the thousands of pleasantries that had to float out of my mouth, a sense of it being just the two of us, old friends and child-hood sweethearts finally reaching the natural conclusion of something we had started many years before. But then the rest of my life would come into focus, and I would catch a glimpse of the person I used to be, was, in fact, just months ago, the sort of person who would travel across the world to dig whale bones out of the ground, and in those moments I felt as if I was battling a phantom, a woman who haunted my otherwise perfect life.

Then, one day, Rashid went back to work at the factory. He got up in the morning, showered, dressed in slacks and a shirt with cufflinks, pulled on the watch my parents had given him as a wedding gift, and got into the back seat of his car. I watched all of this while still in my pyjamas, leaning out of the second-floor balcony and listening to the car door close behind him with a heavy snap. Then, contem-plating the day ahead, I crawled back under the sheets and buried my face in the bed.

I flipped through the books on my shelf and found *Moby-Dick*, remembering how you had teased me that day at the airport. *Moby-Dick* got me thinking about Diana, still trapped underground, maybe even desecrated by now if what they said about unrest in that area was true. I imagined indifferent hands lifting her bones out of the ground, disturbing what had lain undisturbed for millennia, and this made me think about time and its inevitable forward march, that I too would be bones in a grave someday, that I would be dead, and then I started counting all the things I would regret if I were dying, and lying in bed on a Monday with nothing to do but read *Moby-Dick* was not on that list. I would not look back at my life and declare it well spent if this was what I had spent it on.

Again and again I thought of the conversation Rashid and I had had on our wedding night. I wanted to ask him about it again, to find out the details of how he had come to discover my secret, and why they had all – Dolly and Bulbul and Rashid and Abboo and Ammoo – decided never to offer me the comfort of their collective knowledge. But I didn't want to see him laughing it off again, didn't want him to reassure me and tell me it was all right, implying in his own way that, somewhere deep within, I owed him a debt for not minding, for treating me as though I were anyone else, a person with a bloodline that people could trace and rely upon. So I kept quiet, repeating the pattern of unsaying that had begun with my birth, and after a few weeks Melville became a friend, and the parties subsided, and I came to an accommodation with the fate to which I had submitted.

I don't often think about my wedding, Elijah, but I have a photograph I carry around. I even brought it with me on this trip. I look beautiful, in the way of a person who has made an effort to look good for a camera. The sari Ruby and Dolly had chosen was tasteful and suited the copper tones of my skin. I had allowed a make-up artist, a friend of Sally, to paint my eyelids and blow a light dusting of glitter across my forehead. I am not as pretty any more, Elijah – in fact, by the time you arrived on the beach, that particular sheen was long gone – but in your presence, as you know, I was beyond pretty: I was majestic, a sovereign, like the Queen in Rokeya's story.

Prosperity Shipbreaking

And now we come to the time when you arrived at the beach and our lives turned to face one another again. The year I lived in the shadow of *Grace* and watched that great leviathan stripped down to her very bones. The year I broke your heart. I love this part of the story, not least because you are in it, but also because those few weeks we were together tell me everything I need to know about the rest of my life. Sure, it paints a picture of me that I am loath to remember, much less resurrect. But in order for us to come crashing down so decisively, we had to climb to those heights. We had to be those people whose fingertips brushed the atmosphere. I will always be grateful for that.

It is a year after the wedding. Rashid and I have been living in his parents' house with the swimming pool on the roof and the locked bedroom doors. Anwar, in the meantime, is back in his village, carrying his secret, which is also my secret. He hasn't begun to search for Megna, and he hasn't yet arrived in the city where we will eventually meet. How I came to be there myself has to do with blood. My period was late. I had been assigned a car and a driver by the stern-looking man who managed Dolly's household. The driver was young and skinny, and sank into his seat so that all I could see from the back was the sleeve of his shirt and his elbow as he manoeuvred the gearshift. I asked him to take me to the pharmacy in Gulshan 1, the one under the ice-cream parlour. The shopkeeper was standing behind a glass counter that was crammed with sanitary pads, and while I was searching my mind for the Bengali words for pregnancy test, I found myself re-annoyed by the fact that all the pharmacies were arranged in this way, and that if you wanted something embarrassing you had to ask someone to pull it down from a shelf or to open a cardboard box hidden in the back room. I decided my people were all terribly indiscreet. You couldn't walk down an aisle and pick up condoms or tampons or haemorrhoid cream. The shopkeeper took my money and wrapped the rectangular box in a brown-paper bag. And then I went home and the two blue lines appeared immediately and I thought I would explode with rage.

Instantly I experienced an onset of symptoms. I felt a sharp pain in my abdomen and my legs were heavy and I wanted to devour a hamburger. I also had the overwhelming sense that my body had betrayed me by allowing this little seed to take root. What an ignorant little thing it was, didn't it know that nothing had been right since the wedding, or earlier, since I agreed to marry Rashid, maybe even before that, when I had decided against the possibility of love – didn't it know that it shouldn't commit this one act, this act that had been denied my mother, and summed up an equation that had remained unsolved within me?

I sat with it for two weeks. Every morning I willed it to be over. Every morning I cursed this being whose provenance was more sure, within the first moments of life, than mine would ever be. I ate like the proverbial pig, ate everything, was repulsed by nothing except the little cluster of cells with my name on it. Every time I went to the bathroom I stared down at my blank, perfectly clean underwear. I contemplated dangerous acts, such as excessive drinking or jumping from high places, but I had never been courageous that way and I wasn't about to start now. Dolly threw a party one day where everyone was asked to wear black and white and she put a tent out in the garden and hung strands of tiny lights from the trees, and I took a full plate up to my bedroom and ate what felt like an entire side of lamb.

The television was switched to the Discovery Channel and there was a programme on algae. Algae, the building blocks of life. At that moment, with the meat sitting densely in my stomach, I developed an attachment. I thought about meeting a person who was related to me by blood, something that had never happened to me before. Kin. I clutched my belly and took back all the things I had whispered to it. In the background an animated male voice said, *The giant kelp is a large brown alga that may grow up to fifty metres in length*, and I smiled and smiled to myself at this strange accident.

I told Rashid.

I don't know how he had experienced the first year of our marriage. He seemed always upbeat and cheerful, and we'd had a few holidays together, a honeymoon in Thailand, a week in London, a business trip to Hong Kong to which I had tagged along. He had been right about the travel – it took the edge off of living in Dhaka. There were parties and family dinners and trips back and forth from Dhanmondi to see my grandmother. Sally and Nadeem's baby was born in the summer, and we had watched them stumble clumsily around parenthood. The months passed. I read a lot of books. A hundred times I watched a YouTube video of Glenn Gould playing the thirteenth variation but that was the only paean to you I maintained. Although I still had had no word from Bart, a part of me was clinging to the possibility that he would suddenly summon me to Dera Bugti, so I didn't look for a job.

As soon as I told Rashid I was pregnant it was as if I'd crawled into his head and turned on all the lights. He didn't know how close I'd come to not saying anything, how many times I'd contemplated having an abortion. But it was – and I must tell you this, Elijah, though it will pain you – it was a moment of communion between us. When I woke up the next morning, there was a tray on the bedside table with tea, vitamins, and a bunch of tulips. God knows how he'd procured the tulips. I was thrilled when he agreed not to tell his parents, and we spent the next several weeks on a conspiratorial high. Every time we looked at each other, we widened our eyes and smiled. Every chance he got, he put his hands on my belly. We did things that people have done throughout the ages. We guessed the sex. We argued over names. We made cooing sounds to it, to each other. He told me repeatedly how beautiful I looked. He made love to me with extreme tenderness. It was everything it needed to be, and for the first time in our marriage I experienced a complete absence of dissatisfaction.

And then, as suddenly as it had appeared, the little knot of cells vanished. We were gathered around the top of Dolly's twelve-seater dinner table, the five of us – Rashid and me, Dolly and Bulbul, his brother Junaid – and we'd just been presented with trifle, Dolly's favourite dessert, served in a very large glass bowl. Rashid was passing the bowl to me, and as I turned to take it from him I felt a hot, abrupt pain scissoring through me. I grabbed his elbow as the pain intensified, watching in horror as a crimson stain travelled across my lap and towards my knees. Rashid was still holding the trifle bowl, and he set it down. The others were eating, dessert forks clipping against porcelain, custard and Jell-O smudged across their plates.

Rashid stood up and asked his father and his brother to leave the room. Junaid protested, saying he wasn't finished, but Bulbul saw the look on Rashid's face and ordered the boy out. When they had gone, I said to Dolly, 'I'm very sorry, but I'm afraid I've spoiled your dining chair.' The upholstery was stained beyond repair, I knew that even before I stood up, because I was sitting now in a pool of blood, the remnants of that much cursed, little-wished-for, newly coveted being smeared all over the cream-and-navy fabric. Dolly and Rashid pulled me up from that chair, very slowly, and Dolly wrapped a shawl around my waist, and we went up the stairs and into the bathroom, where I climbed quietly into the empty bathtub in my clothes. It wasn't until much later, the tub filled, swirls of light and dark pink filtering into the water, that I let Rashid pull the kameez over my head. And then I lay there for a long time, swimming with the evaporating atoms of my child, utterly, excruciatingly alone.

It was suggested – after the doctor, and the scans, and the assurance that no irreparable damage had been done – that I should spend a few weeks in the southern port town of Chittagong, where Rashid's family owned a country house. I had been there twice before – once on a summer holiday with my parents, and again just after the wedding, when Dolly and Bulbul had held a reception for that branch of the family. I agreed easily when the proposal was put to me, but I didn't want anyone else to come. I thought they might refuse to let me go alone, but I found there was some power in what had happened, and I was allowed to dictate the terms, at least for now.

I also insisted that my parents shouldn't know anything, especially my mother. Ammoo was preparing for the trial of Hossain Hashmi Kubul, a notorious war criminal who had spent the last forty years bragging about his wartime exploits, daring anyone to prosecute him. He had invested in land just after liberation, then started a cement factory that supplied all the building companies in the capital, and he was a powerful man – in the last government, he had even been given a ministry. Everyone knew he had done things, that he was a Razakar, but the tribunal needed witnesses, and Ammoo had found a family who had known him in '71, a farmer and his ageing father who had seen Kubul ordering the Razakars to mow down all the men in the area and torch their houses. She was with the lawyers day and night, preparing the witnesses, finding supporting documents, scouring the area for anyone who might back up their story. She couldn't know about my little hiccup. Every time I saw her I told her how wonderful everything was, and the clouds parted around her face, and I saw that there was no space in her for anything but the lightest of conversations.

I packed a suitcase of my old clothes and took the first flight out on a Wednesday morning. Rashid tried at the last minute to get me to change my mind, but I had to put some distance between us. The spell was broken. I couldn't stop thinking about the look on his face when he realised what was happening, the slight censure that would have reared itself, and him batting it back, shielding me from the truth: that it would have saved us, and without it, we were once again adrift. He drove me to the airport, promising to fly down on Friday. A driver picked me up at the other end, and the caretaker, Joshim, greeted me at the front door.

Khondkar Villa was a modest, two-storey house built by

Bulbul's father in the 1950s. It had a large living room that opened onto a sloping garden. Outside, the bougainvillaea and its bright, flame-like blossoms dominated the landscape, and beyond the garden there were old trees, and more sloping earth, the cars and asphalt of the city nowhere in sight. Chittagong was a smaller version of Dhaka, with the same kinetic pace, the same political graffiti and billboards for shampoo and long-haul flights and mobile-phone packages. But here, elevated above the streets, the city retained its old character as a hill station, a place where the air was cool and empty and lightened by its proximity to the sea.

In the vacant house, the cook, Komola, reigned supreme. She ordered me to wash my hands and then she brought me a tray and ordered me to eat. I was surprised to find I still had a big appetite. The homemade guava jelly and white bread reminded me of childhood summers, when Nanu used to make big batches from the tree in her garden and I would stick a spoon directly into the pot and burn my tongue on the cloyingly sweet paste. Komola filled the guest bathtub and ordered me to get in, but not before she had given me a thorough massage with olive oil. The oil was warm and Komola's hands were comfortably rough, and I slept deeply that night and woke up refreshed.

Rashid came on Friday and declared me better. 'Let's party,' he said, jangling the car keys in his pocket. 'I know everyone in this town.' Komola stood in the doorway with a bowl of rice pudding in her hands. I told Rashid I wasn't going anywhere. I know he wanted to help me fix it, to cheer me out of it, but it was obvious, in this case, that whatever was in his arsenal would not be enough. I spooned rice pudding onto my plate and pretended not to see his disappointment.

He went out after dinner and didn't come back till very

late, climbing into bed beside me and running his hands up and down my body. 'Make love to me,' he whispered, his breath fragrant with alcohol, and I went through the motions, trying to gain comfort from the closeness of our bodies, but eager for the visit to be over so I could be alone in the house again. What would I say to you, Elijah, if we were still in touch? What song title would communicate, now, the complicated forms of attachment that had been promised and taken away from me? We had stopped sending messages soon after the wedding. The last one I sent was an unencrypted sentence that delivered the news in its blandest form. *Married. Happy. Farewell.*

Rashid left Chittagong the next afternoon, and over the course of the following week, I slipped into a routine. An early breakfast, then a walk through the estate with Joshim, he holding a long stick and pointing out the names of the trees. After a few hours of reading, I ate lunch in the kitchen with Komola and the other servants. It took some arguing to get them to agree to let me eat with them, but I told them that I was lonely sitting at the long dining table all by myself. There was another cook, a maid, a guard, and a young girl who did the laundry and dusted Dolly's furniture. In the evening, there was a bath, and more reading, and falling asleep to the sound of the wind through the open window. 'Bou-ma doesn't like air conditioning,' I overheard Komola saying to the others.

I was turning my thoughts to returning home when I received a call from my mother's friend, Rubana. I had, in fact, been thinking of Rubana on the very day she telephoned, recalling the last time I had seen her. It was a few weeks after my wedding, at the home of one of Dolly's distant cousins, Sweetie. Sweetie had invited a large and superbly groomed group of friends to her house in Baridhara, and

Rubana had stuck out in her plain clothes and lack of make-up. I had known Rubana since childhood and had always been a little afraid of her. That evening she appeared bored, looking often at her phone and wandering out into the garden with her hands around a mug of tea. I followed her and she looked me up and down, a giant red teep punctuating her forehead, and asked me what I was doing, not, what are you doing, dear? But *What the hell do you think you're doing?* At least, that is how I heard it. What the hell did I think I was doing, I regularly said to myself. It made me feel a little better in the way that stating something obvious can do. 'I've been thinking about you,' she said now. 'I heard you were in Chittagong.'

'Yes, at my in-laws'.'

'Oh, yes, the hill. Is Rashid with you?'

'No, I came on my own.'

'Escaping already? Wise woman.' Rubana herself was married, but no one ever saw her husband. I imagined a small, whiskery man who shuffled around in a lungi and didn't dare raise his voice above a whisper.

'I know someone who's working on a project. It's in Sithakunda, about an hour from you. Have you heard of shipbreaking?'

Shipbreaking. Yes, I knew what it was. Places on the beach where they tore ships apart. Every few months you would read a story in the papers about how one of the workers had died in a fire or been crushed under falling steel.

'There's a British researcher who wants to do a documentary, but none of the workers are talking to her. You could go and help her make inroads. Translate. We have some local people there, an NGO called Shipsafe, but somehow it's not clicking.'

The prospect of someone instructing me to work, to actually make something happen, gave me a sense of what I had wasted. Except *Moby-Dick*, I couldn't recall the name of a single book I'd read in the last twelve months. I blamed Bart, the failed dig, but really I had just been stubborn, clinging to my coveted title, palaeontologist, not realising that it had been taken away from me and that I should just accept this instead of becoming one of those people I'd always hated. And why hadn't anyone said anything? My mother, who crammed every day with a hundred useful, life-or-death activities, had remained silent as I had slept through the better part of a year.

'I don't know anything about it,' I said.

'Doesn't matter. Use your wits.'

I mumbled an excuse about not being well, and heard Rubana sigh into the phone. She was weighing me up, judging my temperament, and finding me lacking.

'Too bad,' she said. 'It's probably not for you anyway. You'd have to move out of that fancy house and into the office quarters — it's the only way you can have constant access. I don't imagine you can survive without air conditioning.' I found myself telling her about Dera Bugti. The overnight bus to Kashmore. Camp beds. Chiselling in the sun. The prospect of leaving this house, not to return to Dhaka, but to go elsewhere, was a possibility I hadn't dared consider. What would I tell everyone? But if I accepted a job, and if that job took me away from here, then it was out of my hands.

'You're a fairy godmother,' I said to Rubana.

I told Rashid the following weekend, when he came to see me. 'But I'm here to bring you home,' he said. He raked his hair with his long, blunt fingers. I was exhausting him, but he couldn't deny me, not after what had happened. At Dolly's house, the dining chair would have been removed from the table. I wondered where the chair was, whether it was sitting discarded in a storeroom somewhere, or whether it had been sent back to the shop so that the fabric could be replaced, and who was doing this task, and how it been explained, and did they have to pay extra for the blood, for the workmen's disgust?

I left it to Rashid to break the news, both to my parents and to his. He tried to persuade me to stay at Khondkar Villa – the driver would bring me back and forth – but I refused, hoping the accommodation in Sithakunda was terrible, suddenly yearning to get far away from the plush, unpopulated spaces of his house. I said goodbye to Komola and Joshim, meaning it when I said I would miss them, promising to return whenever I needed a good night's sleep or a proper meal.

The next day Bilal, the Shipsafe coordinator, picked me up in a battered jeep. I climbed into the front seat beside him and we sped down the hill. Bilal had recently married, and he flicked through photographs of his wedding on his phone while navigating us out of the city. I commented on the loveliness of his bride. She looked not unlike how I must have appeared just last year, a line of tiny flowers in the parting of her hair. We took a route that skirted the sea. Oil refineries lined the road on one side, and high walls separated the road from the coast on the other, and, out in the water, giant oil tankers and container ships waited to load or dump their cargo. Then we turned inland, getting stuck in traffic almost immediately. Hunched over the steering wheel, Bilal simultaneously complimented his wife's beauty and complained that Chittagong was no better than Dhaka, now that trade was booming. He pointed to a gate. 'See,' he said, as if I should understand. The sign said EXPORT PROCESSING ZONE. Then the traffic cleared and we sped through, leaving the low buildings and overhanging wires of the city behind, turning to a sky that was bright and open.

A few miles into the Dhaka–Chittagong highway, the gentle hills breaking up the horizon disappeared, and we were suddenly confronted with the complicated detritus of broken ships. Bilal gestured to the vast scrapyards of things that looked like they'd been rescued from a warzone: broken refrigerators, oxygen tanks, rows and rows of lifebuoys, toilet bowls, washing machines, metal cages he referred to as compressors, and then a string of antique shops that housed, he told me, compasses and brass trinkets and lanterns and other things that had been found on board. Then, passing a number of furniture shops, open storefronts displaying battered sofas, bunk beds, filing cabinets, office desks, he said sometimes they pretended the stuff came from the ships when actually it was made right there on the road.

Bilal kept casting curious glances my way, because I had hardly made a sound or exclaimed at the strangeness of the landscape, which must have been rare; he was probably used to people talking about how bizarre it all looked, like a glimpse into an apocalyptic future where everything was salvaged and half-broken. But I was numb to all of it, pleased by the sight of something that matched the chaos I felt within me. It was only when we passed through the gates of Prosperity Shipbreaking, and I saw an oil tanker in the final stages of being pulled apart, a felled dinosaur of metal lying on its side with the curved blades of its propeller exposed, that I was unable to hold back from cursing out loud. 'What the fuck?' I blurted out, and Bilal smiled, as if he'd just won a bet.

The Shipsafe office was on a small paved road off the

highway and just a few steps from the beach. There were just two rooms – one in front with a veranda overlooking a small patch of grass where someone had planted onions and coriander, and another adjacent to the kitchen that served as a small meeting room. I was assigned a heavy wooden desk with a glass top in the front room. There was a caretaker who was in charge of keeping the place clean who did a reasonable fish curry for lunch. In the evenings I would have to fend for myself.

Bilal filled the kettle and we shared a pot of tea on my new desk. I asked him a few more questions about his wedding, and he showed me another photograph, this time of himself sitting on the dais with his bride under a red-and-yellow canopy. Then he brought up Gabriela, the British researcher who I had been brought on to help.

She had recently landed in Chittagong after four years on the *Rainbow Warrior*, and was here to complete the initial interviews for the film, after which the director and the crew would arrive in several months. She spoke a few words of Bangla, learned in London before she had set off for Chittagong. 'Why hasn't it worked out?' I asked him. I saw him look out into the garden. 'She's foreign,' he finally said, lifting up his shoulder. 'She asks too many questions.'

'Isn't that why she's here?'

'Mind if I smoke?' he said, taking out a box of Benson & Hedges before I could reply. He brought an ashtray over from his desk on the other side of the room, and then he said, 'I don't trust her.' I tried to press him further, but he withdrew into silence, leaning back in his chair and pulling hard on his cigarette. After a long time he said, 'It's a cruel industry. For years we've been working slowly, patiently with the owners. Suddenly she comes and tells us how terrible things are. A film isn't going to change anything.'

I didn't want to get drawn into a debate about the purpose of art. Bilal had a long scar running along his forearm, which he exposed as he flicked his cigarette stub to the ground. I asked him about the scar and he said his father had taken a razor blade and sliced through his flesh once when he was about twelve because he had been caught kissing his cousin. 'On the mouth,' he said, putting a finger on his lip. 'The servant found us and she dragged me outside by my ear. Abba was shaving.'

The story seemed to relax him. He pulled another chair towards us and stretched out his legs.

'Sometimes people prefer talking to strangers,' I suggested.

'Nobody is going to tell that woman anything,' he said.

The apartment was much nicer than the office, with windows on two sides, one looking onto the road, the other through to the beach beyond. There were two bedrooms and a small sitting area, a dining table, a chair and a few large square cushions on the floor. I took the smaller, empty bedroom. After unpacking my bag and stringing up my mosquito net, I pulled the chair over to the window and ate the noodles Komola had packed for me, listening to the distant whine of the shoreline smelter. Dusk was quickly followed by darkness, and just as I was about to switch off the overhead light and try to sleep, the front door opened and Gabriela entered.

She stopped for a moment, then, realising who I was, bounded over and threw her arms around me. She was fortyish, tall and muscular, with reddish-brown hair. 'Thank bloody Jesus you're here,' she said. I returned her smile. Without sitting or putting down the large bag slung over her shoulder, she began to bombard me with questions. Why were the workers so young? Where had they all come from? Where were their parents? And why on God's great earth would anyone choose this beach, with its glassy water and buttery sand, to destroy ships, rather than sunbathe and swim and fall in love? She had been there for a month and the workers had refused to talk to her.

'It's like their mouths are sewn shut.'

I knew why already, five minutes into meeting her. The way she dressed, for instance. Her shirt was open two buttons too far. She had rolled up her sleeves past her elbows, revealing the articulated muscles of her upper arms. Her jeans were tight and her ass was exposed because she had tucked in her shirt. How would anyone know where to look, much less open their mouths and tell her anything? She had pierced her nose, and three studs up each ear, and there was a small jewel above her lip, where a mole or a birthmark might be. She reminded me of a vintage cigarette advertisement, with the woman flexing her biceps. A cross between that and a hippy and a biker. I was a little disgusted but also thrilled to be in the presence of someone so completely out of context.

Gabriela offered me the bigger room, but I declined. 'Come and lounge on the bed for a few minutes at least,' she said. 'There's nowhere comfy to sit.' She opened a bottle of tequila and insisted I take a swig. 'This shit is the only stuff that keeps me sane.' I was going to say no, but then I thought, what the hell, it's not like I'm pregnant. I tipped the bottle into my mouth and it burned a hole all the way down to my stomach. She kept telling me how glad she was to see me. 'Tell me what we're going to do. I'm at a dead end here.'

'I don't know yet,' I said, replying honestly. 'Give me a few days to think about it. Humans aren't really my specialty.'

'Really? Rubana told me you were good at this kind of

stuff. She said you were unusually perceptive. And she said something else, I can't remember what.'

'I'm a palaeontologist.'

'You're joking,' she said, slapping her hand on the bedcover.

'My subjects are mostly dead.'

'You're wasted.'

'I am, actually. Just a little.'

'No, I mean Rubana – she said you were wasted. I wasn't sure what she meant, but I assumed you were in some dead-end job or something. But you're into dinosaurs, that's not what I expected.'

I laughed, leaning back on the bed. 'Well, Rubana and my mother have a very specific definition of a meaningful life.'

'And you are way hotter than I'd imagined.'

'I had a miscarriage,' I said, confessing before I realised what I was doing.

'Oh shit, I'm sorry.'

She passed me the bottle and I took another swig. I leaned back further and saw the ceiling swimming above me. When I was too tired to keep my eyes open, I made my way to my own bed, my head throbbing, and retreated under the mosquito net.

The next morning Gabriela took me to the beach. It was my first proper sighting of the Prosperity Shipbreaking. You are reading this now and so your image of the place is as fixed in your mind as it is in mine. What I remember thinking, when I first set eyes on it, was that it was a place where I could punish myself as much as I liked without anyone noticing, because it was the least alive landscape in the world, not because it was ugly, but because it was beautiful, and ruined.

The ship I had caught sight of the day before – its name, I was later told, was *Splendour* – was still lying on its side, its propeller pointing towards the sky. Its bridge was gone, its hull sliced away like meat from a carcass. On the shoreline, the smelter was going at full speed, and the air was thick with the astringent smell of burning metal. I stood there for a long time with a sense of being at the edge of the world, where a person might see, or do, anything. Gabriela pointed out a man in the distance, suspended from the deck of a skyscraper-high ship with only a rope around his waist. 'Can you believe this shit?' she said.

The shipbreaking yards consisted of narrow rectangles of oceanfront. From the highway, you could see a high wall with double gates every hundred yards or so. But once you entered one of the yards, you could look across the whole expanse of the bay, at one ship after another in various states of decay. You could look east or west and see a mile-long oil tanker, or a container ship, or a fragment of something that used to be seafaring and was now only a collapsed stretch of metal. And if you looked closer, if you really concentrated, you would see the tiny shapes of people hanging from the ships, breaking them apart with blow-torches and hammers.

My first look at this scene made me profoundly sad. Or, rather, it took the sadness that already existed within me and magnified it. I felt I was made of something unmalle-able, something hard and alien. It took me time to realise what I was really mourning, and perhaps I am only coming to an understanding of it now, all these years later. It was the pregnancy, of course. I hadn't reckoned with my need to be of the same blood as another person – I had never thought about that before, and being presented with the possibility, and having that possibility taken away, made my longing acute in the multiplied hit of a desire for something that is a new, but also very old.

But more than that, I recalled the initial feeling of bitterness when I saw those two blue lines and realised that it wasn't that I didn't want a baby, it was that I didn't want a baby with Rashid. I had allowed myself to be carried away for a moment by the prospect of a child bringing us together, but fundamentally I did not want to be heavy with a being that would bind us together for ever. Rashid was not that man. The knowledge, earned on that first day on the beach, was a little grain of doubt that added, hourglass-like, to everything else. And like all the other little grains of sand, I pushed it aside and went on as before, refusing to add everything up.

Although Gabriela tried to persuade me to meet the workers right away, I wanted to become a familiar figure on the beach before approaching anyone. I spent most of the first week at the Shipsafe office reading through the documents Bilal had gathered on the industry. There were apocryphal stories about how it had all started – a cyclone in the Bay of Bengal, a ship banked on the shore, a group of scavengers, the discovery of steel, and then, eventually, businessmen who turned ill-fortune into profit.

Mirza Ali, the manager of the shipyard, was my first point of contact. He worked out of a narrow building with a corrugated tin roof and windows that faced the beach. Inside, he and his staff drank tea and argued about whatever ship they were taking apart. I waited for Ali to invite me to meet him, and when he did, I knew what do to – my year as Rashid's wife had prepared me well. I dressed in a sari and sipped tea with him, setting him at ease by complimenting him on his operation. Ali reeled off statistics of how many tons of steel his yard had sold to the construction industry. I listened politely, taking in his long white tunic and his prayer cap, the shiny bruise on his forehead that marked him as a man who prayed five times a day. He asked me repeatedly if I was comfortable, hinting at the unsuitability of the accommodations in the Shipsafe flat, but I smiled and assured him all was well. I could see why Rubana had sent me here, and it was of course because of class, because Ali would be flattered by my presence, his natural suspicion averted, and I would ease Gabriela's way onto the beach.

My arrival coincided with the purchase of a new ship called *Grace*, and soon Ali was inviting me to witness the ship's arrival. 'The beaching of a ship is a unique experience,' he said. 'A combination of skill and God's will.' He invited me to come and see it for myself, agreeing reluctantly to let Gabriela accompany me. 'As your guest,' I said, knowing that Ali would want to appear hospitable in my eyes.

On the morning of *Grace*'s arrival, Gabriela and I were instructed to wake up an hour before dawn and make our way to the shore. Outside my window all was black, except for a few bursts of orange from the kerosene lamps of the workers' dormitory. In the distance I could hear the sound of water swooning towards the bay.

I knocked on Gabriela's door. There had been a brand-new moon during the night, and the tide had grown higher by the hour. 'Is it time already?' she called out.

Grace was a decommissioned cruise ship. At almost a thousand feet, she was the biggest passenger ship ever to arrive on Prosperity's beach. Ali had shown me a photograph of a white zeppelin with red trim, gleaming decks and rows of tiny windows. It would take them three, maybe four months to take it apart. Passenger ships were few and far between on the beach; a photograph had been passed around the office and there was much excitement around its arrival. For a few days the ship had been waiting in Chittagong Harbour, its customs inspection passed, for the tide to reach its highest peak. The reason they beached ships in this particular location was because the water was shallow for almost a mile out and then suddenly very deep, making it easy for the vessels to wedge themselves firmly into the sand while the tide was high. Then, when the water retreated, the ship would be marooned, ready for the workers to cut into its hull and begin taking it apart. This was the answer to Gabriela's question that first night.

It was because of Ali's boss that Gabriela and I had been allowed on site. For years, Shipsafe had been campaigning for a ban on the whole industry. Rubana had won a few injunctions in court, but this had only slowed the work for a few months; soon the appropriate palms were greased, and the court orders were ignored and the ships began to arrive again. When Gabriela and her film crew proposed to tell the story of the shipbreakers, Rubana decided to try a different tack. She went to Prosperity, the biggest shipyard, to suggest a compromise: if Shipsafe was allowed access to the site to observe and report on the working conditions on the beach, she would recommend the grant of a compliance certificate by the environment ministry. As a part of this agreement, the company would allow Gabriela's team to make a film about the workers.

This proposal appealed to the owner of Prosperity, a man called Harrison Master. Harrison had, from humble beginnings, built a series of industries on the Chittagong coast: garments, cement, natural gas, fertiliser. He had bought a hill at the edge of a lake – a far bigger hill than Bulbul's – from where he oversaw his empire. He liked the idea of being the only shipyard to be chosen as the subject of a film, swayed by the thought of rising above the other companies in the area, not just in the size of his business (he had already done that), but in the quality of his operation. Which is how I had been given my job: Gabriela and I would interview the workers and report on the breaking of one ship, *Grace*, and submit our findings. Gabriela would make her film and Harrison would get his certificate.

I knocked on Gabriela's door again, and she bolted out, her hair packed tightly into a headscarf. I took in her tight T-shirt and jeans that ended a few inches below her knee. I had mentioned something to her about her clothes, but she had somehow taken this to mean that she should cover her head.

Morning was on the horizon, and Ali was waiting for us on the beach. A few of the workers had come as well, and they formed a small party, some with their hands held up to their eyes to see who could spot the ship first. Ali brandished a bottle of non-alcoholic sparkling apple juice, ready to twist it open when *Grace*'s crew descended. Further along the beach, a tent had been pitched and breakfast was being readied. The captain would weave *Grace* into the Prosperity yard, making sure she remained perfectly upright as she was beached. It was a particular skill. Ali had explained all of this to me the day before, pointing to a red flag in the water. 'Once Captain crosses the flag, he's home safe.'

The light came in as we waited, and then there it was, a sliver on the horizon. We watched as it grew. More of the men arrived, wiping the sleep from their eyes. The curve of the ship began to appear, and now we could see the gleam of the hull, a poem of curves rising out of the remnants of dark, and suddenly it was before us, as if it had turned a sharp corner, white, immense, violent. 'It will seem to run us over,' Ali said, 'but that is just an illusion.'

Grace became audible, her high whine tempered by the rush of water as she approached; then there was a pause for a long minute before the final push to shore, the grunt of the slowing engine, the scrape of metal against sand; and all the while Ali and the others had their hands up in the air as if they were summoning her from the sky; then she banked, parting the shoreline, suddenly immense, her heaviness exposed, tons and tons of steel without the sea to buoy her up. Against *Grace*'s enormous hulk, we were tiny and frail. Ali muttered a prayer under his breath, then blew the air out of his cheeks, spreading the blessing.

We walked towards her. She was painted so bright we had to squint and shield our eyes. 'See,' Ali said, 'I told you she was pristine.' The workers gathered three, four deep around the hull. They looked afraid. 'They've done this many times before,' Ali had assured me. 'They are experienced, and we will take all the necessary precautions.' But standing before the ship now, the black trim wedged deep into the sand, so tall, did they wonder how they would ever take it apart? Fewer than fifty of them, with only the strength of their arms against the mass of the ship – a ship put together somewhere else, somewhere with machines and scaffolding and helmets and time-cards and minimum wage – yet it was their job to bring on her death. They would touch every inch of *Grace*; her heaviness would imprint itself on their hands, and she might, in the course of things, despite their best intentions, take a life or two on her slow way out.

The workers clapped and cheered, sounds to make themselves bigger. After a few minutes a figure appeared on the lip of the deck. He scaled the rim and climbed over, looking as though he was about to throw himself overboard, but really placing his foot on a camouflaged ladder bolted to the side of the ship.

Ali pushed against the crowd, but the workers wouldn't budge, taking in the prettiest, newest thing they had ever been asked to dismember. Ali told me that *Grace* had drifted for five days on the Atlantic after the previous captain had died aboard, setting himself on fire in the engine room. Two tugboats were sent to pull her to shore, and a week later she landed in Portsmouth. Then, after a few months, she set sail again, only to be struck by a virus. *Grace* had stood in the harbour for a month, her passengers quarantined while food and medicine were dropped by helicopter. The owner of the company, a Swede with a superstitious streak, had decided to cut his losses, and *Grace* was decommissioned, a footnote in the history of unlucky ships.

The captain was helped down by the many arms that reached for him, cushioning his landing. He wore a white uniform with blue-and-gold lapels, tight around his shoulders and thighs. He reached out and shook Ali's hand. 'Welcome, captain,' Ali said.

'Call me Jack,' the captain replied, taking off his hat and smoothing down the fine mat of hair underneath, his forehead already streaked with a band of red. 'Hot here, isn't it?'

Gabriela rolled her eyes. 'It's not an Arctic expedition,' she said.

The bottle popped. The rest of the crew descended, and Jack introduced a pair of Koreans, an engineer from India, and three Nepalese men who had boarded in Lisbon and been offered a free ride in exchange for cooking and cleaning.

'So, madam, what do you think of her?' Ali beamed. The

others were already making their way up the beach towards the tent. Gabriela was walking with Jack, her headscarf lifted by the wind, revealing the copper swirl of her hair.

'It's hard to believe it will be gone soon.' I said to Ali.

'In four months, it will be nothing but scrap.'

I stopped, turned my eyes to *Grace*, imagining her in pieces, like the *Splendour*. 'Is it true that she's exactly as they left her?'

Ali reeled off the soon-to-be-destroyed virtues of the ship. 'Casino, cinema, restaurants, swimming pool.'

'What's going to happen to all that stuff?'

'Sold, madam. People coming from Dhaka tomorrow, they're going to give us a price.' He crossed his arms over his chest, a satisfied note in his voice. 'Hotels are interested.'

For some reason, this made me very sad. I kept stopping and turning back.

'Madam, this is the cycle,' Ali continued. 'One ship sets sail, another comes here.' He looked over at me. 'You are unhappy, madam.' He considered me for a moment. 'What about I take you for a personal tour, you would like that?'

I eyed the narrow ladder to the top. I had always been a little afraid of heights, and the thought of being alone with him on an abandoned ship did not appeal. 'I don't know.'

'I will personally ensure your safety.'

'I'm not the adventurous type,' I said, repeating my own catchphrase of defeat.

We ate breakfast in the tent, sitting on wooden chairs at long, rectangular tables. The air was stale inside. Ali insisted I join him at the head table, which was decorated with a red-and-white tablecloth and a small bunch of roses, resembling a shabby version of my wedding. Gabriela was showing Jack how to eat with his fingers, rolling up his sleeves for him and explaining how important it was to get close to the food, to smell it on your hands. Ali opened a bottle of mineral water and filled my glass.

'Is it true the ship is cursed?' Gabriela asked Jack.

'That's what they say.' He tore off a piece of bread and dipped it in his curry.

'Bad luck is finished, now you are on Prosperity Beach,' Ali said. Then, eager to change the subject, he told Jack that I had lived in America.

'So what are you doing here?' Jack asked.

'We're making a film,' Gabriela said.

He raised an eyebrow. 'Hope nobody dies taking this thing down!'

Gabriela tapped his arm. 'That's a fucked-up thing to say.'

Ali took a bite of his bread. 'Shipbreaking is important for Bangladesh. We need steel. Lot of construction everywhere.' He pointed south, towards town.

'Hey look, as far as I'm concerned, you got a giant recycling operation here,' Jack said. He had finished eating. A waiter was summoned with a bowl of water and a small piece of soap.

'Will you have sweet, sir?' Ali said.

'What?'

'He means dessert,' Gabriela said.

'Oh, yeah. Great.' The waiter returned with a bowl of rice pudding in a shallow clay dish. Jack looked around for a spoon.

'Use your hands.' Gabriela said, indicating to Jack that he should dip his fingers into the clay dish.

'How about I take you both aboard, one last hurrah before she gets crushed?'

Gabriela's eyes widened. 'Really?'

'Sure, why not? Ali, you game?'

'Of course, I was telling madam Zubaida just now, we must go up.'

When I peered, at that moment, towards the horizon and saw *Grace*, how white and still and majestic she was, I felt a tug in my chest, and I knew that the breaking I was about to witness would involve giving something up, because I was used to imagining the lives of things that were long dead, and I would do the very same for *Grace*. I would imagine not only the lives that had been lived aboard, the trips and holidays, the food that was eaten, the icebergs escaped, barnacles studded to her underside, dolphins following in her wake, but the ship herself, her disappointment at having spent so little time afloat, her sadness at being consigned to the scrapyard, her pain at being taken apart. I felt all of this, and also, perhaps, I had a premonition that *Grace* would yield more treasures than I could know, that she was a mystery beyond my comprehension. I looked over at Gabriela and allowed her to accept the invitation, a part of me hoping I would maybe slip and fall down that metal ladder and into the warm, shallow water below.

Elijah, I'm on the beach now, and *Grace*, our totem, has arrived. I am about to meet Mo. And Anwar. Are you starting to love me back? Who am I kidding, of course you're not. You see how I tease myself, here in the prep lab, and in the empty apartment with only Nina to keep me company, telling myself it's just a matter of time, and words, before you return to me, knowing, in fact, that the possibility of our ever being together will require an altogether less linear, less knowable set of possibilities, an alchemy of which I am neither the scientist nor the author.

It has been snowing for eighty hours. I have been holed

up at the lab, surviving on vending-machine snacks. Nature Valley. Cheetos. Vitamin Water. My tongue is glued to the top of my mouth. Diana accuses me of losing my sense of history. The hands that arrange her bones, that brush away the layers of earth that weighed heavy on her for fifty million years, those hands should be light and unattached, not heartsick, that embarrassing word, not longing for human touch, for the particular grooves of another person's lifeline, but something else entirely, a pair of moving parts mindful of all that is ancient, and endures. I bristle at her rebuke, knowing she is right.

In the morning Ali had changed his mind. 'Too dangerous,' he said, shaking his head. I looked up at *Grace* and found myself insisting it would be all right. Gabriela and Jack backed me up. 'It's nothing,' Jack said, 'I've been up and down that thing a dozen times.'

'Let's be explorers,' Gabriela said. She had swapped her headscarf for a bandana and tan workman boots, which she wore over her trousers.

Ali passed his hand over his forehead, lifting up the prayer cap, smoothing his hair, and lowering the cap back down on his head again. 'We have never allowed it before,' he said, 'I would not forgive myself if something terrible happened.'

'Come on, man,' said Jack, who was wearing a pair of shorts and a baseball cap with a Yankees logo on it. The rumour had spread that a small expedition was going on board, and a few of the workers had gathered around. I was starting to recognise some of them, and when I passed by, they looked down at their feet to acknowledge they knew who I was. It was fully day now, light reflecting harshly off the white hull. It didn't seem possible to climb all the way up, there must have been a hundred little rungs, narrow and cylindrical and slippery.

Gabriela went first, followed by Jack. They seemed to ascend easily, wind-licked and beautiful, as if on a cable car on a snow-capped mountain. Then it was my turn. The rungs were cold and my legs trembled as I took the first steps.

'Look only straight, madam,' Ali called out from behind me.

I started to climb. Rivets. Thousands and thousands of rivets. How would they ever unbraid this machine? A clear sky now, and the sun struck me full in the face, and in the distance, I heard the cry of a lone gull.

'We have reached halfway,' I heard Ali say. His voice was dampened by the wind and the growing distance between us. I hadn't realised it, but I was rushing, putting one step after another in quick succession.

I couldn't help but glance downwards: a mistake – my stomach lurched. I stalled. The crowd had grown below us. Would they catch me? I believed they would, they were used to rescuing each other, every day on the line with the welders and ropes tied around their waists. I told myself to take one step at a time. My palms were slippery, but I pushed ahead and climbed steadily, one hand over the other, my calves straining to keep a strong foothold, knowing that if I stopped the sensation of falling would overtake me, and finally the ladder curved over the hull and I pulled myself up and over and found myself on a large green square with a circle drawn in white in the middle. A helicopter pad.

The rest of *Grace* rose above me, three more storeys of staterooms, ballrooms, restaurants, and whatever other delights cruise ships contained. I stepped aside and Ali followed, panting and whispering another prayer under his breath. Jack and Gabriela had already crossed to the other side of the white circle and were leaning over the railing and looking out onto the horizon. Everything was quiet and shining. I felt the skin on my face burn in the reflected light. We followed Jack, who led us across the deck and around the promenade, passing the closed doors of passenger cabins. Beyond lay an empty swimming pool.

'What does everyone want to see first?' Jack said, holding his arms out. 'How about the engine room?'

'It will be dark,' Ali said, handing me a flashlight. 'Please madam, be careful.'

'Where that captain killed himself?' Gabriela asked, pulling her bandana down and letting it hang around her neck.

'Yep.' Jack took her arm and they began walking to the other end of the ship, passing a bank of lifeboats. Ali rushed to catch up with them, motioning for me to follow.

I lingered behind, peering over the edge. Sea on one side as far as I could see, and on the other, the beach, the tent still there from yesterday's party, and beyond, the workers' dormitory, the bamboo shacks that had accumulated around it, and in the distance, the Dhaka–Chittagong highway, the markets flanking it on either side, soon to be adorned with the takings from *Grace*. I recalled being up high before, behind a wall of glass on the top floor of a new high-rise in Motijheel, or one time when Rashid had come to Boston and we had gone up to the top of the John Hancock building, but this was different, because everything around was so flat, the broken copper sand, the bay with its outstretched arms. Not a living thing in sight, not a gull or a fish breaking the surface of the water, unless you looked down towards the sand, to the men waiting on the beach.

They were still gathered below, in knots of three and four. One of them waved. I hesitated, then waved back.

When I turned around, I found I'd lost sight of the others. I walked away from the prow, and back towards the helicopter pad. I found a doorway with rounded edges that led to a stairwell. I climbed down. The stairwell seemed to narrow as I descended. I turned on the flashlight and waved the circular beam of light around but there wasn't much to see; the walls were white and unmarked except for a few scuffs here and there. I went around a corner and through a passageway and down further, deeper into the ship, where the air was cool and dense and tinged with metal. Finally, on what seemed like the lowest level, I found a hallway with many doors at regular intervals. I stopped and tested one. It was locked, and so were the next three I tried. The forth swung open, revealing a small square room with a low ceiling. There was a bunk bed against one wall. I traced my finger over the chair bolted to the floor. The ship was not meant to be so still. It was meant to move, to sway, to resist a force stronger than itself.

In the top bunk was a sleeping boy, his arm flung over his eyes. I considered waking him up and asking for directions to the engine room, but instead I just held my flashlight over him and saw his chest rising and falling. His hand that was closer to me was curled into a loose fist, and the fingernails of that hand were clean and neatly trimmed. For this reason, I quietly slipped out of the room and closed the door behind me.

I crossed that hallway and another, zigzagging past more closed doors, then went up a few flights. I caught flashes of daylight. Now I was on a promenade deck that circled the ship, and the cabins that opened on to this were spacious, trimmed with metal and glass. I saw deck chairs, fire extinguishers, showers and televisions and refrigerators. I went across and down again. On one of the lower levels, I opened a set of double doors and found a small library of hardbacks arranged alphabetically. Dickens was present in abundance, *Anna Karenina*, not at all. None of the books appeared to have been touched. I creaked open *Robinson Crusoe*, hunted, and found, my favourite phrase: 'For sudden joys, like griefs, confound at first.'

I was going to lean back and read the whole thing from the beginning, fully in thrall now to being lost and on my own, when I heard someone coming into the library and saw that it was the sleeping boy. Upright, he was small and wild, his hair cut very close to his scalp, his shorts torn at the cuffs. I was happy to see him. 'I've gotten lost,' I said to him in Bangla. He smiled with his mouth, his eyes, his forehead – his whole face – and offered to direct me. I followed him through a door on the other side of the room. We travelled down a flight of stairs, peering through a circular window into an enormous kitchen. Then we were in the passenger area again, a wide courtyard open three storeys to the sky.

His name was Mo. He looked like a lot of the street children I had seen in Dhaka selling flowers or little square packets of popcorn on the street. They smiled at you as if they were going home to air conditioning and train sets. Even when they begged it was with a laugh behind their eyes, a secret only they were privy to, the secret being that if they cried, or looked unhappy, or gave away something of their lives, something you couldn't possibly stomach, you would walk away without parting with a single taka. Mo had the look of one of those kids who was used to making himself so friendly and indispensable that whoever was passing him little scraps of food or money would decide it was less of a hassle to keep him on than to get rid of him. I didn't know anything about him, but I knew this: his friendliness was a façade, and behind that façade was a decade or so of terrible things I would never know about.

I couldn't tell if we were lost, or if Mo was taking me on his own personal tour of the ship, and I wasn't sure why I was following him, but I wanted to be in his company a little longer. He said, 'Apa, I would like to tell you something.'

'My name is Zubaida.'

'Last night, I climbed the ladder and slept here.'

'In that little room downstairs?'

'No, a bigger one with sheets.'

'Was it nice?' I asked.

'I didn't steal anything,' he said.

Mo stopped in front of a pair of double doors. At first when I pushed against one, I thought it might be locked, but it was just heavy, opening with a swishing sound. Inside, I found an unpunctuated darkness. 'Torch,' Mo whispered. I pulled the flashlight out again, and he plucked it from my hand. The carpeted floor tilted downwards, and we followed it, our footsteps silent, until we reached a small wooden stage. I turned and looked behind me and saw row upon row of upholstered chairs. We followed the lip of the stage and climbed up a few steps. A thick pair of curtains bore the name of the company: HEAVENLY CRUISES. We pulled aside the curtain, weighed down with a thick chain. Mo waved the flashlight into the darkness. I saw a wall of ropes and pulleys. I reached out my arms and felt the polished, satin curve of an instrument, the wood warm against my palm. Mo moved the light slowly over it, revealing its legs, trimmed with brass, bolted to the floor, its castors removed. I reached over, pulled back the lid, the white keys shining and alien, and put my hand over Mo's thin wrist, guiding the beam of light over the keys, where a piece of paper rested, crumpled by the lid. It was sheet music, the notes crowded together and incomprehensible to me. Over the top was written: *Shostakovich: Preludes*.

Ali heaved an exaggerated sigh of relief when he spotted me. 'What happened to you, madam? I have been very worried.'

'I got turned around,' I said.

Ali noticed Mo and grabbed the back of his neck. 'How did you come here? Go back to your group.'

'He helped me find my way out,' I said.

'He doesn't work here,' Ali said.

'Oh, come on,' Gabriela interjected, 'we all know that's not true.'

I complimented Ali on the grandness of *Grace*. 'She's exquisite.' I told the others there was something they should see in the big auditorium below. Ali released the back of Mo's shirt.

'You mean the piano,' Jack said. 'It's really something.'

Ali told us that the hotel owner, Mr Reza, would be inspecting the piano along with everything else on board. But he wasn't hopeful. 'No market for pianos in Bangladesh. We are not a cultured people in that way.'

'Not in Western instruments,' Gabriela said, 'but you have a rich musical tradition of your own.' Last night, at Gabriela's request, I had outlined the highlights of Bengali culture. Tagore. Nazrul. The language movement. I had even told her about Rokeya and her imaginary utopia. We had huddled around my laptop and read *Sultana's Dream* together, and she had laughed at this line: 'The men should not do anything, excuse me; they are fit for nothing.'

I urged everyone to follow me downstairs and take a closer look at the piano. We returned to the auditorium and gathered around the instrument, our lights casting yellow petals onto its mirrored surface. I felt a rush of pride when someone behind me emitted a gasp. I was already attached.

Gabriela volunteered to play. She pulled out the piano stool and placed her hands on the keys. She wasn't very good – I thought she might play the Shostakovich, but it was beyond her – yet the sound moved powerfully through the room. We felt the notes under our feet. No one seemed to want to hold up their torches any more, so the scene dissipated, Gabriela herself invisible but for her foot on the brass pedal.

She stopped abruptly. 'It needs tuning, she said into the darkness, 'but it's a lovely instrument – something almost human about it.' We heard the lid snap shut. 'You shouldn't sell it to the hotel, Mr Ali.'

'We had this guy, this piano player, who loved that thing,' Jack said. 'Think he was Hungarian. You should've seen the tears when we told him the ship was sold.'

We shuffled back through the auditorium. I tried to imagine the old Hungarian man playing the Preludes as *Grace* cut through the sea on her way here. I asked Jack what had happened to him.

'Don't know,' he said, blinking against the equatorial brightness as he opened the door. 'Once you get to shore, everyone goes their own way.'

I am not a superstitious person, but the piano and the sheet music were telling me something. A smoke signal. I hadn't forgotten about you in the year that had passed, Elijah, but I had found a way to push you out of my mind, because there were already too many complicated things, too much to regret. I got used to the dull feeling of longing I carried around with me all the time, telling myself it wasn't just you, but Diana too, and Rashid, and the baby I now wanted; my whole life, and somehow this made it easier, spreading the grief around. Occasionally I would look down at my phone and be tempted to dial your number, but I never got past the initial urge: I would have no idea where to begin. There was too much to tell, and I was morbidly full of all those unsaid words, but now the piano was giving me an excuse – a compulsion – so I called you and left a message, struggling to keep my voice steady: *hello, it's me, Zubaida. It's been a long time, I know, but I was hoping we might talk. Please call me back.*

While I waited for you to return my call, I allowed myself to become friends with Mo. He ran with a few other boys in a sort of gang around the shipyard, and though he was smaller than most of them, they seemed to regard him as something of their leader. I once saw him herding a group of six or seven boys into the water, and when they were about waist-high he pushed them in, one by one, like he was launching paper boats, and then he made them hold hands and float on their backs, all in a line, and they squealed with happiness and the tickle of salt water in their ears. I wasn't sure what work Ali had Mo do, but though he was often rough with him, I believed there was some affection between them, and that Mo's position, if far from comfortable, was at least secure (on this count, as on many others, I was wrong, Elijah. I wonder if you soften towards me because of my honesty, or if it disgusts you to know how blind I was, not just on my own account, but on that of others).

I couldn't put off meeting the workers any longer. The first interview was arranged by Ali, and took place in his office. Gabriela set up a camera and a flat mic. In the evening, at the end of a shift, about a dozen men filed through the entrance. They wore helmets and thick rubber boots. Their hands were encased in protective gloves, and over their legs they sported the sort of thick, waterproof waders I recognised from watching television programmes about fishermen. I started by asking their names, and they belted out introductions. Rubel! Suren! Malek! Then they proceeded to tell me how wonderful Prosperity Shipbreaking was, how kind the owners were, that they were always paid on time, and that it was the best job they could hope for, that they were putting their children in school – not just the boys, the girls too – and that they were thankful to God for bringing the blessing of the shipyard to their part of the country.

Gabriela had already told me she had reels of this sort of footage. I talked for a long time, hoping it would warm them up, a monologue about how I had never been to Chittagong before and was looking forward to seeing the sights, Patenga, the hills, Foy's Lake. They told me a few stories about their families. I asked them where they had come from, and they were all from within a few miles. I saw one of them raise his eyes, and I had a fleeting moment of hope, but he kept going, past my face, and up, fixing his eyes on the fan that was bolted to the ceiling above our heads. After about twenty minutes, I turned to Ali and said, 'Perhaps this is not the best place to talk.'

'Ei,' Ali scolded, looking up from his phone, 'say something to Apa. She's come all this way.' Then they all started talking at once, but just repeating the things they had said in the first place, about the kindness of God and the generosity of their benefactor, Ali.

I stood up. 'Thank you,' I said to them, packing away my tape recorder and notebook. I had expected something like this, yet I found it disconcerting. I tried to scan their faces as they left so that I might remember their names, but as soon as Ali dismissed them they were gone, jostling each other on their way out of the office and making tracks towards the beach. 'You are wasting your time,' Ali said, making a show of pouring me a cup of tea. 'Everyone here is happy.'

The last of the men filed away, his boots shuffling on the grey cement. A thought occurred to me. 'These are not the men that pull those large sheets of metal up the beach,' I said.

'No, madam, they are the cutters.'

'Can I talk to the other men?'

'Who, the pullers? Madam, those boys are fresh from the village. They don't know how to talk to a person such as yourself.'

So that's what they were called. The pullers. I had seen them take apart the last of the *Splendour*. Everything else was gone and it was just a matter of getting the propeller to a truck waiting on the road. A group of men tied ropes around the blades of the propeller and hauled these ropes over their shoulders. As they dragged their feet through the shallow water, they reminded me of the biblical films my parents had encouraged me to see as a child in which people were tortured and whipped while building pyramids, their bodies thin and molluscced with sweat. These men with their grey faces and mouths pursed so tightly you would think they were incapable of speech until their cries of Hey-yo! Hey-yo! Hey-yo! came punching out of their mouths. They wore their lungis folded up between their legs, their feet were bare, and sometimes, on top of their heads or over their mouths, they had those rectangles of checked cloth that used to be a bright colour but were soiled now by dirt and sand and sweat. Everything smelled of the chemicals thrown up by the ships and the burn of the metal as it was processed, but their faces bore no trace of disgust, no recognition that the very air they breathed was poison. 'I don't mind,' I said.

'They are uneducated.'

'I won't keep them for long, just a few questions.'

'Why don't you give me the list of questions? I will ask them and then you will have your information.'

'It won't work that way, Mr Ali.'

He gave me a look that was intended to make me feel he was taking me seriously. 'Of course. I am only trying to be helpful.'

I retreated to the apartment and told Gabriela everything. 'I told you it was a set-up,' she said, rummaging in her bag for a cigarette. 'There's no way Ali's going to let us talk to everyone. And even if he did, they're not going to talk in front of their boss. We have to meet them somewhere else.'

'It's not like we can invite them over here.'

'That's a fantastic idea,' she said, lighting up and taking a deep breath. 'Let's do that. You could cook.'

'I am a terrible cook and that's a terrible idea.'

'Why not? They look hungry, the poor sods.'

'No, they don't. They look quite well fed, in fact. And they're wearing all the correct protective clothing. Have you ever seen them wear that stuff when they go out onto the ships?'

'It's all for show,' Gabriela said, tapping her cigarette into the sink.

When Rubana called, I had to confess I hadn't made much progress. She told me to keep trying, agreeing that it was essential to get the men out of Ali's office, to identify the ones who weren't just window dressing for the film. 'Peel back the layers,' she said.

On a Friday I returned to Khondkar Villa. Komola took

some satisfaction at the sight of my dirty clothes. Why hadn't I come sooner? I sat in the garden and smelled the jasmine, shedding the grime of the last few weeks, remembering the piano, and Mo, and the little bunk beds that sat at the bottom of the ship. I wasn't so far from the beach now, but it could all have easily been a dream, a vision of a dark past or a dystopian future, far beyond the reach of my imagination, and I wondered, again and again, why you were not returning my call, what was making you take your time, was it another woman, had you fallen in love, or, worse, had you relegated me to the category of a casual acquaintance who did not require an immediate reply, someone you had once known yet with whom the possibility of serious connection had passed for ever? With every day and every imagined reason for your silence, the picture of you grew stronger, like liquor in a cask.

The first thing, Ali informed me, was to get everything on *Grace* valued and assessed, and then sold. He had three weeks to get rid of all the goods. Once she was stripped, the cutting would begin. I was still at an impasse with the workers, and every time I asked Ali if there were others we could meet, he put me off, saying he would look into it, that a suitable place had not yet been found, all the time smiling and assuring me that my comfort and safety were of the utmost importance. In the absence of actual workers, I began to record the dismantling of the ship and documenting, in detail, what each worker was responsible for doing. So far, I had a list of professions: foreman, salesman, engineer, tank cleaner, cutter, puller, welder, roller. Each crew had its own leader, its own hierarchy, and the teams themselves fell into a sort of order, with the engineers at the top and the pullers at the bottom.

One day I returned to the apartment and found Gabriela in the kitchen with Mo. The two were bent over the stove together, looking at a pair of pooris browning in a pan of oil. I stood in the doorway and watched their easy way with each other, Mo holding a long metal spatula and Gabriela exclaiming at the way the pooris puffed up into perfect little spheres. Something about the scene irritated me. I went into my room and put away my notebook and camera. The smell of oil and fried dough wafted through the apartment.

'Gabriela,' I said, calling out from the living room, 'can you come here for a minute?'

When Gabriela emerged from the kitchen, rubbing her palms along her jeans, I lowered my voice and said, 'What's he doing here?'

'You mean Mohammed? There's a room and a toilet behind the kitchen, did you know that?'

'Yes, servants' quarters.'

'Well we don't have servants' quarters where I come from, so I didn't know. I offered to let him stay there and he's going to do some cooking for us. He was showing me—'

'Pooris, I know.' I recognised the look Gabriela was giving me, a mixture of naivety and moral superiority. 'He has a perfectly fine place to live in the dormitory.'

'It's filthy.'

'We can't change everything and then just leave and go about our business.'

'Who said anything about leaving? I'm not going, are you?'

'Not right now, but eventually. Don't pretend you're going to be here for ever.'

'Good, so he stays.'

I wondered what my mother would have said. I remembered

once when she had hired an acid-burn victim to work at our house, bringing her out of the kitchen and insisting she serve the guests. Her name was Limi. I remember the fruit cake she made on Fridays, and the way people would stare at her scarred hands when she spooned powdered milk into their tea.

'Are we going to pay him?' I asked Gabriela.

'He needs a family.'

'So now you want to adopt him?'

Gabriela threw up her arms. 'I'm not saying that. I just want to – I want to do something. We've been sitting on our hands and we've done fuck all. Don't tell me you're not as fed up as I am.'

When we returned to the living area we found that Mo had set the table, placing the pooris in the middle. He was standing back and admiring his handiwork, the table mats, the glasses filled three quarters of the way with water, a jar of pickles, open, with a spoon inside.

'Mo,' I asked, 'where did you come from?'

'The food will get cold,' he said. I noticed that he was wearing a clean shirt with buttons and a pair of trousers, both slightly too big. Gabriela and I seated ourselves around the table. With ceremony, we passed the plate of pooris back and forth.

'Marvellous,' Gabriela said. 'Tell him they are the best pooris in the whole world.'

'Where did you learn to cook?' I asked him.

'Whatever they tell me to do, I do.'

'Ask him,' Gabriela said, folding a poori into quarters and stuffing it into her mouth. 'Does he know the men who work on the beach?'

I translated. 'I know all of them,' Mo said. 'The new boys always come to me first.'

Gabriela clapped her hands together to brush off the poori crumbs. 'Maybe he can introduce us.'

'Mo, can you make tea?' I asked.

When Mo had darted into the kitchen, Gabriela said, 'We've been here almost a month and no one will tell us anything. Maybe he can help.'

This was a much better idea than the one she'd had before, but I was still unsure. For one thing, the others might consider Mo a snitch if they knew he was helping us. I told her so.

'But if they talk to us, we can help them. We can put them in the film.'

When he returned with the tea, I said, 'Mo, can we come and meet some of your friends?'

He put down the tray in front of me and passed me a cup. 'Which friends?' he asked.

'Your friends from the beach,' Gabriela said. 'We want to make a film about them.'

I repeated the words in Bangla. He turned to me. 'What film?'

'A movie about the beach, about the ships and the workers.'

I was sure – and halfway hoping – that he would say no. But Gabriela kneeled in front of him and pulled at his collar, straightening and smoothing. 'It's very important,' she said. 'Will you help us?'

'We need to talk to the men,' I said. 'Not the ones Ali selects for us – the others.'

'Do you want to talk to the day shift or the night shift?' he asked.

'Which shift are you?' I said, but he didn't reply to that, only cleared away the plates and disappeared into the kitchen. I followed him to the back of the apartment, where there was an empty room with a small square window on one side. It was dark, and the cement floor was streaked with dust. 'Do you want to stay here?' I asked him, and he said, 'Only sometimes, when Ali doesn't need me.'

I looked at him closely. His hair sprouted vertically from his scalp, and when I extended my hand to stroke his head I felt a uniform coarseness, the gentle slope of his crown, and the upright tendons at the base of his neck.

'Bring your things,' I said. He nodded and we looked at the room together, the grey floor, the grille crudely fixed to the sill of the window. Mo said he had to go and that he would come by later with his bag. Then he padded away in bare feet, closing the door behind him with a sharp click.

And that is how Mo came to live with us, how he came to be the link between me and the crew of men who worked on the beach. How Gabriela and I came to belong to this place, came to know all the men who hauled the bodies of ships along the metal-flecked sand. Everything that happened in the later chapters of this story occurred because Mo said yes; even you, Elijah.

The dormitory that housed the Prosperity workers was built by Harrison Master's father. He was an old-fashioned sort of businessman who knew the names of all his workers and asked after their wives and children back home, ordered them off the beach in a rage if they talked back to the foreman or got caught in one of the brothels in town. That is what Dulu, one of the men Mo had lined up to talk to us, told me. But the businessman died and his son inherited the place and hired Ali, which was how they all came to be here, crammed into the dormitory, because the son didn't believe in expanding the facility, and anyway they were grateful it was there at all, because the men in the neighbouring beaches didn't get anything, they just lived on whatever ship they were breaking, which was bad news, because if the fires didn't kill you, the fumes from the tanks would finish you off slowly. Not that there was much living to do here anyway.

The men that Mo had chosen for our film were the lowest and poorest on site, the ones who took whatever scrap of metal was peeled off the ship and dragged it up the beach to the smelter. The pullers came from the north of the country, where there weren't any jobs and the threat of famine hung over them every winter. The men that Ali had introduced me to were locals; they were given their jobs in exchange for permission to use their land. They had clout with Ali, setting their own price and acting as supervisors to the other workers. But these men – boys, really – from up north were recruited in the winter, paid by the hour, and sent home at the end of the season, their pockets only a little fuller than when they arrived.

Before they would agree to speak to me, I had to answer a few of their questions. Mo pointed to a young boy, older than him but not by much, and said, 'Shuja wants to know if you are married.'

The others covered their mouths and giggled.

'Yes, I am.'

'Do you have children?'

'No.'

'What is your father's name?'

'Farhan Bashir. His nickname is Joy.'

'How many brothers and sisters?'

'None. It's just me.'

'Hai, Allah!' Shuja said. 'Are they dead?'

'Shut up motherfucker,' Mo said.

'My father was a freedom fighter,' I said.

Shuja asked to see a photograph of my parents. I handed him my phone, and he passed it around. He turned to Gabriela. 'Is that the real colour of your hair?'

'Yes,' she said, emerging from behind her camera.

'Why did you come here?' Mo said.

'Because we want to know about your lives,' Gabriela said.

This seemed to satisfy him. Here, in this room, Mo was in charge, putting himself beside me, gesturing with his hands for the others to talk or be quiet. 'All right. You can start now.'

By the third week, I had memorised everyone's names, and they had started calling me 'Apa' instead of 'madam'. We met in one of the bigger rooms in the dormitory, the boys crowding onto the bunks, me sitting among them with the microphone, Gabriela behind the camera. The sessions began in the evening, after the shift had ended, and went on for several hours into the night. Mo kept a close watch on me, sitting beside me and directing the conversation, saying, this one has something important to tell you, or ask that one about his village, where the water is full of arsenic, yes, you cunt, she wants to know about the arsenic too. The whole story is what she needs. We hadn't said this to him specifically, but somehow he knew that we were there to get under the surface, to hear all the little details that made up the people that made up the shipyard. He hadn't needed a class in ethnographic field methods to know this, he just knew, because Mo was like that, a kind of effervescent psychic, reading our minds and telling other people what we wanted them to know.

One night we started late. The cutting crew had taken a huge piece of metal off the oil tanker that sat next to *Grace*.

The pullers had tried to fix their ropes to get this piece of the tanker up the beach, and as the light had faded they had just about given up, but Ali had pushed them to try again, and they had spent several hours trying to manoeuvre it without success. The cutters would have to break it into smaller pieces the next day, and they would try again.

When I arrived, the boys were tired, their bodies slumped forward as they balanced on their heels in front of me. Mo had come up with the idea that each of them would tell me the story of where he had come from, about his village, his family, the people he had left behind. Last week, there was a boy, Russel, who said his brother had come to the beach to work as a puller the year before. He had sent money, just as he'd promised, but eight months later the money stopped coming. They tried to contact a relation, the cousin who had set him up with the job, but no one could find either of them. So they sent their second son to find his brother, but when Russel landed in Sithakunda he realised how futile the search would be, the locked gates in front of each of the shipyards, the miles and miles of lots. They hadn't even known the name of the company, or the foreman in charge. So Russel just stayed, lucky to have been recruited as a puller for Prosperity, which was one of the better employers. He hadn't been home in two years, just sent the money to his parents, as his brother had done before him.

Now it was the turn of one of the older ones. He cleared his throat and shifted the weight on his feet. With slow deliberation, he pointed his mouth at the tape recorder, anticipating the nods and the shakes of the head that would accompany his speech, the men who knew what it was to be him, the ones who had suffered like him, seen the things he had seen, tasted the bitter things he had tasted. 'It was the Monga, seven years ago,' he began, referring to the famine that grips the north of the country between harvests. 'We thought we had enough rice. It was my mother and my father, my wife, three children, another coming.' I knew what he was about to say, and so did the others, but we all trained our eyes on him and listened. It was two months before the harvest that the rice ran out. He went to sell his labour, but there was no work going. His father walked into the fields one day and didn't come back. But still there wasn't enough. He had a daughter, three years old, and she was the first to go. Then winter set in, and, with it, a fever that spread through the village. The man wiped his face again and again with his right hand, telling the story with his left hand. As he came to the death of his wife, he put his head down between his knees, shaking his arms back and forth, as if he could wipe the story from his memory. Now he works to feed the two remaining children, left up north with his brother.

'Say your name into the tape recorder,' Mo said.

'Belal,' he said.

I asked the men to tell me what had happened that day, and they said that the cutters would sometimes take enormous chunks from the ships, pieces they knew the pullers wouldn't be able to haul up the beach. 'They do it to torture us,' one of them said. The pullers would waste time trying this or that to get the piece to move, knowing all the time that it wouldn't work. Then they would be forced to wait while the cutters split the large pieces into smaller ones. The managers knew what was going on, but they didn't interfere. There was an order on the lot, a hierarchy that had to be maintained and obeyed, and the pullers from the north were at the very bottom.

I passed around a flask of tea. They sipped in silence, gazing into the kerosene lamp. Gabriela and I took our leave, promising to return the following week. We stepped out into the darkness with Mo. The moon was weak but we could still see the outline of *Grace*. Small fires illuminated the darkness as the night shift worked on the remaining sheets from the oil tanker. We passed through Prosperity's gates.

Mo had to return to the beach to finish something for Ali. 'We'll be all right,' I told him, 'it's not far.' He said he would walk with us but I insisted and Gabriela told him to go on, that we would see him the next afternoon when he came to cook dinner. The stories went around and around in my mind. As I was listening to Belal I had made every attempt to remain impassive, but, now that I was no longer in his presence, the depth of his loss slowly sank in. It was quiet and I could hear the sound of the water hitting the shore. Gabriela and I walked in silence until we were home. I almost ran the last few steps because I felt a strange sensation, like someone was following me. At the apartment Gabriela wanted to talk about the meeting, but I was rendered mute by the memory of Belal's face, his thin, sad lips mouthing the story of his daughter's death. Gabriela suggested we go out. There was nowhere really for us to go at that late hour, so I called Komola and asked if I could come over with a friend, and of course she said yes and asked what we wanted to eat.

Gabriela borrowed the Shipsafe car and we drove into the city with the windows rolled down, and immediately I felt better. I was embarrassed when we entered the house; Gabriela looked everything up and down and I could tell I was being cast in a new light, but Komola brought us a tray with ice cream and tinned fruit, and the heaviness that had lodged in me started to dissipate.

'There must be something we can do for them,' Gabriela

said, putting a spoonful of cubed fruit into her mouth. 'How can you stand it?'

'We're doing something. You're making this film.'

Her spoon clattered against the side of the bowl. 'A film seems like a pathetic response. Is there any more of this?' she asked, gesturing to her empty dish.

'I'll ask Komola.'

Downstairs, Komola said there wasn't any more fruit, but that there was some leftover rice pudding in the fridge. She had been chewing betel, and her mouth was lined with red. She reminded me of Nanu, not that Nanu chewed betel – she didn't – but in the way that she regarded me, with a love that she expected to flow in only one direction.

In the morning Komola made us omelettes and we sat in the garden with our tea cups. I was thankful to Gabriela for not asking me to explain about the house or my marriage. Neither of us wanted to go back to Prosperity, so we had Joshim take us on a long walk around the estate. After lunch, Gabriela sketched out a few ideas for the film while I read over my notes from the night before. Finally, reluctantly, we prepared to return to Sithakunda.

It was dusk by the time we set off, carrying plastic tubs of leftover chicken curry and dal. A cool breeze rustled the tamarind trees as we walked down the path to the car. I was feeling refreshed; Belal's story would make it into our film, and though it wouldn't bring his daughter back, it would be something. I was finally making some headway, not just with this project but with my life. The film would be no replacement for Diana, for Zamzam, nothing against the death of Belal's daughter, but at least I could chalk up one small accomplishment, one attempt at making a dent in the world.

As we drove south to Sithakunda, I spotted a clearing in the highway. There were a few cars parked on the side of the road, and beyond, a stretch of beach. 'That must be Patenga,' I said. 'Shall we stop?' Gabriela was thrilled at the possibility of a swim, though disappointed when I told her she would have to go into the water more or less fully clothed. 'You can roll up your trousers a little,' I said, 'but don't go above your knees.'

The beach was crowded by women in shalwar kameezes who dangled their babies over the water. We lay on our stomachs and let the tide nudge us gently towards the shore. In the distance, we heard the sound of a flute among the cries of the gulls and the shrieks of the children. 'This isn't so bad,' Gabriela said, her shirt ballooning beneath her. 'The water is delicious.' As the sun neared the horizon, we climbed onto a large rock on the shore and waited for our clothes to dry. 'I never want to leave,' I said, and Gabriela nodded.

Finally we decided it was time to go. Gabriela had parked in front of a small line of shops. The car came into view and she was jostling the keys in her hand when we saw a man walking purposefully towards us. He stopped and said, 'Megna.' I thought he was calling to someone behind me, so I brushed past him, but he turned and raised his voice. 'Megna, Megna!' Gabriela took hold of my arm and we were almost at the car, but he followed and came right up to my face. I found my voice and I asked him what he wanted. 'Don't you know me?' he said. I shook my head and tried to push him aside, and that's when he did it. He put his hands on my arms and turned me around and held me where I stood, his fingers digging into my flesh. I shouted at him to let go. 'Megna,' he said again, 'don't be angry.' He was saying 'Megna, Megna, Megna' and I was trying to wrestle out of his grip, and then a few seconds later Gabriela was shouting too, and when he heard her voice the man let go and looked over at Gabriela, and then he looked down at my clothes, my long-sleeved tunic and jeans, and he stepped back, his hand over his mouth. 'Allah,' he said, shaking his head, and he turned around and I watched him sit down, right there on the road. Another man came out and dragged him away, and they disappeared into a barber-shop. I bundled myself into the car and cried as if this man had beaten me, punched me straight in the face and broken my nose.

It was him, Elijah. It was Anwar. I can't imagine what he must have felt, believing I was the woman he had been searching for, only to realise I was nothing more than a stranger. And he must have been afraid, because I could have had him arrested. In fact, once I was home, I called Rashid and that's exactly what he told me to do: file a report with the police. We argued; I said the man hadn't really done anything, and Rashid told me I was foolish for always feeling sorry for people who didn't deserve it. Then he said he was leaving for a business trip to China and that he'd be gone for a few weeks, maybe even a month. Did I want to see him before he left? No, I said, angry now because he was so quick to throw a man in jail, and perhaps anticipating another, worse argument we would someday have about this very man. 'I'll see you when you get back,' I snapped, and put the phone down.

This is how Anwar jolted himself into my life. By accosting me on the street and insisting I was someone else. I quickly forgot the woman's name. Megna. Nothing to me, right? Nothing but everything. But that's for later. Don't blame me for parsing out the story slowly, Elijah. These things take time, and I seem to have all the time in the world, because you never appear at the traffic lights any more; I've sometimes waited at the coffee shop across the street, reading *Anna Karenina* and looking up every few minutes to see if I've conjured you, but there's no trace of you there or anywhere else in this cold, cold city.

You are about to arrive on the beach, and the very best and the very worst things are about to happen. These memories, if you choose to linger on them, will be the ones that pain you most. The ones that will make you want to stop, burn this letter, and never think of me again. So, before you read on, read this first: another love story, another quest, that of Anwar, a man who both rejected and accepted his fate, a man who protested silently, for his whole life, against the many injustices the world had decided to mete out to him. Read him gently, dear Elijah; let your gaze on this page soften; remember that he had nothing to do with my treatment of you, so regard him with kindness and judge him like the innocent he is.

The Testimony of Anwar

I   How I Got Everything

Foreman likes to hoist the new ones up, see what they're made of. Some of them have never climbed higher than a tree in their village. Back home the place is flat, flat. I'm here nine years, I know what's what, so I tell them, don't look, don't look. Hold the torch in one hand, like this, and keep your eye on one screw at a time. From here to here, I show them, holding my fingers apart an inch, maybe an inch and a half. Your eye will see this much, no more. Understand?

I don't tell them the whole story. Whole story is this: you look down, you die. You see the world has shrunk below you. You call God but no one answers. You recite the Kalma. You see God is not there. You piss your pants. No one is watching. No one cares about your shitty speck of a life. The people below are specks and you are a speck. God looks down and sees nothing but tiny ants below Him. You choke. You move your legs. You scream. The building shifts, it moves, it throws you up, it throws you over. You're done for, a chapatti. They scrape you off the pavement; they don't even write to your family. Months later, someone will go to your village and tell the news to your people. And that will be the end of your life.

All this I don't say. I say only what is useful.

This new kid won't listen. Came in with a swagger – I spotted it right away, the way he moved his legs and his trousers hanging, his head loose on his shoulder, nodding, doesn't look down when foreman is talking, raises his head and gives two eyes to the boss. Eye for an eye. Foreman smiles. I know that smile; it means I'll take that two-eyed look right out of your skull. Soon you'll be like the rest of them, giving me the top of your head and mumbling into your shirt.

'I have schooling, sir,' the kid says. 'Intermediate Pass.'

Foreman says, 'Crane will take you to the top.' And the kid says, '*Yessir.*' as if he's been given a gift. All that school, he doesn't even know when his ass is being strung up.

Later I ask the kid where his people are. We're on the same sleeping shift, starts two in the afternoon, the shed hot as an animal's mouth. You can't touch the metal rails on the bunk, you just jump on the mattress and pray for a breeze.

He says he's a Pahari, says it with a little edge, like, I'm a Pahari, you gonna fuck with me? I've never seen such pride in a tribal, and I say, 'So what, no one cares here.'

Army took our village, so I had to come here, make some money. He shrugs like he doesn't mind but I can see when he closes his eyes he's going to dream about college, hearing his name in the roll-call, getting his degree and spending his life in a shirt with buttons and getting some respect. Someday, someone might even call him 'sir'. Buy a scooter and get himself a salty wife.

But now he is here. 'Shit,' he says, 'it's like a fry pan inside.'

It's only March. Wait a few months, I tell him. Then

you'll see what hell feels like. Then I give him my two paisa little bit of advice. I tell him, 'Stay away from foreman and keep your mouth shut. And when he hauls you up, whatever you do, don't look down.' The kid nods, but I know what he's thinking, thinking it's not going to be him at the end of a rope.

I go to my bunk and try to sleep. This month I'm in the middle. We take turns, Hameed, Malek and me. Top bunk is hottest, but there's a breeze, if you can catch it, from a small window out of the side of the shed. Bottom bunk is cooler, but closer to the ground and the toilet stink is strong. Middle is the worst, like being sandwiched between two asses, especially because this month I've got Malek on top. He makes the springs creak as he pleasures himself to sleep. I'm used to the steady rhythm of it, I don't say anything. A man has his needs, out here in the desert. Myself, I can't do it. I reach down and Megna's face comes into my head. She won't let me sleep. I see her little tears and she's asking me to stay – 'What will I do when the baby comes?' And I'm saying no, I'm shrugging. I'm calling her a slut, even though I know it was her first time, and I'd told her I loved her and meant it, except my uncle is there too, and he's telling me, 'Dubai, Dubai, son, it's like paradise, shopping malls and television and air con. Marry my daughter and the ticket is in your hand.' 'You're a slut,' I tell Megna, and I swivel around and leave her there, except I don't leave her, because whenever I try to get myself a little something, like a piece of sleep or a full stomach, she comes out and she comes out strong. I want to know what she did to the little seed I planted in her, where does it live, does it know me, and does it have the eyes of its mother? I'm in the dark and I can't sleep. Malek sighs, rolls over, and the room gets hotter and the stink rises.

Too quickly the sleep shift is over and it's time to get back to the site. Pahari kid is about to get his first kick in the head, but he doesn't know it, he just pulls on his uniform like he's the sheikh himself. I have to throw water on Malek's face to wake him up. He curses me and jumps down. The floor vibrates. Next shift is already waiting outside – it's dark, and starting to cool down, the lucky bastards.

The bus drops us at the canteen. Hameed sits at the end of the table so people can bring him the letters. He's the only one who can read. We pay him a few dirhams to tell us the news from home. He reads me letters from my darkie wife, she says, 'Take care don't forget to eat and does it get cold do you have a shawl?' The others are always laughing – 'She's going to tell you how to wipe the shit from your ass,' they say. I laugh with them. Stupid girl. I don't write back.

Hameed says sometimes he changes the letters, because there's only so much a man can take. Last week he read that Chottu's mother had died. Poor bastard's only been here a month, still cries every time he has to stand out in the baking hot, carrying bricks on his head. So Hameed told him his mother was well, much better, in fact, since he started sending money for her asthma medicine. Later, when Chottu gets hard like the rest of us, Hameed will tell him the truth. And by then he won't even stop to take a breath.

The canteen manager is Filipino, so stingy we get a piece of bread, dal and a few vegetables, and even that they cut from our pay. Eid comes he gives us meat, but only bones and fat. One thing my uncle said was true – as much Coke as we want, straight out of a spout.

'Tareque Bhai,' Hameed says, 'your sister has given birth to a healthy baby boy.'

'Mashallah,' Tareque Bhai says. Tareque has been here the longest and he has gone the religious way. Two ways a man can go here, in the direction of God or the direction of believing there is nothing up there but a sun that will kill you whether you pray five times or not.

We wash our hands and head to the site. They've turned the lights on, the buildings are winking. We come to the Mall of Dubai, which Tareque Bhai remembers was only a few years ago a pile of rubble, and Pahari kid says, 'Why don't we walk through here?' And we all look at him like he was born yesterday. Even dumber than I thought.

'You can't go in there,' I say.

'Why, is there a law?'

'Doesn't have to be a law.'

'I'm going in,' he says, loose, like it's the easiest thing in the world. 'Anyone coming with me?'

I think Hameed's going – those book-learning types always stick together – but it's Malek that breaks off and joins him and I'm cursing myself for not grabbing him before it's too late, telling him, don't even smell that, it'll kill you.

The rest of us make tracks, shaking our heads. This month, Hameed and me are in the hole. Two buildings going up side by side. We call them 'Bride and Groom'. Bride is almost finished, Groom still in foundations. 'Fifty-fifty,' they tell us, fifty storeys for Bride, fifty for Groom. Who knows what they'll name it once it's finished? Burj-al-Arab-al-Sheikh-al-Maktoum-al-kiss-my-ass. Shit, if I said that aloud I would be finished. I giggle to myself and Hameed swings his arm around my shoulder, laughing with me even though he hasn't heard the joke.

Bride and Groom make me think of darkie wife. She was the skinniest, ugliest girl I ever saw. I took one look at her and I swear a few tears came to my eyes. To this girl I was going to be tied for life? 'Just do it,' my mother said, 'you won't even see her for years. Who knows what will happen between now and then? But give us a grandchild, something to keep us company while you're gone.'

I did my duty. Girl started to cry and I even felt a little sorry for her, though I was also thinking, two times I've done it and both times the girl has burst into tears – something wrong with me or what? Next day I took her to the cinema, but even Shah Rukh Khan couldn't wipe the sad from her face.

We climb down and the bright lights make the hole turn blue-grey. The diggers are awake and we start to haul the dirt around, everything dry and sucked of life.

I pick up a basket. I wonder if Malek and Pahari have made it out of the mall without getting their eyes pulled out, and just as I'm imagining what it must have looked like, two guys in their blue jumpsuits staring at those diamond-necked swans of Dubai, I feel a jab in my side, and there's Malek, laughing so hard I can see the gap where he lost a tooth last year after biting down on a piece of candy he bought from the Filipino. 'Worth it,' he'd said, 'I never tasted anything so good.' Now he's telling me about the mall, the cold air that made your sweat dry to salt, and the high ceilings, and the women, the women, didn't cover their legs, no, or even their breasts. 'Breasts, man, like you wouldn't believe.' He slaps me hard on the back, shaking up my basket so I can taste the dirt. 'Go to work,' I say, but he's too busy talking, and now some of the other boys, Hameed and even Tareque Bhai, have joined in, and I can see them all thinking it could be them next, them in the ice-cream cold of the mall, gaping and staring and taking a little slice of heaven back to the hole to chew over.

Worst of all, Pahari kid got hauled up to the top of Bride and nothing happened. Absolutely nothing. He swung like a monkey and laughed his way through the shift. Turns out those tribals like floating on top of buildings, hitched up so the whole world is spread below them.

For the next two weeks, every day, Malek and Pahari pass through the Mall of Dubai on their way to the site. They take their jumpsuits in a plastic bag and go in wearing trousers and T-shirts. One day Malek comes over to my bunk with a pair of sunglasses draped over his eyes. 'Look,' he says, 'I'm James Bond now.'

I keep my head down. I have debts to pay, I can't take the chance.

Once, only once, I am tempted. They are going to the cinema – not the cheap, rundown place by the camp, I'm talking a brand-new theatre, air con, seats like pillows. Pahari knows this guy at the ticket stall, been wooing him since day one, going up and talking about home, saying *yaar* this and *my friend* that. And finally the guy gave it up, late show on Monday nights usually empty, come in with the cleaning crew and sit at the back. Four people, max. Don't get me fired or I'll tell the cops everything, even about the girl.

Pahari has a girlfriend. Not even a darkie or a chink, a proper fair-faced blondie, a shopgirl who sells perfume. He leans over the counter and she smiles like she's seen a film star. We huddle close to Pahari, trying to catch a whisper of that girl's smell.

While we're heaving bags of sand to Groom, Pahari and Malek start arguing about what to see. Malek says it has to

183

be the new *Dhoom*. But our boy wants to see an English film. 'What you're going to do with an English film, you little shit?' But Pahari's not thinking about himself, he's thinking of his girl, moving his hand in the dark, cupping her knee, fingering the edge of her skirt, and what's going to make her open up, a movie with mummy-daddy and fake kissing and chasing around trees, or real humpty-dumpty, tongues and blonde hair and New York City?

Pahari has a point, but I'm just hauling the sand, keeping my head low. Wife has sent another letter. April and the waters are going up, up. Last week my brother, who works at a weaving mill, came home with a bad leg. Needs an operation. Can I send money? I shove the letter under my mattress.

Send money, send money. All anyone ever wants. I have to ask for an advance, so I crawl to foreman. He's got a toothpick hanging from the side of his mouth, and he twirls it around and around. 'You Bangladeshis,' he says, 'can't hold on to your money, *na*. Look at this.' He points to a big black book, lines of names. 'Everyone borrowing, nobody saving. You're going to drown, all of you.'

He opens his mouth, toothpick falls out, frayed and shining with spit. Should I pick it up? I stare at my feet.

'How much you want?'

I don't know why, but I don't say anything for a long time. Pahari and Malek are going to the movies tonight. He's going to lean back on that chair and swing his arm over his girl. He's going to sip Coke through a straw and the music will breeze through him, free and liquid.

Then I say, 'I have been loyal, sir.'

Foreman leans back. Chair squeaks like a dying mouse.

'Sure, you never stole.'

'Yes, sir. I always do what you say.'

I lift my chin a little and he knows what I'm talking about, the little cover-ups, taking a few bags of cement off the truck, losing a little cash. The boss, the sheikh with three wives, always wearing a prayer cap and telling us to call him Master Al-Haj because he goes to Saudi every year and kisses the Prophet's grave – he wouldn't miss a few things here and there. A sack of rivets, a few pots of paint were nothing to him.

So you're telling me what, *na*, that I should be grateful? Fresh toothpick in his mouth. Now I'm thinking about Megna, her crazy thick river of hair, how she smelled so good and told me I should be a proud man. Nothing to be proud of, I always said.

'Yes, sir,' I find myself saying. 'Loyalty like that, it doesn't come easy.'

'And I suppose you want something for your trouble?' He's getting up, he's coming towards me, he's going to give me something, a little money and a slap on the shoulder, friendly like. You have to ask for it, I think. All you have to do is ask. Foreman's close now, he takes my chin in his hand, lifts me up so we're eye to eye, and for a minute I see him staring at my lips and I think he's going to kiss me. He opens his mouth. And then he spits, toothpick flying out of his mouth, right there on my face.

'You stinking bitch, fuck off. You blackmailing me?' He makes a fist, sends it to my cheek. I fall, cursing Megna, her hair and her stupid wisdom. I try to make myself small. He kicks me. I feel his shoe in my stomach. I double up, he kicks me again. My face explodes. A tooth comes loose. I taste blood.

'Who pulled you out of the shithole you call a country?'

'You.'

'Louder!'

'You!'

'Who gave you a job when you came crawling?'

'You.'

'Say it.'

'You!'

And then I make the begging sounds, tell him about my brother, about his leg, how they make him sit in those clay pits for eighteen, twenty hours a day, feeding silk into the loom, the cold grabbing his thighs. 'Please, foreman,' I say, 'forgive me.'

'Piece of shit. Get out.'

Pahari and Malek come back from the cinema with smiles so big I can see their back teeth. I show off my broken face.

'What happened to you?' Malek asks.

'Foreman. What you get for thinking big thoughts.'

'You?'

'Ya, me. Surprise.'

Pahari's looking at my face, my swollen eye.

'Uglier than ever,' I say, trying to laugh.

He's shaking his head. 'That's not right. They can't do that.'

'They can do whatever the fuck they like. It's their country.'

'We'll go to the police. He can't just beat you.'

He makes me cheerful with his baby talk. 'It's nothing,' I say. 'Sit. Tell me about the cinema.' I pat the bunk. 'Come, Malek.' But he's pacing the tiny corridor between our beds.

'Bastard, bastard,' he mutters.

I turn to Pahari. 'So what did you see?'

'English film,' he says, raising his eyebrows. 'Lots of shooting.'

'Your girl enjoyed?'

186

He lies back on the bunk, raises his hands to his face. 'Shit, man.'

I could almost remember that feeling, the first time I tasted a woman's mouth. 'Be careful,' was all I could say. 'They put you under a spell and then you're finished.'

'So what you'll do about your brother?' Malek is squeezing himself onto my bunk.

'Brother will have to wait.'

'Let me give you the money.'

'What do you have?'

'I have, I have.'

'No, brother. I won't eat your rice.' I can't help it, my tongue keeps going to the missing tooth, the gap made of jelly. Malek tries to press me but I can't take his money.

'Oh, I almost forgot, brother. We brought you a gift.' Pahari takes a packet of candy out of his pocket. I chew with my good side.

'Sleep now,' I say to them both. 'It will last longer if you dream about it.'

Next day, foreman comes to the camp. 'I have a job,' he says.

Bride is almost finished, she just needs her windows cleaned. Sheikh Abdullah Bin-Richistan is coming to cut a ribbon and everything has to be perfect. 'We're running out of time and job needs to be done in a hurry.' 'I'll go,' Pahari says, even though it's higher, much higher, than he's ever been, but he wants to take his girl out, proper restaurant this time, with people smiling and asking if he wants ice in his Coke and bringing plates to the table.

'I want double overtime,' he says. Foreman smiles and says, 'All right,' and then, because I see something in the boss's eye, I raise my hand too, and before you know it,

Malek is watching us drive off in a truck. Foreman takes us into Bride's lobby, empty and shining, and I give myself a little smile, because I know I put this thing together with my own hands, me and Malek and the other boys, working through the devil's breath of summer. Pahari is looking around, dreaming of when he's going to own the whole place. They've taken off the elevator on the outside, but there's another one at the back of the building, where all the cooks and cleaners and guards will come and go, and we're going up, up, all the way. 'Wear this,' foreman says, handing us a pair of hard hats. Then he slides open a big door, and we are on the roof of the building, flat and open to the sky. I wonder if Pahari's thinking it wasn't such a good idea after all, but he's not one to admit it. When I put my hand on his back he shrugs it away, moving with speed to where foreman is pointing, to a little balcony hanging over the edge of the building.

Clips and ropes fix us to the sides of the balcony. 'I'm going to lower you all the way down,' foreman says. 'You do one floor at a time, slowly. Then you push the button, and you go up.' He shows me how to work it. I see there isn't anything holding us to the side of the building; we're only attached at the top. It's going to sway. I look over at Pahari again, wondering if I should cut out of the whole thing, but he's grinning like it's Eid. 'Don't worry,' foreman says. And he winks.

On the way down Pahari hangs on the edge and makes a strange, low sound which I think is panic but then he turns around and says, 'FLYING!' The bastard is laughing, holding his arms out and shaking his shoulders around like he's hero in a filmi dance sequence. The windows are like mirrors, we can see our reflections. He puts his arm around me and we are floating down, angels from heaven,

Superman and God and people who don't eat shit for a living.

Every window we clean, we go up one more flight. We're shining up that Bride and she's looking good. There's a wind up here, the balcony moves a little, then a bit more as we move higher. Now we're holding on with one hand and cleaning with another. We wash, I push the button, we go up. Wind gets stronger.

'I'm going to marry her,' Pahari tells me.

A man marrying for love. Too good for me, but nothing's too good for Pahari. He wants everything.

'Do it,' I say. 'Is she going to convert?'

'I'm Christian, you idiot.'

All this time, and I didn't even know. That was my problem. I thought everyone was the same, but it didn't have to be that way. Even I didn't have to be the same. I could be different. The wind dies down and we have a moment of quiet so I can think about all the ways I could be different. And then, before my dreaming starts making me big, wind picks up again. This time, it comes with sand. Minute later the air is thick with it, so thick I can only just make out Pahari on the other side, holding on with both arms. 'It will pass,' I shout, swallowing a mouthful of the desert. 'Don't worry. Hold on.'

We wait, turning our backs to the wind, becoming small, small as we can. I crawl to Pahari and I grab his jumpsuit, put my arm through his arm. We groan as the sand comes into our ears, into our clothes, the devil's spit. The balcony lifts, higher on one side and then another. I pull the lever, but we can only go up, not down. Only one way, so I climb us up, slow as I can. Close to the top and suddenly it shudders to a stop, and I push and push but nothing happens. I crawl to the other side, see if I can make the ropes move.

I can't. I ask myself if this is the time to start praying, but no God was going to hear me now, not after all the curses I had sent in His direction. 'It will pass, it will pass,' I keep saying, but Pahari can't hear me now, he's on the other side, and the wind is too high, and before I know it, we're going back and forth like a swing, and it's everything I've got to keep my arm around the bars of the platform, and I do just like what I teach those boys when they first get here, just focus on a small piece of the building, not the tall of it falling away below me, just this little piece in front of me, and I will the moment to stand very still, and then I see Pahari, his arm has come loose, and the ropes that tie him to the machine are floating free, and the sound of him falling is swallowed by the hiss of the desert, that shape-shifting snake.

I'm home now and I've got everything. Because Pahari's dead and they paid me off. I'm the greedy bastard now. I'm the one who isn't the same. The old me would've stayed, maybe made sure Pahari got his proper burial, maybe I wouldn't even have taken their dirty money, maybe I would've made a stink about it, but soon as they handed me that envelope I was gone. Malek told me the sheikh was getting rid of foreman. We shouldn't have been up there, not without better safety equipment. It's not something they can cover up, like the boys who jump because they miss their mamas and can't take another day. We were up there for an hour; lots of people saw, real people who matter. 'We can make our demands,' Malek said, 'ask for better pay, overtime and a good place to sleep.'

But I didn't care about any of that. Because when I was going to die, when I was hanging up there with the storm in my face, all I could think about was my kid. My kid, walking around with no memory of a father, a kid who would look at himself in the mirror and not know where his face came from. Who knows what Megna had told him, though if she said bad, it would all be true, because I was a bastard for letting it come into the world without a name. Now I want it all, I want my fridge and my socks and my name and Megna, my little piece of heaven, and I'm coming to get it.

II I Am a Doorway Man

I am a doorway man. I sit in the doorway and people come. In the morning, they tell me the gossip. So-and-so's wife left him. Lost all his money gambling and she buggered off. Cup of tea and we talk politics. I'm a big man now, the parties are after me – who will I join? Awami League, BNP? They want me, they want my money, my sway with the village. I sit in the doorway while they kiss my ass. I tell the mollahs to go to hell, none of that fake Goddery. I've seen God, I tell them. He's made of sand and he spat right in my eye.

My story gets bigger with every lip it crosses. First I'm up fifty storeys, then a hundred. Two hours up on that balcony. No six. Ten. Hanging by a rope. Upside down. His forehead was lucky, otherwise he would've been dead like the other guy.

Even Morshed is sucking up. Morshed, who took two acres from my uncle to export me to Dubai, lining his pockets with the money of every SOB who wants to go to foreign. Fat from the stink of the desperate. Now he says, let's be partners, I'll give you ten per cent. If I haggle with him, I can get fifty out of him, no problem. But I'm not going to dirty my hands any more. I didn't even answer the letters from the gang, Bride and Groom both finished, now they're building a golf club on a fake island, sand they're getting from the sea. That life is over. Pahari's dead and I have his blood money, and now I'm gonna sit here in my doorway and let the people come to me.

After all the visiting in the morning, I take a walk around the village. I see the chillies like red lipstick around the borders of people's houses. I see the rice, dark green, then yellow. I walk around the mosque but I don't go inside; if it's there to bring me peace, I don't deserve it.

I walk to the market to take a look. It's winter now and all the interesting things are out of the ground. Things I could only have with my eyes before, now going into my belly. Wife is thrifty, she doesn't like it. I gave her some of the money – only a little – and instead of having a party like I told her, invite everyone and slaughter a goat, she bought a heifer and a bull. There's milk in my tea every morning. Rest of the milk she sells on, and the bull she's fattening – Eid comes she's going to sell it and buy two more. I rile her up, say I'm going to slaughter it myself, what she's gonna do? I'll feed the whole village, the beggars will come to me for scraps, I'll be the king, no more dreams of hanging by my fingers to that balcony, Pahari about to marry his Christian girl, falling like a pebble from the sky.

After lunch, I sleep. No one bothers me, telling me feed the cow, fetch the dinner, dig out the vegetables. I sleep for two, three hours. When I wake up they're at the doorway again, telling me how brave I was, how lucky.

Only my mother isn't happy. 'A son,' she keeps on saying, 'it's nothing without a child. No, I won't stop nagging. Divorce that darkie, you don't need her any more. Find another one. Fair, young. She'll give you a son by next spring and I can die in peace.'

I won't. At night after she gives me the dinner, Shathi listens from outside until my plate is clean. Then she comes, pours a bowl of water over my hands, passes me a bar of soap. She dries my hands with the end of her sari. Then she eats alone. In the bed I can hear her breathe, her sigh as she rolls from one side to another, trying not to disturb me while the blood stirs in her. She wants to be touched. Even though she's skinny and from the looks of it there's nothing but bones to her, I know she has blood, I know her blood wants to be moved, circled around, so she knows she's a woman. My hand reaches out to touch her, but I whip it back. There's nothing for me in that body, no comfort. My hand moves again, floating across the valley between us. I reach out and put my hand on her hip. She lies very still but I can hear a tiny breath escape from her lips. My hand gets heavy on her, like it's going to stay there, and then I can feel myself about to shift, nudge myself a bit closer to her, and Pahari and Megna come back to me, and the moment is poisoned. I push her, rough. 'Move to your side,' I say, soothed when I am cruel, then I turn around, I ignore the deep breath she is trying to suppress, the tiny moonsliver of a cry.

Friday and I'm walking around the village and this time I think I'm not going to avoid the mosque. Too early for the prayers, grounds are empty. I go around the side and enter the small door at the back. This mosque was built a long time ago. It was tiled in blue and white, once, before people picked off the tiles and stuck them above their own doors. There was a tiny room at the back where Megna had lived with her mother. The mosque-cleaner and her daughter. They came to this village when Megna was a just a baby. I go inside now, pulling away the thin curtain over the door. I'm waiting to see the cot, the calendar of Ganesh her mother hung under the window. She had wandered into the village and said her husband had died, there was no one to take care of her, and the imam at the time took her in, said the room was empty and she could have it.

What did I expect to find? Megna's mother, the room exactly as I remembered? It's empty, not a mattress or a scrap of clothing. Damp on the walls and ceiling like it's gonna fall down. I put my hand on the wall and paint comes off easy. The way Megna had opened her legs for me, the little slut. My mind goes back to all the things we did in that room while her mother was out sweeping the mosque or planting beans in the small plot in the front. At night, I would knock on the window and she would crawl out of the bed she shared with her mother and we would lie down under the tamarind tree and touch each other like it was the end of the world.

I'm dreaming so hard I don't hear the mullah until he's clearing his throat and spitting a big one just next to my foot. I turn around and he's pulling his beard and looking at me, and next thing I know he's holding his arms out for me and I guess it slipped my mind everyone's sweet as candy to me now, so I don't know what to do, then I remember, I play my part and we do the three-time hug you only do on Eid with your brother. I'm a big man now, everyone wants to be related. Now he's looking at the patch of paint that's come off on my hand and he's saying, Shame, that, mosque in such bad shape, you remember this place used to be much nicer. Take a cup of tea with me, son.'

We go to the tea stall, and the tea-wallah pulls out his best stool. I offer it to the mullah and I squat on my heels.

We drink. 'Village is changing,' he says. 'Boys are going out, they're not coming back.'

'Everybody wants to go to foreign,' I say, already tired of squatting.

He slurps his tea with a loud sucking sound. 'They leave the women behind and that's no good, is it?'

'I suppose not.'

'Times like this, mosque is what keeps a village together.'

I nod, thinking, how much longer will I have to stay here? It takes him five minutes maybe to finish his tea, slurping and sucking, slurping and sucking. Finally he finishes and he stands up. I stand up too, my knees complaining. Then he says, 'Mosque was a place you spent a lot of time in, son.'

He looks at me and for a long time he doesn't say anything, and then I realise he's telling me he knows I used to sneak in here, knows about me and Megna, then he says, 'We have a fund, you know, mosque fund. Been saving for six years, all the gone-away boys have been sending money.' Then he holds his hands behind his back like he's being arrested and I know what I have to do. I say, 'I'll pay. Whatever's left, I'll pay.'

I let him grab me again, even harder this time, so I can smell the flower oil in his hair and feel the sand of his beard. 'Sobhan Allah! You are a true son of the village.' Then he says, like I just asked him a question: 'That woman who used to clean here, she died. Typhoid, I think. Daughter disappeared, too.' I'm thinking, the bastard was waiting to tell me that. He knew all along that's what I wanted, some information about Megna, but waited till I'd coughed up the money, and then he dropped it on me.

I can't sleep that night. For the first time I wonder exactly what happened to Megna after I left for Dubai. Like a film

I'm seeing it: I leave, I don't even say goodbye. Her stomach starts to give up its secret. She tells her mother. Disgusting girl, her mother says. And then what happens? They leave the village together? They pack up their things and take a bus – where? Who will take them in? Who can I ask, I don't know.

The next day, early, before the mullah has called the village to pray, I pack a bag. Shathi watches me, doesn't say a word. I show her where I put the money, locked in a trunk under the bed. Key is on a string around my neck, hanging next to my heart. I take the string, pass it over her head. Like we're getting married all over again, garlands and all that. She touches my feet. She's like a wife in an old movie, black and white, doesn't say anything or ask any questions, just accepts I'm a bastard and doesn't flinch.

I still have to face my mother. I can't think what to say, so I tell her the truth. 'I'm going to look for Megna,' I say. She slaps her forehead, like I knew she would. 'I told you find a new wife, not dig up a girl you threw away.'

I stand quiet, knowing she has to get her words out before I can explain. She stands up. I think she's about to hit me, like before when I was always getting into the sugar, when my father was working in the railroad and we had sugar. 'Do you know where she could have gone?' I ask, thinking, if she's going to hit me anyway, I might as well get some information out of her.

'Girl disappeared the day you left for foreign, no one saw her again.'

Her mother?

'Dead. They said she swallowed rat poison.'

'Mullah told me she caught the typhoid.'

'Same thing, whatever. You'll never find her.'

'Megna told me her father's people were from the south. Near Chittagong.'

She shrugs. 'I don't know,' she says, but then she looks down at her feet and I know she's lying.

'You know something. Tell me. Tell me.' I'm raising my voice.

She puts up her hand up like she's going to slap me and then she says, 'Village is called Chondonpahar. She had an uncle. Rest I don't know.'

I'm sorry for shouting. I'm going to touch her feet, ask for forgiveness. Then she says, 'You going to leave me with that darkie again?'

For a change I decide to do something nice. I grab my mother's hand. I take her across to Shathi, who is putting straw into the fire. 'I've given the key to Shathi,' I say. 'Go on, show her the key.' Shathi takes the key out of her blouse and holds it up but she looks away, so that Amma can't see the grain of smug on her lips.

'You see? She holds the money. The food, everything. You need something, you ask her. You need medicine, she gets it for you. If she wants, she can throw you out. Remember that.'

Amma is so shocked she doesn't notice I'm touching her feet and then I'm gone.

Before I go I take some money out of the trunk and leave it with the mullah. A deal is a deal, even if I didn't get shit in return.

It's late by the time I leave. I take a rickshaw to the bus station on the other side of the market. Bus will take me to the ferry, ferry to the other side of the river.

*

On the road either side of me, all the paddy fields are flooded. Why, I ask the boy sitting next to me on the bus. He's hungry, I can tell by the way he stares at my throat, like he wants to take a bite out. I haven't seen winter rice for ten years, but I know what it looks like, yellow and brown and green. And it's dry by now, January when it's cold and there's no rain. 'That's not rice,' the boy says, with a big sag of his shoulder. 'It's shrimp.'

I look closer. The water's dark. I try to smell it. The little worms are crawling around in there like a giant itch.

The bus stops and the boy gets up. 'I work here,' he says. 'Lot of money in shrimp, if you want I can talk to my boss.'

I was wrong. Boy wasn't hungry, he was looking at my throat thinking, this old bastard needs a job.

I ask a few other people about the shrimp. They say the water's gone salty because the shrimp like it that way. I wonder if that's why Shathi's been complaining about the water in our well. I don't believe her. I think it's as sweet as ever. I tell her, you want to know salty? Stand out in the desert with a basket of sand on your head, then you'll know what salty tastes like – your sweat will make your lips shrink from your teeth. Salt is the sea pounding against the shore, mocking you when you're so dried out you can't swallow and there's an hour to go before the lunch bell. Salt is the tear that humiliates your cheek when you want a woman and you can't go home.

But maybe she's right, maybe the village water is salty and my tongue doesn't know the difference. Another thing those bastards took from me.

An old woman sits down next to me, smelling of mustard oil. After Bagerhat the road is smooth. She takes out a triangle of paan and stuffs it into her mouth. A few minutes later she'll be leaning over me and spitting out the window. Bus speeds up and I'm feeling the wind in my cheeks, and definitely I think I'm gonna find Megna. Somewhere out there she's been waiting for me with my kid. I'm thinking this and I drift off with my head against the top of the window until sure enough, the old woman wakes me up, sticks her head out into the road, and hacks a mouthful of orange sludge into the shrimpy winter air.

I reach Barisal and from there I take another bus. We cross the Meghna on a ferry in the middle of the night. It's cold and I'm wrapping my arms around myself. I fall asleep with my bag tied around my leg, and when the sun rises, I see the land is different, the trees clumped together, the road going up and down, dark hills on either side. I get off the bus and climb into a rickshaw and head for the village. Now it's early morning and there's a thin fog making everything sad, and for the first time I wonder if I won't find her after all, or, worse, if she's married to some other bastard and he's raising my kid.

Here I come, I say to her. I'm your hero. Bollywood chorus follows me everywhere I go. Clapping and an army of dancers. I'll give you all my money, my sins will be forgiven, we'll live together in peace with our little magic seed.

The village is at the end of a narrow dirt road. A cluster of houses in a circle, mud and tin shacks. Villages like this all up and down the country. I'm noticing now the things wife does to make it nice at home, the little border of henna bushes and the pattern she drew on the frame of our door. Without it, a place can look empty, like no one's ever loved it, just used the land for food, the cheap air to keep you from death, the water to drink and clean behind your ears so you can pray to God without filth in your folds.

I ask around for Megna's people. Two or three can't help me. A kid points me in the right direction. Then I'm standing in front of an open doorway and clearing my throat. A man comes out, old man, long arms and a weak chest, a shawl wrapped around his head and shoulders.

'I'm looking for Fatema Ansar's people,' I say, 'from this village.'

'Who are you?'

'I'm her cousin – from the other side.'

'Khulna side?'

'Yes, Labonchora.'

'Come in, come in,' he says. Waving me inside to a room so dark I have to close my eyes for a minute. When I open them I can see a bed, a stove, and a pile of cucumbers on the ground. He squats, peels one, and offers it to me. It's bitter but I don't mind. I haven't eaten since last night and I'm hungry as a goat.

'Labonchora,' he says slowly. 'You came all this way?'

I had prepared an answer. 'She owned some things there, a cow, a small piece of land. After she died the land has just been there, so I'm looking for her people. I want to buy the land, make sure whoever is owed is paid.'

'She owned a piece of land? How much?'

'A katha. Field next to my own. Wife thinks we should plant sesame, you know how women are. Won't let me forget it.'

He picks up another cucumber and I'm hoping he's going to offer it to me. He looks at me strangely and I know what he's thinking, why don't I just take the land, plant whatever I want on it, who's going to say otherwise? She's a woman, and she's dead.

'Thing is,' I say, 'people tell me she cursed the land.'

He looks up at me and nods slowly. 'I can see she might have been a witch.'

'So if I till it, nothing's going to come up. I'll break my back and only rocks. Waste of my sweat.'

'You won't get a single grain of rice out of it.'

'Not a sesame seed.'

He hands me the cucumber and it disappears into my gullet.

'You're looking for the daughter,' he said. He stood up and took a few steps towards the bed. 'She's her only people.'

I don't say anything. I'm holding my breath.

'That girl killed her.'

I'm waiting for him to get his piece out.

'Took the life out of her skin.'

I mutter something he expects me to say, 'God's will' and all that. He wipes his eyes, cloudy anyway.

'What happened to her, the daughter?' I'm trying to ask it slowly.

'We weren't going to have her, not with another mouth coming. She came, but we said no. Sent her away.'

'Back to Khulna?'

'Tried to convince me. Said she'd work hard, take a job anywhere.' He rubbed his hand over his jaw, as if she was still in the room, trying to get him to say yes. 'Chittagong, she said. I gave her the bus money.' Maybe he was feeling sorry for her now. Then he said, 'Carrying around someone's bastard. Couldn't have that.'

'Yes, you never know with women like that.' The mud floor is freezing and I want something real to eat.

'Take up with anyone.'

'No morals.'

'Whore.'

When I heard him call her that, I wanted to break his arm, but it was only the word I was using myself all this time. Calling her a slut whenever I wanted to forget her, pull her face out of my dreams. So I thought, maybe this is the word people use when they love someone they're not supposed to, and with that I left him, said my farewells and gave him a bit of money, and he took it without saying a word, maybe because he was desperate, or because he could smell I was hiding something, and we both knew that if he took the money, if anyone asked, he would be obliged to tell them nothing, only that a relative of the dead woman had come to pay his respects.

'Plant a jackfruit tree,' he said, just as I was ducking my head through the sad doorway. 'They come up hardy.'

Chittagong. It made sense. Big city, she could disappear. But where would she go. And how would I find her? I use my mobile and call Shathi.

'I'm not coming back right now,' I say. She doesn't ask me where I am, or why, and for a second this irritates me, but then I just tell myself to be relieved because here is one less person I have to lie to. But she says, 'What do I tell your mother?' And I feel a little bad, so I say, 'Give her the phone.' I can see my mother holding the phone with two hands. 'Amma,' I announce, 'be nice to Shathi. I'll be back when my business is finished.'

She grunts at me and I know it won't make a difference, she'll still torture my wife by making her pick the grit out of the rice, and she'll make her walk three times a day to the well, and cook her dal fresh every morning even though I bought a fridge that keeps everything cold. Why am I feeling bad? She's a woman, that's what they do, eat shit from morning to night, they must not mind it, they must know it from the minute they're born. When you know what to expect, things aren't so bad. This is what I tell myself as I wait at the station.

III I Go to the City

My bus pulls up to the station and I think, it's not such a big city. Compared to Dubai, compared to Dhaka, it's a village. No way I could miss Megna in this town. Only so many streets. I could walk each one, go into each house. Not the first time I fancied myself a hero, nice song to accompany me, bursting through doors and raising my face to the sun, shoulders jiggling, singing, 'I'm gonna find my girl, whole world be damned.'

First thing I do, I find myself a hotel, somewhere I can put my feet up. I want somewhere nice, so when I bring Megna in, and the kid, I can tell them: here I've come, look, a room to myself, a sink in the corner, electric fan, tube light, I'm your daddy come to rescue you, everything you ever wanted. I even think about a room with AC, but even in my Bollywood dream that's too much. I find it near the station, Hotel Al-Noor. It's clean, a place you can bring a woman and she'll think, man has made something of himself, man is a man, not some kid who ran out of the country like a scared goat. There's a bathroom at the end of the corridor so I wash. Then I go downstairs I eat something at the restaurant, where I share a table with a few other men, not unlike me, I think, until one of them calls me 'uncle', and I think shit, I look older than am, or at least, older than I feel.

'Uncle' he says, 'what's your business in Chittagong?'

I made up a story on the bus ride. 'I'm looking for my sister,' I say.

I have their attention. Five or six men – boys – with their fingers in rice and dal. 'Something happened to her.' It's the same story, the real story, except I tell it like I'm not the villain. 'Guy from my village, we all knew him, lived just on the other side of a few fields – said he was going to marry her. But kids these days, all scoundrels.'

'So what happened, they went secret to the Kazi?'

'No. Said he would. But then he ran off. Got a ticket to foreign and left her cold. I heard she came here, so I'm looking.'

'Why'd she come here? You have people here?'

I finish eating. Lick my fingers and the dal is drying on my fingernails. There's one guy at the table who's a bit older than the others, reminds me of Hameed. Actually the whole thing, men at a meal after a day of work, and for the first time I am having a missing twinge for my boys, Dubai, the sandpit, Bride and Groom.

'There was a child. So she came here.'

Now they know the whole story. I can see them thinking she was a slut because she opened her legs.

I don't know why I give a damn what they think, but I do. 'I think he forced himself,' I say.

'Son of a pig,' one of them says.

'You have a photo?'

'No.' I could hardly even remember her face. I saw it every day but I'm thinking now how much I wish I did have a picture, something I could show around the streets here.

The older guy points to one of his friends, a shiny little guy with a scar from his nose to his lip. 'Shumon here fancies himself an artist. Why don't you draw a picture of his sister.'

The others nodded. 'He'll do it. He's good.'

They were all rickshaw boys. Lived in a row of shacks behind the hotel. Tonight they were celebrating because the ban on rickshaws had just been lifted on the main road and they had made a bit more. Shumon had a wife, three kids, his parents, two younger brothers living with him. The other guy, Salam, was getting married but he still had to send money to his people back in the village. And the older guy was Awal, arms like twists of rope, grey on his beard, five daughters and another kid on the way.

To make a little money on the side, Shumon painted the backs of rickshaws. Women melting in the arms of their lovers, pink faces and tits like mountains.

'He'll make your sister look like a film star.'

Not sure if I want a picture of Megna looking like that. Maybe, I say.

Next day I go to the train station. Girl comes into town, she'll be at the bus station, the train station, or the ferry ghat.

All this time I haven't tried to think about what Megna's been doing for these ten years. In my dreamworld she was somewhere nice like in garments or a beauty salon. All the other things she could be doing, like begging on the street, I didn't think about. Still I go to the train station because if she's a beggar she would definitely be there. Before I go I call Shathi on the mobile. She answers on the first ring, like she's been holding the phone in her hand. 'I'm in Chittagong,' I tell her.

I can hear her breathing on the other side of the phone. 'Good,' she says.

'Are you crying?'

'No.'

'What happened, my mother did something?'

'No. She hasn't been well, she's mostly been lying down.'
'What is it?'
'I had a dream you were never coming back.'

All day while I'm at the train station I think about what Shathi said. I tell my story to all the beggars at the station. People hold out their hands and beg to me, and I think it wasn't long ago I was begging myself, to a foreman to lend me some money for my brother's leg. Now brother is doing fine, he even had a son, boy walks around the village like a little white prince. No one knows Megna. An old woman says, yes, I saw her, give me a few paisa and I'll tell you where. Her eyes are clouded, she's got the cataracts and I know she's lying. I throw her a few coins I don't bother to hear what she's telling me. I think Shathi's right, if I find Megna I'll never go back, I'll just stay at the Al-Noor forever, looking up at the ceiling fan all day with my head in her lap.

I find Shumon's place behind the hotel. There's a whole world back there, tin and paper shacks all stuck together. 'Come,' I tell him, 'get the others, we'll have dinner. I'll pay.'

We meet the hotel owner, friendly guy. He asks me how long I'm staying, I say a week, ten days, that's it. He nods over at a table at the back, where a pair of cops are ordering tea. Word's gotten out about my sister. Everyone knows the cops won't help. They'll put those RAB guys on you and next thing you know, you're the one in jail. Guy owes me a favour, hotel owner says, pointing to the one on the left. Bald circle on the top of his head. 'If you tell him I sent you, he'll do what's right, won't jerk you around.'

I nod but I don't believe it. But I tell Shumon to do his drawing. Just the face, I say. 'I'll pay you.'

'No payment,' he says, looking around at the others, who nod. 'Brother to brother.'

The next day he comes with his paints and a piece of paper. I tell him what Megna looks like, the small, dark eyes and the crazy hair. I can't really remember her nose so he just draws whatever nose he wants. I come up with a few other things I didn't even know I remembered, like a small dip in the middle of her chin, and also that her face was more long than round. When he's finished, he shows it to me and I'm surprised because it's not exactly her but it's not too far either, and there she is, a little pink but it's her, staring out at me. I can't believe it.

'I'm going to start looking for her right now,' I say. 'Thank you, brother.' I give him some money, just for the paint and the paper, and he takes it.

Rickshaw boys say, let's photocopy the drawing, right, put it up around town with my mobile number. I like this idea. I spend fifty paying for everyone's khichuri, another twenty on the copies. Before they can start asking where my money's come from, I say, 'Our parents, as in me and my sister's, are worried, so they sold a bit of land so I could come here and look for her. All this time they were angry because she ran away, but now they're old they're saying let past be gone, and anyway it wasn't her fault, bastard forced himself on her, everyone knows he was the bad egg, went off to foreign and never came back. Parents are soft now, just want to know where she is, what happened to the kid. So they sold a tiny patch of land and sent me.' I'm telling the story and it feels so good I start to believe it, even manage to get a few tears onto my cheeks. Boys are patting me on the back and promising to put the drawings up all over town. 'You'll find her, brother,' they say. 'It won't be long now.'

Shumon and the rickshaw boys put Megna's picture everywhere. Two calls I get on my mobile, saying they know where she is. 'She's working at a shop in Tiger Pass,' the first one says. 'Meet me there.' But when I go it's just a guy asking for money. 'Please,' he says, 'I need it for my father's operation.' I give him ten I tell him to get lost. Second time it's a woman, and my wish is so strong I think it sounds like her. When she says 'Hello?' I say, 'Megna?' And she says, 'The girl you're looking for, I saw her sitting in front of a barber-shop. She looked just like the picture.'

I ask for more but she just gives me the address. Naveed Napith, on the way towards Patenga. 'What was Megna doing?' 'Nothing, just sitting there.' I don't believe her, the barber-shop wasn't even in town, it was near the beach, and why would she go there? I hang up.

The very next day my luck changes. Shumon comes back from work and we're sitting with a cup of tea. 'No charge,' the hotel owner says. 'You're my regular customer now. Tea is free.' I've already paid for the week up front, so he knows I'm good for it. In the morning I'm gonna pay for another week.

Shumon bounds up to the table. 'You won't believe it,' he says. 'We found her.'

'What?'

'Me and Rajib, we've been asking around, you know.' The boy who sits at the front of the hotel with a giant vat of oil has just fired up the gas on his burner. 'We went to Dewanhat.'

'I told you she's not there.' It was a slum, the biggest one in the city. All week Shumon's been telling me to check it out and I've been saying 'Na, not Megna's sort of place. She would never have ended up somewhere like that.'

'She's not there, brother. We just know the big boss at Dewanhat.'

'What kind of boss?' The oil is sputtering now, and the boy is popping his little samosas in there and watching them dance.

'A guy who knows things. A guy who can find out. That kind of guy.'

I can see who he's describing: cigarette, shirt open to his crotch, everything oily. 'Don't want to get mixed up with a guy like that.'

But Shumon's grinning so big the scar on his lip disappears. 'We showed him the picture and he says he knows where she is!'

Now the kid's making jilapis, holding a bag of dough and drawing circles with his arms.

'Did you hear what I said? We're going to find your sister.'

I'm afraid to be happy. 'What exactly did he say?'

'Said he knows where she is, she's right here in Chittagong.'

'Been here the whole time?'

'Don't know.'

'He gave you an address or what?' It's starting to hit me now, like something climbing up my legs. I'm going to get the girl back, I'm actually going to find her. It will be like the last ten years never happened. Shit. God is Great. God is Great. The words come out of my mouth before I even know what I'm saying, and then I realise that, for some people, God doesn't just come in the bad moments, like when you're hanging hundreds of feet from the sky, but in a moment of bliss, when you get everything you want and you can't believe your luck, and you think, there must be something else behind this, some force that gave me my wish – it couldn't just be that I wanted something for ten years and then I finally got it, that would be too good, too kind of the world and we all know it's not that sort of world, at least, those of us who really know it – and I want someone to thank, or at least I want to feel like someone did this for me, to put peace in my heart. 'Thanks be to God,' I say.

'So where is she?' I can smell the jilapis now and they are floating in their sugar bath. I order us a plate and eat one straight away, burning my tongue. 'Give me the address.'

'Thing is,' Shumon says, putting his hands on the table, 'this guy, he doesn't do anything for free.'

I push the plate of jilapis towards Shumon, but he doesn't take one. I'm ready to say no, but already I'm wondering how much money I can scrape together. 'How much?'

'How much do you have?'

'I have.'

He takes a breath. 'Two.'

It's more than I've got. 'I've only got one-seventy.'

Shumon looks around the room like he's going to find the other thirty in a corner somewhere, then he says, 'Okay, I'll see what I can do.' And he gets up, pops a samosa into his mouth and leaves me with the sugary taste of Megna on my lips.

That night I stay up in bed and think about what to do. I stare up at the ceiling fan, which is off because it's chilly at night now, and I can see a dark streak of dust on the blades. I've been putting off a particular question this whole time, which is, what I'm gonna do with Megna when I find her. My wish being says I'm gonna take her somewhere nice and we'll run away together, holding hands and dancing between the trees, that sort of thing. But I know what it's like to be away from home, what it's like to be without people, and I won't do that again. After so many years, Megna's not going to want that life any more either.

So there was only one thing to do. Bring her home with me, not just to the village, but to my house. As my bride this time. Bring her home and tell everyone the whole truth. The child I would claim, and they would both have my home, my name, and Megna would finally get some respect. People in the village would have to swallow all the shit they said about her and kiss up to her just like they did to me. She would get mine. That was it, that was the only way. I owed her.

Now there was just the matter of Shathi. For a long time I thought, when Megna came back I would send her back to her father. Talak, talak, talak, that sort of thing. But, when it came down to it, when it came time for her to take sides, she chose me against her own. Looked after my father till he died. Right now she was keeping my rice, the key of the trunk around her neck, taking care of my mother. She should get something for that.

I could give her some money and send her on her way, but where would she go?

And then I went to the thought I had avoided. I was the big man in the village now, I could have two wives. Two wives, two beds. I had never touched Shathi, and I never would. She could keep living in my house, though, she could tend her vegetables and fatten her cows.

I know this can't work because Megna wouldn't have it, not if she was the same girl I knew ten years ago. But it's the best I can think of. I'm uneasy but decided. I'll call Shathi in the morning and tell her everything.

I'm awake. Can't sleep thinking what I'll say to Megna when I see her. She'll be angry, that I know. I tell myself, be ready for that. Maybe she won't see my face and I'll have to go back three, four times. But she'll melt soon enough, and who knows, maybe the years made her a little softer, maybe she can see that I was young and drunk on the thought of foreign – nothing anyone can do about that when it hits them. I got a chance and I took it. And, see, I made good, got some money in my pocket now, something to show for the last ten years, a home, fridge. What's she got? Well, she's got my kid, for one thing. Raised that kid right, I bet. School and all that.

I'm up and dressed before the sun, folding my towel on the rail and making it all neat, in case a miracle happens and she comes with me tonight. I go downstairs and I can hardly stomach my own saliva, it's bitter and foul in my mouth. Downstairs the hotel owner is waiting for me, hot cup of tea in his hand. He wants to chat but I'm in no mood, I barely swallow the tea he gives me. I just want to sit quiet with my thoughts. Soon enough Shumon comes in, sits opposite me. 'You got the money,' he says, no hello, no nothing.

It's tied up in my lungi, all one hundred seventy thousand of it, a trick I learned from my uncle. He used to fold his wages into the knot of his lungi, a few notes at a time, folding and knotting, folding and knotting. Then he would wear a loose shirt over it, and just look like one of those men with a paunch, maybe a lazy guy, someone who liked eating the fatty parts of the cow.

'Ya, I got the money,' I say to Shumon. 'Take me to her.'

'You stay here, I'm gonna give him the money, come back with the address.'

Something about the way he says it, I don't like. That scar over his lip is looking all twisty-curvy, and all of a sudden I'm not so willing to just hand it over.

'No, I'll come with you. That way when he tells us where she is, I'll just go over.'

'You don't have to do that.'

I order a glass of water and pass it across the table to Shumon.

He looks down at the glass. Takes a sip.

'Why don't we do this: I'll give him the money, then when he tells me I'll call your mobile?'

'Yaar,' I say, all friendly-like, 'I'm coming with you, that's that.'

'Okay, let me make a call.' He takes a mobile out of his shirt pocket and goes outside. For a second he disappears, then I see him talking again, holding the phone to one ear, bending over to close out the street noise.

I'm starting to get restless now, I can't wait to see Megna, my stomach is high up where my heart should be, everything tight, I can't breathe. I down another cup of tea. The hotel owner comes in again, tries to catch my eye, but I can't talk to him now. Shumon comes back and Awal is with him.

'Okay,' I say, 'let's go.'

Awal puts his arm on my shoulder.

'Brother,' I say, 'no rickshaw pulling today?' I know how much his family needs the money. One day out and they're over the edge.

'Important day for you, brother. I'll do the night shift.'

I'm glad Awal's here. If that guy from Dewanhat tries to pull anything, there'll be three of us. Awal and me get into Shumon's rickshaw, and he turns the cycle around, taking us down the main road. Traffic isn't too bad, we only stop at a few lights. Shumon's legs are young and quick. I toss a coin to an old woman at the intersection. This way I'm sending a message to God I'm not ungrateful for what's about to happen. She reminds me of my mother, who still isn't well. Shathi told me this morning when I called to tell her I needed more money. Not a lot, just enough to get me through a few more days here. Did I tell her what I decided last night? No. In the morning it seemed like the worst idea I ever had. Better to just bring Megna home and deal with it later. Nothing anyone can do when you just show up and say what's what. Maybe I felt sorry for Shathi. Maybe I was a coward, who knows. She would find out soon enough, let her wait.

The slum is behind a new shopping mall. Shopping mall makes me think of Pahari, but I quickly push him out of my mind. We leave Shumon's rickshaw and enter an alley behind the mall. We cross a bridge over a canal that's just an open drain, and then we're inside the slum, rows and rows of shacks and a lot of stink. Dark rooms with skinny cats and children and piles of rotting garbage.

I'm following Shumon as we go deep into the stomach of Dewanhat. I can't see the sky because there are wires strung up everywhere, between the houses and over the tin roofs. Dewanhat has electricity. Awal tells me some of the shacks even have cable TV. 'Lucky bastards,' he says. I don't think so. I'm the lucky one. I never had to move to the city. Out there in the village, no matter how hungry you are, you wake up every morning and you smell paddy, you smell mud and earth and dung. Dung is roses compared to human shit. We rule the world but our shit smells worse than any animal's – we had to get brains, big brains, just to find ways to cover up our own stench.

At the end of another long row, we stop and Shumon ducks his head inside. He comes back and he says, 'Okay, now give it to me.'

I'm better than these people. I have the sun in my face

and a house and a little patch of land. I'm even thinking, time for me to go back to earning a wage. Blood money's not gonna last for ever, its gonna dry out, and anyway I want to be working again, sweating over something so my days have a start and a finish. All this I'm thinking while we're walking, so when Shumon asks me for the money I'm not ready to hand it over.

'I want to meet this guy,' I say. 'I want to make sure he knows my Megna.'

'He knows, he knows,' he says.

'What about the kid?'

'What d'you mean?'

'If he knows where Megna is, he knows where the kid is. What does he say about the kid?'

Shumon comes up real close to me now. 'You're going to kill this whole thing,' he says. 'He knows about the kid. The girl and the kid are together, just give me the money and he'll tell you where they are.'

Awal turns when he thinks I'm not looking, so I push past Shumon and before I know it I'm inside the shack.

It takes a minute for me to take it all in. Then I see them all, the hotel owner, the rickshaw boys, the kid making the samosas. All of them.

They're in a room with a table and two chairs. There's a tube light fixed to the tin wall and everything's bright. I'm about to call them by name, and then I see the hotel owner's got an orange stain on his lips. In fact, now I notice they all have orange lips. They've been sitting here and chewing paan and waiting for me.

I start to shout. Words are coming out of my mouth I'm not sure what they are. Curses. Bad words. Threats. They all sit there and stare at me, not moving, all looking me in the eye, and for a second I think, am I crazy? Are these people really sitting here and staring at me? Or is it a trick of my mind, actually nothing is happening and after all these years of not finding Megna, nothing is worse than a bad thing, so I am hallucinating a bad thing, wishing for it – actually these men are really my friends, and in a moment we'll sit around and drink tea and laugh at something rude. I hear a sound behind me and it's two more men – I've seen them before too, the policemen from the hotel, the fat one and his sidekick. They raise their sticks and just before the pain blinds me and I black out, I think, at least I am not crazy, at least I have that.

Before I departed for Cambridge, I called Anwar. I had been thinking of his story – in particular the moment he had been betrayed by his friends. What did he think of them now, I asked. Was he angry with them for giving him hope and then snatching it away, or did he forgive them? And he said, for a long time he'd harboured fantasies of taking revenge on them. Not just them, but also the foreman in Dubai, and his uncle, who had persuaded him to leave Megna in the first place. He said he had sometimes lain awake at night and counted all the ways they might go. But now that time had passed, he had decided to keep his memories of those events at a distance, to tell himself the whole thing had happened to someone else. And now that it was going to be put down in black and white, he could say this: he was grateful to them, because one thing leads to another, and on balance, he had won. It wasn't a religious thing, he was careful to say, he wasn't lying down in front of his fate. But, he said, you can't be angry at the past. Not for ever.

I wish I could be as sanguine as Anwar. I wish, as I wrote

down our story, that I could be grateful it existed at all, that I fell in love with you and discovered there was something beyond, something grander than the mystery of my origins, something bigger than the little life I had imagined for myself. But I am greedier than Anwar, and I want more, and anyway it was me, you see, who had taken you away. I had no one else to blame, no one to murder in my sleep.

IV   I Go to Jail

Someone throws a glass of water in my face and I wake up. My head, heavy as an elephant's, tells me I've been here a long time, but a small window shows me it's still light out. It's still today. That means no time has passed and the worst is yet to come.

The policeman, the fat one, hawks a wad of spit into my face. I try to brush it away but my hands are tied behind my back. The spit and the water stay wet on my face. The policeman heaves himself up, and I curl into a ball, waiting for him to kick me. He's not wearing a uniform. The other guy, who I see now has marks on his face – maybe he got the pox too old – he's there too, standing by the door. It's dark but I can see a little more now, a cot in the corner of the room, a bucket on the other side. A metal door with no handle.

The two of them talk to each other but no one says anything to me. Then the pox guy comes over and pulls me up by my armpits. I make myself heavy and he struggles. Fat one unties my hands – are they letting me go? They don't talk; I'm afraid to ask.

As soon as I'm untied, I feel metal where the rope used to be. Fat one is breathing close to my ear, and the other is pulling something, and before I know it my arms are going up, like a puppet, and they're stretched tight like that, like I haven't seen someone in a long time and I'm opening my arms wide to grab them, and like that I'm frozen, can't move.

Finally the fat one talks. He says, 'You've pissed yourself.' I look down and he's right. My lungi is soaked. The money, of course, is gone – I can feel it straight away.

I'm scared but I'm also angry. 'You stole my money,' I say.

'That's right, country bastard.'

'Then why am I here?'

'We don't like little rats coming from the country and finding their slutty girlfriends.'

'She's my sister.'

They look at each other and laugh.

'You think we bought that, even for one day? Shit, been laughing about it for weeks.'

'So what,' I say, 'you got my money. You skinned me. Why bring me here?'

'Couldn't just let Shumon do his job – you had to follow him. You had to see all of us. You think we wanted that?'

I get it now. I dirtied their clean job. They would've disappeared, no one would have believed me, but now I knew where they lived.

'What happened to Shumon?'

'Bastard brought you all the way to us, didn't he. We took care of him.'

'Good.' So he was dead. 'You gonna kill me too, or what?'

'We could,' he said, 'or we could leave you in here to rot. No one would notice. You know the cells next door? Hundred, hundred-fifty men in each one. Soon you all start to look the same, you're all as dirty and piss-your-pants stink as each other. No one will even know you're gone. Or –'and he looked at me like he could mean anything.

I try to think of what would be the worst bad thing. He could beat me some more, that would be bad. I remember the tooth that fell out after foreman kicked me in the face, shit hurt for weeks and I couldn't eat anything. But it healed up and I got used to a little stiffness in my jaw, nothing big. Worse, he tortures me, filmi-style, pulls out my fingernails, something like that. I shudder. But then I think, not like he's trying to get some information out of me, so what would be the point? No, they won't do that. But they would teach me a lesson. I want to roll my eyes to the back of my head so I don't have to look at whatever he's going to do. I don't want to be in the room with him and me and the cot and his pockmarked partner. He's talking now about all the ways he can fuck me up, his words running right along with my thinking.

He starts to unbuckle his belt. I'm looking at him. There's a slick of sweat on his lip, and he has to try hard to pull the belt off because it looks like it's holding up the whole top half of his body and if he takes it off his body's going to melt off him like syrup.

He pulls off his belt and he's holding it in his hand and for one second that feels like a year it comes to my mind that he's going to do something else, something like sex to me, which is worse, much worse than anything I had thought of and my legs start to go, they go, and I'm just hanging there by my arms, and when I finally feel it, the knot of the leather on my chest, buckle cutting deep, I cry out with the pain, but also with relief, because it's not the worst, worst thing, until the second lash, and the third.

I don't know where I am, nothing, just the fire on my chest, for what I can't say, days maybe or even a week. I think someone's coming in, putting something on the fire, fat cop or pox cop, fat or pox, pox or fat, putting something cold on me, but I can't be sure, I'm just in and out, and when I'm in I want to be out, leave me to my dreams, I don't want to know the square of light in the window, and the hard of the cot, and the feeling of my own shit curling out between my legs and staying there, stamping the truth on my nothingness, a person with no people and no pride, a piece of trash.

It's Shumon. He's pouring water over me, and everything hurts like I'm being hosed with salt, and then he covers me with a bandage, and puts a blanket over me. Then he goes through the door without saying anything. He's talking to someone on the other side, and then I hear him walk away, and then the door opens again and there's food in front of me, dal and rice. I'm surprised to find that my hands still obey, and I eat, then I fall asleep again, like someone has crushed a pill into my rice.

Shumon's back the next day, and the day after that. When I feel a bit stronger I mouth a bunch of curses at him. He doesn't say anything. I reach my hand over to slap him but it comes out soft, like I'm giving him a sweet one on the cheek.

'You need to get more money,' he says.

'Fuck off.'

'They'll let you go, they told me.'

'They told me they took care of you.'

He lifts up his shirt, bandage all across his chest. 'Lucky my father took me to hospital,' he says.

'I'm not so lucky.'

'No.' He looks down at his hands.

'They want two lakhs.'

'I don't have it.'

'Call your father.'

220

'My father's dead.'

'Everything you said was lying?' Says it like his feelings are hurt, the bastard.

'At least I'm not a thief.'

'It wasn't my idea.'

I turn my face away. 'Fuck off.' And he goes.

He nags and nags. Holds up his mobile and says, 'Call someone, get the money. They're going to move you to the blocks; then I won't be able to get you out.'

A few days later and the fire on my chest is starting to fade. It still hurts but mostly when I try to sit up, or cough. I start to think about getting out of here, and when Shumon comes I take the phone and dial the only number I know. Shathi picks up on the first ring.

'Wife,' I say, 'I'm in trouble.'

'Are you alive?'

Before I can tell her what a stupid question that is, I feel a swell of grateful that she would ask this, as if she didn't care about a single other thing.

'Ya,' I say, quiet like.

'Sobhan Allah.'

'I need money.'

'How much?'

'Two.'

'Where are you?'

'Shumon,' I say, 'where am I?'

He tells me. I tell her.

'I'll send your brother.'

'There isn't two in the trunk. Where will you get the rest?'

I hear her breathe on the other side of the phone, little cat breaths. 'Don't worry, I will get it.'

'I gave money to the mosque. Get it back, talk to the imam.'

'Okay.'

I hang up and I start to cry. Like a baby. Like a girl. A girl baby. A suckling goat.

Guard gives me a bucket of water. I pour it over my legs, rubbing my feet together. Even on the cement floor, I can see the water runs black from my body. I'm disgusted by my own dirt, the smell that's coming off my body. My fingernails are long; I chew them; I tear off the extra, scraping my fingers against the rough walls to smooth out the ragged. I go behind my ears, the back of my neck.

Then I sit on the edge of the cot. I wait. Dal and rice come so I know it's lunchtime. Sun sets. My brother's not coming. I tilt myself back onto the cot, killed by another day.

I wake up to the door opening. Shumon. I don't even lift my head.

'You're out,' he says.

'Not going anywhere with you.'

He hovers over me, little scarry lip pressed right up on my face. 'Your money came.'

'Where's my brother?'

'He's not here.'

I can't be sure if this is another trick. I could even be dreaming the whole thing. Or I'm dead and stuck between earth and hell and this is what they make me do, see if I'm still as stupid as I was when I breathed.

Shumon gives me clean clothes. I recognise the shirt, the lungi. 'Where did you get those?'

'Your wife. She's waiting outside.'

I follow him out the door, through the corridor. Nobody stops us, no one even asks, we just stroll through like we're ghosts. Maybe I am dead. But then I see Shathi and she's holding a bag with both hands, so when I go up and hug her she just stands there like a stone.

Shumon gives me something. It's my mobile phone. I snatch it from his hand and walk away as fast as my beaten legs will let me, Shathi beside me, and we don't turn around to see what happens to him, we just keep walking like we have somewhere to go.

Shathi has a cousin who has a friend who owns a sweetshop on Halishar Road. We can stay with him tonight, and tomorrow we'll take the bus home. Wife and I don't say anything to each other. She hails a rickshaw and helps me climb in. She takes a packet out of her bag and passes it to me. She holds me steady over the bumps in the road and I eat, remembering the village.

We get to the sweetshop and the cousin's friend takes us upstairs, to the room he's got above the shop. His wife is as unsmiling as he is. She asks about Shathi's father. She gives us each a chom-chom. It's so sweet I'm gagging for a glass of water. She pours me one in a tin cup. All I want to do is lie down but there's no bed for us – we'll sleep downstairs, once the shop is closed.

Shathi opens her bag and takes out an eggplant, a handful of tomatoes and a pumpkin. The wife seems pleased now with her vegetables from the village. Then she tells me I should take Shathi around the city, show her the sights, which is her way of saying bugger off till after dark, I'm not feeding you.

We cross the road and Shathi bargains for a guava with the fruit-seller. We sit on the edge of the pavement with our feet hanging over the drain, passing the guava back and forth. 'My chest hurts,' I tell her. 'Pain,' I say. 'Pain, pain.'

Someone comes and shoos us away. This is his place —
he's going to set up his chotpoti stall. We start to walk. I
take the phone out of my pocket. 'I'll get something for
this,' I say. 'Maybe a thousand.'

'Okay.'

'Where did you get the money? Did you go back to the
mosque like I told you? Did the Mollah give you the money
back?'

'He spent it already.'

'Bastard.'

'Mosque will have a new roof, everyone will think of
you.'

'What I left you wasn't enough, where d'you get the rest?'

'The bull. I sold it.'

'That much?'

'It was a big animal.'

I'm thinking about all the times she hauled herself out
of bed in the morning to cut hay for that bull. And I had
complained about it, saying it made her stink too much of
the village, and why couldn't we smell different, like city
people, now that we had some money?

'What did my mother say?'

'She was crying about the fridge, and the TV.'

Shit. Of course the bull wasn't enough. 'Let's go to
Patenga,' I say.

People are sitting on the big rocks and eating things and
looking out into the sea. I look too and see a couple of
ships far out. Shathi lays out the end of her sari and sits
down. I'm noticing how everything she does she does slowly,
like she means to. No accidents with her. She pulls her
knees up to her chest and like that, all squashed together,
she's even more like a doll.

'Tell me what we're gonna do when we get home,' I say.

'We'll plant mustard.'

'And?'

'There's the vegetables to pick.'

'Tell me the vegetables.'

'Eggplant, gourd, cauliflower. Beans. Spinach.'

'What else will happen?'

'Nothing. It will go on like before.'

I'm thinking of before, what it was like when I didn't have any money, when I hadn't gone to foreign. I'm thinking of my mother's face, and how many times a day she's gonna tell me I screwed my life up. It's all playing out in front of me, I'm pissed off every time I wake up by that stupid mosque with its new roof and shiny paint, and whoever has bought my TV, I'm hearing that too, across the compound, when I'm trying to sleep, and the voice in my head telling me I should never have taken that money in the first place, no, not without thinking of Pahari and his family.

'I can't go home,' I say.

She get up and starts walking towards the water, skipping over the rocks. I go after her.

'It's not what you think.'

She stops, looks at me. 'I've never asked you for anything.'

True. She had never even said my name. 'I can't go home,' I say. Ask me something else. 'You want to stay here with me?'

'Someone has to look after your mother.'

It's starting to get dark and the crowd is thick now, the light the colour of stones.

'I want a child.' She looks at me again and I'm getting that she has thought about this. And that what she's really saying is that she wants more than a kid, that she wants to be a wife, a real wife. I wonder if I can give her this. My dream of Megna will have to go. I'll have to kick her out like I did the first time; then again, I've shed blood for her. That should matter, should open the door a crack for the rest of my life. For Shathi. I reach over and hold my wife's hand and we smell the waves, and the ocean smell reminds me of that water that fell from me when I bathed, only yesterday. We walk away from the sea and past the people, laying out their picnics, scolding their children, cracking open boiled eggs.

We get to the bus stop she doesn't let go of my hand. Something's stirring in me; it's so strange I don't even know what it is at first but then I get it. It's my blood, pumping on the inside. Hard now, my chest hurts from it, my legs too. On the bus there's only one seat and I stand over Shathi while she sits. It's dark and the bus pulls away. I see the ships in the sea, standing still, but my hand is moving, holding the back of Shathi's neck, here is her ear, here her jaw. Here is where her skin ends and her hair begins. I'm not looking at her, I'm staring out the window and reading all the shopfronts, but I'm seeing her for the first time, with my thumb, my rough thumb, her cheek, MOHONA BIRYANI AND KEBAB HOUSE, her jaw, KAZI BROTHERS CEMENT, the fold of her lip, SHAMMI RESTURA, her chin, NAVEED NAPITH (GENTS), and lower, as I get bold, the blood is booming in me now, the skin between her breasts is soft as milk, and suddenly I remember something, and with my thumb still on her skin, I squat down and I whisper, 'Please, wife, forgive me. I don't deserve it, but if you can, please try.'

Then I jump off the bus while it's still moving, and I hit the pavement with a crash, crying out in pain, and after a few minutes someone helps me up, I dust myself off, I walk towards the barber-shop, remembering the phone call from a few weeks ago, telling me that Megna had stayed here, on the way to Patenga Beach, at a barber-shop with a rhyming name.

Naveed is shaving the armpits of a guy who is obviously about to get married. He smells like coconut oil and everything's shiny about him. I get straight to the point with Naveed. 'I'm looking for Megna,' I say. 'Is she here?'

He holds the blade up and looks me over. 'You her people?'

'Yes.'

He pulls the blade up, collecting foam, wiping it on a towel draped over his shoulder.

'She stayed here for a few months. When she came to the city, I let her stay.'

'With who?'

'With no one. Just here.' He points to the floor, between the chair and the wall. He wipes the groom's armpit, moves to the other side. The groom lowers one arm, lifts another. Naveed starts to lather.

'What happened to her?'

'How the hell should I know? Stayed here as long as she paid me. She was lucky, too. People talked, wife wasn't happy. Girl like that.'

'Did you see the child?'

'No. But my wife said she was in a bad way – had to go to medical.'

'You haven't seen her.'

'Not since then.'

He's done. He examines his work, runs his finger along the smooth armpit.

It's dark now and the kerosene lamps are all on. I miss Shathi already – no way she's gonna take me back now. I find a shop and sell the phone, they give me seven hundred for it. I paid five thousand. Now I can't even call home.

I need to eat. I need money, a job, food. Can't believe I'm back to this after everything, and my mind flashes to when I was a kid, always hungry, rooting around my mother's ankles for a scrap of something.

But here I am. No point getting sentimental. Naveed says best thing is to ask around the shipyards. 'Nah,' I say, 'I'm a builder, not a breaker.' I find a construction site and the foreman hires me. Fifty taka a day, rice in the afternoon, a place to sleep. The building's almost finished, they're doing the floors now. He gives me a pair of rubber gloves, says to pick up the piles of bricks the old women are breaking by the side of the road, bring it over to where it gets mixed into concrete to make the mosaic, chunks of brick mixed in with the sand to keep it solid.

The women sit in a line with their legs spread and pound the bricks with their little hammers. Their faces are covered in dust. Some, the clever ones, have strips of tyre around their fingers. I'm feeling sorry for them, out there in the hot sun, beating on their own fingers, but I don't go up, don't say, hey, baking out today, can I bring some water – because I'm new and I know everyone's looking. Plus what do I care about a couple of old hags anyway.

I pick up their broken bricks, haul the basket on my head, make my way across the site to the mixer, unload and go back for more. My chest is still bandaged but it's scabbed up and I can see where the scar will be thickest, right up near my neck. If I ever wear a shirt again, proper one with buttons and a stand-up collar, it's going to show, like if I was one of those people who had an operation on my heart.

I don't make friends. I make a small place to sleep by

hanging up my lungi, keep to myself, eat my rice away from the rest of them.

I work on Naveed, finally he lets me ask his wife if we can find out about Megna at the hospital. I tell him everything, about Megna, the baby, how I'm trying to make it right after all these years. I've got nothing left to lose, no need to spin a story. He's got some hard lines around his eyes from looking into people's faces and pulling the blade over their necks, but when I tell him that, whole sad story, lift up my shirt and show him the lines from fatty cop's buckle, his faces goes soft and I think, maybe he'll help me, maybe not, but at least I told the truth.

V   I Find Megna

When I first got to the city I was getting my footprints all over the place and wearing out my sandals with the picture of Megna in my hand. Down the roads with my head swivelling all around, staring into the faces of all the women, catching the long of one's hair here, the small hands of another. They would look back, sometimes like they were angry, other times almost grateful, like, no one looks at me like that, a look without any kind of want or danger, just a frank glance, and I thought, women deserve to be given eyes into their eyes, and I wonder when was the last time, if ever, I gave Shathi that sort of a human thing. Probably never. But by the time I got to Naveed's I'd given up, you know, stopped staring at every living thing like if I stared hard enough they might turn into my girl.

But then, I see her. The whole real-as-flesh girl of her, standing right in front of me like a wrapped-up gift from the heavens. It's evening and I've finished my shift and I'm on my way to Naveed's. She's with another woman, a foreigner, but I don't notice that at first, I just stand there like I'm hit by a stone. She's right in front of me, not more than an arm's length away. It's her. Hair like a pile of electric wires, eyes tilted up, and so beautiful I can't breathe, and then she's gone past me, and I call out to her. 'Megna. Megna.' She keeps walking like she doesn't know her own name, and I try again, louder, even the back of her head is known to me, because I held her there, I held her everywhere, and when she keeps walking I say, 'It's me, don't you know?' Other people turn around. I run after her. She sees me and she stops. I don't recognise the look on her face. I'm waiting for a string of curses to come out of her mouth, but instead, she says, 'Who are you?' Like she never saw me in her whole life. 'It's me,' I say again, and I think it must be the dark street, so I put my hands on her shoulders and she's wriggling out of my hands and that's when I get it. She's pretending. Ha ha, very funny, I think, don't be that way. She's twisting around and I have to let go. Even then I just stand there while she turns away from me, disgusted, and then, finally, I see the foreigner beside her who is saying something in English. They both start screaming. Megna's turning away and Naveed comes out of his shop. I'm running behind her and he grabs my arms and holds them behind my back. He's stronger than he looks, and I can't get out of his grip. 'Sorry, madam,' he's calling out to Megna, and she turns and I notice her clothes, nothing like what my Megna would wear, not in this life, and the smell of her that's rubbed off on my hands is a smell from somewhere else. Not her. I'm going crazy, seeing my Megna in the face of another woman, and when I look again, she's nothing like my girl, nothing at all, and I squat right there, right there on the pavement and cry into my hands, because even

God is playing tricks, teasing me with the sight of her, which is only in my head, which is where she only ever is.

Naveed feels sorry for me and convinces his wife to take us to the hospital. We pick a Friday and I buy some clothes, a clean pair of trousers and a T-shirt so I don't look like a total bastard. I've got some things at the hotel, but no way I'm going back for it. If I see those rickshaw boys my cuts are all going to split apart open and start bleeding again.

Naveed's wife is tall and pretty, skin pale as new milk, and she does him like he knows she should've married better. He's nervous around her, telling her how nice she looks, all assy-kissy, and she puts it all away like notes down her blouse. I'm polite and thank you-ing as much as I can stomach, and secretly I'm glad she looks so fancy, because no village wife is gonna get us anywhere at the hospital.

I'm thinking about Shathi, my own village wife. Hard to sleep at night knowing there's two women out there who hate you. I'm so out of sorrys I don't even try to call her, but she's in my dreams now, right next to Megna. I'm remembering her on the beach, the smell of her hair on the bus. She deserved better, little bird.

We take a bus across town. On the way I tell them everything I know about Megna, whatever will help to find her. Her name, age. Naveed's wife helps me count the months and we figure when she might have been there. The bus stops and we walk the rest of the way. It's the medical college, no fancy people here. Already at the entrance you can see it's the poor man's place, there's sick people lying in the corridor, or curled up by the stairs, they reach out and grab your ankles, starting a long story and begging for a few paisa. Shit. Naveed's wife knows her way

231

around, end of the building, up some stairs that smell like piss, down another corridor full of people squatting on the floor and pointing to their rotting limbs, aching stomachs, waiting to see someone, crying for a doctor or a nurse, anyone in a white coat.

Naveed's wife spots a nurse and she goes up all haughty and clapping on her heels, and they talk for a minute. Then she comes back and holds out her hand to me. 'Give me some money,' she says. I've heard this line before, it sends the crazy to my blood, but I knew it would be this way, so I hand over all I've got, minus a little for food. She twirls around and disappears down the ward.

Naveed wanders off to buy cigarettes. I look around. There's a man with a little girl. Kid's in her father's arms, all limp and tired-looking, then she coughs, goes stiff, then quiet again, leaning her head against his chest. I look over at him and he nods at me. 'TB,' he says. I've heard of that, took some people in my village a few years ago. I got the letter in Dubai, sent some money.

'She got medicine?'

'We fed her the pills for six months. But she's getting worse.'

I look at the girl. She opens her eyes, sleepy-like, and gives me a slow smile. 'Hello,' I say.

'You got kids?' the father asks me.

'Yah,' I say. 'Nine years old. Lives with her mother.'

He nods. The girl starts coughing again, and he hugs her close, putting his hands on her forehead. Then I see his lips move. He's praying.

Naveed comes back. He opens the packet, offers me a smoke, and we light up together. I ask him about his wife. 'I can't believe it myself,' he says, 'why her people said yes. I guess I was a handsome kid.'

'Not any more,' I say, and he nudges me in the ribs. I wince, it's still a bit sore there.

Time passes, we sit down in the corridor like everyone else. Naveed offers me another smoke and I take it just to pass the time. We're thinking of going out for a cup of tea, leaving a message with the kid's father, but Naveed's wife comes back, folding her hands across her chest when she sees us sitting on the floor.

'It's filthy here, let's go.'

'Did you?'

She stops, looks down at us. 'No.'

'What happened?' I say.

'I'll tell you when we get outside. This place is full of sickness, get me out.' And Naveed's on his feet in a flash, clearing the way so she can pass through without touching anyone.

As soon as we get downstairs I stop and make her tell me everything. Outside, it's hot and my eyes are swimming in the sun. Naveed's wife makes fists and puts them on her hips. 'You look like a crazy bastard,' she says, 'but inside you're just a worm like everyone else.'

She's not telling me anything I don't know. 'Did you find the doctor? What did he say?'

'You think they have all their papers in a neat little pile and whenever someone comes off the street and asks them, they just tell you what you want to know?'

I'm looking at Naveed, then at his wife. My tongue's gone dry and heavy. 'You didn't find him.'

'Of course I didn't find him. No one would even talk to me.' She runs her hands down her kameez like she can't believe anyone would turn down a woman who looked that good.

My head goes so low I think it might fall off and roll

around on the ground. Naveed puts his hand on my shoulder. 'We tried,' he says.

We shuffle over to where the rickshaws are waiting. Naveed helps his wife get in and I wave them away. 'I'll walk,' I say, my feet as heavy as ships.

VI   The Shipyard

All the time I dream of my kid, dark hair like her mother's. She has my nose and Megna's little eyes. And maybe my lips. Nice lips I've got, at least that's what Megna used to tell me. Who knows what's left, I haven't looked in the mirror in a long time.

The building on Chowrasta is finished. Carpenters coming in to do the doors, kitchen marble going in. Foreman pays me my last week's wages and I'm out again in the street.

I wander from one building to another but there are no jobs. Or maybe there are, but when they look at my face and see the life stamped out of me, they say no. My money runs out quick. Naveed says I can sleep in the shop, so I make my bed there for a few days. I want to ask Naveed's wife if she'll teach me a few letters, but I haven't seen her since that day at the hospital. Can't believe I went this long without learning a single damn thing. She called me a worm, and she was right – a stringy little insect that crawls through the dirt and eats everyone's shit.

I'm hungry but when Naveed offers me his rice, I say no. My stomach goes soft and achy when I'm alone in the shop at night with the smell of soap and the little hairs Naveed can't catch with his broom.

In the day, when I'm not looking for work, I look into the shops along the highway, and I see strange things. In one, giant metal lanterns, long lengths of chain. Clocks and brass instruments. Shopkeeper tells me it's all from the ships that get broken further down the beach. They sell all the bits and pieces here, the cheap stuff. Everything else goes to Dhaka. He's is a nice guy, old, he has a lot of time on his hands. Tells me there used to be nothing here, then a storm and ship that got washed up and stuck in the sand. There was a foreigner, a Captain, he started the whole thing. I don't believe him, just let the old man talk – what's left when you're old except the ears of the young? I can't call myself young any more but I do, I do because I messed up so bad I still have so much I haven't finished, like bringing a kid into this world and raising him right, teaching him to respect his elders and listening to their stories, no matter how long or made up.

'You looking for work?' he asks me.

'You know anyone?'

'Always something in shipbreaking. I could put in a word. Guy's coming to sell, I'll ask him. Come back tomorrow.'

I tell him I'm grateful.

'It's hard work,' he says, 'dangerous too.'

'I don't mind,' I say.

Next day I scrub up as best I can and wear the trousers I bought for the hospital. When I show up at the shop, shopkeeper tells me to wait at the back. There's a guy with a van on the street, piled high with junk. All I can see are metal legs, cables, things that used to work but now they're just broken parts.

At the back of the shop there's a bunk bed with metal bars, reminds me of our dormitory in Dubai. Wonder where those boys are now, who's building and who's gone home.

I sit down on the bed and wait a long time, then I hear steps coming in my direction and I sit up, straighten out my shirt.

Shopkeeper comes in. 'Here's the one I was telling you about.'

The guy is squat and has a nose like a dog, all squashed up against his face. He's breathing hard and sweating like fat people do. He looks at me like I'm a chicken he's thinking of buying. 'You done construction work?'

'He's used to working hard,' the shopkeeper tells him.

'I worked in foreign, in Dubai,' I say, hoping that will sway him. People are always impressed with talk of foreign.

'You got any schooling?'

'No, sir.'

'Pity. I could use an assistant. But never mind. You come tomorrow, I'll put you on the ship. We got some tankers that need finishing up. Give this to the man at the gate, he'll let you pass.'

He gives me his card. Before I can ask him about the pay, he's out the door, his doggy breaths getting faster as he walks away.

When I was a kid my father made me dig out the latrine. It was supposed to run to the river, but two, three times a year it got stuck, all the shit clogged and flowing up to the ground. He sent me in with a shovel, said nothing, just pointed to the river. The stink was so strong I gagged for weeks after just thinking about it. I hated my father for making me to do it, but I see now that I should've waited, because I'm hanging off the side of a ship with a flimsy rope around my waist, and I realise, this is hell, not the latrine, not the desert, not even up there against the glass with Pahari. But this is what I deserve after all the bad I've done. This work at the end of the world.

I do what they say. Tell me to climb to the top of a broken ship and hang there like a tree-snake, I do it. Tell me to tie a rope around my waist and cut the flesh of a metal beast, that's me. No word, no talkback. Pahari, if he was here, he'd be ashamed of me. What he wouldn't say about the pathetic road I chose, all coward and no brave. What could I do, Pahari? After you died and scared the shit out of me for ever the only thing I could think was, I just want to hide in Megna's sari, and my kid, just want to protect my kid. All coward and no brave. In my head Pahari says, I died for nothing, and I tell him, people like us always die for nothing. And he's shaking his head, loose, like he used to, as if he didn't get his bones ground to dust, as if every wish he ever had hadn't disappeared into the desert like a drop of water on a leaf.

Now every day is latrine day. Every day I fall to sleep with poison in my blood. I get one day's teaching from a guy who hands me a blowtorch and says, 'When I tell you to cut, you cut.' Today I'm up on the east side of the ship. Rope's around my waist, goggles for my eyes that's getting cut from my pay. Sparks come out of the blowtorch and land on my legs like a line of ants, sun burning my back, and all for a scrap of money. For that little scrap I'm all cut up from the metal, arms about to fall off from carrying it, and so hungry I'll eat anything, sleep anywhere, thirsty like I've never known, not even in jail.

There's a row of shacks behind the yard and they offer me a bed for a sum I guess is about half my pay. I don't have a choice so I take my things and sign up. Mostly I decide to keep to myself, but after a few days I let myself make one friend. His character is black and he's a real bastard of a guy, which tells me at least he's honest, no tricks at the last minute thinking he's a winner and then realising he's out to cut my throat.

We share the hut with four others. The first day, he points me to the pallet by the door, says, 'That one's for you. It'll break your back but nobody gives a shit about the new guy.'

He's from the north, where there's never enough food. 'You'll die on this beach,' he says. 'Something will fall on your head and you'll crack open like an egg. Or fire. Or poison.'

'Thanks,' I say. 'No one will miss me, so.'

'Yah, another miserable son-of-a-bitch with no one to love him. Plenty of us around here, na?'

The others ignore him.

'You'll die alone like the rest of us. But at least we won't be happier than you.'

He climbs onto his bed, farts in my direction, and goes to sleep.

My bed isn't broken, it's slanted. I sleep with my feet a few inches lower than my head. Next day, I find a piece of wood and I fix it. My friend, Dulal, is impressed. Tells everyone what a useful guy I am, soon I'm fixing all kinds of things. The leaky tap at the end of the row of huts where we line up to brush our teeth; a broken ladder. I'm not an expert but I know my way around. All this I do at night. During the day, I'm on the shitty little rope, the blowtorch, giant squares of metal dragged down the beach. We chant as we heave, 'Hei-yo, hei-yo, hei-yo.' Look, we're taking out the trash. Feet sink into the sand, grey and oily. 'Hei-yo, listen up, nobody in this world for me.'

I think about going home, but no way I can do that. Shathi's not going to open the door for me, not now. And there's the fingernail of hope I'll still find Megna and the kid. But how? I'm so tired from the ship I can hardly move my legs at the end of the day. I haven't even seen Naveed since I went to tell him I wasn't going to sleep at the shop any more.

It's going to be Eid next week and they're giving us a day off.

I go back to the beach. I'm hollowed out now, I'm done. Thought when I started, I could look for them for years, my hair would turn grey and still I'd be on the hunt. But my bones are dead. I'm stupid and my luck is over. I have to give up. I'm an even bigger fool if I don't see that my girl and my kid are never going to be found, that the world swallowed them up and I'll never see them again.

The hut is quiet. Everyone else has somewhere to go. No one's going back to their village – too far for most. But they're not here. I crawl onto my pallet. Now I wish it was still slanted, because I can't stand the sound of blood pumping to my heart.

I close my eyes, wishing for sleep. Maybe I drop off for a minute, because someone's beside me, breathing on my face. I smell booze. I open my eyes and it's Dulal, drunk, his face inches from mine and grinning like a fool. I'm so fed up with my life it's like I'm drunk too, so I say, 'I don't even know if it's a son or a daughter.'

He nods, serious, not like he's laughing at me, and then he shows me what's in his hand and it's a bottle. I take a swig, it goes down hot and burning, right to my stomach. In five minutes I'm drunk. Thank God. My tongue is loose and he's not listening anyway, so I tell him the whole stupid story. He comes in sometimes, saying things like 'You fool' or 'Shit, brother, you had that coming', but mostly he's quiet, and when I'm finished he repeats some of the stuff I've just said, like 'poor bastard Pahari' or 'Policemen, they're all crooks'.

After I'm done, he stays quiet for a long time and I think

he's asleep. I think I should sleep too, it's getting late, and I'm about to head to the toilet when he sits up in his bed and shouts, 'I'm a genius!' And then: 'There's one place open on Eid day.'

He jumps up, pulling my arm so hard I have to give his hand a good slap.

We go downstairs and throw ourselves into the empty street, not a rickshaw or a cigarette-wallah to see us as we walk crooked. Everything is quiet, all the shops closed, everyone at home with their fathers and children. 'The street is sadder than the hut,' I tell Dulal. I want to go back, but he's saying, 'Don't worry brother, you're going to thank me,' and he's passing the bottle back into my hands, and it's going to my blood, so I just follow him. Who cares anyway, I think. I carry the sad inside me, one place is the same as the next.

We go around a corner and walk for what feels like a long time, though I'm not sure, everything is moving around. Dulal's talking the whole time about Eid, and there's blood on the street from the cows they've just slaughtered. Shathi had to sell her bull, maybe it came here, nice fat one for a rich guy's table. He's eating its liver now, the bastard.

Finally we get there. I see a broken-down building, two floors with a veranda upstairs, saris hanging on the washing line. We go inside and there's a chair with a few women sitting around, wearing clothes like they might be going to a wedding, except if you look close, it's all cheap. Eid Mubarak, they say.

I know what it is. I've been to one when I was a kid, before Megna, brother and me and a couple of boys from the village. I told them all I'd done it, pretended I was a real man, but I couldn't. I was shit scared of the woman, her sex staring at me like a little cat. I can't remember what she looked like, except I know she laughed at me, in a bored sort of way, like she sees that sort of shit all the time. Probably a lot of guys couldn't make it happen at the last minute. It's harder than it looks.

Even through my drink I can smell perfume. Dulal slaps me on the back. 'What I said! Only place open on Eid day!'

The madam, bloated arms with paint all over her face, looks us up and down and says, 'Money first.'

Dulal makes me pay. After I get my cash out, the madam is all smiles. There's a line of girls and she says to choose one. Last time I can't remember them being so young. Maybe it's the drink but the whole thing's making me gag – kids, perfume, madam and her fat arms. But this time I'm not going back. You'd think I was Jesus for all the sex I haven't had. I look at Dulal. I look at the madam, laughing now, teeth at the back all orange from chewing her Eid paan. I'm not going back. I stare up at the girls, find one who doesn't remind me of anyone. Dulal's already picked his, a tall girl, skinny, they're arm in arm like he's known her since his village days. I'm getting mine and he pokes me with his elbow. 'Just like your Megna, eh brother? Arre, Megna, your hero's coming! Megna! Megna!' He says her name like she might appear if he says it loud enough. If only. He takes another swig from his bottle and he's gone behind one of the curtains.

Girl takes me up to her room. I try to get turned on by the look of her ass swaying in my face as she climbs the stairs. We go behind a curtain and the bed's narrow and bare, just a sheet and a few long pillows. There's a calendar and a mirror with a broken corner. We lie down. She pulls down my zip and takes my dick out of my trousers. I put my hand on her head. She puts it in her mouth. I look up,

I see lizards hiding in the tin roof. I feel good. I pull the girl's hair and she climbs on top of me. Her face isn't pretty but it's not mean. I'm sliding into her, easy, like it hasn't been ten years I've been hating my own cock. When it's going to be over, I grab her and pull her face close to mine, so I can't see anything, only eat the lipstick off her face and taste the sex in her mouth, and I hang on to her like I'm falling out of the ship and she's going to save me, a little dinghy in the hard boil of a river.

After, she says, 'I had a friend called Megna.'

Madam comes in, says, 'Your time is up.' I take out the last of my money and buy another hour. Girl keeps talking. It's her. Megna was her friend, a good friend. Always sharing her rice. I'm patient, I don't try to rush her. The men didn't always like her, she had a mouth. But she never complained, always said this was her fate.

Girl says, 'We all took a little bit, here and there. Sent some home. But Megna, she was paying off a big debt. Everything eaten, never had a paisa put aside.'

'By who?'

'Madam, who else?'

The debt meant that Megna had to do whatever. The perverts. Old men. Policemen who got freebies so they left madam alone.

I want to tear the skin off my face. Sun's rising through the door. I don't have long, so I finally ask, 'Did she say anything about a kid?'

Girl looks around at the broken mirror like it's going to tell her something. 'I don't know what happened to the kid. But kid's why she owed madam all that money.'

Madam comes in again. 'Out,' she says. 'Come back when you have more money. And get your friend out too.' She stands there till I drag myself out. Girl comes down with me. Dulal made a mess. I clean him up, throw a handful of water on his face. 'What happened to her?' I say again, heaving Dulal up, putting his arm over my neck. 'What happened to Megna?'

Girl keeps talking while we drag Dulal to the door. 'The sickness took her,' she says. 'Died last year.'

My arms go limp and Dulal slips to the floor.

'Ei,' says madam, 'I said get out.'

Girl helps me get Dulal up again. 'Did you bury her?' I whisper.

Madam is watching, hand splayed across her hip. We drag Dulal out on the street.

'We took her out and put her in the water,' girl says.

'Which water?'

She points in the direction of the sea. 'We borrowed a dinghy. We all went, every girl.' And she runs back inside, her footsteps as light as a rat's.

I call Shathi. 'She's dead,' I cry. Shathi listens, quiet. 'Come home,' she says. She's right. That I still have a home is a miracle. I should go, start all over, pay my penance somewhere else. Is my kid dead, too? I'll never know. If I could just see Megna's face one more time. There's no face like hers in the world, no eyes dancing like that, hair like she rode with her head out of a car window. Just one more time. I think about the time I thought I saw her, that woman with the fancy clothes who played tricks on my mind. All this time, she was dead, fish-eaten, not even a grave to rot into.

Dulal and me, we have the morning shift. No way he's going to make it, so I go to the Boss and make an excuse. Diarrhoea. Boss gives me words on cutting Dulal's pay and then I'm back in my harness. My eyes are cloudy, I can't see through the goggles. My torch burns through the metal. I'm remembering my Qur'an, saying a prayer for Megna. Died of the sickness. The sickness of paying off a big debt. She was a whore after all, but only because I made her one. All the stories I had dreamed up for her life, new start in the city, kid going to school – none of that was ever going to happen. Shit like that doesn't happen to people like us. Any chance she had of a life, I took from her.

Sun beats down hard on me. No wind, everything so still, and me baking in the hot, now with a dead girl around my neck.

I don't know how the day passes. Later, we're eating a few scraps together. Dulal's up, he gives me a wink when I sit down next to him. He's telling me about the girl he did, how luscious she was, best Eid he ever had. 'They should make it part of the day,' he says. 'You kill a few cows, roast their livers, then go fuck a few cheerful women – everyone's happy. I should be Prime Minister.'

I stare down at my food. 'Want it?' I say. 'Have.'

He grabs my plate. 'What happened to you? Whisky got you?'

'Megna's dead,' I say.

He keeps eating. 'Shit.'

'And she was a whore. Worked at that place.'

'Nothing wrong with being a whore.' He's chewing fast, as if someone's going to steal it right out of his mouth. 'Whoring never killed anyone.'

I go for his face. He crashes to the dirt floor, holding his jaw. Then I'm on the floor too, my arms around him, touching his blood, and I'm bleating like a goat while the other guys stand around and stare.

Dulal's nose is broken. I say I'm sorry but he waves

me away. 'Man's gotta do sometimes,' he says. Later, we're about to bed down and he has rags stuck in his nostrils. He asks what I'm going to do now.

I've been asking myself this question all day. I say, 'I wait to die. Nothing left for me. I lost my money, my wife, my kid. Now this girl's blood is on my hands. I die, then God sends me to Hell, that's all.'

'Motherfucker,' he says. 'Shit wasn't all your fault. But you're in a hole, I can see that.'

One of the other guys is smoking a biri, I can see the little orange light. I close my eyes and wait for sleep, wait for death, cursing the blood that flows stubborn in my veins. I think, God made us hard to kill. It takes a knife, a bullet. Your heart breaks, you still go on living.

Dulal's got an idea. We're carrying a piece of the ship from the beach to the road, a big piece of metal that cuts into our shoulders. Ten of us on each side of the metal, Dulal right behind me, guy at the front counting our steps.

'We gotta go back to the whorehouse,' he says. 'The madam, she knows something.'

'Can't do that,' I say. 'No way.' Also, I don't tell him, I spend all my days thinking about what Megna had to do. Men she had to fuck. All the ways she had to fuck them. It's a sex cinema in my head, except nobody's getting hard, I'm just making myself sick. And worse. At night I've been going back to the whorehouse. I don't go in, I just hang around outside. Lights go on, go off. Sometimes from the street you hear the women laughing.

I put these people into my picture. This guy with the long arms, he held down my Megna, he forced it into her mouth. These two guys, sharing a cigarette, they took turns with her while the other one watched. All day I think of this, and at night I fill my picture in a little bit more. I don't tell Dulal about the poison in my head.

'I'm not going back in there,' I say. 'I'll kill that woman if I see her.'

'Let's kill her, then,' he says. 'Cut that bitch's head right off.'

'I'm tired. I can't fight any more.'

'That's a lie, brother. You broke my nose.'

I almost laugh, but the weight of the metal is killing me.

'Nothing left for you but your kid,' Dulal says.

'Kid's probably dead too. Nothing left for me.'

'Don't be an asshole. Madam's gotta know who she left her kid with. Where she sent the money.'

It makes sense. But so many times I thought, I'm close, this is it, and look where I am, I'm nothing. Lots of guys looking for their people in this town. They all have a story, some sad tale of getting separated at a mela, or their kid ran away and got mixed up with the wrong people. Happens all the time. I'm just one sorry bastard in a city of lost people. Nothing special about me. I didn't love Megna any more than the other people looking for their lost ones. The kid doesn't even belong to me, never even clapped eyes on it. So why should I keep looking? What makes me think I'm going to find my girl when everyone else's girls are lost too? I don't deserve it, that's for sure. No doubt about that.

Dulal presses me. 'What's it to you?' I finally say.

We're almost to the machine now, the one that flattens the metal. We take a few more steps, and then the man at the front calls out, and like a dance we all let go of the metal at once, jumping back as it crashes to the ground.

'Same shit here every day,' Dulal says. 'Ship comes, we take it apart. Sometimes a guy dies, or one of us gets cut, loses a leg. It's black. So if you have a chance you take it.'

We head back to the ship for another piece of metal.

'Okay,' I say. 'But don't think we're gonna find that kid. Nothing good is ever happening me to me again.'

It's late on a Friday and the place is busy. Men coming in and out, the smell of sweat and horny everywhere. I ask for the madam. When she comes out she doesn't recognise me, but when she sees Dulal, she says, 'Eid, I remember. You want more?' She's chewing her paan again, little bits of green and orange on her mouth.

I let Dulal talk. On the way over here, I said, 'This is your party. You want something to do, you do it.'

The scars on my chest are itching. Guy brushes past me and I swear I've seen him on the ship. They probably all come here. Boss too. Maybe his whores are more high class, maybe not. You never know with richies, they always surprise you by being more perverted than the rest of us.

'We're looking for someone,' he says. 'Megna. She used to work here.'

'No one like that.' She spits her paan into the gutter. 'I'm busy. If you don't want a girl, get lost.' She turns. Dulal grabs her, arm so soft he looks like he's squeezing a loaf of bread.

'Bitch,' he says. 'We know she worked here. We know you worked her till she died. No use lying.'

She looks him up and down.

'Yes,' she worked here. 'But nobody killed her, ask anyone. She got sick, I even paid for the doctor. Now you know, so get out.' She points to the alley.

But Dulal's just getting started. 'Tell us about the money.'

'What money?'

'The money she borrowed.'

His fingers get tighter on her arm. Now her face is red and puffed up.

'Listen, you son-of-a-bitch. Get your dirty hands off me. I know where you work. I'll tell everyone. I know you like boys – you want people to know? Bokul here, all dressed up pretty, has a surprise between his legs, and you almost sucked it right off him, you sick little bastard.' She laughs, her mouth slick with spit.

Dulal lets go of her arm and looks at me. I shrug. I don't give a shit.

'Listen, I say,' coming between them. 'We're not here to spoil your business. Just tell us about the kid – we know she had one.'

She's rubbing her arm, about to turn away, and for a minute I think she's just going to keep laughing and tell us to fuck off, but she stops and turns to me.

She breathes deep. 'The kid was here. I'm only telling you because she's more trouble than she's worth.'

She. A girl. My heart stops. I die, right there in front of her. 'But that other whore told me she was somewhere else.'

Madam laughs. 'They tell you what I want them to tell you. You think I would let a girl go? A girl who's going to carry me when I'm old? I'm going to starve with so much stupid.'

'Where is she?'

The bitch smiled like she was enjoying torturing me. 'She's gone.'

'What did you do to her?'

She spits. 'I was getting rid of her. She was too much trouble, always crying over her mother. And there was a man, had his eye on her.'

She waves her arm.

'He was going to keep her, I don't know what she was complaining about. Then, yesterday, she cuts all her hair off.

Fuck knows where she got the scissors, but she looked like a bald chicken, the little cunt.'

I double up over myself and gag into the street.

Madam spits at my feet. 'Get out of here, I don't have anything for you.'

It starts to rain, hard like someone's hurling it out of the sky. Finally the rage devils into my body and I lift up my head and drive it into her stomach. I'm pounding madam's stomach with my fists, thinking about Megna and Pahari and Shathi and my father who made me dig out the latrine, and my poor little seedling who was in this hellhole all the time, just past my fingertips, until madam slumps against the wall and through the blood bubble at her lip, she says, 'Go to the beach called "Prosperity". There's a kid that hangs around, a boy. Your daughter's with him.'

VII   My Girl Falls from the Sky

Dulal and me run all the way back down the road and the rain feels like fire on my back and my scars are beating with my blood. Dulal slows down, his hands on his knees, but I say, 'Come on, we have to find that kid.' I'm not letting myself think about anything except finding him. We go all the way up and down, asking which yard is called 'Prosperity' and we're wetter than dogs by the time we come upon a group of men standing around in the dark and the rain. 'What's going on?' Dulal asks.

'Do you know what they're doing, these richies?' someone's saying. 'They're sending an air-conditioned truck to pick up a piece of furniture. Yep, ship there, there's a big, black chair, bigger than any chair you ever saw. Owner's selling it to some rich American, won't even let the thing come out into the air, wants to take it to Dhaka like a bride, wrapped up and protected from the hot. Can you believe it? A chair's got a better life than us.'

'We don't want trouble, we're just looking for a kid,' Dulal says.

'Someone's going to die getting the chair out.'

We always die, I think. That's why we're here. Even when we live, we die.

Dulal gives up. 'Let's get out of here.'

'We have to find him,' I say. 'He's got to be here.' I don't give a fuck about this chair or whatever asshole is taking it to America. 'A kid,' I say to everyone I see. 'I'm looking for a kid who hangs around here.' No one's listening. I raise my voice. 'Ask Selim,' someone says, 'he's in charge.' He points to the front of the crowd. Dulal and me follow the men down the beach till they turn into an alley.

We walk a few shanties down and go into a long room. Inside, there's a mess of arms and legs. Everyone got something broken. They show me their stumps and their scars. They have arsenic and all kinds of shit in their veins and all over their skin. So this is how it's going to be. Even Shathi wouldn't have me this way, not even she, the saint who forgives everything. You couldn't love a man broken like that.

Selim's a big guy with long arms and a chest full of meat. He's saying they're going to march onto the ship with the chair and bring the whole thing down. In the morning, holding the chair high above their heads, they're going to walk all the way from the beach to the town. There's a foreign girl who's going to put the whole thing on TV. I keep shouting for the kid. 'He has my girl,' I say to everyone. They look at me like I'm bringing all the crazy into the room. I try to push my way to Selim, and when I find him he looks me up and down and says, 'There's a boy here, it might be him. Come to the beach with us.'

Soon we're making our way to the beach, holding kerosene lamps, torches, whatever will get us through the dark. It's raining so hard everything's blurry and we can't see more than a few feet in front of us. The shipyard gates are locked but all we have to do is get out onto the water and cross over. 'Which one is it?' 'The pretty one,' Selim says, 'all white like it's dressed up for a party.' Selim carries one of the broken men on his back like it's nothing. We wade through the water, across the end of a tanker, past a pair of propellers on their last cutting, and finally we see it, a pretty little cruise ship half broken.

'What do we do now,' we ask Selim. 'Where's the kid?' I say. 'Hey,' he shouts, 'where's that kid?' No one's seen him. We wait for the chair to come out. 'See – there's the men, they built a ramp halfway up the ship because the chair's so heavy.' We stand around and wait for something to happen. The rain lets up for a few minutes, then hardens and throws bullets of water onto our heads. Soon the sky starts to turn yellow and it's about to be morning, and just as the light is making its way onto our little piece of the beach, we see something coming out of the ship. 'It's here,' Selim yells. 'The chair is coming!'

A crate's loaded onto the ramp. Six men are holding on and one of them's shouting. Now that it's light I start making my way to the front to see if I can find the kid. Instead I see a woman. She's got hair plastered to her back and she's shouting to the chair guys. 'Hai, Allah,' we say. Our stomachs are in our mouths watching this crate like a boulder rolling down the ramp. It's going fast now, faster than it should, and we're watching as it speeds up, running away from the men, and then, like a bar of soap, it slides off the ramp, and we're all running back until we hear a crash, something so loud and crazy we scream back at it like it's going to eat us alive.

We circle around and I see pieces of the black chair scattered like giant grains of sesame. I see a woman, hair plastered across her face, a trickle of blood coming out of her head, and there's a boy pinned under the crate, and then another kid, head shaved clean, and that's when I start to cry, 'My girl, my girl, my girl,' because even without the curl of her hair, I know she's mine, that face, that blessed face I thought I'd never see again.

You see now why I had to tell you, Elijah – or rather, why he had to tell you? I wasn't the only one in Chittagong in search of a self. I wasn't the only one who felt like the loneliest person in the world. The whole time I was there, as I made friends with Mo and got to know the workers on the beach and fell in love with you, he was right beside me, carrying around my secret like a talisman dangling from his neck.

It's time to turn now to the matter of us, to your days on the beach, that perfect bubble of bliss I couldn't help but shatter.

The Arrival of You

Did you know, Elijah, that I was named after the Abbasid princess Zubaidah bint Ja'far, who inspired *The Thousand and One Nights*? My mother, who everyone calls Maya but whose formal name is actually Sheherezade Haque, was herself named after the narrator of that great epic, the Persian queen Sheherezade, a name given to her by her father, Iqbal Haque, who died of a heart attack when my mother was only six. Zubaidah bint Ja'far herself was not called Zubaidah at birth, but Sukhainah. And my name at birth – well, I will never know that, will I? There was some debate as to whether I should, like my mother and most of the people we knew, have a nickname as well as a formal name. The privilege of choosing the name was given to my dadu, my paternal grandmother. She chose the name Putul, which means 'doll', and would not be persuaded to change her mind, even after my mother protested that no daughter of hers could possibly answer to the name Doll.

In an effort to remove the name from its meaning, my parents shortened it further, and Putul became Putlie, Pootsie, Poo, Potla, Potlu, and Potato, until finally only one stuck: Poots. Poots was the girl I was back home, when it was just my parents and me. Poots was what my dadu and my nanu and the servants called me. When my friends came over I went to great lengths to make sure no one would call out to me from the kitchen or accidentally let slip that I had the most embarrassing nickname in the world. In high school I put a ban on Poots, the sobriquet by then completely revolting to me, and my parents obeyed, settling on the diminutive of my formal name, Zee, which is also what Rashid and all my school friends and even some of the people I knew in college and graduate school called me.

It was at some point in the first hours of your coming to Chittagong that I told you my nickname. You said the name aloud to me a few times. Putul, Putul, Putul. Perhaps it was the unfamiliar sound that made it a softer, sweeter word in your mouth, the emphasis on the second syllable, and for you it did not carry the baggage of its meaning in the same way. After hearing you say it, I began to grow fond of the name, and later it even became the way I began to refer to myself. Zee was the girl who married with a gold chain fastened to her head; Putul was the girl who hated the smell of henna on her hands and left home to find a new patch of air among the scrapheap of the world, Putul the bird who flew south in search of a warmer climate and a place to spread her wings.

It was early in the morning when you finally called me back; I was lying in bed and watching the sky brighten through the gauze of my mosquito net. 'Hello,' you said. 'It's Elijah.'

You sounded distant. 'How are you?' you asked, formal.

'I'm well,' I said, trying not to cry.

'I'm sorry it has taken me so long to return your call.'

'Were you busy?'

'No.'

The tone of your voice told me everything. You weren't busy, you were angry. Disappointed. What could I say to you now, knowing that I'd been wrong about you? I started telling you about Dera Bugti, leaving long pauses for you to murmur your sympathy for my failure, for Zamzam, but you didn't. You let the silence sit between us. Then you asked me what I had worn to my wedding, and I described with shame the brocade sari that had hung so heavily on my shoulders and cut into my waist.

'Can I see you?' you asked finally, and we migrated to our laptops and I noticed that you had grown your hair over your ears, and something glinted in the hollow above your collar – a grey, porous stone attached to a leather string around your neck. I was talking to you but I was taking note of all of this, and for some reason I couldn't understand I experienced this alteration as a betrayal, a sign that time had passed, time in which we had done everything but be together. And of course this was my fault. I had married Rashid – all you had done was grow your hair out and put a piece of string through a rock.

It was late by the time we finished talking. I promised to call again the next day. The next day, I had my speech all planned. The first thing I said to you was: 'Please come to Bangladesh.' And you said, 'I don't think so, Zubaida.' I gave you all the arguments I'd prepared: I said it was because of the piano, that you had to hear it for yourself, and that you would never again have the chance to see a piano bolted to the floor of a ship, and then watch that very ship get taken apart. 'That has got to be,' I said to you, 'one of the strangest and weirdest things one could possibly witness.' The sheet music was still there – I had left it exactly as I'd found it, wedged between the keys and the lid. You would have to come and you would have to play that music on that piano. I have no idea what went through your mind, but you resisted for a long time, for the rest of that phone call and the several others that followed, but I kept pressing you, and finally you relented. When you agreed I thought you might fix a date in the distant future, and I was getting ready to argue again, to remind you that the piano may not be on *Grace* for much longer, but you said you would be there the following week. I know now that you are the sort of person who can do that, get up and materialise on the other side of the world on short notice, but at the time I remember being surprised, and then deciding, not for the first time – and certainly not for the last – that everything about you was tinged with magic.

At Chittagong Airport, I watched you help a man manoeuvre a refrigerator-shaped box onto a trolley, then lift your own suitcase from the carousel and drag it behind you. You were easy to spot through the panels of glass that separated the arriving people from the waiting people on the other side. You wore a shirt with a round collar and those same loose trousers I had seen on you that first day. You were walking through customs when an officer looked you up and down and motioned you over to a desk. Worried you'd be stopped, I made my way towards you and waved my arms.

You looked up and met my eyes through the glass. The customs officer put his hands deep into your suitcase and began to remove your things. A pair of trousers. A T-shirt. He opened the zippered case of your toiletries bag. Toothpaste. You were beautiful. That's all I could think as you held my gaze, tilting your head to the side. Smiling hello. A sandal. A square package wrapped in red tissue. You tried to stop him but he shook his head, tore open the gift.

Dark blue silk melted out of the paper and onto his hand. Embarrassed, he passed it to you. You turned and held it up, showing it was for me. I smiled. Thank you. Three paperbacks. Underwear. A linen shirt. The other sandal. My heart was exploding in my chest. Shampoo. At the bottom of the suitcase the officer found a heavy container with a green cap. He pulled it out and thrust it at you. You tried to explain. The officer shook his head. You held up your hands. Wait, please. You twisted off the cap. Lifted the jug and poured a little of the contents into the upturned cap. An offering. What's happening? Wait, please. You gestured to the officer to put his finger into the liquid and taste. He did. You smiling. The officer smiling. Screwing the lid back on the jug. Patting each other on the back. Tucking a strand of hair behind your ear. Repacking your suitcase. A pair of trousers. T-shirt. Toothpaste. Sandals. A silk blouse. Maple syrup. I watched you put everything back in its place, pull the zipper back around the suitcase and start walking towards me.

I had practised again and again what would happen when you arrived. What we would say to each other. I believed the time that had passed had made us both more distant and more intimate, the trick of a long separation and those cryptic song titles. But when I caught sight of you, gesturing to me through the glass, I was struck with the one thing I had not rehearsed, the one thing that was entirely unanticipated. I had practised warmth, I had practised small talk, a little awkwardness, and, yes, also disappointment (a person thought of so often, and used in my imagination in such diverse ways, how could he measure up?), but I had not practised what occurred, which was this: terror. When I saw you, I felt you were coming to me after the separation of war, a feeling at once desperate, pathetic, stomach-churning, want-heavy, and entirely unwelcome. It wasn't possible, it couldn't be, to fear someone so much, to be sickened, at the very moment of their arrival, at the prospect of their ever going away again. As you approached me, I thought of being apart from you, that I would never be able to tolerate that again, that the distance between us right now, the several feet, was horrible, and as the space narrowed, as your face came into focus, there was a lightness on the horizon of my vision, the sensation of floating, your image multiplying as my eyes watered from longing to see you more; and then, the collision of our bodies as you hugged me over the railing that divided us.

I was trained in the art of keeping up appearances, and I wonder if you knew, when I greeted you politely, that I wanted to dig my fingernails into your bearded cheeks. I may have told you later that when you leaned over the railing and hugged me that I had the urge to blame you for everything that had occurred in the last year, because if it hadn't been for you, I would have been a happier person, but that in your presence, happiness was immaterial – you had taken that away from me. But I didn't say any of that. I believe I displayed all the appropriate reactions, keeping my fists to myself, words hidden under my tongue, fingernails safely away from your cheeks.

'Hello,' I said, inhaling your shoulder, the hair tucked behind your ear.

We had to walk side by side for a long time until the divider ended. Then you pointed to one of the plastic chairs. 'Let's sit here for a moment. Hello.' You took both my hands and pressed them together between your palms. I was aware of the size of you, of your physical presence that seemed to make everything else shrink. I pulled my hand away, knowing people would stare, and when I tried to look down at the floor, which was littered with cigarette butts, your eyes followed me. 'Hello,' you said again.

We remained on the plastic chairs for a few minutes, not speaking. I passed you a bottle of water and you twisted off the cap and held it for a while before taking a sip. Then you straightened, and said, 'I wasn't going to come. I almost turned around at the airport and went home.'

At this moment, Mr Ali walked past us. I stood up and introduced you. He had come to pick up another potential buyer, after the first one, Mr Reza, had commissioned most of equipment on *Grace*, leaving behind the electrical appliances, the furniture, and the piano. You shook hands. My attention drifted for a moment, then I heard you saying, 'And thank you for allowing me to visit your ship.'

'Oh, you are seeing the *Grace*. Miss Zubaida did not tell me.'

I had wanted to bring it up with Ali slowly, once he'd gotten used to the idea of having you around. 'Sorry, Mr Ali – I hope it's all right,' I said. 'My friend is a pianist, so I thought he might like to see the instrument on *Grace*.'

'Yes, yes of course. You are most welcome,' Ali said, holding his hands behind his back. 'But you must give me some time to organise the visit.' I said of course we would wait for his permission. It was his ship, after all.

I had considered meeting you in Dhaka and showing you the sights: Louis Khan's parliament building, full of sharp, grey angles, or the bank of the Buriganga, which had once given Dhaka the ambition of calling itself the Venice of the East; and more personal landmarks, the graveyard where my grandfathers were buried, the fancy school I was admitted to when we moved to Gulshan, but I had decided to meet you in Chittagong instead. When I think about it now, it seems unlikely I would have urged you to visit if I had remained in Dhaka, married or not. It was only in this third place that our meeting, and all that followed, was possible.

We stepped into the heavy damp of the morning, pushing through the crowd until we reached the car. I watched you put your bags into the trunk, and you slipped beside me into the hush of the back seat.

'Thank you,' I said. 'For coming in the end. For not turning around.' And then, because I didn't know what else to say, I asked, 'Did you watch any movies on the plane?'

You pulled a book out of your shoulder bag. *Anna Karenina*.

I realised, at that moment, that you were always going to come, that you had been waiting, all these months, for my invitation.

The car was held up on the link road out of the airport. You rolled down the window and let the air in, thick and warm. A train, painted a long time ago in ivory and blue, clattered past, passengers standing between the carriages and leaning through the bars on the windows. The car moved and you closed the window.

'A lot of things happened,' I said.

'You got married.' Your voice was flat.

'I did. I did.'

The car lurched to a stop again on the turning to Chittagong town. I wanted to sound an apology for rushing into the alliance with Rashid, but if I started apologising I might not be able to stop; I might go on and say sorry for the shabby look of my country, the tacky billboards advertising halal soap and mobile phones and air conditioning, the tangle of the telephone wires that hung between poles on the side of the road, the roads themselves, narrowed by trash and people braiding their edges with their hands out, showing off the empty spaces where their limbs should have been, and the air itself, its smell and texture, heavy with missed chances, everything chipped and messy and never quite beautiful, and I would say sorry for not waiting for you, for not believing in our few days together and assuming it was nothing to you, but if I did that, I would not be able to stop and we would begin and end with nothing but a string of sorrys, and that was precisely why I did not want to be your lover, because everything about my life seemed poor when I looked at it through your eyes.

Instead I sat back in my seat, waiting for the traffic to clear so I could point out some of the landmarks on the way.

As we stopped on the main Chittagong roundabout, I thought about Boils Man, and hoped he wouldn't show up today. Not because you wouldn't be able to handle it, the sight of a naked man with small tumours protruding from every inch of his body, but because you would have to see me turn my face away and refuse to look at him, which would tell you too much – everything, really, about my place in this world.

We stopped, the lights changed, horns blaring behind us.

'Tell me again what happened with your trip to Pakistan,' you said.

As I recounted the story I felt acutely the distance between the moment I had said goodbye to you in Boston, and this moment, all the things that had crowded into those months coming back to me in a rush. Sitting there in the traffic, I felt that *Ambulocetus* couldn't be further away, and when I had been picking at the red sequence in the shale of the Tethys, Cambridge and Shostakovich were only distant memories, and that night when I met you, it was as if my long history with Rashid had never taken place. Every episode of my life seemed to exist in its own articulated space. I wondered what would have happened if I hadn't started thinking about my adoption, if I hadn't met you that evening, if Zamzam hadn't been Didag Baloch's son. I had always told myself that marrying Rashid was an inevitability, but so much had happened to frame that event, so much before and so much after – Prosperity and *Grace* and the pulling crew – that it didn't seem possible that they weren't all occurring as a result of one another.

On the way home, I thought about my dadu, my father's mother. Her name was Mehrunessa Bashir and she was born in a village in Trishal, in Mymensingh District, the fourth of seven children. Her father, a munshi, taught her how to read and write, but, though they weren't poor, no one expected Mehrunessa to remain unmarried past puberty. When she married my grandfather she was thirteen and he was twenty years older, already a practising lawyer. It wasn't until a decade into their marriage that Mehrunessa showed herself to be an exceptional wife. She demonstrated frugality in the administration of the household expenses, spreading the small sum my grandfather brought home every month to stretch between five sons and the various relations who came to live with them. She oversaw the purchase of a small plot of land in the town and moved the family there so that her boys would not have to grow up in the village, where school ended once help was needed in the fields. A few years later, she insisted they move to the capital, even though they could not afford it at the time, and, for the first few years, when her husband's clients were few and far between, Mehrunessa found ways to ride out the lean. My grandfather then became well known for a case he fought against a corrupt judge of the Dhaka High Court, becoming the first Bengali lawyer to successfully sue a British lawmaker.

The memoir he wrote of that trial, *Amar Shikha*, was transcribed and typeset by Mehrunessa, who had an eye for typographic detail that her husband lacked. My grandfather died of liver cancer a few months before the war, so he did not witness the destruction and rebirth of the country. He was not there to bury his youngest son, a revolutionary felled by an enemy bullet, his body carried for miles by his fourth son, my father, and buried in an unmarked grave near the village he helped to liberate. He was not there to see the expansion of the family's fortunes, not there to witness his eldest son become a successful barrister, the house growing to two, then three storeys, and he didn't see the arrival of the film star Shalaila Mehndi, or the marriage of his other sons and the birth of their children, or the arrival of me from an unknown woman's arms. That was all Mehrunessa, growing severe in her old age, as if there was work yet to be done, children yet to raise, boys yet to be turned into men. All her life she had brought my grandfather his morning tray and placed it on the table by his bedside so that the smell of simmering tea would wake him up, and she had watered down his dal so that he could afford it at every meal, and she had made sure his shirts were ironed and his children washed and sent to school, and in every way that can be counted, she was ordinary, doing the things that wives do, resolute, undeterred, a woman made entirely of her time and age, and in this simplicity, she was her own life's magician.

These are the kinds of wives that pre-dated me, Elijah. Invisible, magic-wielding, food-stretching, loyal to the last breath. This is the world you crashed into, not a world with people who behaved exactly as they should – of course they didn't – but who always exceeded what was expected of them, no matter how small their mandates.

We turned onto the highway and I kept glancing over at you to see if I could discern your mood, whether you were angry, or disappointed, wondering if maybe some part of you had thought I hadn't gotten married after all, but I knew now that you hadn't moved on as I'd imagined, that I had betrayed you, and despite all that, here you were, your voice marked by the wound I had inflicted.

I had booked you into a small guest-house near the beach, and I suggested we go directly there in case you wanted to freshen up, but you said you wanted to see the beach first. In the car, I was getting ready to point out the scrap-yards on the highway, but by the time we had wound our way out of the city, you had fallen asleep, your head tucked against the bend of your arm, your mouth slightly open.

When we arrived an hour later, I gave you a small nudge. 'You missed the build-up,' I said. The car passed through the Prosperity gates, and *Grace* appeared in her eerily pristine form, all three thousand feet of her, white and regal.

I was nervous as you stepped out of the car, as if I had to prove it was worth your coming all this way. You shielded your eyes against the glare of the sun, taking in the ships in the adjacent lots, some already in their last weeks of cutting, and the workers, scattered and small.

'This is it,' I said. Together, we looked at *Grace*. A few men were on deck, lowering what appeared to be a bathtub to the crew waiting below. The bathtub, fastened with rope, knocked against *Grace*'s hull as it came down. We watched it hit the sand. The men pulled the ropes away, and then two of them turned it upside down like a canoe and marched it up the beach. They passed us, and I recognised Russel, and called out to him, but he didn't hear me. In the distance, another large object crested *Grace*'s deck.

You put your hands behind your head and gazed up at the sky. 'I don't know what to say. This place needs a new language.'

'Deconstruction won't do?' I joked. But I was relieved, because you could see it too, the scale of what was happening.

'No,' you said. 'Even Derrida would struggle.'

The tide started coming in and before long the water lapped at our sandals. We agreed we should return later, but you didn't move for a long time, your eyes going from *Grace* to me and back again. Then, after a few minutes, we turned together and headed up the beach. 'My mother said to tell you hello,' you said.

'How is your family?'

'They're fine. We haven't seen a lot of each other lately. That's the thing about big families, no one ever assumes you need company.'

'When you're an only child everyone figures you're lonely, but they can't do anything about it. No one can be your sister or your brother.'

You told me you had never thought about it that way. You said your brothers were close, that you saw them often, but that you were the only one who had ever wanted to leave the country.

This surprised me. 'You don't all share the same restless spirit?' I asked.

'They travel,' you said. 'But they don't wish they were somewhere else.'

I had always, I told you, had my adoption to blame on my sense of not belonging. Every time I wanted to do something weird, or if I liked something that my parents didn't – chocolate, for example, Ammoo hated chocolate – I told myself, my mother would have liked chocolate. Not that she probably ever tasted chocolate.

You told me that biology wasn't everything, but that it must be hard, not knowing. And I told you I'd never really thought about it till I met you.

It was lunchtime and I invited you to the apartment for something to eat. It was the first time we were alone, and you were careful not to touch me and I was careful not to touch you. I made elaborate moves so that we weren't in too close proximity to each other. At the dining table I made sure we were across and not beside each other, in case our hands accidentally reached for the same thing and the back of my palm, or a finger, overlapped with the back of your palm or your finger. And yet I thought all the time about what it would be like to hold your hand, to feel the bristles of your cheek against my face. The terror I had felt upon first seeing you at the airport had softened somewhat, but I could still feel it churning away inside me. The more I wanted you the further away I stayed. It wasn't like before, in Cambridge – I was married now, and there were other people to consider – but I wasn't guilty. I can't really explain why, but nothing about it felt wrong, or like I was doing violence to someone else, or that I was breaking a promise I had made. And, anyway, I hadn't done anything, not yet.

We talked endlessly about the strangeness of the place, its ugliness and beauty, how the effluent had turned the sand dark grey, and I told you about the sound of chanting, like a keening, as the men carried the heavy sheets of steel on their shoulders, and the insults they would hurl at each other in order to make it from the carcass of a ship to the rolling machine without giving up and letting the metal crash to the ground.

As the sun set and the light in the apartment turned yellow, then orange, it became easier to be in your presence, and I felt myself relaxing, laughing with you as you narrated a story about your recent attempt to learn the ukulele. Mo arrived to make our dinner, and the two of you played a card game that went late into the night. I had feared Gabriela might resent your presence, but she took to you immediately, and it was as if you had always been there, as if you had nowhere else to be but with me in that shabby apartment by the sea. After Gabriela and Mo had gone to bed, you pulled the blue blouse out of your bag. 'I meant to give this to you earlier,' you said. There was a silk flower on the neckline, and a panel of lighter coloured fabric along the hem. I thanked you, believing it was the most intimate thing anyone had ever given me. I recalled the suitcase full of saris that had arrived from Rashid's house on the morning of our wedding, the matching shoes and handbags, the six sets of jewellery, each in its own velvet case. It was disloyal of me to compare that experience with this one, but I couldn't help myself, trying and failing to stop from imagining what it would have been like with you, wedding and gifts and moving in together and sharing a home, copies of *Anna Karenina* united on a bookshelf.

'Oh, and the maple syrup,' you said. 'Tomorrow I'll make pancakes.'

It was almost already tomorrow. I could smell the heat of the day approaching. You leaned back on the floor cushions and tucked your feet under you. It was too late now for the guest-house so I suggested you get a few hours' sleep. I fetched a blanket and draped it over your legs. Your eyes were heavy and you murmured something about how glad you were that you had come, and before I pulled myself towards you, never again to be free, I retreated to my bedroom and tried to sleep.

We spent the next few days waiting for Ali to give us permission to go aboard *Grace*. The days seemed longer and shorter with you in them; I felt myself doing everything in a hurry and also with a sense of ease, eating meals with you and listening to music on my tiny wireless speaker and watching you make line drawings of *Grace*. We took long walks along the shore, your skin darkening quickly as we made our way past the half-broken ships in the adjacent lots. Mo followed you around everywhere with an expression of glee on his face, as if he had been reunited with a long-lost friend.

You liked to run in the early mornings, and that was how you met a few of the workers. You became known as 'Bharmon', after one of them asked you to tell him what was written on your T-shirt, and not able to pronounce the 'V' of 'Vermont', he spread the word that this was your name, Bharmon. 'Bharmon is from America.' 'Bharmon can play the instrument in the belly of the ship.' 'Bharmon runs all the way across the beach to Patenga.' Now, when I walked down to the shipyard with you, they gathered around, unafraid of Ali. I don't know what you talked about, or even how you communicated, but in your mutual hand gestures there was laughter and camaraderie.

They told you stories about the ship that I hadn't known, for instance, that there had been an ice-skating rink, that three thousand people sat down to dinner every evening and hence there were freezers as big as trucks and pots as big as bathtubs, and that it had all been sold and the only thing remaining was the piano. Nobody wanted it.

Ali telephoned one day to say that one of the buyers was coming to inspect the ship, and they were going to rig a special lift for him, a system of pulleys that would be handled by men from on top and below. We could see the piano, then join Ali and the buyer for lunch. When we arrived at the beach, Ali introduced his guest. 'Please meet Mr Sakhawat Sakhawat,' he said with a small bow.

Sakhawat Sakhawat flashed the gold rings on his fingers and shook hands with you. We crowded onto the flat platform and were lifted up along *Grace*'s hull, the curve of the beach retreating from view, the brackish blue of the Indian Ocean deepening the higher we rose. I noticed little of the scene, however, because your hand was on my elbow and I was aroused by the graze of your knuckle against my rib.

When we reached the top, I held you back and allowed Ali to lead Sakhawat to the staterooms on the top floor. Mo was waiting for us on the promenade deck. He had three kerosene lamps lined up against the railing. I let him lead the way, knowing he would get a thrill from revealing the piano to you. It had been his discovery, after all.

As we made our way across the ship, I noticed a few things missing. All along the deck, the doors had small round gaps in them where the doorknobs used to be. Ali had told me that Harrison Master had asked for a few things from the ship for himself, for a guest-house he needed to furnish on short notice. Perhaps the doorknobs were on that list, or perhaps they were in a hotel in Dhaka somewhere. *Grace* was already being scattered across the country.

We reached the auditorium and Mo disappeared inside. You held the door open for me and we entered together. There was the navy darkness, and the particular scent of wood and velvet. We held up our lamps. 'It's behind the curtain,' I whispered, but you and Mo were already making your way to the stage. I decided to remain in the audience, choosing a seat in the front row and setting my lamp on the floor. Then I closed my eyes and waited, nervous now in the compressed hush of that big and silent room, and it came, the scrape of the piano stool as you sat down, and the first note, like a question mark.

I realised I had never heard you play, not seriously, and I was glad to be listening without seeing you. When the music began, I knew I had heard the song before, but I could not remember now what it was called. You played softly, the sound muffled by the curtain, and occasionally I heard you stop to press down on one of the notes a few times, testing the sound. I thought I heard you humming along with the song, but I couldn't be sure.

You played a scale, and then another song. I might have fallen asleep, not because I was tired, but because it was hypnotic and slightly surreal, sitting in the auditorium of a beached ocean liner listening to the sound of a resurrected piano played by the hands of a man who appeared as if from another world. Then you began to sing. Your voice was soft, cloaked in the dark and muffled by the curtain.

> All of me
> Why not take all of me
> Can't you see
> I'm no good without you

It was so quiet I could almost hear the breath that accompanied each word of the song. I matched my breath with your breath, my head light and without a thought.

> You took the best
> So why not take the rest

Eventually the sound of the notes faded away. I heard the whine of the lid's hinge, heard the scrape of the stool as you pushed away, heard the curtain part, heard your muffled footsteps coming towards me. You weren't with Mo and you weren't holding your lamp. When you sat down beside me, I thought you might say something about the piano, but instead you whispered a story to me about your childhood, something about those two years on the farm, about a rosemary bush your mother had planted outside the kitchen window when you had first moved to that remote part of the country. Sometimes when it rained you leaned out of the window and caught a whiff of that rosemary bush. The house was at the edge of a steep hill, the land falling away from it on three sides, the view of trees and the mountains beyond clear for miles. Then you said, 'When I started playing that piano, it was like the rosemary bush outside our kitchen window. As far as I can tell, everything about home, everything I can remember, comes from that smell, everything human and amazing and old. I'm so glad I came, Zubaida. Thank you for bringing me. Thank you for showing me this.'

I swallowed away the lump rising in my throat and closed my hand around your hand. I was reminded again of your strangeness, and also of the way you were both more sure of yourself than anyone I had ever known and yet also unmoored, as if you had never managed to find something to attach yourself to. You moved your hand and you were touching my elbow, and then my back. I shifted closer to you, wanting to tell you that, however glad you might be that you had come, you couldn't possibly be as glad as I was, because, holding your hand now, I was obliterated by feeling.

I wanted to stay in that room forever, the weight and warmth of your hand on my arm. But a moment later I was suddenly claustrophobic, realising we were trapped in a tight, airless bubble, and so I stood up abruptly and led you out and up the stairs, not quite sure where I was heading, following the air and the light until we were back on the promenade deck.

By the time we emerged, the afternoon was in full force, the sun descending brutally, the workers below huddled in the shadow of the ship, seeking a patch of grey among the bright, bright white. You unbuttoned your shirt and your skin shone between the open panels of fabric. I gestured to the men that they should work the pulleys and we floated down as if from a stage, the real world below us in all its ugliness and sorrow.

Something had happened, something I couldn't name. We walked back up the beach without saying a word. I remembered we were invited to have lunch with Mr Ali. I said maybe I should try and get us out of it.

'We should probably oblige him,' you said. But I saw the pulse leaping at your throat.

Ali had laid out a table on the second floor of the Shipsafe office. There were a number of meat and fish dishes, each one topped with a slick puddle of oil. Sakhawat was already seated with a full serving in front of him. Ali piled rice onto our plates and we helped ourselves to the curry. There were no utensils and I saw you making tiny pyramids of rice and placing them carefully into your mouth.

'Mr Ali, what will happen to the piano?' you asked.

'It wasn't possible to sell it.' Ali said. 'No one wanted such a big thing.'

'What will you do?' I wondered aloud.

Sakhawat licked the grease from his knuckle. 'We could give it to one of the shops, see if they can sell it. But it would be very costly to get it out of the ship. There is a chance of damage.'

'It's a very precious instrument,' you said.

Ali motioned for one of his men to clear the plates away. 'We will do our best,' he said. The man returned a few moments later with a bowl of water and a bar of soap and we all washed our hands.

'There was a storm once,' Sakhawat said, 'out of season. And the water came in so high it flooded all the ships. There was a whale trapped in one of Haroon's ships, you remember that, Ali?'

'A whale?' I said.

'It was the cyclone in '91, a long time ago,' Ali said. 'A lot of people died. Strange things washed up on shore. One of the neighbouring shipyards had just bought a cruiser, like *Grace*, and the thing was trapped in the swimming pool.'

'What happened to it?'

'Nothing we could do,' Ali said. 'It died a few days later.'

'People came from all over to see it. It was thrashing around, skin all dried up. Making horrible noises.' Sakhawat made a gesture with his hands to illustrate the whale's suffering, pinching his thumb and forefinger together.

I wished Sakhawat and Ali had not told me this story. Sakhawat replaced the gold rings on his stubby fingers and leaned back on the chair with a soft belch. The stranded animal was probably something smaller than a whale, maybe an Irrawaddy dolphin from upstream, or perhaps it was a short-finned Pilot whale. I tried not to imagine the end of its life, the people staring down as it struggled in the shallow water, its blowhole wheezing and squeezing shut. I glanced over at you and found that you were swallowing this story and that it was changing your relationship to this place, making it more terrible, and yet somehow enchanted, a place where people tore ships apart and whales died in swimming pools and tides threw up the trash of the entire world.

That night, you accompanied me to the dormitory for my next set of interviews. The men were happy to see you, shaking your hand and offering you a share of the cigarette they were passing around. You let them light it for you and you took a drag and then you sat among them on their bunks instead of beside Gabriela and me. We set up our equipment and the light from Gabriela's camera illuminated the room.

'It's my turn,' Mo said.

I was surprised. Mo had avoided all of my questions, and Gabriela's, about his childhood, only informing us that his parents were dead and that he had grown up on the beach. 'Tell us,' I said. 'Start with where you were born.'

'Story is not about me.'

'It's about his girlfriend!' Belal said, snapping his fingers.

'You have a girlfriend?' I asked. I looked over at you and you kept your gaze steady on Mo. Mo didn't answer yes or no to the question about his girlfriend, he just said, 'Her name is Shona. She lives with a man.'

'What kind of man?'

'A bad man.'

'Can you tell us more?'

'Madam sold her. Now she has to live with the man. He beats her, I saw the cut on her face.' He drew a finger across his cheek.

'He's lying,' Belal said.

'He's always making up stories,' another of the crew said.

Mo shook his head. 'It's true,' he said. 'I want to kill him.' He stood up, made a stabbing gesture. He stood over Belal and pulled at the loose collar of his singlet. 'I want him to be dead.' We watched as he made his way from one of the men to the next. 'Like this!' he said, his hand wrapped around an imaginary knife, going up, going down.

Once, when I had asked Ali how Mo had come to live on the beach, he said simply that there were worse fates for a boy, and I assumed that meant Ali considered himself to have rescued Mo from somewhere else.

'Sit down, Mo,' I said. 'Tell us about your friend.'

'Her mother died and left her with the madam.'

'Did you know your mother?' I asked.

He stopped, his hand in mid-air. 'My mother was a whore.'

'Don't insult your mother,' someone said.

'No one believes anything that comes out of your mouth,' another one said. 'Remember that time he claimed his father was an English captain? What, no English ever came to claim him.'

A murmur travelled around the room. Mo stood in the middle of the circle, his hand still clenching the imaginary knife. 'I never lie,' he said, raising the pitch of his voice. 'I never lie!'

At that moment, you stood up, walked over to Mo, picked him up, and carried him out of the room. Gabriela emerged from behind her camera. She wiped her face. 'I can't take it any more,' she said, pulling the camera off the stand. 'This place is hell.'

I tried to start up the conversation again, but no one wanted to talk, and after a few minutes I shut off my tape recorder and followed you out to the beach. You and Mo were sitting on a small raised sandbank and staring out at *Grace*, not saying anything. Gabriela and I joined you. The sand was cool and packed tight beneath us. We watched the sparks from the night crew's blowtorches, listened to the waves breaking and retreating. Finally, I suggested we go home. It was late. You stood up, brushing the sand from your trousers, but Mo seemed reluctant to move. 'We'll join you later,' Gabriela said, taking Mo's hand, and so we left them together and made our way to the apartment.

When we got home you disappeared into the bathroom. By the time you emerged, I had heated some rice and dal on the stove and brought everything to the table. Your cheeks and your chin were pale and shining. 'You shaved,' I said. 'Why?'

You held both of my hands and directed me to the sofa. 'Come, sit with me,' you said. Your face appeared naked before me. I could see everything when you swallowed, the motion of your jaw and your neck and your Adam's apple. I was amazed by your mouth, which was beautifully pink. You leaned towards me and I closed my eyes, waiting for the touch of your lips, anticipating the heat of your breath floating over my face, but you didn't kiss me, you just pressed the side of your face against the side of my face. The smell of soap was overpowering. I opened my eyes and saw over your shoulder to the rough metal bars on the windows, the frayed paint on the shutters, the rusted latches. Now your chin was resting on my shoulder, and my chin was resting on your shoulder. Your hair was soft against my mouth. I opened my mouth and took a strand between my teeth. My mouth filled with saliva. 'Elijah,' I said. 'I'm in love with you.'

Later, after I drove you from the beach, after everything had ended so terribly between us, I thought back to that night and remembered everything about the way you held me, and kissed me, and fluted your breath across my fingers, that you traced the line of my jaw with your hand, that your hair swung down onto my skin and touched me before your mouth touched me. I remembered the words we said to each other. Telling you there was nothing in the world except that I loved you. I remembered laughing. I remembered the weight of your palms on my palms. I didn't remember speaking. I didn't remember being sad. I remembered crying. When you cried, I licked the salt from your chin. I remembered the edge of your thumbnail, inadequately trimmed, scraping a tender patch on the inside of my thigh. I remembered the inside of my thigh. Hello, inside of my thigh. Hello, Zubaida, Putul, Abbasid princess, orphan, provenance unknown. Hello Mrs Rashid, meet the inside of your thigh, meet your mate, this man, only this man, your only mate in the world, your only relation, because you know no one whose blood matches your blood, well, here is a man whose presence obliterates the need for blood, because you are made of the same things, you are nothing and everything alike, because your taste in his mouth is all the closeness you will ever need, the bed is hard beneath your bodies, the bed of a person who has never left this country, the smell of this country is the smell of the sun on the paddy, were your parents farmers or beggars and were there children after you, sons, maybe, that they kept? You don't know and you don't care. You want to find your parents. You want to say sorry to your parents. You want to say sorry to yourself, and to this man, because you loved him from the first moment that you met, but you turned away from this certainty and sank your hopes into history, and now there is nothing except holding him, and kissing him, and fluting your breath across his fingers.

Afterwards, I said, 'Tell me what to do.'

You turned your mouth towards my ear and spoke so softly I could hardly hear you. 'I can't.'

'Please, love me.'

'I love you desperately.'

'Then tell me.'

'I'm not going to do that, Putul.'

I leaned back and examined your face. There was so much more of you, the skin around your mouth clear so I could see the tiny green flecks where your beard used to be.

'Why not?'

'Because it has to be you.'

I closed my eyes again and pressed my mouth against you. You were holding me now, and stroking my hair, and telling me I was the love of your life, and my blood burned when I heard your words, burned under my cheek where I felt your face against mine, and on my shoulder that had housed your chin, and where you had whispered, that place between my neck and my ear, that was scorched too.

Because I was in love with you, I absolved myself of the feeling of wrongdoing, even though I knew I was betraying Rashid with every hammer of my pulse. Because I was in love with you, I told myself things would work themselves out. Or perhaps I didn't think about it at all, because we created a closed world between us, and there was no one else in that world, not even our other selves who might have raised a finger of doubt.

We couldn't bear to be apart. We got up to eat and change the music on my laptop. Mo left things for us on the dining-room table, and when he came back they were eaten and there would be some money left for him to go shopping. 'Let's go somewhere,' you said. 'Okay, let's go. Let's go to the Hill Tracts.' We would hire a car. You need permission to go to the Hill Tracts, Bilal at the Shipsafe office said.

I telephoned Rashid. 'You sound happy,' he said. I told him yes, I was. I was eager to get off the phone, but he told me a long story about dinner with his Chinese partners. I would see him in a few weeks, when he was back from Shanghai. 'Za-jian,' I said, remembering the greeting from my undergraduate Mandarin class, feeling clever and immortal and like I was on top of the world.

What will you do? You, the other, didn't ask. Instead, you sent me messages, sometimes from the other room, or from the beach where you were running. *Black is the Colour of My True Love's Hair*. And: *Feeling Good*. And: *All the Things You Are*. I had trouble replying. Once, I wrote: *I Wish I Knew What It Is to Be Free*.

I told Bilal I needed a few days off. We went to Foy's Lake and convinced one of the boatmen to remain on shore while you rowed. 'I was on the crew team in college,' you said. 'What, a hippy like you?' But you steered the boat expertly, keeping your eyes trained on me as you moved your arms in large, even circles. We stopped in front of a set of stone steps that led out of the lake and into the forest beyond. 'Shall we get out?' 'Of course.' The dangers of the jungle were nothing against the force of our bond. After a few minutes the trees closed behind us and you kissed me while mosquitoes hummed in my ear. I didn't care, even this sounded to me like music. 'Let's get out of town. We'll pretend we're married. Let's get married.' I looked down at my wedding ring.

After a week, Gabriela insisted I continue with some of the work we had begun, so I left you at the apartment with Mo while I collated my interviews and detailed the ongoing destruction of *Grace*. On one or two evenings Mo and I had our meetings in the dormitory with the pulling crew. At night, you and I behaved as if we were free to do whatever we liked, free to kiss in public or marry each other or just do what people did these days, fall out as easily as we had fallen in. We said nothing to each other about when we would meet again, or under what circumstances, but our fantasies carried us out of Prosperity, out of Chittagong and Bangladesh and out of this hemmed-in moment. You insisted on making no plea to me about Rashid. You would say things to me like 'If you think these pancakes are good, you should sample the ones my father makes. When you come to Vermont, you can try them.' Or 'Let's go to Paris.' Or 'Should we have three children, or four?' And 'What do you think about a bathtub at the foot of our bed?' Instead of 'Why don't you leave your husband and marry me?' When I asked, you just repeated what you had said to me that first night, that I had to decide, that everything was up to me. You said I would have to have the will. This terrified me, and I didn't bring it up again.

There were things about you that I noted would annoy me later. Your feet smelled vinegary. There were towels draped over the backs of chairs and glasses half full of water on the floor by the bed. You would get engrossed in what-ever you were reading, or listening to, or you would plug in your headphones and run your fingers along the chipped edge of the dining table, and I would suddenly cease to exist, and because I had been in your orbit just moments ago, this would feel like a slight, and I would be jealous of your book, your headphones, the chipped edge of the dining table. After we undressed, out of habit I reached over to play some music, and you stopped me. Everything was embarrassing to me and nothing to you. You didn't care if Gabriela could hear us, or if I spied you from an unattrac-tive angle. There was no music to float between us, caulking an awkward moment. And you said things. Out loud. Not loving, tender things, but particular things about the particular act and my particular body and its parts.

There had been no sex education in my life. They didn't teach us at school, and my mother was prudish on the matter. I thought sex was pornography. Or the other thing, whispering and moaning while the slap and shuffle of bodies was muted by the blanket pulled over your head. Actually, it was the saddest thing in the world. Afterwards, I thought I would die.

Whatever I'd been doing before couldn't be called sex any more. Or maybe what you and I were doing couldn't be called sex – I wasn't experienced enough to know the difference. All the same, things happened. Unbuttoning. The graze of cheeks, one bristly, one smooth. Tongues. Orgasms. But it wasn't anything like the familiar motions I had made before. It was whatever made all the blood rush to the lower half of my body, whatever made me dream of your mouth, whatever made me want to say the word 'pussy', whatever put the scent of you in my head like a song I can't shake when I am trying to devise a taxonomy for whale bones, whatever that is. Call it love. Call it insanity. Call it coming home for the first time. Call it my mother, living in my blood. I am yours and you are mine. Call it the beginning of the world. The sex was everything and it was nothing, only a small fragment of the whole, magnificent truth of it.

When the weekend came around again we took a bus to Noakhali, crossing the Brahmaputra to Bhola, then on to Khulna, where we found a boat bound for the Sundarbans. It did not occur to me until the moment we boarded that I might be recognised, but there were only tourists: a group of Korean men who worked in a glass factory in Chittagong, an elderly German couple, a Swedish diplomat and his family.

You paid attention to every small thing about me, every scar, every pucker of my skin. We slept together in the lower bunk of the tiny cabin and I felt you breathing into my ear all night and when one of us wanted to turn around we would both have to turn, because the bed was so narrow. You held me and stroked my hair and sometimes, after we made love, you would cry softly into my shoulder. When the boat stopped at the mouth of the Bay of Bengal, we were ferried down a tributary and led through a patch of trees to a beach with black sand. I rolled up my trousers and waded into the water. You tore off your shirt and disappeared underwater. I thought almost constantly of your death, that if you were in a plane crash or if you had a heart attack on your way home, no one would think to tell me. I would have been the closest person in the world to you, but no one would have known it. You repeated this to me every day. You said, 'You're the closest person in the world to me.'

We came back from the Sundarbans with plastic bottles of forest honey, promising to write to the German couple. 'Let's get an email address,' you said. 'That way we can write to people together. As one.'

Despite all of this, you were a stranger to me. When I asked you what the future held, your answers were baffling. You were still not sure if you wanted to return to graduate school. You said you wanted to make a collage replica of the Liberty Bell. A sculpture out of captured air from every country in the world. You wanted to write a piece of music that would sound the same whether you played it forwards or backwards. You wanted to sing a different song to me every morning when I woke up, all beginning with the sentence 'Your mouth smells like honey.' You wanted to play the piano for forty-eight hours straight. You wanted to have twelve children and name them after jazz musicians. You wanted to learn Bangla and watch the films of Satyajit Ray in their original language. You wanted to crowdstitch a piece of cloth that went all the way around the world.

Your intensity was contagious, and when I was with you I was brighter and smarter and everything about the world was terrifying, because it was all possible, and this made the prospect of parting with you seem violent, and also a little comforting, because who could live like that all of the time, sick with wanting, everything but the two of us dull and irrelevant?

On the bus back from Khulna, I felt a tiredness in my legs, the last two weeks coming back to me in slow motion. Days in bed. The mangrove, the guides pointing out *Orcaella brevirostris*, the pink river dolphins that swam beside the boat, and the crocodile we saw sunning itself on the bank of a tributary. You had a habit of waking up early, though through silent agreement you were always back in bed before I got up. 'I went for a run,' you would say, or 'I was meditating.' The hair on the back of my head was matted and tangled. You have a love dreadlock, you said, carefully pulling out the knots with a comb and a small dish of coconut oil.

You frequently mentioned the piano. You believed it was built in a factory in Queens between the two world wars – the best Steinway years, in your opinion; it had a warm, milky tone you had never heard before. Wasn't there some way we could get the piano out of *Grace* to restore it properly? With a lot of care, the instrument could be returned to its original sound, the one it was meant to produce, a timbre that contained all of its history, its travels across continents and decades, enduring the tides of oceans and time.

I asked you why you loved me and you said love's arguments are always teleological. You love someone because you already love them. You love their particular qualities, because you love them in the wholeness of their being. And because you love them in the wholeness of their being, you love the things about them that wound you.

You quoted Rumi: 'The wound is where the light enters you.'

'This was a more complicated answer than I bought,' I said. 'I was going for the five-dollar answer.'

'The five-dollar answer is: I don't know. But I love you despite, perhaps because, you break my heart.'

'If you had a choice, perhaps you would choose to love another person. A better person.'

'Maybe.'

One day, I suggested I might be able to meet you in Cambridge in the fall. I could go back and talk to my adviser, figure out if there were some way to write up the *Ambulocetus* data without access to the fossil itself. We were in the middle of a card game. You threw the cards on the table and I thought it meant the game was over and you had won, but instead you went into the bedroom and slammed the door. When I followed, I found you inside the mosquito net with the sheet pulled over your face.

'What's going on?'

'Get out,' you said.

'I haven't done anything,' I said. I knew, as the day of your departure approached, that it was getting harder for you. 'But I'm sorry anyway.'

You dragged the sheet away and sat up. 'What did you think was going to happen when you made me come?'

'I don't know.' I had taken off my wedding ring and stuffed it into the back of my underwear drawer, but I often caught you glancing at the pale double band of skin that marked where they had been. I don't know what I thought was going to happen. We didn't utter the word 'divorce'.

The faces of my parents and Rashid and Dolly and Naveed were all blank, everyone a ghost except you. 'I just wanted to see you, to be near you.'

'Don't ruin it,' you said.

'How am I ruining it?'

'I'm not having an affair with you.'

'What do you think this is?'

'This can't be what we're doing, Zubaida.' Your lips were drawn tight around your mouth, and I could tell you were trying to keep from shouting at me. 'It has to be better than that.'

'You never propose an alternative. You never say, "Come to Cambridge, we'll live together on Prospect Street, I'll play the piano at Ryles, you can teach, we'll buy brownie mix at Trader Joe's." Why don't you do that? Paint a picture, Elijah. Tell me what it's going to be like.'

I hadn't known, until that moment, how much I had resented your not doing all that work for me – making it real, making it comfortable. I was raising my voice now, and for a minute, as you moved inside the mosquito net, I thought you might climb out of there and leave the room and run away from me, but you pounded your fist against the pillow so hard that the whole room seemed to shake, so I went in after you and lay down on top of you while you sobbed, my hands braided through your hair.

We argued again the next day, about Mo. I had seen the way his eyes followed you around the room, the way he mouthed words after you had said them. He arrived to make lunch for us and there was something about the way he held himself that seemed defeated, as if he had just failed an exam or lost his favourite trinket – I knew he liked to hoard things he found on the ships, that he had a collection of tiny objects, a brass compass, the cap of an expensive

285

pen, the broken clasp of a necklace – so I asked if I could help him prepare the food. When he hesitated, I confessed I was a terrible cook, and he relented then and gave me some instructions, showing me how to cut the okra diagonally while he peeled a small pumpkin.

We worked together in silence for a while. Then Mo said, 'Will you and Bharmon get married soon?'

His delicate elbows were resting against the sink. I said: 'In foreign, people don't marry so quickly.'

'In Desh they do.'

'You want to get married someday?'

He blushed. He had recently shaved his head, and I saw the colour rising up around his neck and his small, pointed ears. 'As soon as I can marry her, I will,' he said. I asked him to tell me who, but he refused. He passed me a bigger knife. 'Apa, now cut the begun,' he said, passing me an eggplant. Then he squatted in front of the black stone pestle and began crushing an onion. As I began working on the eggplant, he said, 'You lived in bidesh?'

'For a long time, yes. I was a student in America.'

He finished the onion and started on another, passing the heavy black rolling pin over it and pulling it back towards himself, back and forth, till it disintegrated into a pale lilac mush. His eyes watered, and he moved his head so he could brush his face against his shirt. 'I want to go there,' he said. 'Do you think Bharmon will take me?'

'I don't know.'

'He said he loved my cooking.'

I started to understand something. I left the eggplant and crouched beside him. 'I don't think so,' I said, noticing how small his arms were compared with the rolling pin, how narrow his feet as they rested against the stone. 'It's very difficult to take people to foreign.'

'He called me "brother".'

I wanted to tell him that I knew the feeling exactly, the feeling of being at the centre of your world, that your hunger seemed insatiable and particular, that I too was in its thrall, and also afraid of where it would lead me.

Mo was crying openly now, and I went back to my eggplant to give him a moment of privacy. He leaned forward on the stone, pulverising one onion after another. Then he scooped everything into a bowl and lit the stove, working quickly, not bothering to wipe his face.

I wondered what I might offer Mo at this moment, something to make up for having taken away his trip to America. 'Do you know reading, Mo?' I asked. He stopped stirring and turned around to face me.

'No.'

'You never went to school?'

'No schools around here.'

'I'll teach you,' I said. 'We'll start tonight.'

He started to cry again. I felt the urge to hug him, but I sensed for some reason that this would not be what he wanted, so I just kept my eyes on him as he finished the cooking and put the curries into bowls and set the table.

The food was very spicy and I could hardly eat it, but you didn't seem to notice, crowding the dishes onto your plate. I wasn't hungry anyway. Mo came around and poured water into our glasses. When you thanked him, he slipped into the kitchen without replying. 'Is there something wrong with Mo?' you asked.

'He thought you were taking him to America.'

'Really? Oh.' You were getting good at eating with your fingers, mixing, as I had instructed you, each dish with a little rice.

'What did you say to him?'

'Nothing. I mean, nothing intentional. But maybe I should've been more careful.' You licked the tips of your fingers. 'I could, you know.'

'You could what?'

'I could take him with me.'

It was just like an American. You had probably never lined up outside an embassy, wondering whether your visa application would be rejected, never listened to your friends plotting the various ways they could get out of the country for good, never had that sinking feeling in the pit of your stomach when you produced your green leather passport to an immigration official at a foreign airport.

'You'd have to adopt him or something.'

'I know.'

I took a long sip of water. 'No, you don't. You don't know anything.'

You looked down at your empty plate. 'If you're trying to tell me I'm ignorant about what it's like to come from here, you're right. But don't doubt my intentions.'

'You make everything sound so easy when it's not.'

'Sometimes we think things are difficult – impossible – but we just have to do them.'

Of course you were talking about me. But how could you know whether it would be easy or hard when no one had ever had any expectations of you, when your parents didn't mind if you dropped out of graduate school or never had a career or married some strange girl you met at a concert? 'You don't know anything about me,' I said. 'Not the first thing.'

'You have more will than you give yourself credit for.'

'Because I'm a little orphan girl who made her way into the light?' And this, of course, was my way of telling you what I was really afraid of – not the disapprobation of

Rashid or Dolly or Bulbul, but that I would lose my parents, the family I had neither earned nor deserved, everything, really, that my life was based on. But I didn't say this out loud, I just assumed you knew, and later when there came to be nothing but a thick silence between us, I wished I had made myself clearer. I wished I had told you that I had lived my life in fear that they would somehow take me back to where I was from, return me, that though I'd been loved and cherished by them my whole life, I had never been able to surrender the suspicion that they might, someday, change their minds.

I found you awake in the middle of the night. 'I can't sleep,' you said. 'You married him. Why did you do that?'

'Rashid and I were practically married anyway.'

The moon was behind you and I saw the outline of your face but not the expression on it. 'Fuck you.'

I had never heard you say that word in an angry way, only a loving one.

'I had a whole life before you, Elijah.'

'You broke my heart. Back there in Cambridge. I won't let you do it again.'

'How am I doing it now?'

'I shouldn't have come,' you said. 'And we should never have taken it this far.

My instinct was to argue that I hadn't cheated on you; we had never promised each other anything: my engagement to Rashid pre-dated whatever it was that had happened between us, and that if anyone had a right to accuse me of betrayal, it was him. But that wouldn't have been entirely honest of me. Of course we had made promises. That day together in Cambridge, walking along Mass Ave, the Glass Flowers, your grandmother's funeral – it was all one long preamble to a pact. That was why I had vowed to remake myself in Dera Bugti, why I had waited with my heart in my stomach for every message you sent me, why I had taken it so badly when Zamzam was arrested and the dig was cancelled. It was because I knew, from the first note the pianist played after the intermission, that you would become the promise that overcame all my other commitments. I had cheated on you by getting married, and now I had to break everything apart in order to remedy that. I threw my arms around you and buried my head in your neck, your piney scent still lingering on your skin though it was tamped down by the sea, the damp heat of early summer, and I repeated, again and again, how sorry I was to you, meaning also that I was sorry to myself, to the whole enterprise of our togetherness. But there was only one thing I could say that would make it right. 'I'll do it,' I said. 'I'll tell him. As soon as he's back from China, I'll tell him everything.'

Some part of you didn't believe me, I know that, but the rest of you wanted to so badly that you accepted my promise and allowed yourself to return my embrace, and for that moment, we were fully together, neither one of us the guilty, neither one of us the wounded.

Looking for Mother

You will, of course, have remembered all of this yourself. But I write it to you now so that you know that it is burned onto my memory, every moment, every word of it. And if, by chance, your regard for me has sunk so low that you have pushed all thoughts of me out of your mind, that you have forced yourself to forget, I am here to remind you. We were in love. We were real. There were witnesses, and I am one of them.

I am at Bettina's house for Christmas. It's a modest townhouse in Astoria with a tiny front lawn and neighbours who have known the family since they first moved in four decades ago. From the little guest-room on the top floor, I can smell the malty flavour of the turkey and the bacon that is draped across its breast. Bettina's mother tells me I need to eat, and I am reassured by this echo of mother talk, the same words I hear from Ammoo and Bashonti when I am at home in Dhaka.

My father lived in New York once. He moved here after the war and drove a taxi and shared a room above a restaurant in Jackson Heights with a Bangladeshi man named Asif who told him never to take a fare above 116th Street. 'Black people are all criminals,' he said. My father had been in a war, and this made him unable to take such statements seriously. He soon befriended George, who also drove a cab and sometimes ordered eggs at the counter of the diner where my father picked up his morning coffee (an acquired taste, this, but one he had come to love). George had black and grey dreadlocks down to his waist and wore a tweed jacket with leather elbow patches. He lived in Flatbush, in a house he shared with a dozen or so other people. They had a dish rota and read aloud to one another every evening after dinner, which they cooked using vegetables they grew in the back garden. When my father visited, a young woman answered the door and said 'Namaste' with her hands folded, and my father was going to explain to her that in his part of South Asia they didn't say 'Namaste' but 'As-salaam walaikum', but then he realised, when the doorbell rang again and she greeted another person, this time a young man in a beard, that she used this word to greet anyone, not just someone who looked like he knew what it meant, and he couldn't decide whether this lack of specificity was good or bad. Later, he read a few stanzas of Nazrul's *Bidrohi* to the assembled group, which included an assortment of people who could be loosely classified as hippies.

I am the rising, I am the fall,
I am consciousness in the unconscious soul . . .

I am the rebel eternal,
I raise my head beyond this world . . .

Afterwards several people came and hugged my father. This was the first time since he had arrived in America that he had been touched with such affection. The embrace made him cry, because he had never mourned his brother, who had died before his eyes on the battlefield. He considered leaving the apartment in Queens, the smell of cigarettes and homesickness and people wearing too many layers in November. But that night, when he went home, he heard Bangla in the corridors of the building, and he knew he had to stay, so he settled for spending weekends with George, listening to Joni Mitchell on the reel-to-reel, planting a banana tree in the sunny part of the garden. Slowly, the wound of his brother's death began to heal. He wrote long letters to his mother, composed while stuck in rush-hour traffic, taught the hippies to play cricket, and even brought his roommate, Asif, to the commune, where he sat uncomfortably on the edge of a patchouli-scented sofa and listened while the group chanted 'Om.' By now, my father had been in America for four years, and his visa was about to expire. He considered going home, but he was too ashamed to admit that he had done nothing but drive a taxi the entire time he had been in New York. His brother had set up a successful brick-making factory on the banks of the Buriganga, and he knew he would get roped into joining him if he went home without a purpose. He brought the problem to his few acquaintances. George told him to consider the political implications of choosing to participate in the military-industrial complex by remaining in New York. His landlord, the owner of the restaurant downstairs, offered him a share in the new branch he was planning to open in Alphabet City, his first in Manhattan. It was Asif who suggested to my father that, if he wanted to extend his time in America and take advantage of the opportunities in the land of opportunity – which he had not yet begun to do on account of his planting things and teaching people the correct way to bowl a cricket ball – the easiest thing for him to do would be to get married. There were networks for such things, people who knew people who knew people. But my father did not want an anonymous match. He gave himself three weeks to fall in love. He walked up and down the streets and tried to look into the hearts of the women he passed. He glimpsed into the rearview mirror at his customers. He glanced to the left and right of himself on the counter at the diner. But there was no one. No one would look my father in the eye. At the commune, the Namaste girl offered to marry him, and he refused politely. Finally, George introduced him to a friend, a rich Uptown girl who wanted to say fuck you to her parents. They got married in the back yard of the commune, flanked by the banana tree and the upright vines of tomatoes without a single relation on either side. Later, after my father decided he wanted to return to Bangladesh after all, his memories of the war now tamed, he was not saddened by the divorce, or by the letting go of his beloved taxi, or by moving out of the apartment he shared with Asif, but by George, who cried and said, 'Man, you are a strange kind of people,' and gave him a copy of *Another Country* to take with him on the long journey home.

Does this explain my behaviour? No. I did not live above a restaurant in Jackson Heights. I did not drive people around in a taxi and wait tables and save every bit of money I earned. My father erased his history behind him and made everything in my life easy. But, when I thought about it, this story gave me permission to make excuses to myself: I was not the only one who had married to solve a problem.

You wanted to play the piano one last time. 'Can you take me up on the ship again?' you asked Mo.

We went to the beach together. *Grace* was starting to look battered. Her hull had been breached; just that morning, the cutters had sliced off a rectangular section of her starboard side. There was no way Ali would allow us on board now. You and Mo made plans to sneak in. Mo described the exact route – he had taken it many times when scavenging on *Grace*. Not for the first time I realised Mo had a life beyond our gaze, that I should work harder to find out which of his stories were true and which were made up. But like so much else in my life, it didn't seem urgent. All I could think about was you, and thinking about you was also thinking of myself, of what I would do with you, and when I look back I think of it as a selfish time, a time when I put myself at the centre of the universe, and perhaps that is what love is, a moment of abnegation as well as a moment of greed, a person at once invisible and fully present to the rest of their lives.

Because one side of *Grace*'s hull was now cut away, we did not have to be pulleyed up to the deck in order to board her. We followed Mo to a rope ladder that had been hung out of one of the lower elevations of the ship, and once we had climbed on board we followed a complicated route through the remaining corridors and stairways, till finally we crossed what looked like a bridge, but must have been a gangway, into a section that I could recognise as the level that had housed the auditorium. Our voices echoed against the steel, our footsteps clanging like bells. The door to the auditorium was gone – now it was just a hole cut out of the shell of the ship. The chairs had been pulled up, the carpets stripped away. The shape of the proscenium arch survived, but not the wood that had framed it. The curtains were gone, but the stage remained, with the piano legs still fixed onto its surface, as if it had survived a bombing, black and gleaming and the only flash of shine remaining on this canvas of rust.

The piano stool had disappeared so you played standing up, leaning over the keys with your arms outstretched. I heard the familiar notes, the scale rising and rising. Variation 13. Little twists, an error here and there, places where you paused – it didn't come naturally to you, Bach in the hands of a jazz pianist – but it was beautiful imperfection. Mo stood beside me and I slipped my arm around his shoulders, the music and the dark giving us permission to touch as if we were brother and sister, equal to each other in our love for you.

Even to my untrained ear, I could tell the piano did not sound as it should. In that way, I thought, it was very much like you and me. Every day that passed, we were exposed a little further to the elements, every day we became a bit more fragile, showing how easily we might be destroyed. How much we needed to be saved.

On the day of your departure we looked at the photographs we had taken together. There was an image of you leaning against the knotted roots of *Heritiera fomes*, the Sundri tree. The dark blue light of the forest cast a deep melancholy on your features, your usually bright eyes half closed, your lips pressed together without a smile. There were happier poses, you holding the oars at Foy's Lake, you and Mo making sand angels on the beach, you and me up close, just an arm's length from the camera, that first time we boarded *Grace,* but that one was my favourite because you were offering to leave a little piece of you in the frame, a glimpse into your darkest fears.

The driver was coming to pick us up at three o'clock. I was going to take you to the airport and then I was going to come back and do one last interview with the workers. Then I was going to go home, wait for Rashid, and tell him I was leaving him. I looked at the time, willing the hour to go by quickly so our goodbye could be over. We got into bed and made love. Afterwards, you covered my face with the palm of your hand. I closed my eyes and thought about what it would be like if I was going with you, packing my suitcase now and saying goodbye to everyone at Prosperity. Telling my parents. I felt a surge of anger at you for not pressuring me to come away now, for leaving it up to me to decide when and how I was going to break with my life.

We got up and started clearing up the last bits of your packing when it happened. I had wrapped the plastic bottle of honey in a bag and sealed it with tape, and I was leaning over your bag and slipping the honey into the side pocket when we heard a knock on the door. Mo went to answer it, and there, on the other side of the threshold, was Rashid.

He did not appear surprised. He walked right up to you and shook your hand, as if he had expected to happen upon his wife packing another man's suitcase. I felt my legs giving way under me, so I walked over to the window and leaned against the wall and watched the two of you introducing yourselves. 'I'm Elijah,' you said, your face lacking a single shred of remorse, and Rashid said, 'You must be a friend of Zubaida.' He may have even have said something like 'Welcome to Bangladesh', though I can't recall the exact words because a roaring began in my ears and I was afraid if I opened my mouth I might have to shout in order to drown it out.

I try and think of how a better person would have reacted. A better person would have taken the moment as an opportunity to bring everything out in the open – after all, if I

297

had really meant what I'd said, if I was really going to leave Rashid, what better time than now? A better person would have told the whole story, in calm, unambiguous terms. A better person would have marked out her loyalties – not only to you, the man I was now in love with, but also to herself. But I was not that person, not even in the better light of your presence.

The only sign that Rashid had noticed anything at all was in the slight force of his breath and the way he was lifting up various things and putting them down again, like the jar of pickles on the dining table or the camera Gabriela had left on the bookshelf. I finally found my tongue and stammered something about you coming to visit. You were waiting, I know, for me to say something truthful to Rashid, but I knew from the moment I saw him that I would not. He knew it too. We stood around awkwardly while you both waited for me to act, to set the terms for the conversation we were about to have. I was still holding the bottle of honey, and I walked over to you, Elijah, and placed it in your outstretched hand. 'Don't forget this,' I said. And then I asked Rashid about China, and Rashid said it was a good trip, that it had ended early, that the car was waiting downstairs and if I was ready we could leave straight away. 'The traffic gets bad in the evenings,' he said to you, as if you too were planning to drive to the other side of town and spend the night in a frangipani-scented villa on the side of a hill.

'I met Elijah at Harvard,' I said to no one in particular.

'Yes, I assumed that,' I heard Rashid reply, though my eyes were on you, your back bent over the suitcase, your posture so terribly, terribly sad. It was starting to dawn on you now that I was not going to tell Rashid anything, that I was going to go home and leave you there at the apartment. I noticed

Mo hanging around and I was afraid he would say something to give us away, so, with a wave of my hand, I motioned for him to leave the room. It was the sort of shooing gesture I had often seen Dolly make to her servants, and to this day, of all the things I am ashamed of, my gesture to him in that instant is what I regret the most.

You went into the kitchen and I heard you talking to Mo. Then you both came out and shook hands with each other. Rashid and I stood and watched. You slipped a folded-up note into the front pocket of Mo's shirt. He wrapped his arms around your waist and you had to peel him off. We heard his bare feet on the steps, the movements of a wounded animal.

'You can collect your things later,' Rashid said, and I nodded mutely, and turned towards the door and walked through.

And as we parted, Elijah, right there in front of my husband, do you know what I was thinking? Not that I would regret, the moment I left the apartment, the way I trashed everything that had passed between us in the last weeks, not my treatment of Mo, not abandoning you without even a proper goodbye, not the bland expression I gave you as the last image of my face, not the way I allowed Rashid to circle my waist with his arm — no, none of that. All I could think about, as we descended the stairs and stepped into the air-conditioned car, was that if only Rashid had arrived a few hours later, I could have spared him the sight of me gazing at you as if I had just been born, and everything could have gone back to the way it was, and I would have had nothing to explain, no story to tell, no guilt weighing me down like stones around my ankles.

Anna said to Vronsky: *Don't you understand that from the day I loved you everything has changed for me?* It did for me, too, Elijah. But not enough. Everything did not change enough, not enough for me to have the courage to tell the truth in the moment that the truth demanded, not enough for me to stand by you and leave behind all the unanswered questions of my life. Too much remained the same. Don't read this and forgive me – I know you won't – don't forgive me yet. There is so much more to the story, you will see; for now, I will only tell you this: I wanted desperately to be the person who would upend everything and thrust myself into the unknown, but the future was not the only thing that was unknown to me, and because I was already unmoored, I could not cut the threads that held me in place. Not yet.

In the days that followed, I was a puppet. He instructed me to eat chicken soup, so I did. Told me I should stop taking walks around the estate with Joshim because the daytime mosquitoes might give me dengue fever, so I spent the mornings inside. He drove us to Patenga, where we dipped our feet in the sea and listened to the sound of gulls and peanut shells cracking beneath our feet. He was patient, solicitous, as if he had found me in the throes of a terrible illness. But at night he kept to his side of the bed and never touched me, not even the barest graze of his knuckle against my skin.

I couldn't sleep. My body was cold and I caught a whiff of you in the crook of my elbow, as if my arm had brushed a dark and very private part of you. I didn't shower, afraid the smell would disappear. I lay awake at night, trying to cover over the wound, and every morning, as the day hit my eyes, it would open up like a flower as I remembered everything, the way the light poured through the windows and pooled around our feet that afternoon, and the grate in my voice as I dismissed Mo, and the streaks of dark in the cement of the stairs as I climbed down, because my head had been bowed and I had concentrated on nothing except putting one foot in front of the other.

At the end of the week, we returned to Dhaka. I couldn't face the beach, or Gabriela. I called Bilal and told him I was sick, that I needed a few weeks off. 'Is it typhoid?' he asked. 'There's been something in the water in Sithakunda.' 'No, it isn't typhoid,' I said, wishing it was something measurable like that, something that could be treated with drugs. Maybe I'll go to Nadeem and ask for some pills. Of course I knew I wouldn't. There was no point in seeking oblivion now.

In Dhaka, it was my mother's birthday. My parents came to dinner and we sat around the table while Rashid and his father told us about China, marvelling at the height of the Shanghai skyline and the fact that the electricity never went out. My father was animated by this conversation; as an old leftist, he had a lingering fondness for the Chinese. Everyone was jolly, even Ammoo, though I knew she had recently returned from another trip to visit the rape victims in Sirajganj. When the cook brought out a cake to celebrate Ammoo's birthday, I realised I'd forgotten to buy her a present and was about to apologise; but Rashid came out with a grey velvet box, inside of which was a necklace of milky pearls. 'This is wonderful,' Ammoo said, her eyes shining and wet, 'this is unimaginable happiness.'

In the morning I resolved to tell him everything, starting with the music and Sanders and the way I'd felt the night before we were married and how I hated being called 'Bou-ma', daughter-in-law, by Dolly, as if she had brought home an injured animal from the zoo. But I didn't. I ate white bread toast and scrambled eggs. I went to lunch with Rashid at the golf club and watched him practise his swing, a solid figure against the gently undulating blanket of green.

You had said something to me about having courage. About my will. But I was nothing but a coward. Just looking at Rashid, the way he twisted his hip as he raised the club, made me afraid.

One day my clothes and books and laptop – the things I'd left behind at the apartment – appeared at Rashid's house. He must have asked Joshim to pack everything up. I didn't ask him about it and he didn't volunteer anything. Among my things I found a T-shirt that belonged to you. 'Had you left it for me to say, I am still here, I understand, I will be patient, I will wait'? Of course not. Joshim would have found it bunched up at the foot of the bed and he would have folded it into my bag. All the next day I walked around with VERMONT written across my chest.

It was a Friday morning, dull with rain. I was about to get dressed, had just peeled the covers off the bed, when Rashid appeared in front of me, wielding my laptop. He held it high in his hand and then threw it against the wall, making a bright, clapping sound.

When he started yelling, I raised myself off the bed and sat very still at the edge, my feet balanced on a chair ('What is that fucking T-shirt you wear all the time, and that look on your face like someone just slapped you?'). He was pacing the room, and occasionally stopping and turning to look at me. I concentrated on a small square of marbled floor under my feet. He pulled out a cigarette from the drawer of his bedside table, lighting it with shaking fingers and inhaling deeply. 'Don't smoke,' I whispered, and at this, the first words I had spoken, he shouted, 'What the fuck?'

And I said, 'Don't smoke on my account. I mean, don't punish yourself because of something I did.'

There was a knock on the door. 'Breakfast!' Dolly chimed. On Friday, everyone ate together in the dining room, Bulbul at the head of the table, French toast arriving hot from the kitchen. We looked at each other and called out, in unison, 'Coming!' Then Rashid, changing his mind, holding the cigarette behind his back, opened the door a crack, said, 'Ma, Zubaida's not feeling well, can you just send something up?' and there was a brief exchange about my symptoms, whether a visit to the doctor was called for, a list of things I must do (the word 'gargle' was repeated), and then finally Rashid closed the door and came back inside. He opened a window, ushering in the sound of the rain hitting the thick leaves of the jackfruit tree that leaned against the eastern side of the house. For a moment I considered leaping out of that window and falling softly onto the grass below. Then, in answer to his question, I said, 'He's someone I met at Harvard.' To which Rashid said, with a sadness that could only be whispered, 'You already said that.'

It had come up before, when our engagement had been announced to the extended family. That I, having attended the elite college in New England, and then Harvard, would be more educated than Rashid. 'More qualified' is how people put it. But nothing had come of it – Dolly and Bulbul had mentioned it casually, and my parents had dismissed it, saying, how could this small thing matter when the children had known each other for years? Surely they would have discussed it and worked things out. But we hadn't. What was there to say? How would such a conversation begin? Hey, I'm cleverer than you, what should we do about that? Should you read more books so you can know what I mean when I refer to Stephen Jay Gould's *Cerion* snails? In retrospect, I wondered if we should have said something to each other. Perhaps Rashid should have read a few more books. *Anna Karenina*, at the very least. I remembered now how casually he had unpacked my boxes and put my books on the shelf in the study of our little suite, treating them as if they were all the same. My rare edition of *Jane Eyre*, for instance, with the lithographs, he had placed beside a paperback of his own, a Scandinavian thriller with the image of a white wolf on the cover. If I told him to read *Anna Karenina* now, he would get fifty pages in and say I was turning to Tolstoy for an excuse to cheat.

Rashid was saying something to me, but he was facing the open window and I couldn't hear him. I was suddenly very tired. He tossed the cigarette from the window and turned to confront me again. He wanted, of course, to know the details. When and how. And why. There was a knock on the door, and a trolley was wheeled in with a jug of tangerine juice, a steel cloche, and a pot of tea. On a plate next to the teapot was a tiny pile of chopped-up ginger and a small dish of honey. The honey made me think of the mangrove, of that plastic bottle – what had you done with it? Rashid pulled up the cloche and asked me if I wanted something to eat. I shook my head. The smell of eggs made the bile rise in my throat. I knew I should keep talking, tell Rashid how sorry I was, tell him it was over, that I would never do something like that again. But I couldn't bear to utter the words. I was emptied of will. Nothing happened. It was nothing.

'Should I move out?' I said finally.

This made him angry. 'So like you,' he said. 'Running away when things get messy.'

I saw him battling with himself: on the one hand, giving himself licence to rage, on the other, measuring, calculating, bookending his anger. He came over and sat very close to me, and I saw his hands holding each other. I was suddenly filled with an old affection for him, the man who had been my childhood friend, and I leaned into him, and then the words, the things he wanted to hear all came pouring out, the sorrys, the desperate pleas for him to forgive me. All the time I felt you listening and your heart breaking, and now I was trying to tell a story, a maudlin, nonsensical story that was an explanation of what I had done and why.

We lay down together on the bed. Rashid pulled the sheet over our heads. A small amount of light came through and I could see the outline of the room, the heavy curtains framing the windows, the pair of Shakoor paintings, a present from my parents, on either side of the bathroom door. Oh, God, my parents. I would have to tell them. I turned around and buried my head in the pillow. I had ended up on Rashid's side of the bed and I smelled his sleep smell. I could hear him breathing on the other side, and wondered if he was crying. But he wasn't. I heard him get up and cross the room. At the door he turned around and said, 'I'm joining my mother for breakfast.' And as I heard the door closing behind him I realised he had been waiting for me to say I loved him, and that I hadn't, not once.

About half an hour later he came back. He was holding the newspaper in his hand, and a bottle of cough syrup. I was on the bed where he'd left me. I had allowed my thoughts to drift back to that early moment on the beach when we climbed aboard *Grace* and you played the Steinway for the first time. I remembered the smell of the auditorium, already turning briny, and how you pierced the silence with your playing, as if it was the first sound in the history of the world. I might have slept, because when Rashid started talking it was difficult to open my eyes. He looked at me and sighed, long and deep, and sat down on one of the matching armchairs that faced the bed. 'Did you tell your mother?' I asked him.

'No. But she knows something's wrong. You'll have to come out for lunch, at least, or she'll call a doctor. She loves you. Everyone loves you.'

There it was again.

'I love you too,' I forced myself to say. And then, a truer statement: 'I don't want to lose you.'

The day dragged on. I took a shower and dressed in something Dolly would approve of. At lunch I was given broth and broken rice. In the afternoon everyone went to their respective parts of the house and it was very quiet, so I went outside and destroyed a few ixora flowers by pulling them from the bush and squeezing them between my fingers. A few of Rashid's relatives came after dusk, and snacks were wheeled out on a trolley, and Dolly made excuses for my silence by claiming I had been ill for the last few days, and an uncle put his hand on my forehead and declared me feverish, after which I was excused and given dinner in my room, everyone taking a certain amount of pleasure at my frailty.

Later, in bed, Rashid turned away from me and I swam my palms across his back, overcome by a deep longing to be held. When I tapped him on the shoulder, knowing he was awake, he turned around and I said it all again, the sorrys and the forgive mes, genuine this time, because how could I want for anything, here in this house that had welcomed me, Rashid even now willing to lie beside me on the bed, and I said how undeserving I was, how I would try and make it up to him, that I did love him, I did. He kissed me on the forehead, his breath grave with smoke, and that is when I realised he hated me – you both did, except one of you would do it from afar, and the other from up close.

I couldn't sleep and neither could he. I felt him twisting and turning on his side of the bed. At one point he got up and paced the room, finally settling into the armchair with another cigarette. He turned on the lamp by the dressing table, casting a lean shadow against the wall. When he finished smoking, he changed into shorts and running shoes, and I thought he would leave then, for the gym, but he switched off the light and sat back down. Every so often I would open my eyes and he and his shadow were still there, gazing back at me.

As the hours passed, I felt a small seed of rage taking root inside me. It occurred to me that I was owed something in return for what was happening. What was happening was that I would never be touched in the way that you had touched me, that all the things I had said to you as we made love would come back to you and you would be disgusted by the thought of me, and if I was going to have myself live in your memory as a woman who had no will, who, given all the freedoms and choices in the world, would choose this, if I was going to fall that far in your regard, then I would demand something in return.

The logic was faulty, of course – I have told you before, there had never been any explicit demands, no ultimatums or threats. And yet I felt as if they were all holding my life to ransom. What would I ask for in exchange? What could be as big as this? Even as the question was posed in my mind, the answer came catapulting back: I would seek out the woman who had eluded me my whole life. This was the only reasonable exchange, the only bargain I was willing to strike. And with this resolution firmly lodged in my mind, I fell into a thick sleep.

A few hours later I woke to find Rashid packing for an overnight trip to the factory. He was rolling his socks into cylinders and while he was placing them in a corner of his bag, I told him I had decided to find my birth mother. He paused, a pair of trousers folded over his arm. 'How does that make anything better?'

'I've decided,' I said.

'Look,' he said, 'you're confused. I can see why you think looking for your – for this woman – is going to help, but it won't.'

'How do you know?'

'Because there are probably things you would rather not know.'

I recalled our trip to Savar, his proposal by the rectangular pool. 'What are you trying to say, that I'll find out I have adulterous genes or something?'

'Zee, don't bullshit me, I know you know what I mean.'

'What, that I couldn't help myself so I cheated on you?'

'What the fuck do I know why you lied, cheated, what-ever the fuck you did with whatever fucked-up stranger you met in America?' He turned away from me and I saw he had an old scar just below his cheekbone on the left side. I had never noticed that scar before. What kind of a wife did that make me? I was a poor companion to him even before you came along. Then he said, after a long time, 'Are you in love with him?'

It was the first time he had asked me, and I knew it wouldn't be the last. I was tired and my head was heavy. I leaned against the soft upholstery of our bed. I considered telling him the truth, that not only was I in love with you, but that there was something out there called love, something

I had never believed in because I thought it was beyond me until I met you, and now that I had, this did not make the love more desirable – perhaps even less, because of the wreckage it would leave in its wake – but unassailable, something enormous and fixed, a piece of architecture that would remain in my consciousness no matter how hard I tried to deny it.

'No,' I said.

'Thank God for that.'

'No,' I repeated. He asked for assurances, and I gave them to him. I swore up and down the walls and past the corridors, and my sorrys spilled out into the garden outside, where the thick-leaved trees stood still. But I was resolved, and his resistance had only made me more determined. I was full of rage, against him, and Abboo and Ammoo, Dolly and Bulbul and all the other people who knew and had refused to talk to me all this time. The rage made it so that giving you up was the best thing I ever did, Elijah. Do not allow this to wound you, because in my anger – at my own cowardice, at the chain of events beginning with my birth that had conspired against me, against love, against all that I longed for in my body and breath and soul – I was finally released. I would do something, I would jump out of my own scissored self and traverse the difficult and treacherous chasm of history, and though I didn't realise it at the time, because all I could feel was the missing-limb ache of your loss, the start of this journey prompted a small, electric joy.

To find my mother I would start with my mother.

I called Ammoo and found she was on her way to a sari shop in Gulshan Two. I asked if I could meet her there, and, always suspicious when there was a spontaneous change in plans, she asked me repeatedly why, and when I refused to say, she relented and gave me the name of the shop. 'Fifteen minutes,' she said. 'Unless the traffic is bad.' When I arrived she was already there, sifting through a pile of printed saris. I observed her for a minute before entering the shop, noticing how, lately, she had become more beautiful, something in the way her face had settled into middle age made her appear gentler, almost placid. She had chosen a sari now, a blue cotton, and the shop attendant was opening it up to show her how the pattern changed across the six yards of material.

I pushed open the glass doors, slipping into the cool of the shop and remembering a joke I sometimes shared with my father about Ammoo's moods, referring to her as a thermometer. 'What's the reading today? Fever?' 'No,' he would reply, 'chills only.'

Ammoo spotted me, leaned back and frowned. 'This was a strange place to meet. Is something wrong? Where's Dolly?'

I had thought about it on the way over, rehearsing the scenario in my mind. 'I wanted to buy you a gift,' I said.

'Why?'

'Because I've saved some money, and I thought I should get you something. How about this one?' I said, pointing to the blue cotton.

'Are you all right?' she asked again. She held my elbow so she could face me fully.

I went on the offensive. 'What, I can't buy my mother a present?' I glanced at the price tag. I wanted to buy her something expensive, something flashy that would glint every time she opened her cupboard, but I knew she would never go for that. 'This one's too cheap. Won't you buy a silk or something?'

'Jaan, really – this one will be fine. Something wrong with Rashid?'

The short drive to the sari shop had given me a chance

to rehearse what I was going to say, but I wanted to begin the conversation on my own terms, and Ammoo had a habit of unsettling me. Already the energy of the morning was starting to dissipate. 'While we're at it, let's get something for Nanu too.'

We chose a grey pastel for Nanu. I paid. 'Now,' I said, 'there's a café next door, and I'd like to go there, and I'd like to talk to you about something serious.'

I led us out of the store and down the narrow street beside it. A metal staircase bolted to the side of the building led to a café on the second floor. Inside, the room had a curved wall on one side, and a set of tall windows on the other that looked down at the traffic on Gulshan Avenue. We sat down on a pair of soft armchairs with our backs to the view. The menu listed a variety of cupcakes and fruit juices.

We ordered coffees. 'I'll have the chocolate soufflé,' I said to the waiter, 'I hear it's very good.'

Ammoo leaned back in her chair, slipped off her sandals, and tucked her feet under her. I had rarely seen my mother sit any other way – sometimes even at her office, she led meetings in bare feet, crossing her legs over a conference chair or leaning a bent knee against a boardroom table.

'How are the trials going?'

'There are twenty-seven Birangona women at the centre in Sirajganj. One of them told me the people in her village still won't let her draw water from the tube-well. It was supposed to be a name that helped them, but it's become a label for life.'

'Will there be more convictions?'

'Sometimes I think it's a pointless exercise. But then I meet these women and at least I can look them in the eye and tell them we're doing something. That we haven't forgotten.'

'We haven't,' I said. I was beginning to understand why she had pressured me to change my major in college. My mother went to sleep every night knowing that she had played her tiny part in making the world turn. I had always told myself that *Ambulocetus* was no different, but I knew now that it was. Mo had taught me that, the way he had attached himself to you and me and made us feel that we belonged together, and to him.

'So, what was it you wanted to talk to me about?'

The coffees arrived, and I busied myself with a packet of sugar. Of course now that I was here, in this moment with my mother, I didn't want to do it. 'There's a boy who works at Prosperity. Can't be more than eight or nine. His parents are both dead, or missing, I can't be sure. I've been teaching him to read.'

We'd had three lessons before everything fell apart. Mo quickly memorised the alphabet, and his hand was steady as I had him trace over the letters. I had even gone into town and bought him books, with simple words accompanied by images: 'ma', 'kak', 'bok'. Late into the night, the light remained on in the kitchen as he placed the book on the floor and squatted over it, not touching the pages, just leaning forward and mouthing the words. 'Those men at Prosperity, they need people like you,' I said. 'People who care what happens to them. I'm trying to understand you. And I wish you'd try to understand me too.'

'Is that what's bothering you? I'm sorry, you're right. I never really got my head around your studies. I won't complain about the whales any more. But what's going on? Are you finished with Rubana's project? You come and go without explaining anything.'

I had rarely seen my parents argue. Sometimes I would

notice a brittle silence between them, or my mother, hypertensive, would put a large pyramid of salt on the edge of her dinner plate. I don't think either of them was used to apologising, at least not overtly, though perhaps something passed between them when I wasn't looking, a pattern of recriminations and sorrys that occurred behind closed doors.

'You know your father and I are proud of you. We thought you'd be a professor one day.'

'I don't know if I should have married Rashid,' I said. It was as good a place to start as any.

Ammoo reached out and touched the edge of the table. 'You can't say that. Don't say that.'

'He's suffocating me.' There, it was out.

'You don't know that for sure. You haven't given him a chance. It's hardly been two years.'

'Why are you defending him?'

'He's always been like a son to me.'

It was just as I'd suspected. That Rashid was the child my mother had never had. 'He's your son more than I am your daughter?'

It took a moment for her to realise what I meant. Her face fell as if I had hit her, her gaze dropping to her lap, her mouth twisting and drawing inwards. 'I can't believe you said that.'

'It's true. You love him more than you love me, I've always known it.' I had started in this brutal vein, and found I couldn't stop.

The soufflé arrived. I broke the surface of the chocolate and plunged my spoon inside. It was burnt and dry. Ammoo started to cry.

'I don't know what you're talking about,' she said, pulling a tissue out of her handbag.

I dipped my spoon into the dessert again. 'This is disgusting.'

Ammoo carried the soufflé away. I watched her arguing with the man behind the counter. A few minutes later she came back, removed her sandals again, and sat cross-legged on the chair. 'They're bringing another one,' she said, her voice clogged with tears.

'I need to know more. About my adoption. We never talked about it and you never told me anything. It's my fault too. I never dared to ask.'

We looked at each other. For an instant, I thought she might reach across the table and hold my hand. We would stay like that for a long time, talking about everything. Then we would walk out of the café with our arms intertwined, the burned soufflé forgotten, perhaps even having neglected to pay, no words, only the heavy truth hanging like a hammock between us.

Ammoo started laughing, a hollow, sharp laugh. 'I have no idea what you're talking about.'

'You're saying it's not true.'

'I'm saying I don't know what you mean. We told you and then there was nothing else to talk about. I can't believe it. My own daughter.'

That's just the thing. Not your own daughter. 'I'm just asking to have a conversation.'

'You sound so American,' Ammoo said. That meant I was cold and heartless, that I didn't care about hurting my mother. That I wanted to talk about things. 'I want to stoke the American in you,' you had once said. Well, maybe that's exactly what you'd done.

'I want to know, Ma.'

'Why don't you ask Dolly?'

What was this obsession with Dolly? 'Because I'm asking you. Don't pass me off to my mother-in-law.'

Ammoo was shaking her head. 'Dolly arranged everything. She brought you to us and had us sign the papers. She told us your mother had abandoned you and wouldn't come looking, that's it.'

The replacement soufflé arrived and when I took a spoonful I discovered it was identical to the first, grainy and overcooked.

'Why you insist on bringing me to these pretentious Gulshan-type places, when you know they can't even make a decent cup of tea?' Ammoo said. 'Let's go.' She pulled a note out of her handbag, flung it at the table, and marched out of the exit, not looking back to see if I was following. I took another spoonful of the soufflé, then another, scraping the sides until it was reduced to a rubble of chocolate crumbs at the bottom of the dish and my mouth was filled with the taste of burned chocolate.

The driver opened the car door and I got in beside Ammoo. As we were about to pull away, we saw the waiter rushing towards us. He tapped on the window. 'Madam,' he said, 'I'm very sorry, but bill was eight hundred and sixty taka. You only gave five hundred.' He held his hands behind his back while Ammoo counted out the money and passed it to him through the car window.

We were silent until we reached the Gulshan roundabout. 'So you're telling me that Dolly and Bulbul brought you a baby and you didn't bother to find out where I'd come from?'

'It was a mercy,' Ammoo said, wiping her face with the end of her sari. 'You wouldn't understand.'

Outside, it began to rain. Abul Hussain turned on the wipers.

'You don't know what it's like to want something so badly, to try, and keep failing. Your father and I – we couldn't bear it. Thank God for Dolly and Bulbul.'

'I'm in love with someone else.'

Ammoo threw herself back against the seat of the car and put her hand over her eyes. 'I'm not listening to this.' And then: 'It's that American boy, isn't it?'

'Elijah. His name's Elijah.' Where had she heard of you? I thought for one paranoid moment that Rashid had told Dolly and that it was all over the family now, but then I realised I had spoken about you soon after I'd returned from Cambridge, using any excuse to say your name aloud. Ammoo had probably suspected something and decided to ignore it.

For a moment I thought Ammoo was going to slap me, but she was defeated, staring up at the roof of the car. 'Rashid knows.'

'Oh, God.' I could almost hear my mother thinking, my poor boy.

'I'm sorry. It was my fault. I take responsibility for everything.' After the roundabout, the traffic came to a halt. A boy with an armful of white roses knocked on the car window, pleading with me to buy a few flowers.

'You take responsibility, but at the same time you want to blame us for not talking to you about this – this adoption thing?'

'I'm not blaming you, I'm just saying, a little transparency would have gone a long way.'

'What's wrong with Rashid?'

'I can't stand being in that house. I can't breathe. They're just like any other rich family. The kind of people you taught me to laugh at.'

'I don't recognise my own daughter. Why are you talking like this?' She pulled out her phone. The little boy knocked again, and Ammoo waved him away. 'I'm calling Dolly.'

'I don't want to talk to her.'

She put her phone away. 'Do what you like, but please, don't tell her about this other boy, it will break her heart. And she'll never forgive me.'

The traffic eased and we pulled away from the little boy and his flowers, passing the market and turning left at the park. The collective disappointment of everyone I knew pressed down on my chest and made it difficult to breathe. And yet at this news of my adoption – could it be true? Was it really all Dolly and Bulbul? – I felt a small lifting. Now that my mother and Rashid knew, even though things were messy and they were all about to gang up against me, at least it was out in the open, and things that should have come out many years ago were finally being said. I would ask Dolly for the whole story. I hadn't given up my right to know.

When it came to it, I didn't have the courage to confront Dolly. I woke up every morning and promised myself I would ask her at breakfast, but then Bulbul would be at the table, or Rashid's brother would walk in just as I was about to bring it up. I saw her ordering the servants to tidy up the garden or organising menus for dinner and decided she looked tired, or busy, and I would put it off. The questions gnawed at me, but my mother's look of disappointment reverberated in my mind, making everything seem impossible.

Sally came over one day with her baby, her second (as she had predicted herself, she'd had two in quick succession). They had named the girl Nadia. She passed him to me as soon as she walked in the door, blowing on her freshly painted nails. 'I just got a manicure,' she said. 'I think of that as winning. Today is a winning day.' She had tried to

cheer up her skin with a heavy coat of make-up, but underneath her eyes were dark and sunken.

'I'm so fucking tired,' she said. I offered her a coffee. 'I
can't drink caffeine,' she sighed. 'It goes into my milk.'

The baby stirred in my arms, batted a hand against my
chest, and fell back asleep. I lifted his head to my face and
kissed the mellow indent at the top of his head. He smelled
fragrant, yet unperfumed, a kind of sweet loaminess that
came from deep within his skin. I inhaled and inhaled.

'There's a rumour you and Rashid are on the outs,' Sally
said, leaning back and putting her head against the rounded
armrest of the sofa.

'People are always trying to break us up,' I said. 'Remember
a few years ago, when there was a rumour he was sleeping
with you?'

Sally blew on her fingertips again. 'Assholes.'

'And then there was another story about him and some
Indian girl who worked in garments.' I was getting a little
agitated, remembering all the rumours about Rashid and
other women.

'So there's nothing to it?' Sally said.

The baby stirred again, his mouth opening and closing,
so I stood up and shifted my weight from one foot to the
other. I considered telling her everything, wondering
whether she would laugh it off and declare me finally –
finally – human, capable of making mistakes like everyone
else, or whether she would hold it against me for ever, even
if she pretended to take my side. 'No, there's nothing,' I
said. 'Just the usual. Marriage isn't easy.'

'You're telling me. I married a man who still calls his
mother every night before he falls asleep and tells her what
he ate and how many shits he did.'

I laughed. 'Seriously?'

'No fucking joke.' She sat up, pulled a cigarette out of her bag and clamped it between her teeth.

'You're smoking?'

'No I'm not fucking smoking. I'm just holding onto my brain by chewing on a Benson's.'

The baby screamed. I swayed more aggressively but I was ineffective, so I passed him back to Sally. She swivelled around to check that no one was looking, pulled at her kameez, and guided a dark, enormous nipple into the baby's mouth.

'Yes, I know. My tits are fucking incredible, but Nadeem won't even touch them. He says they're for the baby and that creeps him out. I'm so horny I could screw the driver.'

'It was never true, was it? About you and Rashid.' My eyes were lemony with tears.

Sally drew the baby closer and looked up at me, the unlit cigarette still dangling from her lips. 'I'm going to tell you something honestly. Don't be mad.'

'Okay.'

'I would have. Seriously, I would have. We're all a little bit in love with Rashid. You know that.'

I did know that. Everyone, my mother and my friends and random people I had never met, telling me how wonderful he was, what a perfect man. The baby suckled fiercely, his cheeks pulsing as he swallowed.

'Did you do it?'

'No. But not because of you. Because he wouldn't. He would never touch anyone but you.'

I let out a breath, letting the tears fall freely against my cheeks. We didn't speak after that. Sally held her baby upright until he burped wetly and softly on her shoulder, and then she left, leaving behind the fragrance of curdled milk and tobacco.

That night, I examined Dolly as she ate, careful to open her mouth just wide enough to prevent her lipstick from smudging. Bulbul was narrating a story about a telecommunications secretary who had asked him for a bribe that morning. 'Nowadays they don't dance around the subject,' he said. 'They just put out their hands and tell you how much.' Rashid complimented the lamb chops, and Dolly said it was all down to the meat, which she had procured at great expense from the German butcher. Who by the way, Rashid interjected, now sells bacon. Bacon? The eyes of the assembled group widened, even mine, more out of surprise than horror. 'What's the country coming to?' Dolly lamented.

'I actually like bacon,' I said. Rashid swung his knee towards me under the table.

'Tawba, tawba,' Dolly said, slapping her own cheeks.

Bulbul pushed his chair back and said, 'Every time I go to Bangkok, we eat the noodle soup. Then someone told us it's made of pork.'

'We had to stop eating it,' Dolly said.

'But we haven't,' Bulbul said. 'We had it the last time. And you know the sausages at the breakfast buffet aren't chicken.'

'Of course they're chicken. Five-star hotel is full of Arabs.'

'Everyone pretends they don't know what's in it.' Then he pointed at me and said, 'Just don't go telling everyone your secret.'

After dinner, instead of following Rashid up to our bedroom, I lingered at the table and asked Dolly if I could borrow a necklace. Rashid and I were invited to a wedding the following night and I wanted something to go with my sari. Her annoyance at my pig-eating dissipated and she led me up to her bedroom, where, inside a panelled bank of closets, she turned the combination lock on a safe. 'Do you want just gold, or some kind of colour? Ruby, emerald?' Her voice was high and melodic and I realised she was practically giggling with joy. So this was what she had envisioned when she thought of my future in this house, that we would coo over her collection of trinkets, coordinate our outfits, share handbags and earrings. I must have done something to give her the impression that this future was possible, and I remembered now that when she had proposed shopping trips to London or Singapore, I had smiled and agreed, because some part of me wanted a mother like that, a mother who wasn't tempering every conversation with some new angle on how terrible the world was. Dolly lifted a three-stringed ruby necklace out of its velvet box. A diamond clasp bound the necklace together. I took it from her and held it with both of my hands. Then I said, 'Ammoo told me that you arranged my adoption.'

Dolly kneeled in front of the safe and pulled out another box. She popped the button and opened it, and inside was a wide gold collar. I was reminded of a *National Geographic* spread on an African tribe whose women wore thick brass cords to stretch their necks. 'This story is racist,' my mother had commented, taking the magazine from me. 'Don't read it.' I shook the memory from my mind and focused on Dolly, attempting to read her expression. I returned the ruby necklace to its box and dabbed at the gold collar. 'This is nice. It looks old.'

'It belonged to my mother-in-law.'

'Ammoo said you set everything up. She called it a mercy.'

Dolly turned back to the safe, so I couldn't see her face when she said, 'By then she was desperate. Bulbul and I couldn't stand to watch her suffering any more.'

I pictured my mother, and found it was easy to imagine her younger, to cast grief upon her features. 'Can you tell me where it was – where I was from?'

'Do you want to wear the gold?'

'I'm afraid it might be a bit formal,' I said, retracting my hand. Looking closer, I saw how gaudy the piece was, how crudely the jewels had been placed in their setting.

'You always go simple,' Dolly said. 'Weddings are for dressing up.'

'It's just – I don't know the couple very well and we're just going to drop in for an hour.' I hated these things, but Rashid said he had promised the groom's father, someone he did business with.

'I don't remember anything,' Dolly said, closing the box and returning it to the safe.

'Was it an orphanage?'

'No, it was a girl. A girl in need.'

'I'll wear the ruby,' I said.

She passed the box to me and then I watched as she put everything back in its place, and I wondered if any of the servants knew about the safe, if they had pressed their hands against the door and tried to guess the combination. 'You don't remember anything else?'

'No,' she murmured.

I didn't believe her. 'There's no documentation? Birth certificate, adoption papers?'

'There was. But it was all lost when we renovated the house.'

She sighed, as if she had told me this story a thousand times. 'Your parents were upset. We did everything we could to make it easier. Bulbul even greased some palms at the registry and put Joy and Maya down as the mother and father.' She moved to her dressing table, which was crammed with perfume bottles and small cylinders of lipstick, and began to unravel her hair. I was dismissed. As I turned to go, more in the dark than ever, she said, 'I can't tell you what to do. But you should stop eating that filth.'

Rashid and I attended the wedding the next evening. I wore the rubies around my neck and tried to hold onto the feeling I had experienced at Sally's confession. I made light conversation with the other wives and ate biryani with a fork and wondered what, after all, was holding the universe together. Afterwards I fell asleep in the car on the way home and stumbled into bed. In the morning Rashid woke early and I started telling him what his mother had said. The air was heavy with his aftershave. 'No one will talk to me,' I complained. He opened his side of the closet and stood there for a moment, sliding a tie from one of the articulated hangers.

'Did you hear what I said? I'm not getting anywhere.'

'Maybe they don't know anything,' he said. He wrapped the tie around his neck.

'How can they not know? A baby, a whole live person, appeared out of nowhere. I wasn't immaculately conceived.'

'Why don't you drop it, Zee?' he said, pulling the silk through its loop.

I peeled the comforter off the bed, ready for a fight, but I was at a disadvantage because he looked and smelled so much better than me, so I folded myself back into the blankets and banged my fist against the pillow. Rashid left with a curt goodbye, reminding me to call Nanu because she was having a check-up that afternoon and I should ask about her sugar level. How did he hold such a catalogue of mundane information in his head? No one loved Nanu more than me, but I was hardly going to keep track of her diabetes. I whispered a curse under my breath as the door slammed shut.

I called my parents – no reply on either phone. I sent them each an identical text message. I waited for what seemed like the entire day, but was probably a few hours. Finally, I went to their apartment and Bashonti opened the door. Ammoo was in the centre of a small tornado of people in the living room and I could smell something frying in the kitchen. I stood on the fringes of the group, catching Abboo's eye a fraction of a moment before being noticed by a woman – one of my mother's friends – who smothered me against her chubby shoulder. 'It's good you came,' she said. 'We all need to be together at a time like this.' I nodded, pretending to know what she was talking about. Bashonti emerged from the kitchen and passed around a plate of samosas. I couldn't tell if the moment was a solemn or a happy one, but I was hoping for solemn, because then no one would notice if I looked preoccupied or upset. It was always something I'd hated about people, the way they looked into your face and felt they had to make a comment about your appearance, like 'You've lost weight' or 'Are you depressed?' when I wished they would say 'Tell me why the sperm whale carries oil on the front of its head', which would have been a question I was equipped to answer. Not that the location of the spermaceti was an evolutionary puzzle anyone had thus far been able to solve, least of all me. But as a topic of conversation it was far superior to what I was usually offered.

'How's your gorgeous husband?' my mother's friend asked. So nobody had died, then.

'He's fine, thank you.'

I tried to detach myself, but she grabbed hold of my

arm. 'Newlyweds. So romantic. Better enjoy it before the babies come.'

I felt a hand on my shoulder, and it was Ammoo. 'I'm going with Salma and the other lawyers – do you have a car, or do you want to go with your father?'

'I'll go with Abboo,' I said. 'What are we doing at the courthouse?'

She squeezed my hand. She had forgiven me, or perhaps forgotten altogether. 'They're opening it to the public today.'

I stuffed a few samosas into my mouth as the plate hovered near me, and then followed my father downstairs and into his car.

'The road looks clear,' Abboo said, looking ahead to assess the traffic.

'I have no idea what's going on.'

He peeled his eyes away from the road. 'Don't you read the newspaper? They're announcing the Ghulam Azam verdict today.'

Of course. Only a person whose head was buried deep in the sand wouldn't know that. I was reminded again of the difference between my parents' household and Rashid's – the conversation around the dinner table last night had been about the rising cost of labour and how so-and-so had to shut down their factory because the workers had gone on strike. 'I'm sorry. I've been busy.'

'A big day for your mother. Try to be supportive.'

'I am supportive.'

'She feels you don't care about the trial.'

A car stopped abruptly in front of us, and Abboo jammed his hand on the horn. I knew my parents questioned whether I cared about the country as much as they did, and I had never really felt the need, or had the courage, to confess that I did not. I was proud that they had been in the war, proud to call my parents freedom fighters, but in reality I resented the space that it took up, the way all their conversations would eventually rotate back to reminiscing about the war, as if there was nothing but a bead curtain between this moment and that, so that all it needed was a brush against history to reveal the shiny betterness of the past. It was difficult to compete with, even more difficult to imagine that my life would ever amount to anything significant. They often said that the country lived in the shadow of that moment, that because the deaths had never been fully accounted for there was no way to move on, but what they never admitted was that it wasn't just the dead, or their families, who felt the dark cloud of those nine months following them wherever they went, but the rest of us, the children of the people who survived, all of us burdened with what we couldn't do, our imaginations limited by the protean, whereas theirs were set free by having done the impossible.

We pushed through the crowd of reporters and cameramen who had gathered at the entrance to the courthouse. I had only seen the building from the outside – a classical façade made grand by its brilliant white colour – and now, up close, it was impressive, wide marble corridors with double doors leading to the individual courtrooms. As we followed the group up the stairs through the corridor on the upper floor, we found Ammoo. She caught my eye and waved, and I noticed that her features were somehow rearranged, made bigger by the event, and I wondered if this was the face she had worn throughout the war, the look of majesty that comes over a person when she is assured of her role at a crucial moment in history. She entered the courtroom and the doors shut behind her, and we stood and waited outside. Abboo reached over and took my hand. I couldn't remember a single question I wanted to ask him; all the curiosity I had gathered up the evening before vanished in the dusky light of this afternoon and the cluttered murmur of the crowd. I saw a few familiar faces, friends of my parents, colleagues, people who I might have gone to school with. A chant rose up and gathered volume. 'Death!' I heard. And then: 'Hang him!'

The door opened and we fell silent, but it was just someone leaving. He waved his hand to indicate his irrelevance, then shut the door behind him and ducked away. I saw a woman holding the hand of a small child, and remembered a story my parents liked to tell me about how they had taken me to Suhrawardy field to attend the mock trial of Ghulam Azam. Back then, twenty years ago, only a fake trial for this man could be held, with actors playing the prosecution and a stuffed effigy in place of the real villain. He had been found guilty, sentenced, and executed at that trial, but it had all just been play, not like now, when Azam and the other men like him were in fear of their lives, their pasts finally catching up with them. That's why my mother defended this government, no matter what its other sins might be, because it was the first time, and the only time, that anyone had made Azam account for what he had done. The man was heavy with the dead, and now he was standing in front of a judge and being asked to explain the deaths of children, and he would have nothing to say. He was old now, over ninety. His reckoning had come late, but it had come, and I was here to witness it. I swelled with the weight of the moment, understanding what it was, possibly for the first time, to be my mother's daughter.

The door opened again and the news spread in a ripple, passed on from one person to the next until someone announced, 'Life imprisonment!' Cheers clashed with shouts of disappointment. Everyone started talking at once and trying to push into the courtroom. Abboo's hand was still gripping mine, and we were moved along until we were close to the doorway. I peered inside and saw a group of people surge towards the front of the room, raising their hands up to the bench to get the attention of the judge. People held their cell phones above their heads and took photographs. Finally the crowd became so thick that I couldn't hold on to Abboo's hand and we were separated.

After a few minutes there was a commotion as Ghulam Azam was led out of the courtroom. A ring of policemen surrounded him, but they could only move very slowly, and as they passed me I took a good look at him. He was in a wheelchair, his feet apart but his knees pushed together. His hands were cuffed in front of his body, a cap stiff and large on his tiny face. One of the policeman had placed an almost kindly hand on his shoulder as they processed slowly out of the courtroom. Ghulam Azam would be taken to prison that day, and a year later he would die, mourned by people all over the world who didn't know, or didn't care, about what he had done. My mother would repeatedly curse her computer screen as she read the stories of the crowds that showed up at his funeral, her triumph diminished every time he was referred to as 'Professor', every time he was written about as a religious leader rather than what he really was – a murderer. But that was later. On this day, the satisfaction was substantial, if not complete, a guilty verdict, a sentence, and he sitting birdlike in a wheelchair with only a policeman for company. As for me, catching those glimpses of the man, my own father solid and devoted somewhere in the room, I hung in the balance. My own discovery contracted and swelled like the chambers of a heart, and one moment I decided I didn't need to press my matter forward, because, as Rashid had reminded me, I was loved and that should be enough. But in another, the desire to resolve my story, to call time on the silence that had surrounded me, was inescapable, and finally it was this urge that won, and as soon as the scales had tipped, I couldn't wait another moment. Ghulam had trumped me, but now that he was finally defeated it was my turn. I jostled my way towards the exit, pushing against the tide of people, the only one going the other way, until I was spat out of the building, struggling for breath as I reached the gardens outside the courthouse.

I hailed a rickshaw, too impatient now to wait for Abboo, and pointed in the direction of Nanu's house in Dhanmondi. As we crossed Mirpur Road I took out my phone and sent a text message to my parents. *I have to know the truth*, it said. *Otherwise I am leaving home and never coming back.* I couldn't help sounding hysterical, suddenly all the years I had not known clambering on top of me. I peeled back the rickshaw's sunshade, trapped in my own chest, unable to fill my lungs with enough air.

The front door was ajar and there were voices coming from inside. I entered and saw a man seated on the sofa with his back to me, a massive back, broad and padded, a white turban on his head. He turned to face me and then quickly turned away.

'It's only Zubaida,' my grandmother said.

The man stood up and came towards me. Under the turban, the pair of thick-rimmed glasses, the beard that brushed his chest below, he had a beautiful face, dark, soft eyes and a kind mouth. 'As-salaam alaikum,' he announced.

On his forehead was a black bruise like Ali's, only wider and darker, shiny from years of prayer. 'How wonderful it is to cast my eyes on you.'

'Your uncle is visiting from America. He just arrived this morning.' Nanu was smiling in that wistful way she did whenever she mentioned my uncle. I myself had no memory of this man. He had come to Dhaka only once, as far as I could remember. He had given me a Kit Kat and frightened me with a story about the heat of hellfire. My parents often talked about him. Before the war, Ammoo told me, Sohail was a charismatic young man who kept a copy of Mao's *Little Red Book* in his front pocket. Their father had died many years before, and in their modest bungalow in Dhanmondi it was just him and Ammoo and Nanu, and something about being surrounded by women had made him delicate, almost fragile. Certainly not a fighter. So it came as a surprise to everyone when he crossed the border and joined the Mukti Bahini. Sohail, Ammoo says, did not distinguish himself as an assembler of crude explosives, or as a crack shot or a fearless running-into-the-line-of-fire type. He is rumoured to have baulked at crucial moments, like the igniting of a device or the running over of an army checkpoint. But what he lacked in skill, and courage, he made up for in conviction. When it came to believing what he was doing was right, Sohail was unbeatable.

But Ammoo doesn't recall what he did in the war as much as what he became after the war was over. It was not fashionable then, as it is now, for young people to make the pilgrimage to Mecca, or to encourage their wives to cover their heads, or to pepper their sentences with appeals to God. But Sohail Mama adopted the cloak of religion just after the war and did not shed it for the decades that followed, not through the death of his son, or the shifting of the world order, or the isolation from his friends and his past that were demanded by this new, lean life. In his own way he was a man who pushed against the tide, breaking hearts along the way, mowing over his friendships and his family because he was convinced he was doing the right thing, no matter how high the price – the highest price being that he and Ammoo rarely spoke, and whenever Ammoo mentioned his name or told me anything about him, she would always end with a sigh and say that it was as if her brother, like Abboo's, had died in the war.

I sat down beside Sohail now and he offered me a plate of dates, which he said someone had brought to him from Mecca. The dates were stuffed with whole almonds. I put one in my mouth and when I bit down I tasted a cloying sweetness. We said very little, regarding one another openly. I consumed one date after another. Sohail occasionally peered over his glasses and exhaled deeply, pulling and smoothing his beard with one hand, then another.

I wondered about his sons, whether, if I happened upon them, I would find them at all familiar, or if they would be just like all the other bearded men at airports and shopping malls, their wives trailing a few feet behind them. 'Nanu,' I said, turning to my grandmother. 'Rashid said you were getting your diabetes checked.'

'Sweet boy,' she said, smiling. 'He sent me his car so I could go to the doctor.'

Bastard. 'What did the doctor say?'

She waved her hand. 'Nothing to worry about. I'm not going to stop eating my Toblerone.'

'I came to ask you something.'

Somehow Sohail's being there made me believe that it

would all finally come out. In fact, I was unsure whether anyone would be capable of lying in his presence, and I wondered whether this was the secret to his success, the reason he was able to convert many dozens of Americans every week, not only at his mosque, but also as he went about his life, shopping at the supermarket, refilling at the gas station, picking up his wife from her Islamic exercise class on the other side of town.

I turned to Nanu. 'Did you know I was adopted?'

Her reply was immediate. 'Yes.'

'From where?'

'I always thought your parents should have told you, but they had their reasons. They asked me not to talk about it.'

'Did you know?' I asked Sohail.

'Your mother wrote to me. But she told me it was in confidence, and I haven't spoken of it since.'

The doorbell rang. 'Don't answer that,' I said. 'Tell me more.'

'I don't know any more, jaan,' my grandmother said. 'Come, sit beside me.' She patted the cushion, upholstered in pink.

I wasn't sure how or where to direct myself. The doorbell rang a second time, and I found myself leaning against the door. 'Are any of your children adopted?' I asked Sohail.

'Mine are not. But our Prophet, peace be upon him, was himself an orphan.'

I nodded, remembering what I had whispered to you that night at Sanders. The bell rang for the third time. Then, my father's voice. 'Sweetheart, open the door.'

'Is Ammoo there?' I asked.

A pause. 'Yes.'

'Let them in,' Nanu said gently.

I opened the door and found my parents in the corridor,

standing slightly apart but holding hands. 'Sohail Mama is here,' I said.

I stepped aside and they followed me in. Nanu rose from her seat, leaning on her walker. 'I'm going to get more tea,' she said. 'Sohail, come with me.'

'I can't, the servant girl is in there,' he said. He observed purdah and the only women he would glance at had to be related to him by blood.

'For God's sake,' Ammoo said, 'you haven't changed.'

Sohail turned to Ammoo and hugged her, unoffended. She shrugged him off. 'I'm here for my daughter.'

'Something of a daughter,' I said.

Nanu closed the kitchen door behind her. Sohail, enormous, made himself invisible by looking up at the ceiling and mouthing something – a prayer, I assumed. Ammoo began to make galloping, strangled sounds into her hands. The noise echoed around the room and then was swallowed by Abboo and me. We looked at each other and I nodded to him so he would know it was okay for him to start explaining. He leaned forward, his elbows on his knees. 'You know, don't you, sweetheart, that I was captured during the war.'

So he was going to start with that. I couldn't be angry about that, could I, because he was a war hero with war wounds. Maybe that is how I should have been thinking of myself all along, as a war wound, a throbbing reminder of something bad and something good that happened all at once.

'After I was released, and the war ended, and your mother and I married – well, we tried for a few years, but as it turns out—'

I was afraid he would detail his torture so I finished his sentence. 'You couldn't have children.'

'Something like that,' he said. Sohail finished his prayer and withdrew his gaze from the ceiling. We heard Nanu moving around the kitchen, the clatter of plates and cups.

'Looking back,' Abboo continued, 'We made some errors, in the way we—'

'It was my fault,' Ammoo interrupted. 'It was me. There was nothing wrong with your father. I was the problem.' She stood up and circled the room. From the kitchen came the rising and rising sound of the boiling kettle.

'Come here, jaan,' Abboo said, and Ammoo obeyed, returning to sit beside him. I could see them very young now, their faces lean and tired, grappling with things beyond their control, images from the war, and the sparse, mysterious future before them.

'For a long time I didn't think about children,' Ammoo said. 'But then suddenly I did, and when I did I felt a sort of desperation. We tried everything, spent all our money.' She smoothed the pleats of her sari. 'Anyway, the point is, the silence – your father did it to protect me. We never talked about it. The few people who knew, they just assumed it was him, and because of the war, no one asked.'

'But what about me?' I said, wanting to remain angry. 'You never wanted to tell me any of this?'

'We wanted so badly for you to be ours,' my father said. 'We were selfish. We're so very sorry.'

Nanu returned with the tea. She sat down and busied herself with pouring and adding powdered milk, sugar. Sohail passed around the cups, placing one in front of me, patting my head as he moved heavily back to his chair.

'There's more, I know there's more. Dolly said she lost all the records of my adoption. How could that be?'

Ammoo's eyes fell to the floor. 'You tell her,' she whispered. 'I can't bear to think about it.'

I could see Abboo struggling to form the words. I wanted to tell them I loved them, that my life wasn't so bad, that I knew they had done their best. I wanted to feel sorry for Ammoo for the burden she'd been carrying around all these years, but the urge to be harsh was stronger. You, Elijah, of all people, will know that I was capable of being cruel. I looked around and they were all staring at me and the air seemed to wrap itself around my mouth. I ignored my father's outstretched arms, the soft sobs of my mother. 'You know what this makes me? Not knowing who I am? It makes me half a person.'

'It was a terrible time,' I heard Sohail say. His voice was steady. 'We all did things in the war, and we've all found ways to make peace with those things.'

'Did you kill anyone?'

'That's not what he means,' Abboo said. 'After the war, everyone was looking for meaning, for something that would help us to make sense of what happened. For some people, it was their work – lot of money people made. And sometimes' – he looked at Sohail now – 'it was religion.'

'For us it was a baby,' Ammoo said. 'We wanted a baby to erase all our pain.' I looked at her and saw that she was pulling it out of herself with tremendous pain and effort, like a demonic spirit that had lodged itself between her ribs and had to be exorcised. As she spoke, her voice grew in volume and confidence. 'So when we couldn't – when I couldn't – you won't understand, it's something so deep, the inability to bear a child.'

I took a sip of tea, burning my tongue.

'We didn't want to have any contact with – her – your mother. It was too difficult. So we let Dolly and Bulbul handle everything, and then we asked them to destroy the evidence. Once you were legally ours, we just wanted to forget you had ever belonged to anyone else.'

I didn't know what to say. Their reasons for wanting to erase the adoptedness of their child – me – was not unreasonable. It was born out of a need to love and be loved, I could see that now and I believed it. But it also meant they must have, on some level, been ashamed – not in the way some might have thought, and I had always feared – that my roots were somehow contaminated by poverty, or bad luck, or misfortune – but ashamed of themselves, and maybe ashamed was not even the right way to describe it – more that it was a terrible thing, the fact that I'd had to come from somewhere other than my mother's womb, that I wasn't made of them in the way they had so ardently desired, that their solution for the damping of their sorrow had collapsed around them and left them no option but to settle for someone else's child. So although I was grateful for this truth, it made me think of all the nights they might have spent waiting, and wanting, and being denied, and perhaps even after I had come to them, they may have glanced down at my sleeping face and wished I were someone else, the someone who was never to be, and I could see now why they didn't want me to know, because as soon as the image flashed before my eyes, I missed the time, just a few minutes ago, when the knowledge didn't exist, not in the specific, tangible way it did now.

I looked at my uncle to see if he had something to say at this moment, something solemn and meant for moments such as these, but he was leaning back with his hands folded on the dome of his belly. 'I have to find her,' I said. 'I'm going to keep looking until I find her.'

Abboo sighed deeply and tightened his arm around Ammoo, who was wiping tears from her eyes with the end of her sari, tracing the bottom of her eyelid where her eyeliner had smudged. 'How will you do that, darling? We have no idea what happened to her.'

Sohail Mama hauled himself up and ambled towards me. 'I am going now,' he said. 'I'll stay at the mosque tonight.' I saw a shadow crossing Nanu's face, knowing he wouldn't listen if she asked him to stay. All the mothers in the room were longing to cling to their children, I thought, lanced by the memory of my miscarriage. Sohail hugged me and I clung to him. 'Allah sees everything and forgives everything, remember that.' His soft shoulders smelled of rosewater. 'Losing a child is like the end of the world.' I let him whisper a prayer into my ear, knowing that I was betraying Ammoo as I lingered in his arms.

After he had slipped on his sandals and closed the door behind him, I said, 'I'm going to spend the night here. Nanu, can I stay?'

'We'll stay also,' Ammoo said.

I was too tired to protest. Nanu busied herself in the kitchen, emerging with a simple chicken curry and rice. She spooned the rice onto my plate. Once or twice she tried to raise various topics of conversation, but no one took her up on it. I ate with my head down, hungrier than I wanted to be, glancing occasionally at my parents. My mother was pushing her food around with a fork. Finally I went to bed without a word to anyone and fell asleep immediately.

When I felt Ammoo's hand on my face, it must have been close to dawn, because the room was bathed in pale orange light. I don't know how long she'd been there, but she was lying down beside me and her eyes were open. When I started to turn away from her, she stopped me, her palm firm on my cheek. 'When you were a baby I would lie down beside you and pull your mouth open like this,' she said, pressing her thumb down on my chin. 'And I would put my face close to yours and I would try to smell your breath.'

'How did it smell?'

'Milky and sweet. Like custard.'

My mother could beat anyone at hard-luck stories. If you started a conversation with her about something bad that had happened to someone you knew, she would pretend to listen and tell you something so harrowing and dark you would immediately fall silent. I always thought of this as Ammoo's superpower, the ability to make people feel simultaneously better and far, far worse about their place in the world. I realised now, listening to her frayed breathing, her story of catching the scent of the child that had come to her so late, and with such trouble, that she lived within these dark tales. They fed her and she fed them. She was in dialogue with the lives of others, breathing the very air they expelled, those invisible people who were nothing but a blur to the rest of the world, but alive, vivid, to her. I put my palm over her palm on my cheek, and we lay that way for a long time, circled by the years we had spent belonging to each other.

In the morning, after Nanu had fed us all breakfast and we went our separate ways, my mother back to Sirajganj to start another round of interviews, my father to the factory, I considered the failure of my search, casting my mind to the time my parents made the decision to adopt me. The country, at peace, must have been unsatisfying to my parents. They missed the people they had become when their names began with 'Comrade'. Returned to ordinariness, they no longer hummed the protest songs as they fell asleep, now in unstrange places. Too quickly they forgot the tragedies of that hour, and what remained was a lingering sense of loss, because now they were citizens, and the business of citizenship was inferior by far to the business of revolution. What they wanted, more than anything, was an anchoring hope, and that anchoring hope was me.

And that is why I would never know who my mother was. They had destroyed the evidence and started a family in the new country.

I wandered around the city. I walked up road 27 and went into various shops, one displaying only black-and-white saris, another selling handicrafts, its walls decorated with rickshaw art. I bought a postcard. *Elijah*, I wrote, *I will never know who my mother is.* On an impulse, I took a rickshaw to the Dhanmondi Post Office and stood in line behind a string of men in identical pale-blue half-sleeve shirts and I wrote down your address and paid the severe woman behind the counter. Immediately I regretted it, wishing I could reach behind the metal grille and retrieve the postcard, but the lunchtime crowd swelled and I lost my will. Eventually, hunger drove me home, past the parliament building which sat like a giant grey crab on Manik Mia Avenue, past the planetarium and the tiny bookshop tucked behind the old airport, and finally into Banani, where I stopped at a cheap bakery to buy a chocolate Swiss roll that I knew would irritate Dolly. All the while I was thinking, my search is over. I was still the restless being I had always been, but now that I knew there was nothing left to discover, was the mystery greater, or did it shrink?

I could not decide this on my own. There was no one for me to ask, no one to tell me how to feel about this, the failure and resolution of my search, not my parents, not my husband, not the friends I had gathered over the years at home. I realised that I had spent much of my life parcelling myself out, giving a little to this person, a little to that, and there was no one to connect the dots, no one to understand the sum total of all the parts, the orphan, the scientist, the daughter of revolutionaries. Except you, of course. But, in spite, or perhaps because, of that, I had given you up.

I dialled Rubana's number. I knew she would scold me for leaving the beach abruptly, but I suppose I wanted someone to tell me to follow through, to be better. She didn't reply, so I sent her a text message, and about an hour later she called me back.

'I'm filing a case with the High Court,' she said, as if we had been cut off in mid-sentence. 'I'll be using your interviews.'

'I thought they were just for the film.'

'The case studies will make a difference. Put a human face to all the misery. You've done a good thing.'

A good thing. I thought about the way I had treated Mo. 'Bilal told me you left,' she said.

'I'm sorry. I had some personal issues to deal with.'

'I hope your mother doesn't regret sending you to me.' I heard a pause, then a clicking sound, as if she was pressing her lips together and separating them. 'I've heard things, about an American boy.'

Of course Rubana would have heard. My face burned as I busied myself with a crease on my kameez.

'You know I don't really care about these things – your life is yours. But you can't give people excuses for not taking you seriously.'

I felt guilty at the strength with which I wished this woman was my mother. I told myself it was time to stop doing this, a habit I had developed over the years – stop looking for her at every turn, imagining she was this person, or that. Strangers on the street. Women I had known my whole life.

As if she had read my mind, Rubana said, 'You could go back and do a few more interviews.'

'Thank you,' I said, relieved. She was giving me a way out again, and I was taking it with both hands.

'I'm sorry,' I said to everyone. 'Rubana needs me to finish some work.'

Rashid refused the tub of pistachio ice cream being passed around the table. 'When will you be back?' he asked.

'My baby-babu misses his bride,' Dolly said.

'A few weeks.' Under the table, I reached for his hand.

'Can't someone else do it?' Dolly said. 'It's so sad when newlyweds have to be apart.'

'Why don't we all go down for a weekend?' Bulbul said. 'We haven't been to the house in months.'

'It's going to rain the whole time. You'll catch a cold. Rubana is really being unreasonable,' Dolly said.

'I've missed the Chittagong golf course,' Bulbul said. 'If we go down I can play a few rounds.'

Dolly plunged her spoon into the ice-cream tub. 'That's it. You'll drag me all the way down there and disappear for the whole day.'

'Weather is nice this time of year.'

'No, it's not. And Sigma and Pultu will be disappointed if we don't invite them for lunch.'

'Of course,' Bulbul said, leaning back in his chair. 'But Pultu can play a round with me and we can have lunch at the club.'

Dolly and Bulbul went back and forth a few times about whether they should fly or drive down to Chittagong, where they should have lunch, and Rashid excused himself, and we all dispersed before the tea trolley arrived. 'You really have to go?' he asked as soon as we had closed the bedroom door behind us. He pulled his phone out of his pocket, unrolled his shirtsleeves and threw himself down on the armchair.

Rashid had decided not to think about the depth of my entanglement with you, but simply about the fact that I had strayed, because it would then remain a problem to be solved. That had always been his way. And I knew that his main strategy was keeping me close, watching over me and treating me with great care, as if I had developed a hairline crack all across my body that would slowly heal, but only if my two halves remained pressed together for a long time.

'You can come to Chittagong and visit, like your mother said.'

'I wish you would call her Ammoo,' he said, bringing up a conversation we'd had months ago, about what we would call each other's parents once we were married. Rashid had slipped easily into calling my parents 'Ammoo and Abboo' after a lifetime of 'Maya auntie and Joy uncle', but I had been unable to make the transition.

I was in no mood to argue. 'Like Ammoo said.'

He stood up, removed his watch, placed it carefully back in its case, and started to undress. 'I need to get out of here,' I said. 'I feel like someone cut my anchor.'

He looked at me and I saw myself through his eyes, clouded and unreadable. 'I don't understand. You have everything in life. Everything.'

I wanted to tell him about the day before, about what my parents had told me, that I was giving up the search – I knew this would appease him – but instead I unbuttoned his shirt and let it fall to the ground, slipping my arms around him and stroking the ribbed cotton of his singlet. I raised my face to kiss him and he lowered his mouth towards me, but he stopped as our lips briefly touched, pushing my elbows away. 'I can't,' he said. I nodded, stepping away, feeling rejected despite everything. He picked up his shirt from the floor and darted into the bathroom, and I cried while he brushed his teeth. When he came back he lay down on the bed and fell asleep quickly, letting me curl around his tense, bowed back.

Return to *Grace*

Abul Hussain came to collect me the next morning, but at the airport, there were no flights to Chittagong. 'Sorry, ma'am, due to bad weather all flights are indefinitely postponed,' the girl behind the counter said, wearing a surprisingly tight red-and-grey suit.

'When is the next flight?'

'Scheduled for tomorrow morning, ma'am, but that also may not depart.'

I thought about going home, but now that I had set my mind on returning to Sithakunda, I couldn't turn back. I ducked into the car. 'Abul Hussain, can you drive us to Chittagong?' It was a five- or six-hour drive; Dolly and Bulbul had done it regularly in their jeep before the domestic terminal was refurbished.

Abul Hussain glanced at me in the rearview mirror. 'We would have to tell sir.'

'Baba won't mind, I'll call him now.'

'There isn't enough petrol.'

I rifled through my bag, failing to find any money. 'Stop at a bank, I'll get some cash.'

We drove through the city again, going south from Mohakhali to Mohammadpur. Abul Hussain parked in front of a shopping mall, where a uniformed guard opened the door to a tiny air-conditioned cubicle that housed an ATM machine. I had always found it strange that in America the cash machines were exposed, as if there was nothing remarkable about being able to take money out of a cavity in the wall. At the shop next door, I bought a packet of Uncle Chipps and a few bottles of water. Then I remembered I hadn't really eaten anything since the night before, which felt like a lifetime ago now, so I hunted through the mall for a restaurant, finally settling on a place that sold fried chicken. I bought a box for myself and one for Abul Hussain.

In the car, I sent a text message to Abboo. *Ok if Abul Hussain drives me to Chittagong? Urgent business.* Then I gave Abul Hussain a hefty tip and passed him the fried chicken. 'You can stay the night and drive back tomorrow.'

He selected a piece of chicken from the carton, taking a bite and then placing it on his knee, where it remained as he negotiated the traffic. In Mohammadpur he picked it up again and took another bite, leaving an oily stain on the leg of his trouser. I offered him a napkin, guilty for making him drive all the way.

After Mohammadpur the traffic cleared and the dense tangle of the city gave way to low-slung buildings and carts piled high with vegetables, and then, acres and acres of brickyards, everything red, dotted with tall, narrow furnaces that churned smoke into the sky. Eventually, the view turned to farmland, chequerboard patches of land planted with rice as far as the eye could see, everything flat and green to the horizon. I closed my eyes, willing sleep to come and cut out the hours until I arrived at the beach, to Mo and Gabriela and *Grace*.

My phone rang, but I ignored it, knowing it would be my parents or Rashid. I recalled now that Ammoo had slapped me once, when I was eleven, for stealing her make-up bag and wearing lipstick to school. The principal had telephoned, and after a wordless ride home Ammoo had hit me softly across the cheek with a bewildered look, as though her arm had acted of its own accord. When I finally locked myself in my room and Ammoo had called out repeatedly. When I finally opened the door I found her curled up on the sofa. She hadn't seemed sorry as much as surprised. The phone kept ringing. Eventually I decided to answer. It was Abboo.

'Your mother is very upset. Dolly also called a few times. And there's a storm coming.'

'I know, that's why I'm driving.'

'They're saying it's going to be bad.'

'Please, let me go. I know you did what you thought was best. But I can't rest. I can't work, I can't do anything. I can't be at peace.'

'You were just a baby, a few weeks. A tiny thing in my hands. The most beautiful thing I had ever seen.'

I hung up so he wouldn't hear me cry. Last night, when I couldn't sleep, I had written an email to Rashid. It was full of regret for all the things I had allowed myself to do, that there was no excuse for the way I had behaved, but that, perhaps, if he tried very hard, he would see that there would have been no way for us to go ahead if I hadn't at least made an attempt to piece together my past. I had gone over it again and again, but I had been unsure how to finish the message, whether I could tell him now that it was all over and we could begin again, but as a pale baby bird of a sun crested the horizon, I had decided not to send it.

I closed my eyes for a moment, and when I opened them the wipers were on and I could hear the sound of water above and below, rain on the car's roof and on the road. I checked the time and it was only noon, but the rain clouds had smothered the light. We drove on, slowed by the darkness and the dense sheets of water. Abul Hussain switched on his headlights and bent over the wheel, holding on with both hands.

I called the Shipsafe office but no one answered. I asked Abul Hussain to turn on the radio, and the reception drifted in and out. I rifled through the magazines my father had left in the car and found a recent copy of *Outlook India*. There was news about Bollywood, a corruption scandal in the Indian Army, a recipe for Urad Dal. For a stretch of the highway, the sky cleared momentarily and the rain thinned, and I could make out the trees on either side of the road, the landscape changing from flat to gently rolling. Abul Hussain pointed to a sign. 'Apa, can we stop for tea?'

He parked in front of a squat concrete building. I waited in the car while he ordered tea from a young boy sitting in front of a large kettle on a propane stove. When the tea was ready he passed me a small clay cup through the window. After a few minutes the sky thickened and it began to rain in earnest, and after Abul Hussain retrieved my cup, we set off again, seeing very little in front of us except the road ahead and the grey outlines of the hills in the distance.

The shops along the highway to Sithakunda were all closed. The car stalled, water sloshing around the tyres. Abul Hussain switched off the engine, then revved it again, propelling us forward, and we covered the last few miles at a crawl, the sound of the wipers beating back and forth. An hour or so later we reached the Shipsafe office.

The front door was locked. I borrowed a key from the caretaker, who informed me that everyone had gone home early because of the storm. I concentrated very hard on remaining downstairs instead of rushing up to the apartment and crawling on my hands and knees in search of a last fragment of you. Even down here at the office, I felt your presence, your footsteps burdening the air above me.

I switched on the overhead light. There was my desk, the glass chipped and taped together, the ancient computer, the corkboard with edge-curled newspaper clippings, Bilal's battered armchair with the striped towel draped across the back, the smell of tea and biscuits. I had only been away a few months, but I realised I had left long before that, that the moment you arrived I hadn't cared much for any of it. I remembered the feeling of being around you, which is that you swallowed all the air in the room, though perhaps it wasn't you at all, but the strength of my feeling for you. In any case, I had been a poor volunteer; I had not done well by the pulling crew. And Mo I had let down altogether.

I glanced over the transcripts of the interviews. Without sentiment, I began to read. The words were flat on the page, one sad story following another, each starting with its same moment of fracture – an illness, a bad crop, the death of a father – and the long journey south, the bag of things they carried, the tiny pocket of hope, and then arriving at the shipyard and finding the acres of steel and rust, and Mr Ali, the dormitory, the long dark nights, carrying iron on their shoulders to the sound of chanting. I felt nothing, no sorrow, no jolt of recognition as the words I had heard and recorded appeared in black and white.

Then I came to the story of Shahed, a young man we had interviewed together. I remembered the way you held his gaze because he had refused to look at me. He had been sent here only a few months before, and was living not at the dormitory but in a room he shared with a few other strays. Ali had taken him on as an apprentice, and he had yet to be paid. He ate, he said, by begging on the highway at night, and during the day, when the others saved him a few mouthfuls of rice. He had a cut on his arm that looked raw, which we only discovered when you put your hand out to touch him and he flinched, the thin fabric of his shirt sliding from his shoulder. You dressed the wound yourself, telling me later your father had taught you first aid in the days when you'd lived in the house in the mountains and there wasn't a doctor around for miles. Now, reading Shahed's words, and imagining in the pauses your fingers unrolling the bandage, splashing alcohol on the wound, and all the time Shahed not flinching, not making a sound, his lips parting as you finished, wanting to kiss the hand that touched him with as close to a caress as he had known since saying goodbye to his mother in the winter, she with a touch of her palm on the top of his head, you with a careful tap of the surgical tape.

I went upstairs to the apartment to face Gabriela. I assumed she had built up a catalogue of things to say; I had left without a word to her and ignored her many phone calls and messages, and, worse, I hadn't even asked after Mo or any of the other men on the beach.

Inside, the place had been stripped of its last traces of you. Gabriela had cleaned everything up. The grey mosaic floor was spotless. All the dusty corners of the flat, the empty bookcase and the window grilles, had been washed. Even in my bedroom the blanket had been folded and the sides of the mosquito net pulled up so that it formed a flat grey canopy over the bed. As soon as she saw me Gabriela said, 'Where the fuck have you been?' and I braced myself, but she laughed and put her arms around me. I began to explain, starting with your name, but she said, 'First, we drink. Then you can grovel.' We repeated the ritual of my first night at the apartment, though this time the tequila went down easily, and after two big gulps from the bottle I didn't even feel a little bit drunk.

I asked after Mo. Gabriela told me that he had continued with his duties, cooking and cleaning and looking after her. I had thought, for just a whisper of a moment, that wherever you had gone, you had perhaps taken him with you, but I knew this would be impossible. You would have wanted to leave right away, and Mo didn't have a pair of shoes, much less a passport. You would have left him behind, though you would not have abandoned him as roughly as I had. And you would not have abandoned me at all.

'The only thing is, he seems to have run into some trouble with Ali. I'm not sure exactly what – Ali always pretends he hasn't the faintest clue what I'm saying when I try to talk to him.'

'I've fucked everything up,' I said, the alcohol finally hitting me.

Gabriela laughed. 'I was married once too, you know.'

I had never asked her. She had taken the studs out of her top two piercings, and her shirt was loose and fell several inches below her hips. She looked more normal now, yet somehow diminished.

'I should have taken better care of you,' I said.

She waved her hand. 'Don't worry, darling,' she said. 'I could see you were preoccupied.'

'He was – is – a childhood friend. A childhood sweet-heart.' This is how I had always described Rashid. A childhood connection. 'So romantic,' my cousins used to sigh. 'So sweetly old-fashioned.'

'I met Elijah at a Shostakovich concert. Out of the blue. Lightning and thunder and all that.'

Gabriela nodded. She pulled a packet of cigarettes out

of her handbag, a foreign brand in a dark blue box. 'I didn't know you smoked,' I said.

Gabriela inhaled. 'I never needed to before.'

'And what about you?'

She scraped a match against a rough wooden box. 'We were children, we didn't know what we were doing.'

'I sort of feel like that. But that's not an excuse. I mean – for me.'

She laughed. 'He's the director of the film. We're still close friends.'

'What happened?'

'I cheated, he forgave me. I was the one who finally left. Now he's married, he has three children. The terrible thing is, I'm probably still in love with him.'

Something in her face reminded me of Ammoo. Not that Ammoo herself regretted anything, but she was in constant fear that I would have regrets, that if I didn't marry Rashid, for instance, that I might carry around the expression that could be seen on Gabriela's face right now, the sense of having allowed a chance at happiness to pass me by. Ammoo wanted, more than anything, to mitigate disappointment for me. I wasn't sure what to say to Gabriela, and what would it be like for me, ten, twenty years from now? Would I pine for Rashid, for the familiar rituals of our togetherness, being able to anticipate so many of his gestures – would I miss the safety of that or, as now, would I be tired of knowing so much, would I continue to long for otherness, for the pleasures of the alien?

The door opened, and Mo entered carrying a shopping bag. His smile when he saw me was so wide, so undiminished, that I stood up and walked over to him and lifted him up in my arms. He was heavier than he looked, and smelled of sweat and iron.

'Did you hear about the piano?' he said.

I hadn't.

'It's going to America. Elijah is going to fix it.' The sound of your name in Mo's mouth was the first time I had heard it uttered aloud since you left, and it struck me with great force. Mo didn't know the details, but he had heard Ali saying that the American who had been visiting had somehow arranged for the Steinway to be transported to Boston, where it would be restored, and then presumably sold on. I stood frozen as the tears gathered in my eyes, my ears still humming to the sound of your name, and beyond, to the notes you had played on *Grace*.

I wanted to hug Mo again but I didn't. My arms were suddenly without feeling or energy. I asked after the others. 'How is everyone?' I asked him.

'Russel is still looking for his brother,' he said.

'And Belal?'

Mo kept his eyes trained on his feet. 'Belal has gone home.'

'Why?'

'Mr Ali said he was making trouble.'

'Did he do something?'

Mo shrugged. 'I can't say.'

Again I was pierced with guilt for having abandoned them. I tried to remember if there was anything about Belal that stood out. He didn't strike me as the type of person who would get under Ali's skin. Ali had told me once that he would periodically encourage a turnover so that the workers would remember who was keeping their bellies full. I recalled it now, and the way Ali had said it, as if it was nothing to exchange one man's labour for another's. 'You stay out of trouble,' I said to Mo.

'Mr Ali won't leave me,' he said. His belief that there was some security in his life made him seem all the more fragile. I was about to ask him why, whether there was some particular reason Ali would keep him around, but he disappeared into the kitchen, declaring he would make the best spinach curry I had ever tasted.

'Did you practise the letters?' I called out. 'Every day!' he replied, and in those words, in that voice, there was a small measure of consolation.

When I stood up to leave, I was suddenly dizzy, and I had to sit down again.

'You sure you don't want to sleep here?' Gabriela asked.

'I promised Rashid I'd stay in town.'

'Under lock and key, are you?'

'The errant wife.' And, with that, I asked Abul Hussain to take me to the villa, where Komola was waiting at the door, her hands soft against my face.

In the morning, when the car stopped inside the gates of Prosperity, I watched for a long time as a cutter made his final pass and a large piece of *Grace* came crashing down onto the sand. I was wearing sunglasses, a pair I had found in the bedside drawer of my room and had probably belonged to Dolly, and through the sepia-tinged frames I saw the people I had so carefully come to know appearing as vague shapes against the broken silhouette of *Grace*. A tanker had arrived while I was away. Now it was wedged between *Grace* and a half-demolished container ship in the neighbouring lot. *Grace* had been pared down. Her foredeck and bridge had been sliced off, large panels of steel cut away from her hull. She was all gloom now, empty of the footprints of happy people.

Ali was waiting for me in the Prosperity office. 'Welcome

back, Miss Zubaida.' He pulled at his beard, which appeared fuller and longer.

'Thank you, Mr Ali. It looks as if you've made a lot of progress,' I said, gesturing towards the beach.

'By the grace of Allah, we are ahead of schedule with the cruiser.'

He didn't ask me to sit down, but I took a seat opposite him anyway. 'I heard also that you have sold the piano.'

'To your friend, the American. He was very persistent.'

'Yes. He's a difficult man to refuse.'

'And you have come back. Will you stay long?'

'I would like to continue with the interviews,' I said.

'We are always pleased to act as your hosts,' he said. 'And you are entitled to employ who you wish, of course.'

It took me a moment to realise he was referring to Mo. He tapped the desk with the end of a pencil. 'As long as the boy completes his duties, he is free to live where he finds a place, but you will understand that it may cause some disturbance among the other men. As you have taken such an interest in the boy. I hear you are teaching him to read.'

'He didn't get a chance to attend school.'

'Neither have any of the others.'

'Have they complained?' I wasn't sure where he was going. He obviously didn't care if my favouring of Mo had caused problems with the workers.

'Not exactly. But I've known them a long time, and they don't take to change very well.'

'We won't be here long.'

'That's precisely the issue, madam.' He continued to tap on the desk with the end of his pencil. It was mid-morning and work was going at full tilt on the beach. 'After you go, things will have to return to normal. That is the way here. We have been operating for many years.'

'I'm not sure I understand.'

He smiled again, raising his hands in a gesture of surrender. 'Nothing to worry about, madam. All is up to the Almighty. Now I must go, I have some business to attend to.'

Ali appeared to dismiss me. I wasn't sure what had just happened, but I guessed the conversation had sounded different to Ali's ears than to mine. As I turned to go, he said, 'Please give my regards to your father.'

'You know my father?'

'Sir is a respected man, a son of Chittagong. Of course we all know him.'

He was talking about Bulbul. 'Yes, of course.' And I turned to go, still confused by the exchange. Outside, a large sheet of metal was being pulled up the beach. The cutters would come soon with their tools, trimming the sheet down again so that it could be dragged to the equipment at the northern edge of the beach, where it would be rolled and flattened and eventually transported. I looked for Mo, but couldn't find him, so I made my way to the office. As I passed the dormitory, I saw Gabriela coming out of one of the side doors. I wondered what she was doing there, but she swept past me before I could call out to her.

I allowed myself to consider for a moment what would have happened if I'd gone away with you. Hopped on a plane. Goodbye, everyone. Sending Rashid and Ammoo an email, perhaps the same one. *I'm on my way to America*, it would have said, *with Elijah Strong*. They would have considered it a joke. Called me, and then each other. Would they have been any angrier with me than they were now? I laughed to myself, because I knew now that losing you was scarier than any of it, and since I had done that and was still here, it meant I could probably do anything. I wish I had discovered that about myself before it was too late.

When I returned to the dormitory for an interview session that evening, I found Gabriela already there, passing around tea and bowls of puffed rice to the men. Mo hung back, dodging me as I entered, and none of the others stopped to say hello. I guessed I had offended them with my abrupt departure. Only Russel seemed happy to see me, asking after you. You were in America, I said. I told him about the piano, but word had already spread. 'Can we smoke?' Russel asked, and there was a small commotion as the biris and the matches were passed around, and after everyone had lit up, small conversations bloomed around the edges of the group. No one seemed in any particular hurry to start talking.

'So,' I began, 'we are almost at the end of our interviews, but there are a few of you who have yet to tell me your story. I am sorry for the break—'

'Will it be on TV?' Russel interrupted.

'Yes, in my country,' Gabriela said.

'In foreign,' I translated.

'What about Bangladesh?' someone asked from the back.

'We will try,' Gabriela said.

'We don't know,' I said. 'But you don't have to talk if you don't want to.'

Someone raised his hand from the back of the room. 'Apa, what about the other place? Can you take the camera there?'

'Don't worry,' Gabriela said. 'We won't leave anyone out.'

'We are only getting interviews from the pulling crew,' I said. 'The film will focus on your group.'

'I mean the other pullers.'

'She's not supposed to meet the other pullers,' Mo interjected.

'What other pullers?' I glanced at Mo, at Gabriela. I

looked around. 'Where's Belal?' Belal, who had lost his wife and his daughter.

A man stood up. I didn't recognise him – a heavy, powerful face, square shoulders. 'As-salaam alaikum Apa,' he said. 'My name is Selim.'

'Selim has just arrived from the north,' Gabriela said.

'I was here last year,' he explained. 'My father died, so I went home for the winter.'

I was struggling to keep up. Something about the equation between us, and the workers, and Ali, had fundamentally altered in my absence. The group appeared charged up, lacking in the tired resignation that had dominated our previous conversations. I remembered what Bilal had said about not trusting Gabriela, her inability to get the workers to speak with her. And now, the warm, almost intimate way she was sitting among them, passing them mugs of tea, using Selim's cigarette to light one of her own.

I took Gabriela aside. 'What's this about the others?'

'I was going to tell you,' she said. 'There was an accident here last week.'

'On *Grace*?' No one had said anything to me. 'Does Rubana know?'

'They hushed it up. Ali's hiding the wounded workers.'

'That doesn't sound right. Where would he hide them?'

'There's a place down the road. He paid them off, doesn't want them in hospital.'

The sound of conversation rose around us. 'Don't you want to see them?' Selim asked.

I looked around the room, lit by Gabriela's camera and the solitary bulb that hung from the ceiling, and replayed the conversation I'd had with Ali that morning. I knew they were waiting for me to say something. I dialled Rubana's number but there was no reply. I remembered Dera Bugti now, and being inches away from *Ambulocetus*, and having to put all that earth, all its history, back in its place, its secrets packed away for someone else to discover. I gestured to Mo and asked him, first of all, why he hadn't said anything to me. Mo stared down at his feet, and I had to put my fingers under his chin and force him to look at me. 'I didn't want you to be hurt,' he said, and I took this to mean that he was afraid I would get into trouble with Ali. It's you who will be hurt, I wanted to say. And I won't be able to protect you. Again I will betray you.

I turned to the assembled crowd. 'Yes,' I said. 'Take me with you.'

I followed Selim and Mo a few hundred yards down the highway. We turned into the market, which was empty now, past the small mosque, then down a dirt alley. Mo gripped my elbow, helping me skirt the flooded potholes, the loose electrical wires, the small pyramids of garbage. We pushed open the tin door of a small concrete shed. The smell of blood and bleach was overpowering; my eyes adjusted to the darkness and I saw three cots laid out in a row. I saw a man without legs, another who was wrapped all around his waist and his chest, his bandages glowing in the dim caramel light. The third man, lying on his stomach, a thin layer of gauze shielding his burnt skin, was Belal. I would not have recognised him if Mo hadn't whispered his name into my ear.

It wasn't as if I had ignored the fact that they all had a story of death that followed them around like a shadow – a friend or a brother or someone they had only a passing acquaintance with, a man who shouldered a few inches of the weight they shared – a piece of steel crushing a skull, a chest, an errant metal rope escaping from the winch and cutting a throat. I had heard all the stories; I had read the reports and I knew the statistics, but I was unprepared for this. My stomach revolted from the smell and the soft moans coming from Belal's bed. I hung back while Gabriela rushed to one, then another, ignoring everything I had told her about approaching people she didn't know, tracing her fingers over their bandages, holding the hands that were still whole. She had been here every day, knew the progress of every injury, every wound. The amputated man would survive; the man whose chest was split open with the winch that had snapped and struck him would probably not. They weren't sure what would happen to Belal.

I had spent many years thinking about bones. When I studied the fossils of *Ambulocetus* and *Pakicetus*, I told myself the souls of those ancient creatures were in their bones. I knew that the fusing of Diana's pelvis would produce a smooth bowl shape that would tell us how *Ambulocetus* had evolved into an amphibian when her ancestors had been terrestrial. But the bones I had studied, pressed down by millennia, were always partial. I would work with fragments and imagine the whole, fill in the parts that had been broken by history, and this was how it should be, because our knowledge of the past could only ever be in pieces, left there for us to put together. But now, confronted by these fragments of people, a room in which the atmosphere had been thinned by the fleeing of hope, my knowledge of bones gave me nothing, no explanation, no prescription. I could not imagine these men whole, no matter how expert I was at putting things together.

'We have to take them to a proper hospital,' I said. 'They can't stay here.'

'They won't go,' Gabriela said. 'I already tried.'

'Ali's paid them,' Selim said. 'Says he's going to take care of their families.'

The bandaged man whispered something. Mo went to a metal drum in a corner of the room and filled up a glass of water. The man lifted himself up, struggling to reach the glass held out by Mo. I couldn't bear the sight of him, the tendons of his neck straining towards Mo, his mouth open and dry, his arms pinned down by their bandages, and I ran out of the shed, my foot catching on the raised wooden threshold and flinging me violently into the alley outside.

Gabriela and I stayed up late talking about what we should do.

'It seems so pointless to make a film,' I said.

'Exactly,' Gabriela agreed, 'it's no fucking good.'

We couldn't go to the police; Ali had already paid them off. And what would we charge them with, if the men themselves wanted to remain where they were? We discussed the possibility of alerting the press, and I left another message for Rubana.

'My mother would know what to do,' I said, a surge of feeling for Ammoo coursing through me. The sight of those workers, the ones Ali had gone to such trouble to hide from us, who even Mo had deemed were too dismembered to take part in the interviews, changed what I knew about this world and my place in it. It made everything else shrink – my little quest to find my origins, even the wound of your absence. Ammoo would know what it was to be overcome by the discovery of something ugly, of secrets that are just below your gaze and unnoticed by you until a terrible moment breaks it all open.

Gabriela and I sat in silence, then, for a long time, until it was almost morning. I had to leave – Rashid would arrive in a few hours. We agreed to return to the injured workers' hut the following afternoon, with Mo, and decide together what to do about the film. I left Gabriela dozing in the brightening day, her arm thrown over her eyes, as if she wanted to go back in time and erase the sight of everything she had seen in the last months.

I went to pick Rashid up at the airport. I don't know what I expected to feel when I saw him; I was raw from the night before, tired and full of uncertainty, and I thought maybe if I tried to reach out, tried to tell him something about what had happened, we might make a connection. He had just seen me, and we were waving to each other, and I was telling myself I was doing the right thing to let him in, when he stopped to talk to a man in a dark suit. The man put his arm around Rashid's shoulder and they passed through the gates and came towards me.

'Darling,' Rashid said. 'This is uncle Harry.'

Harry reached out and shook my hand. He was wearing gloves. 'What a pleasure,' he said. 'I have heard so much.'

'Zubaida's been staying here. Taking in the Chittagong air.'

I smiled distractedly, wondering how long we would have to stay and make small talk. 'Yes, I know,' Harry said. 'Ali has told me everything.'

I turned to Rashid. 'Ali?'

'Uncle Harry owns the shipyard,' Rashid said.

Harrison Master. Uncle Harry. 'Prosperity,' Harry said. 'My father loved that place. I don't care for it much, but he made me promise we wouldn't sell.' He took a tube of chapstick out of his pocket and smeared it over his lips.

Here was my chance. Gabriela and I had wondered, time and again, what sort of people would own businesses like these – well here was a man standing right before me, and I could ask him anything. How do you feel, sir, about lining your pockets with the broken backs of poor farmers from the north? And was it your idea to take a group of injured men and lock them away for the sake of your business? Of course I didn't say anything. I even managed a smile as we parted, watching Harry's companion, a man I hadn't seen at first, pull a comb out of his pocket and smooth Harry's hair before they exited the airport.

In the car on the way home, I exploded at Rashid. 'You couldn't suck up to him any more if you were a mosquito on his leg.'

'Oh, hell, Zee I was trying to be nice. For your sake.'

'That man should be thrown in jail. No, shot by a firing squad.'

'What are you talking about?'

'You have no idea what they do to these people.' I was angrier at myself than anything else; a lifetime of living with my mother should have taught me better. Of course the stories were worse than they first appeared; of course Ali was hiding the really dark truth; of course there was something dirtier, something more frightening, underneath.

It started to rain. 'You can't fix everything,' Rashid said.

'Everything? I haven't fixed a damn thing.'

'If you want to feel guilty about something, there's a lot to choose from.'

I had given him a lifetime of ammunition. He would forgive me, I knew that, but I could see now that he would be free to throw it back in my face at any time. Isn't that what people do, accrue debts they end up paying off for the rest of their lives, waiting for something to happen that will narrow the difference between themselves and the people they destroyed? I couldn't tell him any of it, I could see that now. We rode home in silence, beside each other in the back seat of his car, and I wondered if I was the only one who felt we were far, far away from each other, or if he, too, felt the distance stretching open between us.

Komola and Joshim greeted us gaily at the door. The rest of the family would arrive soon. 'Go upstairs,' Komola said, 'dress up for your mother-in-law.'

I went upstairs and saw that Komola had laid out my clothes. A green silk sari, the matching blouse and petticoat were all ironed and on the bed. Rashid was still steaming over our argument. 'I'm going to play golf,' he said, changing into shorts and a polo shirt. 'I'll be back in time for dinner.'

I showered, trying to put aside the sight of the injured workers, but there was too much there, Mo and Gabriela and you, always you hovering at the edge of my thoughts. I lay back on the bed, my hair blotting the bedcover.

When it was time to get dressed I realised I needed help putting on my sari. Komola wasn't in the living room or kitchen. I made my way to the back of the house to the servants' quarters. A narrow cement staircase led to the rooms above the garage. The washing — a checked lungi and a red petticoat — hung between two metal pegs at the top of the stairs and created a barrier over the open door. I called out and waited, heard nothing in return, and was about to turn back, already feeling like an intruder, when I heard shuffling from inside. Komola came out, fiddling with the soft cotton folds of her sari.

'Sorry,' I said. 'I'm disturbing you.'

'I was praying,' Komola said.

'How long have you lived here?' I asked, catching a glimpse of her cluttered room, the trunks stacked up against

364

the wall, clothes folded in an open shelf, a small round mirror nailed to the wall.

'Since I was a girl,' Komola said, pinning her hair with a quick motion of her wrist. 'Before you were born.'

I was about to ask her more, about where she had come from, where her people were, but Komola was uncomfortable, closing the makeshift curtain behind her.

'Can you help me with my sari?'

She followed me back inside and up the stairs. I changed into my blouse and petticoat and started on the sari, but Komola took it from me, searching for the correct side, controlling the long, liquid fabric. I thought about how she always looked at me slightly indirectly, her head tilted down or to the side, but she was bold now, folding and tucking. 'Apa, there's something,' she said. 'I heard you crying in your room. Why?'

Had I been crying? I couldn't remember. 'It's nothing; don't trouble yourself.'

She made pleats, holding the end of my sari between her teeth. 'I knew you when you were a baby, you know.' The words came out narrow.

I took a moment for this to sink in. It wasn't unlikely – my parents had brought me here as a child to visit Dolly and Bulbul. Perhaps she had seen me then, peeling leaves off the banana plants. I swallowed the lump in my throat. 'You've been here a long time,' I said.

She passed the anchal behind me and over my shoulder. Then she crouched down and took hold of the pleats. I looked down at her and I could see the wide parting of her hair and the grey streaks that fanned out on either side. This was the head of a woman who had been parting her hair the same way her whole life, committing the same rituals, washing, oiling, braiding. Perhaps, as an occasional indulgence, she had once or twice bought herself a clip.

When she was finished with the hem, she took a safety pin from her own blouse and started attaching my anchal. Her touch was light, her fingers papery, their lines deep and serrated. 'Tell me,' I whispered, 'did I seem all right?' What I meant to ask was, did I seem *different*, as in, different from the rest of them, born fully into privilege, but I couldn't quite get the words out.

'You were a sweet child. Maybe a little lonely.'

She was finished. I sat down on the bed. My hands started to shake and Komola took them between hers.

'I feel lonely now.'

'God has blessed you.'

The breaths came so sharply out of me that I could hardly speak. 'My mother – was she – did she love me?'

Komola put her arms around me, her body as soft as a whisper. 'She followed you like a hawk.' She kissed the top of my head and retreated. I had embarked on what I must have thought was a heroic journey, but all I had done was wound the people I loved, starting with my mother, that wild bird who had been tamed and chastened by her desire for me.

An hour passed. I waited in the bedroom, draped in the green silk, until I heard Dolly and Bulbul at the door, and then I descended the stairs to the living room.

Komola and Joshim had gone to great trouble with the house. The furniture was primped; the glass cabinets that housed the family's baubles – the porcelain shepherdess that Dolly had collected on a trip to the Wedgwood factory, the blown Venetian glass, the gold painted Thai woodwork – were dusted and polished so that their contents gleamed from within.

The formal living room was opened and I was able to

see it for the first time. It was such a large room that Dolly had made four separate seating arrangements within, each with its own colour scheme and design. There was the leather suite on the eastern side, where the coconut trees cast their narrow shadows; the blue sofa and loveseat looked west; along the north–south axis of the room, a grey corner unit and a French-looking suite with carved wooden armrests faced each other. It shouldn't have worked, but it did, in the peculiar way of excess. When I entered the room, I asked myself how Dolly chose between one sofa and another. Did she enter the room and think to herself, I'm going to enjoy the sun on the leather settee today, or today I want to pretend to be Marie Antoinette so I'll make myself at home on the gold-tipped chair? Now Dolly was sitting upright on the blue loveseat, and when I entered the room, not for the first time I was a little afraid of her. She was heavily made up, a pair of thick gold bangles wrapped around her wrists, reading the newspaper with her Pomeranian, Clooney, draped across her feet.

'Hello,' I said. 'How was your flight?'

'Fine. But your father-in-law is exhausted, he went to take a nap.' She folded her hands on her lap. 'Tea, darling?'

'All right.'

Dolly pressed a button on a small rectangular object – her calling bell – and Komola appeared. 'Bring bou-ma her green tea. And snacks.'

'Aren't we having dinner?'

'It's early,' she said, looking at the slim gold watch on her wrist. 'Baby Babu isn't even home yet.'

Dolly watched me lift a roast-beef sandwich from the trolley. 'You skipped lunch, didn't you, sweetheart? I told you, you have to eat.'

I nodded, taking a large bite.

'And I've heard all about your . . . friend.'

The white, crustless bread swelled in my mouth. I remembered reading a story about how several people die every year in Japan while attempting to eat mochi rice cakes. I had tried mochi once, and found it quite disgusting. I wished now that it had killed me.

'I thought you looked a little unsettled. So I made a few phone calls. Everyone knows everything, my dear. You should have been more careful.'

I felt the sting of tears behind my eyes. 'I'm sorry.' How many times had I said that?

'Does Rashid know?'

I took a sip of tea. The lump of sandwich travelled slowly, painfully, down my throat. 'Yes.'

Clooney shifted, raised himself up, and reapplied his torso over Dolly's feet. Dolly lowered a bangled hand and scratched behind his ear. 'Poor Baby Babu.'

'I didn't mean to—'

'Of course you didn't. But you did.' She sucked in her lips, redistributing her lipstick. 'People warned us, you know. But I told them there was no way you would disrespect Rashid, or us.'

Lately there had been a few stories in the papers about how Bangladesh was built on a major fault line. That the apartment buildings in the big cities were too close together, put up without any regard for safety, and even a tiny tremor would be catastrophic. If ever there was a time for an earthquake, this would be it. The house would slide down the hill and this conversation would end. The rest of the sandwich sat in my hand. 'It was a mistake,' I said, using my free hand to wipe my mouth. For a few minutes, there was only the sound of me sobbing, and the rustle of my sari as I shifted to find a tissue on the side table.

Dolly summoned Komola again. 'Take the trolley away,' she scolded. 'Can't you see she's finished?'

When the tray was cleared, she turned to me again. 'I've been trying to protect you all these years. Making you feel it didn't matter where you came from. Treating you like you were my own daughter. But you have disappointed me. And I can only assume it's your bad background.' She dropped it in casually, like a cube of sugar into a warm mug of tea. I looked up to see if she regretted the words as she uttered them, but she looked at ease with herself as she always did.

I was emboldened by this revelation of fact and prejudice. 'If it was so bad, why did you agree to the marriage?'

Dolly ran her hands up and down the armrest of her chair. 'You're not a mother, you wouldn't understand.'

It would be easy to assume she had hated me all along, but I knew this was not the whole truth. There was loyalty in her acceptance of the match, a genuine regard for my parents, and not a small amount of affection for me. I had squandered all of this.

'Anyway, what's done is done. I don't know if Rashid will forgive you. That is between you. But you will never be the same to me. And I'm no longer willing to protect you.'

I wasn't sure what she meant; I could only assume she would speak openly and publicly about who I was, so that if word got out about what I had done, or if Rashid and I were to break up, she would have an easy explanation.

'I had a servant girl,' she continued. 'She heard us talking about your parents – we talked about it all the time, the tests, the doctors. They tried so hard. This girl came to me and told me a girl in her village was – that she needed help. We went to Mymensingh, we met the girl. The husband

369

had abandoned her. She had no money, nothing. We paid her twenty thousand.'

'You bought me?'

'Don't be naive. The girl needed money.' It was hard – impossible, really – to imagine myself at the centre of this drama. That money would have exchanged hands. And then, me, a salve for my mother's wounds. Komola appeared at the periphery of my vision, switching on a lamp in a corner of the room. I heard the distant rumble of thunder. In a few minutes, I would hear water pounding the trees and the lawn. Dolly shifted; she was going to get up and leave me there in the dark room with my red face and the sandwich still in my palm. 'And there was one more thing,' she said, pointing her toe. 'I haven't wanted to mention it, but like I said, I don't consider you mine any more, so you might as well know. The girl didn't tell us at first, but when we got to the village, there were two babies.'

The breath stopped in my chest. 'Twin girls,' she said. 'Everyone in the village was talking about it, two babies and not one of them a boy.'

'That's impossible,' I said. Surely if I had been a twin, I would have known it. I would have felt an emptiness, like a phantom limb, throughout my life. There would have been the imprint of this womb-sister, a voice inside my voice. My loneliness would have multiplied; my loneliness would have been halved. Dolly was lying.

'We wanted to take both, of course. But she refused. So stubborn. Insisted on keeping one of them. We argued but there was no persuading her. Idiot girl. What could we do? We couldn't tear the child from her arms.'

'Did you tell my mother?'

'Of course we didn't. She'd been through enough.' Dolly turned away, dismissing me, and now it began to rain, dark sheets of water pouring off the guttering, and the sound, a hush, like a mother trying to quiet her baby. I smoothed the folds of my sari and got up, feeling myself crumble from within. I turned to leave. 'Please can I go now?' I whispered.

Dolly regarded me for a minute, looking me up and down with naked distaste. 'Poor Baby Babu,' she said. 'Ruby was right.' And then the door closed behind me.

I went upstairs and lay on the bed. I should pack a suitcase, I thought. Call the driver and ask to be taken to the airport. But I couldn't move. I stared up at the track of lights on the ceiling. The blouse of my sari was tight under my arms and around my chest. I thought of the pair of Shakoor paintings that hung in the bedroom in Dhaka. Two similar-looking women, strong faces, big noses, bands of primary colour across the top and bottom edges of the frame. A parrot sat on the head of one, a flower adorned the hair of the other. Twins. I hardly allowed myself to think about what might have happened if my parents hadn't adopted me. Of the life I might have had. Hunger and cold. Want and lack. The absence of comfort. But now not only was it possible to imagine this life, there was actually someone out there living it, someone who looked exactly like me, same curly hair and wide mouth and long, elegant fingers, fingers that may have never known the gentle weight of a pencil. I wondered, if I lay here, very still, without moving, if this new knowledge might disappear from my mind, in fact, history itself might be altered, so that all of this truth telling could be reversed. I might stay here until there was no longer a twin, no longer a woman who took money for one child so she could raise another, but time moved in only one direction, though I wished it were not so, wished it could be anything but so.

It rained and rained, and the sky grew darker until it was night, and still I lay there. After a long time I heard the door opening and footsteps approaching. A warm, dry hand was cupped over my forehead, and I saw the cufflink and smelled the familiar scent of leather and aftershave on his sleeve. Rashid.

'I'm leaving,' I said, pulling myself upright.

'Don't go,' he whispered into the dark. He leaned over me, pressing my face into the collar of his shirt. My sari rustled as the fabric collapsed between us.

'I've ruined everything.'

'Stay with me. Stay and don't leave my side.'

I was comforted. He held me tighter and I considered falling asleep in his arms. But I wondered how he could be so easily duped, that he could imagine me returning to him and continuing with our lives as if nothing had happened. Erasing you from our history. How naive he was, how foolish.

'What time is it?'

'Nine thirty. Are you hungry? I can have something sent up.'

'I have a sister. Did you know that? A twin sister.'

He sighed. 'This again.'

I sat up. 'A sister, Rashid. There is a woman out there in the world who looks just like me. And your parents never told me.'

'You know everyone was just thinking of you. What's best for you.'

'Your mother said I had a bad background.'

'She's upset.'

'I should at least know for myself. How bad it really was.'

He released me. I went to the bathroom and splashed water on my face, and when I returned he was calling someone. 'Here,' he said, handing me the phone, 'your father wants to talk to you.'

'Putul,' Baba said, 'what's going on? You don't answer your phone.'

The tears came back, fresh and bitter. 'Dolly's angry. She hates me.'

'Come home, sweetheart, we'll talk.'

'Did you know about my sister?'

I heard him take a deep breath. 'A sister? What do you mean?'

'Dolly said there were two of us. Twins.'

A pause. Maybe he was wondering if I'd gone mad, whether I was making the whole thing up, but he didn't let on if he did. 'I didn't know, sweetheart – your mother and I – we would have never kept something like that from you.'

'I want to say sorry to Ammoo.'

'Please don't cry. Take the first flight, I'll pick you up at the airport.'

'I don't know. Let me think about it.'

Rashid extinguished his cigarette and went into the bathroom to brush his teeth. I suddenly felt the need to be anywhere but in that room, in that moment, with the rain outside and the smoke inside and Rashid with his face puffed up with forgiveness. I looked out the window, and I was angry now that I couldn't just go outside and take a bus or walk on the pavement, because I didn't come from the sort of place where someone like me could open the gate and let the dust of the road onto my shoes. I wanted to be somewhere else, not just away from this house, but from this country. What if I had been adopted from some other country? China, perhaps. Or Vietnam. Anywhere was better than here. I lay back on the bed and closed my eyes, trying to imagine the next few days, the silence around the table, the words 'bad background' echoing in my ears, and later, if we patched things up, living with Dolly and Bulbul and hoping she wouldn't run into me on the stairs, wondering idly if Rashid had ever considered building a separate entrance for us, or if we might, at some point, move into our own place, or if he just assumed I would live with his parents for ever, eating Friday breakfasts around the big table, entertaining guests in a living room with four sofas.

Finally I fell asleep, only to wake a few minutes later with an image of my twin, a beggar on the street, her palm out, her lips drawn tight around a mouth that had never known anything of pleasure, not a kiss, or a teaspoon of sugar. I told myself I was assuming things, that perhaps she had enjoyed a perfectly all right life – maybe not a life of privilege, but a comfortable enough life. Maybe she had a home. A pond. Laying hens. A vegetable patch. Maybe it wasn't so bad. She would have at least known her own mother, which is what I, with all the money in the world, had never had. This is what kept me awake, long into the night, as thunder pounded the sky overhead.

In the morning I packed my bag and went downstairs to see if Joshim would drive me to the beach. It was pouring as I stepped out onto the terrace, and I watched for a few moments as the lime tree and the bougainvillaea danced with the weight of the rain. When I turned back, my hair plastered against my forehead, I found Bulbul lying back on an old rattan armchair in the living room.

'Come here,' he said, waving his hand.

He was holding a small tumbler of whisky. I sat down on a chair as far from him as possible without seeming impolite. He pointed his drink at me and held my gaze for a few moments. Then he said, 'Your mother was a shit-poor woman from nowhere. And now you are the daughter-in-law of this house.'

I smiled, delighted by his rudeness. 'Lucky me.'

'We were worried you would turn out ugly. Or a darkie. Who knows who your father was – he could have looked like anything.'

I had burned my bridges with Dolly and there seemed little left to lose. And he would probably not remember any of this tomorrow. 'I hate you,' I said.

'But when the girl brought you to us, we all fell in love with you. Me, Dolly, your parents. Sweetest baby anyone had ever seen. How does a woman like that have a baby like this? It's one of God's mysteries. And two of you.'

There it was again. My sister. 'Did you see her?'

Bulbul put his drink on the flat wooden armrest of his chair. 'We did. Spitting image.'

'And what did you do? I asked, my voice shaking, 'Choose one?'

'Something like that.'

Again I questioned my own ignorance. I knew all the clichés about twins, how they sensed one another's presence, how if one was injured, the other would feel pain. I had never felt anyone's pain but my own – did this mean my sister had lived a life as untrammelled as mine? I knew this could not be. There had been pains and wounds and injuries: I had just been ignorant of them. And what about my mother – what did my mother do? Try and love one child as if she was loving us both? Put one mouth to her breast and imagine the other mouth on the other breast? Take some comfort in knowing that one would never go hungry, while the other would know her love?

'Did I have a name?' I asked. 'Did she?'

He slid further down the chair. I could see the roof of his mouth when he spoke. 'Your name was Mohona,' he said. 'And her name was Megna.'

Megna and Mohona. Mohona–Megna. Mo and Meg. Megna.

'Megna what?'

'Oh, people like that don't have surnames. Of course your mother wanted to choose a new name for you, so then you became Zubaida. Our little Zubaida.'

Mohona. Megna. Where had I heard that name before? I couldn't remember. Megna–Mohona. Then I did. Shouted across a street by a stranger. Could it be? No. It was a common enough name. A common mistake. But he had been so sure. He had looked at me and seen someone else. I tried to remember his face, but it was getting dark and I had just wanted to get out of there, afraid of his heavy hands on my shoulders, the way he looked at me, hungry, as if he knew something about me, something buried. Perhaps he did. Perhaps he had seen the me that was in someone else, a me that had been lost until this very moment. No, it couldn't be. But what a thought. What if I were to run into this man again – ridiculous to think that he had known my sister, but what if? I imagined myself clinging to a window ledge, my fingers slipping, and this man holding out an arm, a small gesture of hope. I would never find him again, I knew, and even if I did, the chances were – well, they were minuscule. But if no one had kept track of my mother, if none of the people who were responsible for my life had thought that I might someday want to know something more about my past than simply that I had been saved, my only chance was to do something for myself, to go somewhere I might have a scrap of hope.

I turned to go. Bulbul's eyes were closed. I almost felt sorry for him, seeing for the first time the smallness of his life, how he was hemmed in by the legacy of the rich father who had built this house and founded all the businesses he so diligently managed, that every time he entered a warehouse, or factory, or office building, he would be watched by the framed portrait of the patriarch who had started it all. I left him there with his hand still curled around the tumbler, the tiny blossom of possibility springing up inside me, giving me hope, that most mercurial of things. 'Thank you,' I whispered to his sleeping form.

The barber was squatting at the entrance to his shop with his lungi hanging down between his knees. He had a pile of peanuts on his lap, and, as he gazed out onto the street, he picked up a peanut, smashed the shell between his fingers and tossed the kernel into his mouth.

'As-salaam walaikum,' I said.

'Walaikum as-salaam.' He looked at me apologetically, gesturing to the peanuts that prevented him from getting up.

'I'm looking for a man,' I said. 'A man who attacked me a few months ago. Do you remember him?'

He shook his head. 'No.'

'It was right in front of your shop. You came over, argued with him. You pulled him away.'

He sifted through his lap, pulled out another peanut and smashed it against the floor with the heel of his hand. 'You must have got the wrong street. Lots of barber-shops around here.'

It had stopped raining, but the air was packed and humid and I could see sweat gathering in droplets through his thinning hair. 'You don't remember me?'

He gazed up and stared into my face, as if to be absolutely sure. 'Forgive me.'

I stepped back so I could read the sign above his shop. NAVEED NAPITH, that was it. I was so sure. If Gabriela had come with me, she could have confirmed it, but I still hadn't been able to get hold of her. I paced back and forth to the shops on the left and right. There was a cigarette stall a few feet away, an electrical shop selling batteries and bits of wire, and a tailor's. No one remembered me. I crossed the road, silently mocking myself for making the trip, ready to give up, when someone called out for me to wait. When I turned around I found a woman in red heels and a kameez dotted with sequins. She had short hair, a pointed chin and bright, clever eyes, a face that seemed out of place on this street.

'I know who you want,' she said. 'My husband won't tell you because he thinks you'll call the cops.'

I grabbed her wrist. 'You know him? What's his name?'

She snapped her head back. 'Why d'you want to know?'

'I need to speak to him. It's important.'

She tossed her chin towards the barber-shop. 'Anwar. Keeps looking for some girl called Megna. All day long he's saying Megna this, Megna that. And also a kid.'

My heart dropped several inches into my stomach. 'He has a child?'

'He's not a reliable type. He comes and goes. One day he's working in construction, the next day he's a shipbreaker. Lost a lot of money too, I heard.'

'What's he doing now?'

She crossed her arms in front of her. 'He disappeared a few weeks ago. We haven't heard anything. You related to him?'

The back of my shirt was plastered with sweat. 'Something like that. Where was the last place he worked?'

'You don't look related.'

'Not exactly related. Did you say shipbreaking?'

She took my arm and pulled me back towards the barber-shop. 'Let's ask Naveed,' she said.

Naveed was brushing the last of the peanut shells from his lungi. 'I remember now,' he said, looking his wife up and down and chewing the inside of his mouth. 'It was Chittagong Shipbreaking.'

Naveed's wife wove her arm through his. 'There's no such place as Chittagong Shipbreaking. Now tell this poor lady the truth, can't you see she's not going to snitch?'

'I won't,' I said, 'I won't tell anyone, I won't get him into trouble. Please.' There was a rough breeze coming from the shore, and I was almost shivering now as my skin dried and cooled.

Naveed was still chewing his lip when he said, 'It's Dhaka-Sylhet Shipbreaking partners,' he said.

Chittagong. Dhaka. Sylhet. He was just naming cities. 'Are you sure?'

'He's sure,' the wife nodded. 'He wouldn't lie in front of me.' And she grabbed his cheek between her index and middle knuckle and pinched hard.

'Okay. Thank you.'

'Give us a name,' she said as I turned to go. She pointed to her stomach, which I could see now was protruding. She must have been six or seven months pregnant.

'Mohona,' I said, already speeding down the lane, pulling my phone out of my pocket to see if I could find a number for Dhaka–Sylhet Shipbreaking.

★

'Where have you been all day?' Gabriela said when she saw me.

It took me a moment to realise what she was talking about. Oh, yes, the injured men – we were supposed to meet them again today. 'Sorry. Something came up.'

'Were you with Mo?' she said. 'He said he'd be there, but he didn't show up either.'

'No, I was – I was trying to find someone.'

'They're saying there might be a cyclone tonight.'

'Do you remember that guy, the one who came up to me near the beach?'

'You mean the guy who thought you were someone else?'

'I was looking for him.'

She tugged on her shirt, impatient. 'We need to finish the interviews before we get those men into trouble.'

I wasn't in the mood to hear a lecture, so I let my thoughts drift, trying to remember Anwar's face, trying to remember exactly what he'd said to me. 'He called me Megna, right?'

'I don't know. I suppose so. You understand what I'm saying?'

I nodded vaguely. Then suddenly she was very agitated about Mo, and said we had to go and find him immediately. 'If Ali finds out he's been helping us, it's going to be a fucking disaster.'

It had started to rain. I tried to convince Gabriela to wait a while, until the weather improved, but she wanted to leave right away. It was getting dark, and usually you could see the light of the cutters' blowtorches from the bedroom window. I looked now but it was impossible to make anything out, thick sheets of rain covering everything, and no moon.

'You can't even see anything.'

'I have this bad feeling.'

I was tired. I leaned over the dining table and rested my face in the crook of my elbow. 'I'm sure he's fine, Gabi. He's been here longer than any of us, and they have storms here all the time.'

'Please,' Gabriela said.

I closed my eyes and leaned back on the sofa. I was hungry. In the fridge, there was a bowl of chicken curry covered with a plate. I fished out the chicken with my fingers, eating it cold. Mo would have cooked it. I thought of his arms, those delicate elbows, leaning over the stone pestle.

'Let's go to the beach,' I sighed. 'We'll find Ali and he might have some idea.'

I found an umbrella in one of the closets, and we set off on foot. It was only a few yards between the apartment and the Prosperity gates, but in the dark and the rain our progress was slow. Gabriela was trying to tell me something, but I couldn't hear her. We locked arms. The gates were closed, but there was always a gap between the gate and the wall, and we had squeezed through before. Gabriela had wrapped a scarf around her head and face, but I could feel the rain pounding my exposed shoulder and splashing onto my neck. Passing through the gate, we saw a light on in the Prosperity office, but when we stepped inside, it was empty, the chairs pushed under the desks and Ali's computer switched off. The wind picked up, tossing a scattering of sand against the office windows.

I told Gabriela we should wait. 'Maybe Ali's gone to check on everyone. It's unlocked, he might come back.'

Gabriela unwrapped her sodden scarf and draped it against the back of a chair. 'Mo was trying to tell me something, but I didn't understand the Bangla,' she said. 'Something about a girl.'

'What girl?'

'That girl he tried to tell us about before, you remember?'

I wandered over to Ali's desk. I knew he kept food in his drawer, and I rifled through his desk, fishing out a packet of Marie biscuits and offering them to Gabriela. 'He never said anything after that day.' Mo hadn't confided in me – of course he hadn't. I couldn't be trusted. I bit down on the dry biscuit, the flavour of butter and nigella seeds flooding my mouth.

'He came home the other day with a cut on his face.' Gabriela tapped her eyebrow. 'Just here. So I asked him what happened and he said "Ma". That means mother, right? His mother?'

We waited to see if Ali would show up. I tried him a few times on his mobile, but the lines were down.

'Isn't there someone we can call, the police maybe?' Gabriela asked.

'There are so many stray children,' I said, repeating something I had heard my mother say many times.

'I want to check the dormitory,' Gabriela said. 'Come with me or I won't be able to talk to anyone.'

They would find it strange, two women turning up after dark with wet hair and clothes. I thought about explaining this to Gabriela but I knew I wouldn't get anywhere. Outside it seemed the rain had abated somewhat, though we still had to duck forward against the strength of the wind. We made our way as quickly as we could, our feet making impressions on the sand. As my eyes adjusted to the dark, I caught glimpses of *Grace*'s truncated hull.

All the dormitory doors were shut. 'Upstairs,' Gabriela shouted into the wind. I heard the dull clap of thunder in the distance, and the rain came down hard again, pouring over the concrete steps as we attempted to make our way up. I banged on the first door. When there was no reply, I travelled down the corridor and tried the other three, pounding my fists as hard as I could. Gabriela too. They probably couldn't hear anything. We went back to the first door and tried again, shouting to be let in. It finally opened and we were ushered inside before the rain followed us in. Tube lights illuminated the room, windowless except for a small opening near the ceiling, which was criss-crossed with metal bars. Rain was coming in through this opening, and someone had placed a bucket and a few bits of clothing underneath.

There were maybe twenty men in the room. I didn't recognise any of them. 'Mo?' Gabriela said. 'Mo?'

'Have any of you seen the boy?' Zubaida asked. 'We're looking for him.'

'Who sent you?' someone asked.

'No one. But he's been missing all day and we can't find him.'

Someone offered me a dry cloth. I wiped my face and passed it to Gabriela, who did the same. 'Could he be somewhere in the building?' I asked.

'Could be.' Two men offered to search, ducking out into the rain. It was awkward, looking around for something to do while we waited.

'Are the storms always like this in summer?' I asked one of the men.

'Worse,' he said.

'Which crew are you?'

'Cutting,' he said.

I nodded. The beds were bunked three high. Underneath the beds and against the walls their things were jammed together, battered trunks and plastic buckets and cups and plates made of tin. A clothes line, heavy with lungis and gamchas, hung between the beds. Some of them had photographs of wives and children pinned to the side of their bunks.

'How long has Mo been on the beach?' I asked. 'Does anyone know?'

'Was here when I came,' someone said. 'That was three years ago.'

'They tell me he was born here,' another chimed in.

Again, I was struck with how little I knew. How few questions I'd asked. 'Doesn't he have any people?'

The door opened again. The two men who had gone in search of Mo reappeared. 'No one's seen him,' they said, water pooling around their feet. 'Boss sir says you should go back.'

'Mr Ali is here?'

'In the office.'

'We're going,' I said to Gabriela.

'Can you tell him,' one of them said, 'that you came to look for the boy? He doesn't like us to walk around.'

Gabriela said to give them my phone number. 'In case Mo turns up.'

I obeyed, writing it down on a piece of paper, knowing they didn't have mobile phones, and that they probably couldn't read anyway, but it made me feel better too, because now I was also starting to worry. I had never known Mo to be anywhere but on the beach or at the apartment. Sometimes he shopped for our food at the market. But the market would be closed now. I wished again that he had told me more about this girl, his friend. The guilt pricked at me again, but there was no point in staying here. I was wet and cold. We would explain everything to Ali and then go home.

Ali was calling someone on the landline when we struggled back through the storm and into his office. I was aware of the clothes sticking to me, and of Gabriela, whose pale blouse was showing the outline of her bra. Ali gestured for us to come in, listening to someone on the other end. 'Yes, sir. Of course. We will do all the accounting, of course. Storm came without warning, sir.' It must be Harrison. 'Very sorry, sir. Yes, yes. I will do it immediately, of course.'

'Something the matter?' I asked when he'd hung up. I noticed we had neglected to return the biscuits to his drawer.

'It's the storm. We are trying to assess the damage.'

His phone rang again. He excused himself and wandered into the corridor, speaking in a low voice. 'Forgive me,' he said when he returned. 'Sir is very concerned. Please, sit down. You were looking for me? In this storm?'

'We are in search of Mo,' Gabriela said. 'Have you seen him?'

I didn't have time to signal to her. 'You came out in this storm to look for the boy?' Ali was confused, almost offended, that we would make such an effort and put ourselves in an embarrassing situation just for the sake of Mo.

I rolled my eyes and lowered my voice. 'It's her,' I said, glancing at Gabriela over my shoulder. 'She's become . . . attached.'

Ali nodded knowingly, as if foreign women came to the beach and took people under their wing all the time. 'I understand,' he said. 'But I'm afraid I can't help you.'

'You could send out a search party,' Gabriela said, putting her damp palms on his desk. 'We haven't been able to find him anywhere.'

He moved his eyes to his lap, to the other side of the room, the ceiling, anything to avoid looking at her. 'Please don't worry, madam. The boy is used to these types of storms. You will see, he'll turn up tomorrow, grinning from ear to ear. I assure you, he's perfectly safe.'

Gabriela shook her head, looking as if she was about to cry. 'I have a bad feeling,' she said again.

'Gabi,' I said, 'Mr Ali knows what he's talking about. Let's go home. Maybe Mo's come looking for us. And if he's still missing tomorrow, we'll make some calls.'

'Yes,' Ali said. 'If he hasn't turned up by morning – which I'm sure he will – we will investigate further.'

I led her away. 'Thank you, Mr Ali.'

'Shall I escort you home?'

'No, really, it's not far.' At the door, I paused. 'What are you doing here so late yourself, Mr Ali?'

He waved his hand in front of his face. 'There is the matter of your friend's piano. We are going to transport it first thing tomorrow morning. Sir has ordered an air-conditioned truck to carry it to Dhaka. But the storm has made it difficult. Nothing to worry about. Please, go home.'

Outside, the darkness was thickened by rain. We paused for a moment, as if by standing there we would find a trace of Mo. Gabriela suddenly broke away and started running towards the sea. I followed her, and after a few paces I almost knocked into the group of men gathered on shore. I could hear Gabriela's voice asking, in her awkward Bangla, for Mo. More men crowded onto the beach. Through the dense sheets of water, I could make out a milky moon, and as I was forced further towards the water's edge, I saw lights illuminating the breached hull of *Grace*. The crowd grew around me, pressing against me, water falling from above, and, it seemed, also from the sides and from below, and very quickly my hair was plastered against my face and I was soaked through. I felt a hand grabbing my elbow, and when I turned around Gabriela was gesturing for me to bring my ear close to her mouth. 'They're angry about the piano,' she said.

I looked around at the workers. They had pulled themselves into a semicircle, and in the middle was the man
with the heavy forehead who had taken me to see the
injured men. He raised his arm up now, throwing his voice
into the crowd.

'The chair is coming!' someone said. I lost sight of
Gabriela. My eyes adjusted to the half-dark, and I made
out a crude wooden ramp laid against the side of *Grace*. A
few minutes later, a knot of men came out, balancing
something very large and heavy on their shoulders. The
crowd around me shifted, raising their voices higher. The
men on the ramp started to move. It was a large rectangular
crate. There were three men at the bottom, while the others
pushed from above. Everyone started shouting as they made
their way, inch by inch, down the ramp. I stood transfixed,
understanding now that it was the piano – your piano,
Elijah – that they were trying to manoeuvre out of the
ship, and every second seemed to stretch as we waited, and
they were halfway down and the shouts of anger turned
into cheers, as if it had gone from being a protest to a
crowd at a cricket match. I heard laughter. Then, it happened:
one of them hesitated, broke the pattern, his arms going
down when they should have been up, and everything
moved very quickly after that: the crate rolling over on its
side, pulling everyone to the edge of the ramp, the leader
telling them to hold on, hold steady, but from where I was
standing, I could see there was no way they were going to
save it, so I ran towards them and shouted for them to let
go, let go, save yourselves, it doesn't matter, telling everyone
to stand back, because it was going to fall and they would
be crushed beneath it, and they rushed back and allowed
it to fall, twenty, thirty feet below them, the crate breaking
open like an egg, and the sound, a thousand notes being

played all at once, the clap of every hammer against every string, the rain a drone of accompaniment, and then the rip of breaking wood, a tearing, ugly sound, and the instrument spilling out from inside, in pieces of black and bone, and then, a flash of colour, a human cry among the sound of breaking, a body, falling and then another, tumbling together and matching the cries of the piano as it shattered above and below them, and finally we saw, pinned under a piece of the crate and the heavy lid of the piano, their arms around each other, a pair of children. And before I blacked out, I heard a voice. 'My girl,' the voice said, 'my girl. My girl.'

The Last True Story

I went to the place of dreams, Elijah, the place of otherness. I want to say I remained in the rational and saw nothing, but I have been unable to wash out the conviction that I dreamed of you the whole time I was unconscious. In the place of otherness, it was your face I saw, you sitting beside my hospital bed, holding my hand so that the pulse at your wrist galloped steadily beside mine, your breath against my skin as you kissed my bruised forehead. It was only a few hours, but, to my mind on the other side, it seemed far, far longer, years, time measured as it was in the age of *Ambulocetus*.

The age of *Ambulocetus* was forty-nine million years ago, after the Indian subcontinent crashed into Asia, creating the Himalayas and sealing off the mighty Tethys. Even then, *Ambulocetus* still clung to her hind legs, allowing her a few hours on shore every day to lie by the sea and catch the sun that beat down on the northern Asian plateau. But it was in the sea that she was at home, unlike her ancestor, *Pakicetus*, who remained in the shallows, her grazing water only knee-deep. And down through the generations, *Ambulocetus*'s descendants became bolder, travelling to deeper and wider waters, their snouts elongating, their hind feet becoming webbed, their front teeth narrowing to catch prey underwater.

The story of *Ambulocetus* is the story becoming, of transformation, of leaping between one sort of being and another sort of being, of leaving history behind for the wide swathe of the possible. It is not the story of extinction. *Ambulocetus* is no Mastodon, vanished from the earth with the snap of evolution's hand; no, her story is of the rather slower sort, as, generation by generation, she leaves behind the hoofed foot and short snout of the Mesonychid, over time developing the curved bones in her ears that will allow those who tug at her grave to read her like a hieroglyph: here lies a whale, a creature who lives and eats and breathes by the ocean's heartbeat.

I had been injured by a piece of the crate as it broke apart. It was a knock on the head, stitches, a slight concussion, and a fractured elbow. There would be many tests, back in Dhaka, to make sure there had been no permanent damage, but they would all reveal the same thing: that I'd had a lucky escape, given that I had foolishly rushed towards the piano as everyone else had scattered.

It was not you at my bedside. It was not your voice in my head, crying, 'My girl, my girl.' That was my father. It was not your hand in my hand. That was my mother. And it was not your breath on my face, kissing my bruised forehead. That was Rashid.

Mo. When I peeled open my eyes, I called out his name, and they said, when you are better, you can see him. I closed my eyes again, willing them to be gone, willing them to be the dream and you the real after the dream. But when I looked again, there they all were, so selfish in their worry for me. I was hardly injured. At least, not in the common way.

I was in a government hospital. The room, the best they

had, was bare except for my bed and the three chairs that seated my family. It smelled of urine and antiseptic. There was no window, only a flickering tube light fixed to the wall.

I woke up again in the darkness and I screamed and screamed until the doctor arrived with a needle and so I pulled out the IV, and then my father said, 'Let's take her; she has to find out anyway.'

I remember the rest vividly. On the other side of the hospital, in a room with two beds, lay Mo. On the second bed was a girl with a shaved head. They were both sleeping, and unlike me in pyjamas my mother had brought from home, they were in hospital gowns that were too large, their arms protruding like cherry stems. There was a monitor that beeped intermittently. Mo's chest rose and fell.

Their faces, untouched, were perfect.

'There are internal injuries,' the doctor explained.

'Can you operate?'

'Profound injuries,' he said.

I pulled back the sheet. Mo's legs were bandaged all the way up to his thighs, and around his midriff there was a large bloodstain. 'The dressing needs to be changed,' I said.

'Profound injuries,' the doctor repeated. Abboo put his arm delicately around my shoulder and I flinched, feeling a wound where there wasn't one. Mo had been smuggling himself out of the country in the crate. (To you, Elijah.) He heard the piano was being shipped to America, and he wanted to go. And with him, in the crate, was a girl. They were trying to locate her family, but no one had heard of her. She wasn't from the beach and she wasn't from the town. Maybe it was his friend, the girl he said he wanted to marry. When he grew up. Which would now be never.

★

On the second day, a man came to the door and said his name was Anwar. 'You are not Megna,' Anwar said.

I was unmoved. Nothing could surprise me now. A boy had packed himself into a crate to be with you. I had loved you and been loved in return, and yet I was not with you, I was here, in this blue and white room.

'Who are you?' That was Rashid. I gestured for him to let the man speak, my arm weighed down by a thick padding of bandages.

Anwar approached me, getting closer than a man like him could hope to get to a woman like me, until I could see the ridges on his forehead, the plateaued calluses on his palm as he waved his hand over me, disbelieving.

'She was my sister,' I managed. Then I was crying. 'She was my sister.' And he was crying too, his features collapsing together in the middle of his face, covered finally by that callused hand. Someone pulled him away and ushered him out of the room, and I drifted again to the place of dreams, of otherness, of you.

All the time I was lying in that hospital bed, Ammoo whispered into my ear. Telling me how sorry she was to have kept the truth from me, that I was going to come home now and it would all be put right. The silence would be shattered. The unsayable would be voiced. We would find my mother. We would retrace her steps. We would search up and down the country.

On the third day, they let Anwar return. We talked and talked, or rather, he talked, and I listened. Hours passed. I shared a piece of banana bread with him, a gift from Komola. That's when he told me my mother was dead. Before I could grieve for her, which I did with the barest sense of what I was mourning, they told me that Mo had died in the night. They had switched off the machines. Did I want to see him? I shook my head. I had said my farewell the day before, when I had taken the soles of his feet and pressed them against my cheek and begged him to forgive me because I knew he had only loved you because I had led the way, because I had suggested to him that his wishes could grow that big, out of the beach, beyond the country, to a place of pianos and cold winters and childhood.

The doctor said I should be transferred to a private hospital in Dhaka. I needed an orthopaedic surgeon to set my arm properly. Anyway, I was taking a bed. Someone might need it. I refused to be discharged. They replaced the IV and gave me sedatives and I slept and slept.

On the sixth day, Anwar brought the girl to my bedside, and he told me this girl, whose name was Shona, was Megna's daughter and his daughter. And he told me the story of the woman he had once loved and left behind.

She hid behind his legs so I had no idea if she resembled me. 'Come here,' I said, my voice like a broken glass bottle. She remained behind her father but she extended her hand to me and I grasped the tips of her fingers. Again I cried. Again my mother whispered into my ear. My mother was dead. My mother loved me. My mother was a shit-poor woman from nowhere. I had a twin sister. My sister had a daughter. My sister's daughter was also my daughter. On the seventh day, these were the words that came to my lips.

'My sister's daughter is my daughter.' I looked at the three people who were the closest in the world to me. Holding my hand. Blowing prayers over my face. Whispering tender words into my ears. My sister was a prostitute because Anwar had abandoned her to build a skyscraper in Dubai and she had nowhere to go and when she had died, her daughter had been sold and Mo had tried to rescue her and now here this girl was, hiding behind her father's legs, the father who had abandoned her mother, my sister, the woman with my face who had died of a broken heart.

Dolly, who had pointed out the ugliness of my history, had no idea how ugly it really was.

'My sister's daughter is my daughter,' I repeated.

Rashid said: 'She could be anyone.'

'No.' I shook my head. 'She's mine. Can't you see?' I closed my eyes and pictured the girl, who had finally emerged from behind her father and stood by my bedside in a cheap blue dress. Through the pain on the side of my head and the ache in my arm and the unbearable pain of waking up and finding that you were not at my bedside, I experienced a sweet, unpunctuated joy. I know who I am now, Elijah. I saw it the moment I looked into her face. I am her, and she is me. The restless being is at peace at last. Rumi said: look inside yourself; everything that you want, you are already that.

'I want to take her home,' I said. We were alone; my parents had quietly left the room as I had expressed my demand and Rashid his reservations.

'She has a father,' Rashid said. 'She belongs with him.'

'No,' I argued. 'She's mine.'

Anwar had given the girl to me. He had brought her to me and said that she should come home with us, because he had nothing and we would give her a life. Ammoo and Abboo had looked at each other, Bibles of words passing silently between them, and nodded. Only Rashid pointed out how strange this would make our family.

'I've decided,' I said.

Rashid had not left my bedside since the accident, and the strain was showing, the lower half of his face obscured by stubble. 'Wait till you're better,' he said, lightly caressing the small strip of my skin between my hairline and the bandage. They had shaved my head there, I knew, and put in seventeen stitches.

'She looks like me,' I said.

'I hadn't noticed,' he said, his hand resting on my shoulder, running the soft pad of his thumb along my collarbone.

'You wanted to be a father.'

'Yes, to our child.'

'This can be our child.'

He folded his hands on his lap and looked up at the murmuring light of the fluorescent bulb. A nurse entered and checked the level of fluid in my drip. We waited until the adjustment had been made, one bag exchanged for another.

Finally, he said, 'Zee, it's too much randomness.'

'Take it or leave it,' I said, refusing to make my case. 'She comes with me.'

And he said, 'I choose you, Zee, but you can't expect me to take a stranger into my house. My parents wouldn't have it.'

In that moment, I was free of him. There was no turning back from this: his declaration of her as a stranger was also an objection to me, to the randomness of me. It wasn't that I couldn't love a man who wouldn't take this girl into his heart, but that he was making it clear he could only love the piece of me he could imagine, the piece he could know. The mystery of me, my alienness, would always be at best obscured, something to ferret away in shame.

Perhaps it was already too late for Rashid and me – too late the moment I met you, Elijah. And I should be sorry, perhaps, that this is what it took for me to see that Rashid and I could never be together. But if you are reading this, if I have done my job, you will know that it was never going to be enough that I loved you. It would have to be that the whole rotation of the world, my world, shifted ever so slightly, so that everything that seemed acceptable, everything that seemed inevitable, would suddenly become loathsome to me. And that is what happened. A bruise on the forehead. A bruise on the brain. A fallen girl who was my girl, my other, bearing the weight of all the missing fragments of my history.

Ambulocetus was not alone in her day. She had contemporaries: *Takracetus*, *Gaviocetus*, *Dalanistes* – each of these may have been the ancestor of the whale as we know it. Or it could have been another altogether, a genus yet to be discovered. What we do know is that the whale was first a coyote, then a water-curious amphibian, and, finally, the creature that would rule the seas and become the stuff of our myths, our ocean-totems, our outstanding beast, the one who reminds us that long before our time, beings were made on a grander scale, their bones as big as cities. The whale is the fragment of that grandeur, of life writ on a canvas so large it is almost beyond the imagination. And for this to have happened, a transgression had to be committed, an abandonment of limbs, an adventure into water, and the courage to bid farewell to the past, whatever such voyaging may have cost, whatever longings and loves were left behind in the rubble.

Shona and Abboo and Ammoo and I went home together, the four of us a mottled tribe. I said goodbye to Rashid at the hospital. I was hollowed out, numb from all that had happened, so I told him with a dead voice that it was over and he gave me a look of disbelief – it made him feel better, I think, to assume I'd taken leave of my senses. I saw him a few times after that, but we had less and less to say to each other, and finally, about a year later, in front of the same Kazi who had married us, we signed our names again in the black register and were divorced.

Those first weeks with Shona were the hardest. I thought she would cry, that she would ask for Mo, or her father, or someone from her past, but she didn't speak a word to us on the long ride home, all the way down the Dhaka–Chittagong highway, through the city, and past the gates of the apartment building and up the elevator. When we entered, she only gave a small hint of the vast distance between this place and all the other places she had called home by pulling at her eyelashes, a gesture I would come to know as one that conveyed extreme distress. Ammoo took over the care of her. She knew, instinctively, what to do, putting Shona in the bed with her and making sure the rest of us kept our distance, especially Abboo. In the morning we found them curled around each other like human and cat. A strand of Ammoo's hair was in Shona's fist. I was desperate to question her about Mo, to ask where she had met him and how they had come to be in that crate together, but she could barely look at me, her eyes perpetually sweeping the mosaic floor.

Eventually we took her to see a doctor, and there were injuries, ones that pre-dated the accident, that would take their time to heal. It would be impossible for me to accurately describe the recriminations that we all silently carried with us from the moment Shona arrived, all the guilt, responsibility, self-hating that we experienced as we wondered about her life. Shona told us nothing about her mother. She sat at the table and refused to eat. She wet the bed again and again. We made the mistake of putting her in school, believing the company of other children might do her some good, but she was sent home after the first week, having spat at the teacher and punched another girl.

I had to confront, again, the fact that I would never know anything about my mother. I searched in Shona's face for a sign of myself, and I saw that her lips, the particular angle of them when she was angry, or smiled (rare, that), mimicked my own, and her incisors, like mine, were sharp and slightly crooked. Aside from that, she gave away nothing, said nothing.

Bettina is doing research on a group of transgender environmentalists in Nepal. She says we are in the age of Anthropocene, when humans rule the world, dictate the conditions and possibilities of life, shorten or lengthen the survival of the planet. The erasure of nature is a cynical thing, to be sure, but looked at in another light, we can say that, for a moment, until the world collapses, we live on a planet shaped by humans. Not by nature, not by time, or history, or dinosaurs, but by us.

Bettina has inspired me to write this:

Fatema Ansar, My Mother

Fatema Ansar's dreams were too big for her life. Which is to say, her life demanded a small set of dreams, or, better yet, no dreams at all. If she had been one of those people who accepted her fate without a word of protest, who rationalised her poverty, if she said it had all been written on her forehead before she was even born, so that to rail to against it would not just be futile, but against the natural order of things, she might have lived a happier life. She might have lived. Instead, she had thoughts. She lay awake at night when the moon was full and put her on stage like a spotlight, and she would imagine all

*the other lives she might have had. That she might go to school
someday, that she might leave the village and go to Mymensingh
town, that she might marry and have daughters who would
also learn the numbers and the letters, that she might die with
a smile on her lips, satisfied she had done something to advance
herself in the world. But, modest though this set of possibilities
may sound, for Fatema Ansar, they were poison, because Fatema's
life happened at the very heel of fate. There was nothing to
absorb even the smallest dream for a girl like her.*

*It began with some promise. There was no school − her
parents were too poor for that − but she did marry a man
who by all accounts would have probably turned out to be not
so bad, who would have kept her in food and clothes and
might even have given her the occasional tender glance as the
years softened him, had he not been bitten by a snake a few
months after the wedding, which was nothing more than a
kazi reciting a few prayers over their heads and the same food
they ate every day, and after that first night, when he had
made love to her with violence and held her tightly to his
chest, telling her he had put a son in her womb, he left for
the East, because the harvest was poor and he had sold himself
to a farmer in Khulna for the spring planting, and they said
goodbye in the hush of the hut they shared with his parents
and his three younger sisters. And all through the months of
Ashar, Srabon, and Poush, she waited, her pregnancy showing
early, and when the news came that he had died where he fell,
that the farmer was sorry but his body could not be sent home,
the expense was too great, his parents turned on Fatema, and
in the eye of their grief, their only son and their only hope
dead in the bloom of his life, they said, 'Go, you are no longer
eating our rice.' The heel of fate. And she went home, home
to her parents, who had been cursed, as had her in-laws, with
an abundance of daughters, one of whom they had sent to*

Dhaka to work as a servant, not a choice now for Fatema,
because she would be saddled with this fatherless child, and
that is when her sister sent word. That there was a family.
God had not blessed them with an issue. Would she? Could
she? Her parents sat silent over their empty fields and accused
her of being hungry, as if the enormous bulk of her pregnancy
was the food she was stealing from their plates. When the
babies came – yes, there were two – she despaired. Girls. The
heel of fate. Would they take them both? Yes, they would. They
came to the village in a car, their pockets bulging with money.
And, just as she was about to hand them over, as she passed
one and was about to pass the other, the smaller one, her
shoulders pulled away from the transaction, and she said, 'This
one I will keep.' There were arguments, her parents came out
of their hut and pleaded with her, but Fatema's dreams were
bigger than her life, and she stood resolute, numbing the pain
of losing one with the consolation of the other, imagining a
world in which she would never have to give up a child because
she was hungry, and she tied the money to her sari and took
the smaller one away from the village and to the East, where
her husband had died, not knowing if she would find the place
he was buried, but pulled there by the force of her will, and
the farmer, sorry for her, had offered her to the imam, who had
given her a small room behind the mosque, and that is where
she settled, a woman alone with a child, dreams too big for
her life, the first act of will she had ever committed giving her
a small measure of happiness. It wasn't much, but it was
something.

In the absence of knowledge, I choose imagination. I
choose to know my mother through my dreams, and the
words that come from my dreams. I can draw a picture
and then inflate it so that it resembles a life, a history,

something I can hold on to. In the age of the Anthropocene, the human rules, and there is nothing more human than to dream.

Of my sister, I knew slightly more, because of Anwar (and because of me – I knew, had always known, exactly what she looked like). He tells me that when she had believed she was accompanying him to Dubai, she had said she would like to swim in the sea and have her foot brush against a large creature, a timi. 'Timi' is the Bangla word for 'whale'. My sister, too, would have searched for *Ambulocetus*. Perhaps we would have travelled to Dera Bugti together, befriended Zamzam together. Perhaps we would have both fallen in love with you. Never mind, I love you enough for both of us, now that I have fallen in love with you twice and lost you twice and had a twin who has died, making my hopes twice that, you see, of a normal person's.

We tried to remain together, but looking back, it was obvious from the start that it would not be enough to try and become a family when all there was to connect us was a desire, however earnest, to make amends for the past. After four months, we called Anwar and asked if he might like to see his daughter. Perhaps she could stay with him for a while, see if it suited her. We travelled back down the country to Anwar's village in Khulna. I was afraid his wife would refuse to take her in, but when we arrived Shona appeared to relax, squatting on a piri and sifting through the rice with Anwar's mother. We left her there with a measure of satisfaction in our hearts, even though the separation was a complicated one. My mother, especially, struggles with the notion that certain barriers cannot be overcome by will alone. And I had to confront the fact that, even though something of the mystery of my life has now been solved, the fundamental aloneness of it will always be with me, like a scar that flattens and fades but refuses to disappear.

We visit her often. They come to our house for Eid every year and we sit around the table like a family and eat vermicelli and halwa. Anwar's wife tells me she wishes to have a child, but one has not come along yet. I can't say that we are intimate, in the way I imagined we might be. They hold themselves at a distance, expecting, perhaps, that our bond will break apart as abruptly as it materialised. But I live in hope that someday, perhaps when age and circumstance narrow with time, we will achieve an easier connection. I had a small glimmer of this when I asked Anwar to tell me his story. I wanted to know exactly how he had come to be on the beach that day, and he was surprisingly willing. We sat together last winter, and I wrote it down exactly as he told it.

There is the rest of the world, which seems very far away now. If you have read the newspapers, you will know that Ghulam Azam has died, that the country my parents love so deeply is as troubled as it has ever been, but also that it exists in a sort of ecstatic state, an escape artist overcoming, with only seconds to spare, every catastrophe that befalls it.

Shona is twelve now. Mo, whose age I had never asked, would have probably been something of a teenager.

I don't think of you all the time, Elijah. But I remember you on the cusp of every major event in my life. On the day I moved out of my parents' apartment (a scandal, I should tell you, that I should be simultaneously divorced and living alone). On the anniversary of Mo's death. I think about the fact that if I were dying, I would want to be with you. I would want to know what words you would say to comfort me. How you would love me through something like that. When I look back I realise so much of the time I spent with you was spent thinking about death, yours or mine or my parents' or the seed that perished in my body, or even death on a catastrophic scale – that is, the extinction of the species, like *Ambulocetus*, someday all to be bones in the ground – but that's what happens I suppose when you fall in love, because suddenly there is a thread connecting your life and all the lives that went before you and all the lives that will follow. Even when we were together I was filled with a sense of dread, not for the parting that would inevitably occur, but simply because I had a periscope into life, the vast and intimate sadness of it, for the first time, and that this is why I loved you, because even the worst of the world was there to be discovered together, shoulder to shoulder with you, my beloved stranger.

Diana is incomplete. The parts of her that arrived safely – her ankles, her pelvis, some vertebrae, the upper half of her ribcage – were assembled by Suzanne and I and these fragments lie before us in all their broken splendour. She is about ten feet long, and would have weighed between seven and eight hundred pounds. Her spine, as we had imagined, is semi-flexible; her pelvis tells us that she ventured only so far into the water. I look at her bones and they are my talismans, reflecting the future and the past, the lives of animals that came before and after her, and, more intimately, the people I have loved and lost: Mo, and Zamzam, and my sister Megna, and my mother, and you, Elijah, most of all. Everything that endures is in the atavism of her bones, fifty million years of history encased in calcium, iron, and sediment. Perhaps my mysterious friend will send me the rest, perhaps not. In his last package, however, he included the handwritten letter from Zamzam that had started it all:

I will not have a burial, comrade. I will die unmarked, and you will only hear of my death in the whispering of trees. You will never gaze on my lifeless form. But, as if you were preparing my body, washing and wrapping me in the white shroud, take these bones which are the echoes of God, and send them to my friend, who will care for them and ensure their proper place in the chronicle of humans and animals.

Remember, Elijah, how the first words we spoke to each other seemed so arbitrary at the time. Aristotle was an orphan, you said. Well, it was Aristotle, sailing in the Aegean, who first distinguished whales from fish. And later, it was the Arab scholar Jahiz who began to classify animals and hinted at a theory of evolution. I went to London to see Jahiz's book for myself. *The Kitab al-Hayawan is a treatise on animals and the medical properties of the various parts of their bodies, compiled from works of Aristotle and Ibn Bakhtishu*, the caption says. Inside, there is an illustration of a four-legged animal floating in a pool of water. It was probably intended to be a lizard or a salamander, but the image has echoes of *Pakicetus*, the land-loving ancestor of Diana. I looked down at the manuscript and it told me that the connections between us are not spurious or the result of coincidence, but ancient and profound, and yes – even the scientist in me will allow – sacred.

★

I have been putting up flyers. Bart, Jimmy and I are going to display *Ambulocetus natans* at the Natural History Museum next week. There will be a reception for the media, and my small world of palaeontologists will be watching with great interest. Diana is incomplete, but she is magnificent, and there is still much we can learn from her.

I have considered that there is a chance that all of this – Diana's bones being sent to Cambridge, which made me put her back together, which put me at the intersection that day, which made me write it all down – was a ruse, a set of events puppeted by fate to send up a smoke signal to you, Elijah. All so that you would find the flyer tacked to a bulletin board on campus, come to my unveiling, read this story, and collude with me to determine its ending.

My hopes go up and down like paper lanterns in the wind. When I first sat down to write, I thought that if you ever read these words, you would see that although I gave you up, whatever it was that passed between us was no illusion, and here, in black and white, was the incontrovertible truth of it. And then, when I came here and started to piece Diana together, when I saw you on the street and then not again, I lost hope; I no longer imagined you running up beside me as I walked through the Quad, telling me that all was forgiven.

Worse, the more I wrote, the more I realised I couldn't change a thing. I couldn't sand down the rough edges of my words to you, nor make myself turn to look at you with your fingers wrapped around that bottle of honey, because that is how it happened and there is nothing I can do to push my hand back into the black of our past. I have been tempted to bend the truth, to paint myself a little prettier, but I know you hate evasion more than anything, so I have been relentlessly, brutally truthful. I have placed my ugly, complicated heart within these pages, and although the shame hasn't passed, I tell myself at least I have been able to face it. I have been able to look that woman in the eyes, and say, yes, I was her. I was her and I am her. But this truth telling, in the end, is not for me but for you. To bring you back to me. To give you something in return for the pain that I threw at you like a shower of stones.

Now that I have pieced together not just the fossil but myself, I must tell you that this forensic approach no longer satisfies me, Elijah. It is no longer enough for me to uncover the truth. I want to make my tracks on the world, leave my own mysterious scratchings on the walls of history. As I put the finishing touches on Diana, placing her bones in their correct order, and as I finished our story, I asked myself what would happen if I cut my tether to the truth. What would happen if I turned to that place of dreams, the one where I can make up the ending of a story? I couldn't do it with ours − I had to tell it exactly as it happened − but I could do it with others. I remembered my grandmother once telling me that her son had hidden a trunk full of rifles in her back garden during the war, and an idea began to take shape in my mind.

I am buoyed by the prospect of changing her story as I write, giving her a pause of happiness in what has been a long and lonely life. I can start with a true story and I can make the rest up, blunt the edges of a tragedy, or perhaps not that at all, perhaps render it even clearer, but this time, this time I will be holding the brush, I will be the story-teller, and everything − history, and the will of other people, and the hard forward thrust of time itself − will be in my thrall, because you see, Elijah, I am no longer a person written and mutely accepted, I am the scribe, the person with her foot on the brass pedal of the piano, and though you may never love me again, you will always remain the making of me.

I will send this to you now. I am full of those days on the beach when the light was the colour of oranges and the scent between us had mingled so deeply that there was nothing between us but a thin double-layer of skin. It is springtime in Cambridge; I see snow melting on sidewalks and blossoms punctuating the cold. In a few days I will wait for you to come and visit my beloved fossil. You will be late, I know. You will make me lose hope until the very last moment, and then, out of the corner of my eye, I will notice you tying your shoelace or taking something out of your pocket. The moment I see you I will feel myself disintegrating, but you will hold me steadily in your gaze, as you have always done. I have said a thousand sorrys within these pages, and I will say them again, later, but for now, there will be no more words, only eyes. Mine will say: you came back. And yours will say yes, I did, and we will walk hand in hand out of that room – past Diana and the glass flowers and Zamzam and Megna and the war my parents fought, all of our ghosts behind us, and before us the terrible, dark world – belonging only to each other.

Acknowledgements

I am grateful to The Society of Authors, who awarded me a travelling scholarship which enabled me to visit the Harvard Museum of Comparative Zoology in the summer of 2015. Many thanks to Jessica Cundiff for a tour of the collection, including the Agassiz shelves, *Kronosaurus*, and Stephen Jay Gould's writing desk. Thanks to Alice Albinia for introducing me to Usman Qazi, who gave me invaluable feedback on the chapters set in the Suleiman. Mizan Uncle and Jamboo Khan were excellent hosts in Chittagong and Shithakunda, and I thank them for their gracious hospitality. Rezwana Chowdhury and her team at BELA work tirelessly for the rights of workers on the shipbreaking beaches, and I offer them my respect and admiration. Although we have not had an opportunity to meet in person, Phillip D. Gingerich and Johannes Thewissen's work on *Ambulocetus* has served as a great inspiration. Any mistakes or omissions are of course entirely my own.

My personal debts are many. Thank you, first and foremost, to my publishers, Terry Karten and Jamie Byng, who have brought to this book the kind of optimism and enthusiasm a writer can only dream of. Thank you to all my wonderful collaborators at Canongate, HarperCollins, and Penguin Random House India, all of whom have committed heroics at various stages of the process — Louisa Joyner, Meru Gokhale, Jane Beirn, Jenny Fry, Lorraine McCann, Natasha Hodgson, Jaz Lacey-Campbell, and Vicki Rutherford. Thank you to Sarah Chalfant, who is a friend to my intellect, my heart, and my spirit. Thank you to my friends at the Wylie Agency – Andrew Wylie, Alba-Ziegler Bailey, Jin Auh, Jackie Ko, and Charles Buchan. I thank Anya Serota, who has seen me through a decade of writing life and so much more. Thank you to Abrar Athar and Medium Rare for translating my 'girl on the beach' idea into reality. Thank you to Joe Treasure, who patiently read endless drafts of this novel. Thank you to Peter Florence for coming to Dhaka and for all the dreaming that followed. I thank Tash Aw, Michael Puett, and the inimitable John Freeman for their friendship and inspiration. Thank you to Auntie Lona for the precious gift of writing time. To the extended ROLI family, especially Matt Carney, Corey Harrower, Kate Enright, Nataleigh Strasburg, Jean-Baptiste Theibault, and Charles Cook, thank you for making this small corner of London feel like home.

I thank the sisterhood for holding my hand through illness, the bruise of early motherhood, and eventual re-emergence into life, reading, and this book: Bee Rowlatt, Kamila Shamsie, Rachel Holmes, Leesa Gazi, Sohini Alam, Sawsan Eskander, and Eeshita Azad. Thanks to my sister Shaveena, who, by telling a small lie many years ago, accidentally gave me the idea for this novel. Thank you to my grandmother, Musleha Islam, who, with her indomitable spirit, is the muse for this entire endeavour. Thank you to my parents for their love, and for embodying these words by the great Rabindranath Tagore: 'Where the mind is without fear and the head is held high/Into that heaven of freedom, My Father, let my country awake.'

And finally, boundless gratitude to my partner Roland Lamb: we are twelve years, three books, a baby, a company, and several continents later, yet you are still my romantic hero on and off the page. And to Rumi, who has just begun to discover the magic of words, I thank you for filling every day with grace, love, and laughter.

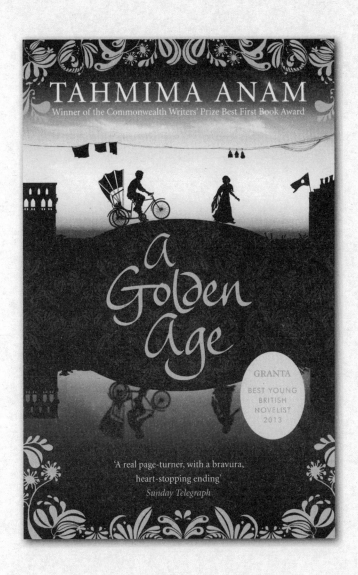

TAHMIMA ANAM

a
Golden
Age

GRANTA
BEST YOUNG
BRITISH
NOVELIST
2013

'A real page-turner, with a bravura,
heart-stopping ending'
Sunday Telegraph

'A stunning debut' *Observer*

CANON‖GATE

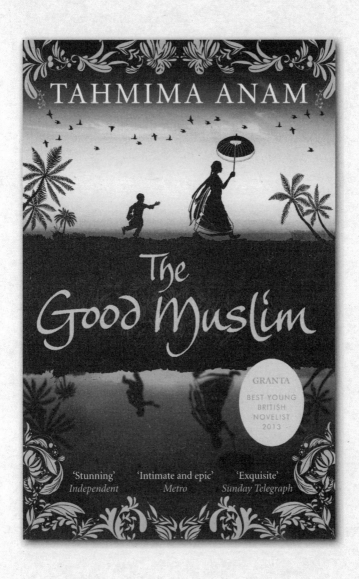

TAHMIMA ANAM

The
Good Muslim

'Stunning'
Independent

'Intimate and epic'
Metro

'Exquisite'
Sunday Telegraph

'Powerful and ambitious' *Guardian*

CANON‖GATE

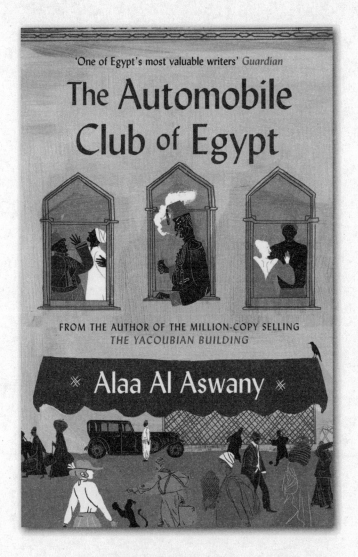

'One of Egypt's most valuable writers' *Guardian*

The Automobile
Club of Egypt

FROM THE AUTHOR OF THE MILLION-COPY SELLING
THE YACOUBIAN BUILDING

Alaa Al Aswany

'A scathing, brilliantly executed novel'
New York Times

CANON‖GATE